P...

Uncommon Pleasu...

"Uncommonly good storytelling."
—Beth Kery, *New York Times* and
USA Today bestselling author

"Scintillating sexual chemistry, wonderfully drawn characters—a total winner."
—Lauren Dane, *New York Times* bestselling author

"Beautifully written and emotionally charged, Anne Calhoun's romances define erotic."
—Alison Kent, author of *Unforgettable*

PRAISE FOR THE NOVELS OF ANNE CALHOUN

"Anne Calhoun is one of the best writers of contemporary erotic fiction."
—Sarah Wendell, *Kirkus Reviews* blog

"One of the best erotic romances I've read in a long time . . . An emotional read with two characters that I can fall in love with."
—*Dear Author*

"Absolutely fabulous."
—*The Romance Readers Connection*

"A must-read."
—*Smexy Books*

"Fresh and imaginative."
—*The Romance Studio*

Unforgiven

ANNE CALHOUN

BERKLEY SENSATION, NEW YORK

THE BERKLEY PUBLISHING GROUP
Published by the Penguin Group
Penguin Group (USA) Inc.
375 Hudson Street, New York, New York 10014, USA

USA | Canada | UK | Ireland | Australia | New Zealand | India | South Africa | China

Penguin Books Ltd., Registered Offices: 80 Strand, London WC2R 0RL, England
For more information about the Penguin Group, visit penguin.com.

UNFORGIVEN

A Berkley Sensation Book / published by arrangement with the author

Berkley Sensation Books are published by The Berkley Publishing Group.
BERKLEY SENSATION® is a registered trademark of Penguin Group (USA) Inc.
The "B" design is a trademark of Penguin Group (USA) Inc.

For information, address: The Berkley Publishing Group,
a division of Penguin Group (USA) Inc.,
375 Hudson Street, New York, New York 10014.

ISBN: 978-0-425-26502-4

PUBLISHING HISTORY
Berkley Sensation mass-market paperback edition / June 2013

PRINTED IN THE UNITED STATES OF AMERICA

10 9 8 7 6 5 4 3 2 1

Cover art by Dan O'Leary.
Cover design by George Long.

ACKNOWLEDGMENTS

I couldn't have written this book without people I'm honored to call friends. Alison Kent got the story rolling; Jill Shalvis kept me going. Jen, B, and the indispensable Robin Rotham all read the book at various stages and guided me back on track when I drifted. My agent, Laura Bradford, believed from the beginning. Greg Oxner, who's crewed on a Herreshoff boat, shared his love of sailing (and Tilley hats) with me, and gave sails, a chronometer, and a rudder to Marissa's dream. Any mistakes are mine, not his.

To err is human. To forgive is divine. Neither is Marine Corps policy.

—Bumper sticker

Hope deferred makes the heart sick, but a desire fulfilled is a tree of life.

—Proverbs 13:12

1

IN LATE SEPTEMBER, twilight turned to darkness with little warning. Turning off County Highway 12, Adam Collins braked hard, and the rear end of his Charger, loaded with what few personal possessions he'd accumulated during twelve years in the Marine Corps, swerved on the mud and loose gravel. He cursed and steered out of the skid, but the car's high beams veered crazily in a white swath across Brookhaven. The house loomed black and huge, sharp-angled peaks and chimneys jutting from the top of the hill into the foreboding gray sky. For a moment the headlights illuminated a woman's curvaceous figure, tall and proud, on one of the second-floor balconies, her outstretched arm pointing through the rain toward the cottonwoods lining the creek at the bottom of the hill. Only after he parked in the first available spot at the bottom of the driveway and began the long walk up the semicircular gravel drive did his tired brain realize the too-still figure was actually a wooden figurehead from a sailing ship.

The incongruity jerked him out of his driving fog, then made him laugh. Whoever owned the house now had a screwed-up sense of place. They couldn't choose a decoration more wrong for a historic mansion looming over the prairie surrounding Walkers Ford, South Dakota.

A group of men huddled under the overhang protecting the door to the kitchen. Cigarette smoke drifted downwind to Adam. He recognized a few of the men by the set of their shoulders or the way they held their cigarette. A whispered, "Adam's here?" reached his ears, but he just gave the group a nod as he passed, moving quickly to retain the element of surprise. Bright patches of yellow light on the grass mirrored the enormous first-floor windows, and excited girl chatter drifted from the open front doors. He climbed the three slate slabs forming the steps to the front door, and strode into the entry hall. Light blinded him and he blinked, as much from the high-gloss clear coat on the polished oak parquet floor and grand staircase climbing to the second floor as the shock of seeing his fiancée in his best friend's arms.

But while Keith Herndon had been his best friend for going on fifteen years, Delaney wasn't his fiancée anymore. She'd been engaged to Keith for four months, and not Adam's for eight. All conversation in the huge room halted as everyone turned to stare at the man who shouldn't be there. His mouth open with shock, Keith's arm tightened reflexively around Delaney's shoulders. She'd frozen mid-gesture, her hands raised, fingers splayed as if she were being held at gunpoint, or pleading for quiet with the elementary school students she counseled. Before the surprise they'd looked happy, his ex-fiancée and his best friend from childhood. A matched pair, really, both the product of Norwegian ancestors that settled in the eastern part of South Dakota, with blond hair, blue eyes, and fair skin still tanned from a summer of sunbathing on the artificial lake on the county's golf course, where the Walkers and the Herndons both lived.

"Well, goodness gracious, if it isn't Adam!" Delaney's mother broke the silence with this genuinely pleased exclamation. A crowd of the town's middle-aged female residents, all cooing and exclaiming, surged around Mrs. Walker, carefully avoiding the cane her Parkinson's diagnosis only recently had forced her to use. Adam had time only to blink before he was engulfed in a cloud of competing perfumes and big hugs from

Mrs. Walker, and Mrs. Lerner, his junior-year English teacher. *Welcome home, we're so glad you're back; a credit to the town; such a long drive, you didn't do it all in one day, I hope,* and similar phrases bombarded him before he managed to get a little space.

"No, ma'am," he said to Mrs. Lerner. "I got as far as Grand Junction and stopped for the night. Came the rest of the way today."

"You should have told someone," she said. "We would have had a reception for you. It's not every day one of our own comes home from active duty service. Are you a civilian now?"

"Yes, ma'am," he said. His separation became official just a few days earlier, but the title of civilian didn't fit. Neither did *former* Marine. Marine was all he'd been for the last twelve years. In January he'd start graduate school in South Dakota State's architecture program. Between now and then, he had a few loose ends to tie up.

Performing the duties of a best man headed that list. He squared his shoulders; crossed the slick, gleaming floor; stopped in front of them; and held out his hand to Keith.

"Congratulations," he said.

Keith reached out and gave Adam's hand a firm shake. "Thanks," he said.

Adam then turned to Delaney. "Congratulations, Delaney."

She said his name in the quiet, tempered voice he'd heard ten thousand times, in person, over the phone, over Skype. The pitch had transformed from girlish to womanly over the last ten years, but always held a note of unshakable certainty. Delaney knew wrong from right when he was still fucking that up.

"It's so good to see you," she continued, "but we weren't expecting you until a couple of days before the wedding. You didn't need to come so early."

He just looked at her, the woman he'd planned to marry when he left the Corps. "I came *home*, Delaney."

She blushed. "Oh. Of course you did."

"I've got some things to do," he said. Find an apartment.

Sort through the boxes stored in his mother's garage for the last twelve years. Start the internship arranged by an organization that helped veterans transition back into civilian life. Among other things.

But Delaney didn't ask, a simple reminder that his list of objectives was no longer her concern. Conversation flowed around them. Delaney's mother and a couple of aunts from Minnesota discussed table arrangements and decorations with a confident-looking woman in a black pantsuit carrying a clipboard, who could only be the wedding coordinator, in town from Brookings to get familiar with the venue.

The acoustics in the enormous room brought him low-voiced snatches, words like *candelabra* and *deployments*, *tablecloths* and *red rose centerpieces, such a strain on relationships, ivy and white lights, candles*, the contingency plan of an awning over the entrance in case it rained on the wedding day, three weeks away.

"Excuse me," Delaney said. "I really should talk to Stacey about the tent."

"It's not going to rain on our wedding day," Keith said confidently.

Delaney looked back at her fiancé. "We should be prepared," she said before the knot of people absorbed her.

"Long drive?" Keith asked easily.

"Fifteen hours," Adam said as he looked around. The last half of the drive had been through a cool, rainy front carpeting Nebraska and South Dakota; his eyes were gritty with exhaustion and strain, and the room looked almost surreal. The crystal chandelier overhead refracted modern electric light while antique-looking sconces cast soft pools on the parquet flooring. Floor-to-ceiling windows lined the west-facing wall, Delaney's family reflected in the glass. At either end of the room a fire burned in a tall fireplace, but while the mantel and woodwork remained intact around the smaller of the two, bricks, plaster, and lathing framed the taller fireplace.

Memory flashed in his mind, the picture made hazy by time and his blood alcohol level at the time. His hands, holding a pry bar and a hammer, as he balanced precariously on a ladder and ripped another square of hundred-and-thirty-year-old oak paneling from the wall. Marissa's face, wet with tears, brown eyes enormous, pleading as she reached up the ladder, her hands plucking at his ankles.

Drunk teens surrounding a fire roaring not in the fireplace but in the backyard. Cheers erupting skyward as he carried more of the paneling outside and hurled it onto the flames. Yeah, he'd gotten that party started, all right. Burning most of Brookhaven's irreplaceable wall was just the beginning of what he'd destroyed that night.

He cleared his throat. "How'd you talk the new owners into clearing out the furniture for a wedding reception?"

"We didn't," Keith said. "Marissa owns the house. Bought it back for taxes owed five, maybe six years ago. She's been renovating it ever since. Jesus, man, you'd think you'd been in Afghanistan or something."

He'd put Marissa and Brookhaven out of his mind the day he left for boot camp in San Diego. So the sprawling, incongruent house belonged once again to the last living descendant of the Brooks family, like the Walkers, a founding family of Walkers Ford. Despite him, Marissa's dream had come true.

Gray shimmered in his peripheral vision. Keeping his gaze fixed on Keith, he absorbed more details. Bare shoulders exposed by the halter-style top, silky fabric clinging to breasts. Arms folded across a slender torso, muscles delineated in forearms, biceps, shoulders. Dark brown hair cascading over one bare shoulder. A ruffled black skirt that stopped mid-thigh. Long, bare legs. Black heels.

His heart slammed into his breastbone, then took off in triple time. "You're holding your wedding reception in Marissa Brooks's house," he said, but it wasn't a question.

"The country club was booked until late January and Delaney didn't want a winter wedding," Keith said, and this time his voice held a hint of discomfort.

Adam didn't bother reminding Keith he knew all about Delaney's preferences for her wedding. For example, he knew the country club was the only place in three counties elegant enough to hold a Walker-Herndon wedding reception, but if couples wanted quiet elegance, Brookhaven would give them a run for their money. He looked around the empty room. "She rents it out?"

"First time," he said. "Won't be the last, either. I hear she's in debt up to her eyeballs at the lumberyard. It's great, but a total fucking boondoggle. She can't live here by herself." Keith stepped away, putting distance between him and Adam by looking around and spreading his hands. "You'd never guess what went on here when we were in high school."

With that, Keith turned and walked away. What went on here in high school was Adam and Marissa almost having sex in every room in this house. Back then the windows were missing, the flooring water stained, filthy, scuffed; the plaster chipped, cracked, or missing. But over the spring of their senior year, they'd almost, *almost* had sex in this house more times than he could count.

She'd been willing. Experienced to his virgin. Despite desire raging inside him like a dragon's fury, he'd stopped just short. Every time. That uncharacteristic discipline cost him. Cost her. Cost everyone in town, but he, Marissa, and Josh Wilmont paid the most.

The presence hovering at the edge of Adam's vision coalesced into a living, breathing woman standing in the doorway leading into the kitchen. He'd seen her since he'd left, but never alone, never up close.

Another woman stood next to her. Adam recognized Alana Wentworth from the newspaper article link his mother sent him, but the town's contract librarian blended into the woodwork next to Marissa. A smile on her face, Alana said something to Marissa, then crossed the room to speak with Mrs. Walker, leaving Marissa all alone.

You can face her. What you felt, for her, around her, is long gone.

One breath. A second, as he fought combustible emotions. With his third inhale he bent his head and counted the strips of wood forming one parquet square, but on the exhale he put his hands on his hips and cut her a glance. One shoulder braced against the kitchen door frame, she didn't move, but the only color in her face was the red on her mouth, a deep, rich color he only saw on models on the backs of women's magazines. No real woman wore lipstick that red.

No woman in Walkers Ford drew that much attention to her mouth. The older females in the room wore skirts and blouses, and the younger ones wore tight jeans and low-cut tops, but none of them radiated Marissa's sheer sexual energy. Back in the day, he and Ris had had enough chemistry to set fire to rain-soaked wood. Today, right now, he stood in a no-man's-land between the wedding party and Marissa, and given a choice between the group planning wedding logistics like it was a two-week reconnaissance mission for an entire platoon and the girl he left behind twelve years ago, he chose the girl. The Marine Corps taught him how to handle himself. Surely he could handle a simple conversation with someone he used to know.

His boots sounded unnaturally loud on the parquet as he walked over and stopped in front of her. "Hey, Ris."

She tilted her head up and looked at him. In the heels she was only a couple of inches shorter than his six feet, and that mouth; that red, lush, wet mouth. Thick black lashes fringed her dark chocolate eyes. She didn't need mascara. Years ago, shaking in the grip of demanding lust, he'd brushed his open mouth over her lashes, her mouth, her cheekbones, past sexual desire, desperate to absorb her in every way possible. Memory sliced into his awareness: of his body pressed against hers as he rocked his pelvis into the soft give of her hip, of sharp, agonizing pressure aching in his cock, of his fingers exploring mysterious, slick heat while her gaze went distant and her lips parted in a soft cry . . .

She peered around his shoulder at the throng of people in the room, then looked at him. "You made that look easy."

Something resembling a laugh huffed from his chest. "Nothing to it," he said.

"Oh, sure," she said, as mockingly casual as he'd been. "Because that's not your ex-fiancée and your best friend planning the wedding that should have been yours."

Trust Marissa to cut right to the bone. "As long as she's happy," he said, a little less casually. "How've you been?"

She shrugged. "Fine."

Twelve years of near silence summed up in a single word, but she had every right not to tell him anything. "The house looks good," he said.

She kept watching Delaney and her flock of attendants. "Good?"

"Amazing," he admitted with a glance over his shoulder.

"That's better," she said, then looked back at him again. "Want a tour?"

Was there a hint of invitation under the simple question? "Yes."

He could do this. He was a world champion at resisting Marissa Brooks. He'd done it since he was seventeen years old.

But now you don't have to . . .

She led him to the center of the room, under the massive chandelier. "The house was designed by Henry Dalton Mead at Josiah Brooks's request when he traveled west from Connecticut in the eighteen-eighties," she started. "He'd sailed to Japan and China before he came to Dakota territory, and he was obsessed with the Japanese custom of sliding walls that partitioned off smaller spaces inside one large family home. So he had Mead build Brookhaven's living space with that in mind." She pointed to paneled places at the ends of the walls. "The panels slide into those compartments when he wanted an open space for parties or dances. Otherwise he would slide them out, along the runners in the ceiling to close off a smaller space by the fire."

"To heat it," Adam said.

"To heat it," she agreed. "My grandfather put in a furnace. I updated it to a heat pump, but it still gets cold in here in the winter."

She set off through the smaller groups still focused on

wedding details, up the broad, oak staircase to the second floor. The upstairs resembled any other large house, with a row of white paneled doors on either side of a long hallway. She held open a door into an empty, square room with hardwood floors, a fireplace, and a large, rain-lashed window. "Each bedroom has its own fireplace. Seven smaller bedrooms share three full bathrooms, but the master bedroom has its own bath and sitting room."

He leaned past her to peer into the room, large enough for a queen-sized bed and a chair and rug by the fire. "I remember cracked plaster. Some water damage to the flooring."

"I got lucky. She was structurally sound, but needed a lot of cosmetic help," Marissa said. "If you remember that, you probably remember her background. Sorry to bore you."

"I wasn't bored," he said, and turned to look down at her. "You loved to talk about the house. Remember?"

And just like that, the space between them filled with the electric heat of the spring of their senior year in high school. They'd ended up out here all the time, officially trespassing because the county owned the house by then. Marissa would wander through the empty, rundown rooms, repeating her dad's tales about Brookhaven and his family's glory years. Adam would follow her, watching her talk, deafened to the point of hearing one word in four by the unsatisfied sexual longing thumping under his skin. Eventually they'd end up somewhere— the barn, if it was raining, by the creek if it wasn't—in a tangle of arms and legs, tongues and gripping hands—

"I remember," she said.

He jerked back to the present to find her looking into the room, heat staining the cheek turned to him. Goose bumps rippled along the pale skin, and her nipples peaked under the gray halter top.

Pretend that's about chilly air, not hot longing that should have gone away . . .

"You're cold," he said, then cleared his throat. "Let's go back downstairs."

That sounded better. He stepped back, she closed the door, and at his extended hand, led him back down the stairs to the comparatively warm, brightly lit main floor.

"It looks great," he said as they cleared the last stair, pitching his voice to carry. "You do good work."

The look she shot him under her lashes told him he might have fooled everyone else in the room, but not her. "Thank you," she said.

No one came to lay claim to him, so he fell back on small talk. She was watching him, her eyes curious, amused, maybe even challenging. "Still living in town?"

"No, I fixed up the servants' quarters," she said, tilting her head to indicate what he remembered as a tiny set of rooms off the kitchen. "I couldn't afford to renovate Brookhaven and pay rent on the State Street house. I moved back here after Chris died."

At the opposite end of the room Keith laughed, the sound rich and easy, his perfect teeth and blond hair catching the light from the chandelier when Adam glanced at him. Delaney looked at Adam, then slipped her hand into Keith's.

When he looked back at Marissa she was watching him again. "You want a drink?"

To do what he needed to do, he had to stay clearheaded. He really didn't need to add alcohol to the hot chemistry sparking between him and Marissa. He wished he could blame it on her mouth, her eyes, the length of her legs, the fact that he hadn't had sex in over a year, but it was him, too. The heat simmering in his veins, slipping along nerves and skin to pool in his cock, fueled those flames. It wasn't him, or her. It was them.

I'm fine sounded in his head, but what came out of his mouth was, "Yeah."

"Come on," she said with a tip of her head, then the swinging kitchen door closed on the conversations behind them. The silky ties of her halter hung between her shoulder blades as she disappeared through a door between the fridge and a closet, returning moments later to hand him a nearly full bottle of Johnnie Walker Black Label whiskey. Adam looked around as he twisted the bottle's cap. He remembered a chipped white sink and a wood counter over Depression-era linoleum, not gleaming steel and granite countertops.

"You did this yourself?" he asked.

"Anything I could teach myself. I got help with the rest, apprenticed myself as free labor. An artist in residence at SDSU did the stained-glass windows," she said, finding glasses in a nearly empty cupboard. "New deck. New roof. I kept it simple on the second floor, and just sanded and stained the floors and patched the plaster."

"You do good work," he said. He ran his hand over the granite while she poured. The joins in the granite were nearly invisible. He tried to remember what her career aspirations had been in high school and came up blank, but he doubted construction had been on the list.

"Thanks," she said, and handed him a shot glass. She considered him for a moment, then poured out two shots. "So, Staff Sergeant Collins, what we should drink to?"

2

WAS HIS RANK an attempt to put some distance between them? Adam couldn't tell. The outfit was sheer sex, the look in her eyes harder to read. "I'm out," he said brusquely.

Her eyebrows lifted. "Really?"

"I start grad school in Brookings in January."

She cocked her head and considered him over the glass. "In what?"

"Architecture."

Her eyes narrowed, somehow at once amused and suspicious. "Architecture. That's what you want to do now that you're out of the Corps. You want to be an architect."

He felt his face go expressionless. That was the plan, back before he'd ended things with Delaney. Once his future was supper for one, not two, architecture school seemed as good a career choice as any. Rural communities needed architects; he was coming home to a rural community, and he needed to do something. "I replaced my destructive habits with something more constructive. You didn't know?"

"No one talks to me about you." She said the words without a hint of inflection, no teasing, no flirting, no anger. That unemotional appearance could stem from total serenity, or a really good cover for a sea of emotions.

You should know . . .

"It's Mr. Collins, now." Fuck, that title sounded foreign, or maybe just wrong. He lifted his glass. "Adam, to an old friend. So . . . to old friends."

Marissa downed the whiskey in one swallow and set the glass on the counter next to his.

"Is that what we are? Old friends?"

He'd been engaged to Delaney long enough to know when not answering a question was in his best interests. He exhaled against the burn. "Hit me again."

With another little smile she poured out two more shots. The warm amber liquid picked up flecks of brown in the granite under the shot glass, and her gray top stood out against the white cabinets and granite.

"Your turn," he said as they lifted their glasses.

"To reunions," she said.

He lifted the glass in salute, and downed the shot. This time the fire seared along nerves already wide awake and tingling, and a glow ignited in his stomach.

He looked at the rim of her glass, free of lipstick, then at her mouth. Big mistake. "That color doesn't come off?" he asked with a vague gesture.

"Special protective layer for shine and durability. Like a clear coat on wood," she said. When he huffed, she flicked him a shuttered glance through her lashes and lifted the bottle. "Want to go again?"

"Hell, yes."

Her hand was steady as she splashed the third round into the glasses. "Your turn."

He thought for a second about coming home, about weddings, about life after the Marine Corps, about loose ends. About the step he had to take, and might as well take now. "To new experiences."

She paused with the glass halfway to her mouth. "You've never been a best man before."

"Nope," he said, and tossed the shot back. He flicked a glance at the full glass she held. The silky halter top draped over her peaked nipples, and another bolt of lust crashed through him, spurred on by whiskey, exhaustion, and a sense of recklessness he thought the Marine Corps had trained out of him. "Try to keep up, Brooks."

She swallowed the whiskey without breaking eye contact, then set her glass on the counter next to his. "It might be easier to score with a tipsy girl at the bars in San Diego, but you don't have to get me drunk. Or maybe you don't remember."

This was why he'd avoided her for the last decade. The lock on the compartment holding all things Marissa was a good one. Solid. Bulletproof. Forged in the kiln of regret and anguish and fear. Walking through Brookhaven's front door somehow warped the compartment's walls. Memories seeped free . . . driving along Highway 12 on his motorcycle, her on the back of the bike, arms wrapped around his waist, her breasts firm and hot against his back, her thighs gripping his hips. They'd routinely done one-ten without helmets. Just riding the bike gave him a hard-on; riding it with Marissa drove him near to breaking, her hair streaming in their wake. Later, sitting by the creek behind Brookhaven, she worked out the tangles with her fingers while he watched, sprawled beside her. Her eyes alight with the same desire flaming hot and low in his belly, while he forced himself to remember all the reasons he couldn't do what she would so willingly do.

Reason number one: you're leaving and she's staying.

Reason number two: no knocking up a seventeen-year-old girl.

Reason number three: feeling this much is more dangerous than doing one-ten without a helmet.

"I remember," he said, and just like that he took another step down the path, found it scarily solid under his foot.

With a little glitter to her smile, she went on. "A best man's job isn't too difficult. Get the groom to the church on time and sober enough to stand up. Give a speech at the reception. They usually fall into two categories," she said. "The first is incredibly formal and stilted, like something out of a high school speech class. The second is absolutely pickled because the groom and his posse have been drinking nonstop for two days, so they're either drunk or hungover. Last year Tom Lewis nearly keeled over on the chancel steps before Father Dobson sat him down and shoved his head between his knees to keep him from throwing up on the altar. They did the abbreviated version of the vows, and then he went into the vestry and threw up in the baptismal font. Leanne still hasn't forgiven him."

He laughed, low and short. "I bet the honeymoon was a little on the frosty side," he said absently. This speech wouldn't be just any best man's toast. All the guests would be watching him to see what he had to say about love, marriage, and his former fiancée and best friend.

From the look on her face, Marissa was thinking about the same thing. "New experiences indeed," she said.

He set down his glass. "But that wasn't what I meant," he said.

A pink alcohol flush stood high on her cheekbones, and her eyes gleamed. Another memory long suppressed slipped under the door locking away everything about Marissa: his first kiss with her, in the pasture behind this very house, her back to a tree; her hands in his back pockets; her mouth open, hot, yielding under his. The kiss lasted as long as it took for sweat to rise at the nape of his neck, slide between his shoulder blades, and trickle down to the base of his spine, where her thumb stroked it back into the skin.

Another hard thump of his heart against his chest.

That's desire. Lust. Nothing more. Still, you should walk away.

He reached past her to set down the shot glass, and when he did, his inner arm slid against the slick fabric of her top, warmed by her body heat. The hair on his arms stood on end, and an electric shock zapped down his spine, straight to his cock. She shuddered, the movement faint, quickly tamed, but he'd seen it.

"If you're looking for new experiences, you've come to the wrong place," she said, her voice husky from the whiskey.

He'd had every reason to say no then, and no reason to say no now.

He stepped closer. At the movement she turned to lean against the countertop, a slight, challenging lift to her eyebrow. Another step and he braced both hands on either side of her hips, bringing their gazes level.

"I'm exactly where I'm supposed to be," he rasped.

Seconds ticked past as the voices just outside the kitchen filtered into his consciousness . . . an earnest discussion about the supper menu . . . then he kissed Marissa Brooks.

The voices faded away. She tasted like whiskey, or maybe he did, but the slow slide of her tongue against his mixed with the bite of the whiskey and sent heat coursing along his nerves to pool in his balls. His cock thickened, straining urgently against the zipper of his cargo pants.

Her hands braced against his ribs and pushed. "You think we can just pick up exactly where we left off," she said, still husky but now unsteady.

"Pick up and keep going," he said bluntly. Not very romantic, but this wasn't about romance. This was just old embers, coaxed back to life by a fifteen-month deployment, fueled by alcohol. Nothing more.

Still looking up at him, she bit her lower lip, ran her tongue over the sore spot, as if tasting them together, considering the implications with a caution she'd never shown when they were eighteen. Then she lifted her hand to his nape, fingers toying with the bristly edges of his buzzed hair, then tightening to bring his mouth back to hers.

A nuclear chain reaction of chemistry exploded between them, and suddenly all he could hear was the blood pounding in his ears. The soft, pleading noise she made vibrated under his hand, splayed against her exposed throat. He stepped into her body, felt the taut muscles of her belly tighten, then relax, against the pressure.

The first sign of yielding shot through him, and he gripped

her ass, pulling her against him, working her skirt up enough
to get his knee between hers. But her hands flattened against
his chest and pushed, breaking the kiss. "We can't do this
here," she whispered. "We're in the kitchen. Your ex-fiancée
is in the next room!"

He hauled open the door to the pantry, gripped her upper
arm and dragged her inside, then closed the door, plunging
them into blackness. The only light in the tiny, windowless
space slipped under the door, and in a moment his eyes
adjusted to see mostly empty shelves lining three walls.

"This is the pantry," she said, amusement clear in her
voice. "The door to my apartment is the next one."

He knew that. It took more than three shots in ten minutes
to disorient a US Marine. He found her by feel, hands outstretched, skimming the rough shelving until he encountered
warm, bare skin. The hollow of her throat, then with both
hands he followed the tendon in her neck to her pulse, then
to the line of her jaw. He cupped her jaw and aligned his body
with hers as he bent his head and kissed her. The inability to
see heightened everything, the scent of her hair, the soft, wet
sounds their mouths made as the kiss deepened into ravishing.
Her breasts against his chest, her hands slowly fisting in his
shirt. So slowly he couldn't tell if she was distracted or savor-
ing sensations, she tugged his shirt free from his pants, and
then her hands were on the bare skin of his waist. One hand slid
around to the base of his spine, and her thumb stroked over
his vertebrae, the motion exactly copying what she'd done
during their first kiss. The difference was that before, her
hand remained outside of his jeans.

Now her fingers flattened at the top of his ass. He growled
low in his throat, and found the ties holding up her halter top.
A quick jerk, then he dragged his hand down her breastbone.
The fabric dropped to her waist, baring her breasts to his
hands, then his mouth. She quivered when he used the edge
of his teeth on her nipple, her fingers digging into his shoulders. Even in the dark he could see white teeth set into her lush,
red lower lip.

He slipped his wallet from his pants pocket while she went at his belt and button fly. His cock bobbed free, bumping her wrist before she turned her hand and gripped him. It must have been his imagination that a pleased little purr drifted into the air when she slowly stroked him from tip to base, then cupped his balls.

Stars exploded in front of his eyes, weakening his knees. She set a slow, firm rhythm, driving him to reach into the darkness, for the shelving unit, and shove cans aside until he found a support and gripped it. He'd stopped breathing. That's what those lights dancing in front of his eyes were. He forced himself to inhale and lifted her hand from his cock.

"Stop."

Was that his voice, rough and low and curt? In the enclosed space the potent scent of her skin and the undeniable scent of arousal drifted into his nostrils, dragging to the surface all the long-buried memories of her body, her mouth. The ache, long dormant, crawled through his blood like molten lava. She shimmied her skirt up and sent her panties to the floor while he sheathed himself. Then he gripped her ass and hoisted her, opened her thighs with his hips and nudged into place. It should have been odd, strange, unfamiliar, but it just felt right. So goddamn right. His awareness collapsed into sensation, hot, slick, tight pressure as he stretched her open and slid inside. Her breathing, shallow and fast. The undulating grip of her pussy as she adjusted to him.

His head was swimming, and not from the shots. He was a *Mister*, not a Marine. Brookhaven looked like something out of an architectural magazine. His ex-fiancée was marrying his best friend, and twenty minutes after coming home he was inside Marissa Brooks.

She trembled when he bottomed out, and he heard a muted thunk as her head dropped back and bumped against a can of something. He curved over her, cheek pressed to her temple, on the edge of losing it in a spectacularly embarrassing fashion, when he heard Delaney.

"Where's Adam? I want to remind him about the tux fittings."

Only a solid-core six-panel door with no lock and three feet of electrified air stood between Delaney and him, bare-assed and balls deep in another woman. An unexpected hot thrill shot through him, just vengeful enough to firm up his control and make his cock throb with anticipation. Marissa's sheath clenched around him in response. A faint whimper drifted the millimeters separating that lush red mouth from his ear. All the little hairs stood on end at the helpless sound.

"Shhhhhh," he said, nearly soundless. Then he pulled out until the tip of his cock nestled just inside her sex, and slid forward again. "Be quiet."

"Did he leave?" Mrs. Walker's voice.

"I didn't see him leave," Delaney answered. "Where's Marissa?"

"Probably showing Alana around," Mrs. Walker answered. "They're good friends, I think."

The words came from just outside the door. Probably she was standing between the pantry door and the door leading to the servants' quarters, trying to decide whether or not to knock. Marissa's face was indistinct in the darkness, but Adam could make out her mouth, lips parted, and the pale skin of her torso, her nipples dark, hard tips on her breasts. As shallowly as they were breathing to avoid detection, their breath still mingled.

Marissa's fingernails curled into the nape of his neck under his shirt collar, her body hot and trembling against his. He wanted to hoist her higher, but any movement in the closet would advertise their location. So he closed his eyes and moved, slow, secretive, stealthy. Withdraw. Wait until temptation becomes torture. Push back inside, parting those slick, swollen walls, feel her quiver as he stretched her, then snugged up against her clit. Her tremors increased but he couldn't stop, couldn't do anything but feel his balls tighten, the pressure seethe in the tip of his cock as he did it again, again.

"He looked different."

Delaney's voice again, but he ruthlessly blocked her out. He needed all his strength and coordination to hold Marissa because she was shaking in his arms like she was going to fly apart. When he stroked in he knew why. She buried her face in the crook of his neck, stifling high-pitched gasps as her pussy contracted around his cock.

She'd come.

Thought flared in his brain in time to the rapid thumps of his heart. He'd done nothing for her except grope her with less technique than he'd used before, then fuck her in what was likely the most uncomfortable position ever, with her back to rough shelves. And she'd come.

Thump.

Sex could be like this?

Thump.

What would it be like if he got her flat on her back, in a bed, somewhere private?

Thumpthumpthump . . .

Endless, erotic possibility opened up before him, snapping his control. It was too much, a decade of denial, her helpless surrender, enforced silence, the imminent threat of discovery, sharing air in the small, dark space. Her heels hooked around his thighs, holding him close as he slammed home once, twice, then came. Hard.

When the blackness receded he said the first thing that came to mind, drawn out of long-submerged dreams. "I wanted that to last longer," he said, low and gruff. The sound of his voice recalled Delaney's, and he glanced at the door.

"They're gone," Marissa said expressionlessly.

Her face was a pale oval in the darkness, her mouth still red temptation. She unwound her legs from around his thighs, and braced her hands against his chest until he withdrew and backed away. The ache receded, but he knew that was only temporary. What remained was a taste of something dark and edgy, yet familiar. The smell of sex layered over damp earth and Marissa's skin. Perhaps it was the rich, bitter layer of revenge, the coppery tang of blood mixed with salty sweat. Maybe it was lust.

Whatever it was, emotionless it was not. The dragon, awakened and hungry, shifted in his chest, stretched leathery wings against his collarbone and shoulders.

"Fuck," he said under his breath.

He could hear her rearranging her clothes by feel in the dark, then she opened the door and peered out. "There's a bathroom across the hall."

He crossed to the small, antique-looking half bath across the way. Inside he ditched the condom, washed his hands, and looked in the mirror. None of the glossy color on Marissa's mouth had come off on his. He checked his neck and shoulder, and realization bloomed. Twelve years earlier, every minute of every hour they spent together dripped emotion. Anger, fear, longing, exhilaration, the temptation of testing the edges of his control. This time it was hot and slick and irresistible on the surface, and like her lipstick, she left nothing of herself behind. The Marine Corps taught him how to hold it all in.

But who'd taught *her*? Where was the passionate girl he remembered?

When he opened the door, she stood in front of the pantry, her arms crossed, the halter hiding the sex flush on her collarbone and neck. "See?" she said. "No big deal."

Her words landed with the impact of a roundhouse kick, but he'd learned his lessons well and didn't so much as blink. "Right," he said. "No big deal."

"Good night, Adam," she said, then opened the door to the servants' quarters and slipped inside.

The bolt shot home with a firm click as he stood there, hands on his hips, and compared the only two women he'd let into his life. In the months since their breakup, he realized he hadn't loved Delaney as much as he'd loved the way she looked at him when he came home on leave before deploying to Iraq the first time. He'd worn his uniform with a self-conscious pride that made him cringe now, and he hadn't been too eager to closely examine the way it caused a sudden and profound transformation in the eyes of Walkers Ford. When pretty, kind Delaney Walker stopped to talk to him, to ask him about boot camp, then invited him to a party at her parents' lake house over the weekend, a sense of relief dropped over his soul, like a curtain over a window framing the black thunderclouds and horizon-searing lightning. Too relieved that Delaney's respect and love erased what he'd done to Josh and Marissa at Brookhaven, he'd never stopped to count the cost. She resisted sex before an engagement, no great difficulty when she was in college and he was deployed; when he'd produced a ring, she'd gone on the pill, and they'd used condoms.

And while the experience was a pale imitation of what he'd felt with Marissa that spring, he'd taken that for a good thing. This was reasonable. Understandable. A manageable urge, as unlike what Marissa inspired in him as civilians and Marines.

But now he was back in Walkers Ford, out of the Corps, tying up loose ends before the wedding, and before he moved on with his life. They'd gotten twelve years of curiosity out of their systems, and besides, he had one more unannounced homecoming to go. She'd said good night. He could return the courtesy.

"Good night, Ris," he said softly. Then he shoved the screen door open and strode down the hill to his Charger, got in the car, and drove away, all the while wondering where the passionate, impetuous girl had gone.

3

W ITH WATERY KNEES and sensitized nerves firing randomly in all her hot spots, Marissa trailed Delaney and Stacey through the kitchen, entryway, and great room, half listening to their earnest conversation about wedding details, but mostly focused on *what just happened*.

Because *what just happened*, namely, a quickie with Adam Collins in her *pantry*, shocked the hell out of her. Worse, it made her forget about Brookhaven for a few minutes, an indulgence she couldn't afford for a number of reasons. She'd said it was no big deal, but that was pride talking. Twelve years earlier she'd loved Adam Collins with the passion only a seventeen-year-old girl could muster. She would have done anything with him, even though she'd known he was leaving.

Back then, everyone had dreams, or at least a plan. Delaney planned to go to college, then to grad school to become a school psychologist. Keith planned on college, then law school, then a job at his father's practice. Marissa was a Brooks, which meant she had dreams, not plans, and no money; like her father before her, she dreamed of restoring Brookhaven to pristine condition. Adam was a Collins, and like his deadbeat father before him, he dreamed of speed. Not stock cars. Motorcycles. In the rare moments when they weren't screaming around eastern South Dakota at ninety miles an hour they talked about dreams. Adam dreamed of getting out of Walkers Ford, as fast as his Hayabusa could carry him. His need to prove himself was as tangible as the humid spring air.

Back then, she didn't care that he was leaving, and she didn't want to go with him. All she wanted was him, inside her, going all the way. Stopping short channeled her desire into love and Adam's pent-up longing into increasingly reckless decisions. Risky moves on the bike. Drinking, something he'd rarely done before that spring. Risky moves, alcohol, and a teenage dare crashed together the night of graduation, at Brookhaven, and the consequences changed their lives, forever.

He left, not for the racing circuit, but for the Marine Corps, and broke her heart. But one fifteen-minute interlude with Adam in her pantry wouldn't risk her heart again. It wasn't likely he'd take an interest in her anyway. The idea of Adam Collins, seasoned Marine and world traveler, settling down in Brookings, South Dakota, was ridiculous. She would finish restoring Brookhaven, her only dream, and go on with her life.

The thought sent her stomach twisting and looping like a ride at the county fair.

Delaney and Stacey stopped in front of the grand fireplace for another moment of low-voiced conversation in the empty room. At Delaney's request, Keith drove Mrs. Walker home an hour earlier. Alana stayed for a while, too polite to ask Marissa where she'd disappeared to for twenty minutes, but even she'd given up and gone home to Walkers Ford. Was that Adam's next stop, his mother's house? Darla Collins kept Adam's bike. Did Adam know it lurked under a shroud in the garage? He'd had a plan, starting with smaller races as an amateur, making money where he could, working his way up to a sponsorship deal. He was fearless, gifted with unbelievable spatial awareness and reflexes. He would have succeeded, if not for—

"Marissa," Delaney asked as Stacey pulled on her coat and prepared to leave. "Do you have a minute?"

Delaney's father wrote her a check large enough to pay off the HVAC bill with some left over for the lumberyard. Their agreement gave Delaney access to the house whenever she wanted, and they both knew it. Or maybe Delaney still felt a tad bit possessive about her ex-fiancé.

"Of course," she said, and closed the door behind Stacey. So polite. It really was impossible to find fault with Delaney. Her father owned the state's largest privately held bank, but Delaney opted for a career as a licensed school psychologist serving three rural counties and volunteering at Pine Ridge once a month. She was pretty, reserved, always dressed on the demure side of current fashion. They made a great story, the good girl and the bad boy turned Marine, until Adam ended things before the storybook finish. The news had rocked not only Walkers Ford but the entire county. Fairy tales starring Marines and pretty school psychologists didn't end that way.

They didn't start with getting fucked in a pantry, either.

The air on the west side of the great room held warmth despite the rapid drop in temperature as night fell; or maybe that was heat lingering under her skin. Delaney waited until Marissa joined her in front of the unfinished fireplace. "The house looks beautiful," she began, genuine approval in her voice. "But the wedding is in four weeks. Will you be able to repair this wall before then?"

Both ends of Brookhaven's great room were finished in floor-to-ceiling oak woodwork panels that mimicked the construction of the sliding panels that defined Brookhaven's unique style. The smaller, less elaborate fireplace in the dining area was intact and polished to a high sheen. The fireplace at the south end of the great room stood under walls stripped to the plaster and lathing. The rest of the house had been done since the spring, but summer's busy season in construction stopped her progress. Or that's what she told herself.

"Not a problem," she said.

"What happened to it?" Delaney asked. "The other fire-place is in such excellent shape."

Memories surfaced from the lockbox deep inside, pushed through her skin as prickling, hot shame. She should have stopped Adam before things got out of control. Even though the county technically owned the house at that point, Brookhaven was hers. Her responsibility. Her obligation. Her dream, even then.

"Vandals," Marissa said shortly.

Delaney nodded, as if agreeing, but said, "Adam looked well, don't you think?"

Marissa kept her gaze on the exposed brick and plaster. He did look good. His hair was still regulation short, the color of aged cedar, his eyes a true hazel, his body as hard against her stomach and breasts as the shelving was against her back.

"A little older, maybe," Marissa said when the silence stretched into unnecessary guilt. Adam no longer belonged to Delaney. Marissa hadn't done anything wrong.

Delaney joined Marissa in her close examination of the unfinished mantel, lifting her smooth, pale hand to touch the exposed brick and plaster. Keith's engagement ring glittered brilliantly in the light, a move Marissa thought was intended to show off the diamond until she remembered Delaney was left-handed.

Delaney smiled, but it didn't reach her eyes. "Thank you again for allowing me to use your house," she said.

"My pleasure," Marissa said. Delaney thought of it as her wedding. Marissa thought of it as Brookhaven's redemption, the final act in her father's lifelong dream, and hers.

Delaney let herself out. Marissa locked the door behind her, then walked around the house, turning off the lights, plunging the room into blackness. As her eyes adjusted, she could see in the distance the cottonwood trees lining the riverbed at the bottom of the pasture that sloped away from the house.

She'd kissed Adam for the first time against one of those cottonwoods. They'd been barefoot and muddy after a mile-long water fight along the creek left her white top clinging to her skin and her hair in dark tendrils on her shoulders. Weak from laughter, turned-on from the newly discovered sensation of being prey to a boy's predator, she'd leaned against a big tree, wrung water from her hair, and found him watching her with the same expression on his face he'd worn in the kitchen tonight. The intensity scared her then, but now he had the body and the demeanor to go with the eyes, and she had the experience to deal with it.

He still left her weak, but not from laughter, and despite the rumors flying around town, he wasn't staying. That dream died long ago, and she of all people knew sex didn't change it.

Now, alone in the house, she pushed through the swinging doors into the kitchen. The whiskey bottle and two shot glasses sat in plain view on the kitchen counter, something neither Delaney nor Stacey commented on while they discussed foot-traffic flow into the great room. She ran water in the sink and washed the glasses and wiped down the counter. Then she carefully tightened the cap on the bottle and put it back in the pantry she used because the servants' quarters had a bare minimum of cabinets in the kitchen.

When the door opened, the slightest hint of Adam's skin and sex wafted past her to dissipate in the kitchen's cool air. Nerves awakened, and barely satisfied, lit up like Brookhaven's porch light on a clear winter night. She set the whiskey bottle in its accustomed place, then stepped out and carefully closed the pantry door—like the proverbial barn door—too late. She wasn't known for playing hard-to-get, but they'd gone from *Hello, Marissa* to the shocking, stretching glide of his cock into her body, with his ex-fiancée right outside, in less than twenty minutes.

Why the hell did you do that?

Because it's been forever and a day since you had a new experience.

She stepped out to the white-painted planks of the tiny porch. Rain dripped cold and steady from the overhang covering the servants' entrance to the house her great-grandfather built when he arrived in the Dakota territory, flush with his inheritance from the Brooks shipping fortune. Succeeding generations ran through the inheritance in true Brooks-dreamer fashion. She and her father had lived in the house until they moved into a rented house in town, taking with them boxes of artifacts from Brookhaven's glory days, memories not of his childhood but his father's, passed down to him, and from him to Marissa.

Her father taught her to dream. Life taught her dreams don't always come true. Her first time with Adam fell more in the realm of fantasy fulfilled.

Why the hell did you do that?

Because for the first time, he clearly wasn't going to say no.

The flashpoint memory of his body pounding into hers sent an aftershock rippling through her.

Her heart had stopped when he walked into the room. Alana was there not as one of Delaney's attendants but as Marissa's friend, and even the smooth, composed librarian faltered when Adam walked on the scene.

Isn't that . . . ?

Yes.

Oh my.

Marissa had no response to that, because Adam wasn't supposed to be there. He'd caught her off guard—that was a handy excuse for *Why the hell did you do that?*—and based on the looks ranging from raised eyebrows to dropped-jaw shock, no one else in the room was, either. Even Keith, normally so arrogantly slick and confident, looked almost panicked. No one expected him until much closer to the wedding, but there he was, wearing cargo pants and a button-down shirt, shoulders squared, jaw set, boots thunking against the hardwood. The room was massive, high ceilings, open floor plan, and Adam dominated it from the moment he strode through Brookhaven's double front doors. Apparently you could take the man out of the Marine Corps, but you couldn't take the Marine Corps out of the man.

But something glinted in Adam's eyes, something that made her heart knock hard against her throat and had her searching for an opening. Now, with her mouth numb from three shots of whiskey, her legs weak from a mighty orgasm, and her shoulders sore from getting sandwiched between oak supports and Adam's hard body, she knew why.

The boy she'd thought was long gone still lived in that straight-backed, broad-shouldered recruiting poster.

The lights of Walkers Ford, twinkling through the steady rain, called her back to the present. Her life rolled out before her like the sodden prairie sloping away from Brookhaven, to the creek and beyond. Priority number one was to cover the exposed plaster and lathing around the great room's fireplace in time for the wedding.

It sounded so simple. Another house built by Henry Dalton Mead lay just east of Brookings, due to be demolished. All she had to do was tear off that house's mantel and paneling, transport it to Brookhaven, and install it. She'd have her dream, for herself, for her dad, for all the Brookses who came before them.

So why can't you turn into the driveway, let alone walk into the house?

She would try again. She would do this. Had to do this. Wanted to do this, even, so this time there wouldn't be a problem. Above all, she wouldn't show any weakness, any hint of hesitation.

You can't even turn into the driveway . . .

A shiver chased up her spine. Nothing a hot bath wouldn't cure. She locked herself in Brookhaven and went to turn on the water.

4

ADAM WOKE WHEN a bolt of pain shot down his arm. He rolled to shift his weight off the futon slat pinching his nerve and consequently rammed the top of his head into the oak support. The bolts holding the futon together squeaked in protest; if he wedged his shoulder against the top arm and his feet against the bottom, he could shatter the frame with one good shove, hatching himself onto the floor of his mother's sewing room like the six-foot-two-inch, two-hundred pound, dragon-slaying Marine from the old television commercials.

"Fuck," he hissed.

Task number one was to find an apartment in Brookings as soon as possible.

With a low curse he slid down, rubbed the tender spot on top of his head, then his eyes, then scraped his palm over his stubble. Through the house's thin walls he could hear the perky chatter of a morning news program and the sounds of eggshells cracking in brisk succession. One, two, three, four, five, a pause for a dollop of milk, then the sound of the whisk against the bowl. After two days of fast food, the last thing he wanted to do was eat, but his mother had been near highly unusual tears when he arrived out of the blue on her doorstep last night. She'd want to feed him. Therefore he would eat.

Wearing only his boxers, he sat up, elbows on knees, and looked around the room. The house was tiny, no more than eight hundred square feet, the size of Brookhaven's master bedroom, and when Adam had left for basic training his mother took over his room. His entire childhood, her machine and all the fabric and notions she used to make clothes, drapes, bedding, and pillows occupied most of the living room. She needed the space, and when he visited home after he left he stayed with Keith. His high school belongings were crammed onto shelves in his mother's single-car garage. He had less of an urge to go through them than he did to eat. What would be in there? Clothes that wouldn't fit. Posters of fast cars and faster motorcycles. He'd never cared about high school sports. The only thing he dreamed about was racing.

Two gentle taps on the door. "Honey?"

He looked at the closed door. "Yeah, Mom?"

"I've got breakfast ready to go, whenever you want it."

The few belongings he'd accumulated in San Diego and his Marine medals and commendations were in boxes in the back of the Charger. Sorting the old stuff would make room for the new until he found a place of his own.

You could store an entire company of Marines at Brookhaven, not to mention a few boxes . . .

Yeah, right. What are you going to say? Thanks for the fuck, and, oh, by the way, can I move into the house I ruined?

She'd clung to him like his body was the only thing on her mind, like she wanted him. Only him. Right then. Then she'd all but slapped him. He guessed he deserved it.

"Honey?"

"Sorry, Mom," he said hastily. "Let me get a run in first."

"Sure, honey," she said.

He got up, pulled on shorts, a T-shirt, and his running shoes, and walked through the living room to the kitchen. She'd redecorated in the year since he'd been home last. This time the theme was cherries. New slipcovers and curtains in mostly cream with tiny red sprigs of cherry blossoms, and new cushions in a dark green with bright red cherries on the chairs around the kitchen table. The banter from the national morning news trickled into the air from a small television on the table.

His mother, tall, slim, and dressed in a blouse and pants she'd likely designed and sewed herself, looked better than she had when he was in junior high and high school, working two jobs and trying to raise a son bent on self-destruction. While she'd never said a word to him about it, over the years he'd pieced together the history. On the verge of starting at design school in New York, she'd spent a summer hanging around with a fast-talking dirt track racer with faster hands. He'd knocked her up, then moved on without a word, let alone child support. Adam's birth effectively ended her dream of making a career in design. With her custom sewing business and the money Adam sent her every month, she'd been able to quit the job at the convenience store.

He bent to kiss her cheek. "The bathroom looks great, and so do the curtains."

"The jacquard was on clearance. I used most of it for Mrs. Herndon's breakfast-nook cushions, but there was enough left over for the valance," she said as she set the eggs back in the fridge.

Inspiration seized him. "Don't worry about breakfast," he said. "I'll get in a run, we can take a look at the garage, then hit the Heirloom for lunch after the church crowd gets out."

"Oh, honey, you don't need to do that," she started.

A lifetime of frugality made treats a rare thing in his mother's life. "When was the last time you had one of their caramel buns?"

She smiled at him. "I do like those."

"So we'll go, and you can eat two." And he'd get coffee and something light, like oatmeal. Or water.

"All right," she conceded, but he could tell she was pleased. "Be careful, honey. Anymore those big trucks act like they own the road."

She'd said the exact same thing to him when he first got his license and took off in a rusted-out Charger for parts unknown. The car spewed oil and exhaust before he'd rebuilt the engine. She'd been right to worry. He'd wrecked the Charger in a single car crash two days after he got the engine purring.

He'd used the insurance money to buy a Hayabusa with a blown head gasket. That spring, the weeks he'd spent tinkering with the bike's engine then driving all over hell and gone with Marissa clinging to him were the closest he'd ever been to happy.

The rain stopped overnight, but the damp chill lingered under a low, gray sky, raising goose bumps before he got to the end of the cracked driveway. He ignored them and set off at a jog down his mother's street at the far edge of town to the county road. Run a mile. Left turn onto another county road, past the golf course where Delaney and Keith's families both lived, pushing hard in the steady drizzle. Left turn and another two miles brought him back into town. He focused on his stride and picked up his pace to a sprint for another mile, past the post office, a few stores that stayed in business only because the nearest Wal-Mart was still forty-six miles away, and the Heirloom Cafe. When he reached the library, the new librarian was unlocking the front door. He lifted his hand in acknowledgment of her wave, but kept going. At the volunteer fire station he slowed to a jog, and turned for home.

The most direct route to his mother's house lay down Oak Street, but without consciously thinking about it, his feet took him on a detour. Right to Elm, a block down Elm, then back left to Oak, neatly avoiding the block housing 84 Oak Street. For the last twelve years he couldn't bring himself to run past 84 Oak Street.

His mother opened the garage and backed her ten-year-old Buick down the driveway while Adam showered quickly and pulled on cargo pants and a T-shirt, then joined his mother outside. She flicked on the bare bulb overhead, revealing the shelves set into the garage's framing, boxes on those shelves, stacks of sewing and fashion magazines, and a large object hulking in the corner, under a protective cotton cover.

He froze, then covered the instinctive reaction by setting the nearest box on the floor and hunkering down to open the flaps.

"Honey?" his mother said.

Inside the box lay clothes he'd never wear again, flannel shirts smelling of damp, faded jeans ripped at the knees, frayed at the hems. He let his hands dangle from his knees, but didn't look at her.

When he saw Josh Wilmont wipe out, sending his brand-new Honda spinning back down the road toward Brookhaven while Josh flew in a monstrous, cartwheeling arc into the ditch, he'd skidded to a halt in the middle of the dirt road and left his bike where it landed to sprint to Josh.

No! No! Jesus God, no!

Josh's death was the end of the destruction he caused that night. And after the ambulance came and went, after the sheriff and the deputies and the fire department and the parents of his classmates and friends came and went, after only he and Marissa remained in Brookhaven's dilapidated great room, the missing paneling around the fireplace as wide and empty as her eyes, he walked away. He left the bike and Marissa, hitched a ride into Brookings, waited until the Marine Corps recruiting station opened, and signed his enlistment papers that day. He was done with bikes, with racing, with his half-baked dream of opening a garage after his racing career was done.

"You should have sold it."

"My name wasn't on the title," she reminded him.

Air huffed from his lungs in dark amusement. He'd bought the bike against her orders, and hidden it in Brookhaven's barn. He owned that bike, and he owned the havoc he'd wreaked with it. *Whoever said you can't go home again was wrong,* he thought. *You can, as long as you can face the demons that live there.*

So why can't you run past 84 Oak Street, where Josh used to live?

Add selling the bike to his list of things to do. Find an

apartment. Write a speech for the wedding. Sell the last reminder of the boy he was.

But that boy would never completely disappear, not as long as Marissa was in his life.

You can do whatever you want, Adam.

The whisper eddied from the depths of his memory to deposit him on the smooth planks forming the hayloft floor in Brookhaven's barn, dust motes dancing in the rectangle of sunlight the same length and width as a bed.

I want you to do whatever you want.

In a moment she was bared to his gaze, her T-shirt tugged over her head and discarded, his already sacrificed to protect her from the dirty hayloft floor. Her hair, her mouth, her tongue, and now her pink-tipped nipples drawn to taut nubs on her small breasts. He couldn't breathe, couldn't think, but he could drive iron nails with his dick. But when he fumbled open the button on her jeans and stripped them down her legs, pounding nails wasn't what he wanted to do. His gaze held hers as he hesitantly laid his hand on the mysterious territory at the crux of her thighs. She looked up at him, open, vulnerable. Willing. His touch grew bolder. Steamy. Slick. What was left of his rational brain reminded him that guys said it felt so, so good, to get a girl under you, to get inside her.

His animal body already knew that, a hundred thousand years of biology imprinted on heart and nerves, muscle and bone.

Please. Adam, please.

He kissed her. Touched her. Pinched her nipples, held her jaw for his kiss, gripped her nape to hold her face to his neck while he wrestled with demon-spurred temptation. She unzipped his jeans and shoved them low on his hips. He rolled onto his back, taking her with him. In the tumble their legs wove together and his cock slid in the sweat-and-precome slick between his belly and hers. With a hot little whimper she gripped his shoulders with both hands and ground against his thigh, but it was the rhythm that sent him over the edge. A minute, maybe two, of them moving together, perfect slide and grip and swivel, her nipples searing into his chest, her mouth open and panting against his. The orgasm blew all his circuits, the sunlight blinding him behind tightly closed eyes as he clenched his hands on her hips and ground into her belly.

Some functioning part of his mind knew girls could come and she hadn't. He had, God, had he ever, but it wasn't enough. He had Marissa in his arms, naked and slick, trembling with the force of longing unrelieved, and it was not-fucking-enough. It would never be enough, because what they had to give each other wasn't what the other wanted. Needed. Dreamed.

Maybe if you'd given in and let yourself have what you wanted and she wanted, spun the roulette wheel of birth control options available to horny teenagers in conservative rural areas, the wildness you couldn't control would have bled off. Maybe Josh would be alive.

Maybe you would have figured out how to love someone.

"I'll deal with it," he said, then pawed quickly through the contents of the box. But later. He couldn't bear to look under the cover and see the bike on rotting tires, or hear the click of the ignition when it wouldn't start. "This one's for the Salvation Army, unless you want the fabric for quilts."

She peeked inside. "I'll keep the material," she said. He shoved the box to the side and hauled down three more. All the while, the bike loomed in the corner.

"You were at Brookhaven last night?" his mother asked as she sorted school paperwork into the recycling bin.

"The interior looks just like it did in Marissa's pictures, without the furniture. Except for the paneling in the great room, the house is finished," Adam said. A check of his watch told him the Heirloom would be emptying out from the church rush. "Ready for that caramel bun?" he asked.

She got her coat while he restacked the boxes, shelved the ones from the back of his car in the space they'd made, and pulled her aging Buick into the garage. The gossip mill had done its work, because his appearance at the Heirloom didn't surprise anyone. They entertained a steady stream of towns-people at their booth, all asking about his plans. He repeated the same story over and over. Yes, he was out. Yes, he was enrolled in the architecture master's program at SDSU. Yes, he planned to stay in the region after he graduated.

Yes, he was home. For good.

A couple of his mother's friends clustered around the booth. He greeted everyone, and when the conversation turned to grandkids, he touched his mother's shoulder. "Stay and catch up for a while. I'm going to take a walk," he said.

He paid the check and stepped outside. The damp air settled against his flushed skin as he looked up and down Main Street. The business district had an abandoned air to it, compounded by the town's unspoken agreement that businesses would remain closed on Sundays. Still ignoring the rain, he walked to the corner of Main and Maple. The police station stood across from him. The next block down held one of the town's two gas stations, across the street from Gina's Diner. When he was in high school the local construction guys hung out in the parking lot before starting their day, and that hadn't changed, either. The current generation of roofers, well-diggers, haulers, builders, and jacks-of-all-trade, identifiable by their Dickies and brown Carhartt pants, stained with paint and caulk, clustered around a crew-cab pickup truck parked at the far end of the dirt lot. Hands on his hips, breathing steady and deep but not hard, he kept on walking.

Red flashed among the gray sweatshirts and fleece-lined denim jackets as he crossed the entrance to the parking lot. Marissa leaned against the tailgate, a silver travel mug in one hand, the other tucked into the pocket of a red fleece jacket, zipped to her chin for warmth. She wore army green cargo pants and scuffed, stained Cat boots, her long hair in braids under a red fleece watch cap. Smiling easily, she studied the dirt parking lot while the cluster of men around her laughed and joked; but when she looked up from her boots and saw him, she froze.

All conversation stopped as the group of guys turned to look at him. He recognized a couple. Billy Olson, a year ahead of them in school, stood between Marissa and Zach Lansing, from their grade. A couple of older guys were vaguely familiar, and younger guys whose older siblings he probably knew by name, if not by face. There was no getting out of this now. He crossed the lot to join the group and nodded at Marissa. She gave him a noncommittal smile over the rim of her travel mug. The coffee smelled like it had started out weak and simmered on the element for three days.

"Well, hey," Zach said, and held out his hand. "Welcome home."

"Thanks," he said over the chorus of *glad you made it back safely* and *good to see you again*. He'd grown up with these guys but hadn't seen them much since boot camp. This crowd didn't mix much with the Herndon/Walker crowd, where he'd ended up spending his time at home.

"You in town for a while?" Billy asked. He stood closer to Marissa, a little protective, a little possessive, but she neither acknowledged him nor moved away. A slight quirk in one eyebrow transmitted *good question* loud and clear. He tried to get a read on her mood. She didn't seem upset or hurt or angry. If anything, she looked almost amused.

Almost.

"Until the wedding," Adam said.

"You looking for a job?" Zach asked.

"I'm starting grad school in Brookings in January," he said.

One of the kids he didn't recognize eyed him. "You went to college and were in the Marines?"

"Yes," he said. It wasn't easy, but it was doable. San Diego State faculty went out of their way to help active duty, reservists, and veterans get their degrees.

There the conversation halted until Billy turned to Marissa. "Guess you finally have to finish the place."

"Guess so," she said noncommittally.

"Come on, Billy," Zach said. "Grandma's roof won't shingle itself."

The group slowly broke up in twos and threes, leaving Marissa leaning against the truck's tailgate and Adam braced up in the parking lot, arms folded across his chest. She looked at him again. "What?"

"You okay?"

"Why wouldn't I be?"

Because despite the tough-girl boots, truck, and attitude, she was eight inches shorter than him, and a good seventy pounds of bone and muscle lighter. Because he'd been anything but gentle, or a gentleman. But the unreadable little smile never left her face. She sipped from the travel mug and looked him over. "It's forty degrees out, and raining. Aren't you cold?"

He hadn't noticed. The Corps taught him to respect the elements, no more. No grunt allowed the weather to impact him. "I'm fine."

"So we're both fine," she said. Her gaze flicked past his shoulder to the diner's door. He recognized Lucas Ridgeway, the Chief of Police, and Alana. She smiled and waved at Marissa, then she and Lucas crossed the street together.

Lucas held out his hand to Adam. "Welcome home," he said.

"Thanks." Originally from Denver, Lucas had spent summers in Walkers Ford with his grandparents. He'd left the Denver PD to take the job as chief of police in Walkers Ford a couple of years ago. The next time Ris told Adam he didn't belong in Walkers Ford anymore, he'd point to Lucas as an example of someone else who'd downshifted and come home.

"Marissa, I'm so glad I caught you," Alana said. "The interlibrary loan books are on their way. I should have them by the middle of the week."

"I may just have you send them back," Marissa said. "I won't have time to read them."

Alana's gaze sharpened. Adam felt his spine straighten under the woman's alert gaze, telegraphing something he didn't understand. Marissa caught the nuances, though, because she continued before Alana could speak.

"Do you know Adam Collins? Alana's the contract librarian the council hired while they decide what to do with the library."

"I didn't get a chance to say hello yesterday, Mr. Collins," Alana said, holding out her hand. "Welcome home, and thank you."

With wide-open spaces diluting Marissa's impact on his senses, he could see the new librarian for what she was: young, her blond hair caught up in a blue scarf wrapped around her neck, with blue eyes and a good grip. She looked more sophisticated than the librarians he remembered from school, and she clearly hadn't missed their sudden absence from the group last night. "Nice to meet you," he said.

"Please stop by the library," she said, hoisting her bag a little higher on her shoulder. "Are you connected with the Veterans Affairs department to help with a job search or your educational benefits?"

"Yes, ma'am," he said. "I'm all set to start at SDSU in January."

Her eyes lit up. "And your program of study?"

Definitely not from around here. No one in Walkers Ford said things like *program of study*.

"Architecture," he said.

"Oh, congratulations," she said, then turned to Marissa. "Are you working today?"

"On Brookhaven," she said. "Not much time left."

"You could save those books for when the house is done," Alana said.

"I won't need them when the house is done."

Alana's brow furrowed slightly. "We should go," Lucas said.

"I'm renting a house from him," Alana explained to Adam. "Plumbing problems."

"Call me," Lucas said to Adam. "We should get a beer and catch up."

The offer sounded good. Adam nodded. "Where's she from?" he asked as they left.

"Chicago," Marissa said, and opened the truck's door.

He flattened his palm against the window and closed the door again. Her mouth was natural pink today, and she looked eighteen again, right down to the daring glare. "About the paneling," he said.

"What about it?" she asked as she tugged an escapist strand of hair free from her mouth.

"You need to replace it because I destroyed the original. That's on me. I'll help fix it, replace it, whatever."

"Brookhaven is my responsibility, not yours." She looked away, the fingers gripping her silver travel mug of coffee white in the cool air. "No one mentioned our little interlude in the pantry. I figured the point of that was for word to get back to Delaney, which won't happen if you don't talk about it."

"That had nothing to do with Delaney," he said.

Her bottomless brown eyes glanced past him again. "Your mom's looking for you."

He looked over his shoulders to find his mother standing under the roof overhang, and just like that, Marissa was in the cab. The door slammed, then the engine turned over with a gruff roar. No girly Ford Ranger for Walkers Ford's tough girl. She was driving a two-ton diesel dualie, and the truck's momentum displaced the air millimeters from his ear as she cruised out of the lot. Hands on his hips, he watched her drive away, like the conversation was over.

It wasn't.

5

NIGHT HAD FALLEN by the time Marissa gunned her truck up the semicircular driveway and into her customary parking spot under the oak tree sheltering Brookhaven's north side. Prickles of pain bloomed in her back when she jogged through the rain that lashed the back meadow to the servants' quarters' tiny entryway. She'd driven through the mist and rain to the house with the paneling, then sat at the end of the driveway for another two hours, trying to force herself to get out of the truck. She couldn't do it.

Oncoming darkness drove her to turn around and return to Brookhaven, letting the whap of the windshield wipers and the patter of rain on the truck's roof dissolve all thought from her brain. The end was in sight, a century of Brooks dreams fulfilled. Even with time allowed for courtesies, the transaction should have taken just a couple of hours, but she couldn't get out of the truck.

Inside her tiny apartment, cold settled into her bones, and another shiver rippled through her. The prohibitive cost of heating the main house wasn't the only reason she stayed in the tiny servants' quarters; the first summer she began renovations she'd slept in the great room, drawn to the spectacular view of rolling prairie and Dakota sunsets, but as the work progressed, the big space created odd resonances of her emotions, distorting what felt true and real outside the house, giving it back to her with sharp edges and eerie echoes. Lately her ears rang even in the snug, shiplike apartment.

The galley kitchen held a dorm-sized refrigerator, a two-burner stove, and a half-sized oven. She'd bought the appliances from sailing outfitters catering to boatbuilders and renovators who felt that smaller, not bigger, was better. She heated a can of soup on the stove, ate while sorting her mail into bills and non-bills, then went into the bathroom and ran hot water into the tub. Steam rose into the cool air while she flicked on the light, turned her back to the full-length mirror on the back of the door, and pulled three layers of shirts free from her pants. Her plain white bra strap bisected her back just under her shoulder blades, and what she saw reflected in the mirror made her blow out her breath in disgust.

The hard rap on her door came unexpectedly. She let her shirts fall back around her waist as she walked into the kitchen, pulled back the curtain, and saw heavy shoulders that could only belong to Adam. Clouds scudded across the sky behind him, and a steady breeze bent the leafless branches of the trees lining the creek at the bottom of the meadow. Anger flared, sweeping through her, making her movements jerky as she flipped on the porch light and opened the door.

He stood on the painted wood porch, wearing a three-button henley shirt loose over a pair of jeans and motorcycle boots; his hands shoved deep into the pockets of his jeans were the only hint he found it cold. Round dark spots dotted his shoulders, and drops gleamed on his bristling jarhead haircut. As she watched, he wiped his hand over his skull and flung the collected water to the side. The open collar of his shirt exposed his throat and nape, the tanned smooth skin oddly vulnerable compared to the braced stance.

"I'm not in the mood to be your unannounced booty call," she said. She'd never quite settled on a reason for having sex with him twenty minutes after he walked into Brookhaven, but his reason came to her in the middle of a sleepless night.

There was no love lost between Walkers and Brooks, and while Delaney would never stoop so low as to feud with Marissa, Adam would know that sleeping with Marissa could hurt Delaney.

God knew his sleeping with Delaney hurt Marissa.

It was the only reason she could come up with for him to finally say yes, after he'd refused time and again that summer twelve years ago. If that was his reason, once was enough.

Except he said it had nothing to do with Delaney.

His expression didn't change. "What's with the tweezers?"

"I have a splinter," she said, because she didn't want him in her living space, her *bedroom*, seeing things he shouldn't see. "No big deal. Go home."

He stuck his foot between the closing door and the jamb. She banged the door against the thick lug sole.

"Goddammit, Ris," he said, turning his shoulder into the closing door. Her stocking feet skidded on the wood floor, so without warning she stepped back. Resistance gone, he lurched into the kitchen, sending the door sharply against the kitchen wall. Her father's favorite old photographs of Brookhaven in vintage frames jumped on the nails. She flashed back to that summer, to the water fight along the creek, the way she'd attack him just to feel his body against hers, feel him restrain her and kiss her until she was helpless and pleading with sound and body.

Based on the look on his face, he was remembering the same thing. It was the first flash of real emotion she'd seen on his face in twelve years.

"Just like old times," she said. He was wet, she was wet, and the sudden sexual charge in the air heated the room to summer temperatures.

He closed the door. "Let me help."

She folded her arms and glared at him. "I don't need your help."

In response he held out a hand and glanced at the tweezers.

"It's a splinter, not a compound fracture."

He made a small beckoning motion, sheer size and presence giving the gesture a hint of imperiousness that sparked heat low in her belly.

"I'm fine."

It was his turn to raise his eyebrows. "It'll get infected if you don't get it out."

"I've been removing my own splinters since Chris died," she snapped. Adam's abrupt departure for boot camp hadn't ended her longing for guys going nowhere at a hundred miles an hour. She'd met, fallen for, and married Chris Larson within six months of graduating from high school, a bad decision that only got worse when married life didn't end his drinking and driving. He'd died shortly after her twenty-second birthday. The tragedy didn't end her taste for adrenaline junkies, but she had stopped falling in love with them. Improvement, of a sort.

The reminder of her husband made him blink, and some of the edge softened from his jaw. "But tonight you don't have to remove your own splinter," he said more softly, making the give-it-up gesture again.

"You promise you'll leave after?" she asked.

"If that's what you want," he said.

She slapped the tweezers into his palm, turned, and strode through the darkened bedroom into the bathroom to turn off the water. The huge, old-fashioned white tub dominated the room. A book holder crafted out of scrap oak, stained the same gleaming shade as the floors and sealed with two coats of clear, leaned in the corner by the shelving unit holding towels and toiletries. She shoved her current choice in reading material behind the towels, then glanced around the room for anything else that might give him ideas.

The room's details distracted him from his courtly quest to fix her ailment. "Mom said you did her bathroom earlier this year. You're really good," he said, eyeing the pale gray subway tiles covering the lower portion of the walls. The upper sections were painted in shifting shades of blue, white, and gray. Two dark gray towels hung from heated towel racks.

Pride wouldn't allow her to make light of her accomplishments. "She was fun to work with. She's got a great eye for color and lines."

When he leaned toward the door to get a better look at the bedroom, she turned away from him and pulled up the hems of her long-underwear shirt, turtleneck, and sweatshirt, shrugging them over her shoulders to expose her back.

Mission accomplished. He stared at her bared back, gaze flicking from one reddened spot to the next between her bunched shirts and the waistband of her flannel-lined jeans. While the flush on his face outside might have been due to the cold, this time it was all embarrassment, and that gave her pause.

"I fucked splinters into your back," he said.

"Pretty much," she said. "Most of the woodwork in the house is smooth as silk, but I didn't anticipate repeated, forceful, bare-skin contact with the pantry shelves."

Expecting ice cold fingers like her own, she sucked in air when he lifted his hand to her back, but his palm was blessedly warm between her shoulder blades. His touch bent her forward a little more. The contact of rough palm to her back tipped her ass toward him, and the look in his eyes went heated, dark, dangerous. *Oh yes.* She looked down at the faucet and broke the connection.

He touched a finger to a spot just below her left shoulder blade, gently pushing the skin up a little. "Here?"

In her mind's eye she saw the tiny, enflamed circle. "Yes."

A moment of concentration, then a slight tug under her skin's surface. The tiny sliver of wood dropped into the sink in front of her, and a long moment passed before another gentle stroke, higher up and just to the left of her spine. "Here."

This time she just nodded. The air in the room was quiet, close, his breathing even and regular while hers sounded shallow and erratic. It was as hot as sex, but in a different way. It was . . . intimate. Sex didn't have to be intimate. It could be emotionless, almost animal. Like it was last night.

This time he gently pinched to force out enough wood to grasp with the tweezers before dropping the splinter in the sink. "I hurt you," he said.

"It's not the first time," she replied.

His gaze flicked up to meet hers in the mirror. After a pause she pulled her shirt over her head and held it to her breasts with one hand while with the other reaching around to indicate a spot on her upper shoulder blade, maddeningly just beyond the reach of the tweezers. He cupped her shoulder and turned her back into the light to remove the last splinter. Without asking, he reached past her and opened the medicine cabinet, found a tube of antibacterial ointment, and dabbed a bit on the tip of his index finger. When he laid the side of his pinky at the nape of her neck to steady his hand, goose bumps rose along her shoulders.

His finger dabbed the ointment on a splinter spot. "You're pretty quick with a door, tough girl," he said.

"It's easier to keep someone out than get them out once they're in," she said.

His glaze flicked up to hers in the mirror, but she didn't add anything. Chris was an unpredictable drunk, with good nights and bad nights, but if he wasn't discussing Delaney, she wasn't dragging her marriage into the ring.

"You're a menace with that truck, too."

"I knew exactly where the mirror was in relation to your head," she said, stung by the slight to her driving ability.

"I don't doubt it." He didn't add anything, and this time when she looked up at the mirror he kept his gaze focused on her back. Heat radiated from his body to her bare back, one hand rested loosely on her shoulder as he dabbed a little more ointment on the last splinter site.

"There were no girls between Delaney and you," he replied without meeting her eyes.

The low-voiced words, so calm and remote and utterly unexpected, stopped her heart in her chest. She watched him trace the length of her spine to avoid looking at her. A drop of steam condensed into water and traveled down the mirror while she processed that detail. "Just me?"

He made a noncommittal noise, but hazel eyes darkened to green around the pupil as the seconds passed, and chemistry, coupled with the touch of his index finger along the edge of her hair where it swept across her nape and over her opposite shoulder, raised goose bumps and pebbled her nipples. He shook his head, and a delicate little quiver rippled low in her belly. To even the ground between them she turned around, dislodging his hands from her body.

Bad move, because he didn't step back. Looking up into his eyes only reminded her how much taller he was. Broader, too. His shoulders took up most of her vision, and only the shirts clutched to her breasts gave her any modesty. "I don't believe you." He was hot as hell; a gorgeous, decorated, focused United States Marine. Getting a woman to sleep with him couldn't be much harder than snapping his fingers.

Except he wouldn't want the ones who spread their legs at the snap of his fingers.

"Believe it."

Unshakable certainty, combined with what she now recognized as seething desire under iron control, convinced her. As a teenager Adam refused sex not just with her, but with any other girl who came his way. He'd slept with Delaney, been deployed in Afghanistan when he broke off their engagement. Stateside for less than a month, home for less than forty-eight hours.

So where did all that energy go? As a boy Adam channeled his sex drive into hell-raising and his motorcycle, and into going as far as they could without having sex. He'd been a virgin only as far as actual penetration. She hadn't been one in any sense of the word.

She was half-naked and trapped between the pedestal sink and his body while they talked about sex, so saying anything other than *get the hell out* was a mistake, but he was looking at her. Her eyes, her mouth, her spine, reflected in the mirrored medicine cabinet above the sink. The tops of her breasts. "What do you want, Adam?"

"You know what I want, Ris." The intensity in his eyes trapped the air in her throat. Then he bent his head and kissed her, his lips full and resilient against hers. A soft sound filtered into the warm, humid air. In response he slipped the tip of his tongue between her lips for a flickering caress. Heat shot through her, lighting signal fires in all the right places. Fire meant warmth, heat, light, but it also meant danger.

She was too experienced, too jaded to fall into bed with a man just because he announced *he wanted her*, even if he used that whiskey-rough voice, even if every nerve in her skin was alive to the heat and desire pouring off him, even if she'd dreamed about him since she was seventeen.

"So you came here to get me?"

Amusement flashed in his eyes. "Actually, I came here to ask a favor. This," he said, and bent his head just enough for his lips, warm and full, to brush her ear. Once, twice, and all the hairs stood up as a chill tightened her skin. Then his teeth tightened on the fragile edge, holding the sensitive skin for the slick flick of his tongue, and her throat closed. "*This* came out of the blue."

"A favor." The shift in the conversation tilted the world under her feet.

"How well do you know Brookings?"

Totally caught off guard, she blinked. "Brookings? Pretty well. Why?"

"I need to find an apartment, sooner rather than later. Many more nights on the futon at my mom's house and I'm going to need a chiropractor."

She gaped at him. "You came here to ask me to help you find an apartment."

"I planned to ask nicely and buy you supper afterwards, but yes."

"Why not get Keith to help you?"

"He's busy." Inflectionless, no details. Keith was pretty

low on her list of favorite people, and it didn't surprise her that he wouldn't take time to help his best man find an apartment.

"How do you know I'm not?"

"I don't. This isn't a command, Ris. I'm asking a favor. Say no if you can't. I'll figure it out on my own. I just . . . wanted company."

Something vibrated under the words, but she couldn't think with him so close, so she pushed against his chest. He leaned back a few inches, but she harbored no illusions she'd moved him. He'd moved for her, and having that powerful body at her command struck at a very feminine place inside.

"I'm not going to sleep with you again."

Big words when she was still half-naked and close enough to feel the heat of his erection against her belly, but she had to retain some measure of self-protection here. She chose bed partners without much regard for rules or convention, but something dark and dangerous occasionally breathed fire under Adam's steel-hard exterior. He had the power to anni-hilate her. He'd done it before.

"Fine," he said. He took one step back, all he could do in the tiny bathroom, giving her enough space to struggle back into her layers of shirts. In just seconds she was too warm, the first time that had happened in who knew how long.

"When?" she asked through her tightly closed throat.

"Tomorrow?"

An excuse to put off doing what she had to do, and no small sense of relief washed through her. When she nodded, he added, "I found a couple of apartment complexes online, and a few other rentals in the older parts of town. I'll pick you up around nine."

"Okay."

"Just so you know . . . if you change your mind, ask any-time." He bent forward and kissed her, soft, hot temptation personified, before he stepped back. "I won't say no."

An image flashed bright on the movie screen of her mind: Adam, in her bed, saying yes to everything she asked. She'd been shocked by electric currents before, and that's exactly what happened now, the charged air between them zapping the breath from her lungs. Leaving the bedroom lights off, he covered the distance to the back door in four steps, then walked out into the rain.

6

ADAM TOOK THE steps two at a time, water splashing up from the depressions worn into the hundred-year-old marble blocks each time he planted his foot. He arrived at the front door of the Walkers Ford library just as Alana, in a long coat and scarf, struggled to unlock the front door with one hand while balancing two cardboard shipping boxes and a tote in the other. "Let me help you with those," he said.

"Thanks so much," she said, and offloaded the boxes and tote into his waiting arms. A plastic container of hummus and another of sliced carrots and celery peeked out from the top of her tote. Lunch, or maybe a morning snack, and not purchased at Walkers Ford's lone grocery store. Based on the weight and her occupation, the boxes held books.

Sheltered from the rain by the portico, she struggled with the lock for a few seconds, jiggling both the handle and the key before it gave way. She stepped through and held the door wide open for him. Large windows let in enough of the day's gloom for him to find the circulation desk and set down the boxes while she went to the bank of switches and turned on the lights.

"That's better," she said with satisfaction. "I was ready for biting cold and snow when I moved here, but not for weeks of rain with no end in sight."

"Give it five minutes and the weather will change," he said, repeating the old saw about weather on the high plains.

"I've been giving it five minutes for ten days straight. So far, that adage holds only rainwater," she replied, her voice more amused than irritated as she adjusted the temperature. Under his feet the furnace whirred to life. She walked to the circulation desk, absently adjusting a display of children's books as she moved through the big, high-ceilinged room. "What can I do for you?"

"I can wait until you get your coat off and your things settled."

"I'll be wearing my coat for the next few minutes," she said, still amused. "I'm sorry it's so cold. The windows are original and leak heat like a sieve. It's not an ideal environment for books. How can I help you?"

Her alert, interested gaze was both disconcerting and compelling. "I need books on giving a speech," he said.

The promise of a day with Marissa, vulnerable and tough all at once, couldn't fully distract him from the upcoming wedding. Online he'd found some simple formulas to construct a best man's speech, but he wanted something to help him organize his thoughts before he planned what to say.

With a brisk nod she led him into the double rows of shelves that ran the length of the single room and stopped in the eight hundreds. Deftly she sectioned off a cluster of books and set them on top of the shelves. "We don't have a very large selection, I'm afraid," she said. "Most of the budget for new books goes to popular fiction and periodicals, but the high school library might have a more recent selection. As a graduate you can continue to check out books there. I can also order books from other libraries around the country. You'll have to pay the shipping costs and it takes a couple of weeks for them to arrive."

A return trip to the high school didn't appeal, and he didn't have a couple of weeks to wait for better books to arrive, but after twelve years in the Marines, he knew how to make do. He scanned the titles and recognized a couple his online research indicated were classics. "I'll take these two," he said.

Alana reshelved the others and led him back to the desk. He looked around at the high ceilings, the white columns beside the doors, the marble flooring. The ceiling itself was recessed paneled wood. "The building needs some work," he commented.

"It does," she agreed. "These old Carnegie libraries are fast-crumbling national treasures, in my opinion, with rural tax bases shrinking as they are." She looked up at him, then added, "The town council's considering how best to upgrade the building and the technology. Marissa's skills would come in handy if they decide to go ahead."

"She won't be the front-runner to get the job," Adam said. He knew how Walkers Ford worked. The front-runner was probably Chuck Matterly, a prominent builder on the school board who'd put up a couple of cookie cutter subdivisions around the county.

Alana's smile disappeared. "I don't suppose you still have your library card?"

He'd never had a public library card in Walkers Ford. "No, ma'am," he said.

"Then let's get you set up with one." She powered up her computer and looked up at him expectantly. "I need something that proves you're a resident of Walkers Ford or Chatham County. A rental agreement, a utility bill, or a phone bill will do," she said.

Invisible chains tying him to the community wouldn't count. "I'm staying with my mother until I get a place of my own."

"Driver's license?" she said without batting an eye.

He pulled the card from his wallet and offered it to her. She transcribed the information into the computer, then began the process of checking out the books. "Due three weeks from today, but late fees aren't onerous, still a nickel a day. Don't make me hunt you down to get them back."

Three weeks from today Delaney would be married and on her honeymoon, and he'd be setting up residence in Brookings. "Understood," he said. "Thanks."

He was halfway to the door before her next question stopped him. "Will you see Marissa again soon?"

"Yes," he said. As soon as he got to Brookhaven. Less than twenty minutes until he saw Marissa again.

Alana opened a drawer, removed a box cutter, sliced open the boxes, but didn't remove the contents. "How well do you know her?"

There was a loaded question. He shrugged, then considered the books in his hand. "I've known her all my life."

Alana pulled books from the boxes and set them on her desk. The room had warmed up enough for her to remove her coat and drape it over the chair. "Marissa ordered these books via interlibrary loan."

"The books she said she didn't want anymore."

"Yes." Alana looked at him. "I think she should still have the chance to take a look at them. Skim them, if that's all she has time to do. Would you take them to her for me, please?"

His boots clunked loudly in the silence as he walked back to the circulation desk. The books, six in all, came from libraries in places like Delray Beach, Newport, and San Luis Obispo. He scanned the bindings for the titles, then looked at Alana. "What's this all about?"

"Oh, just your average, run-of-the-mill obsession." He cut her a look at the lighthearted tone over the stone-cold serious words.

Apparently he didn't know Marissa nearly as well as he thought he did. "What does she owe you for the shipping?"

"Sixteen thirty-four," Alana said.

Adam gave her a twenty, then put the change into a clear acrylic box marked Library Fund. The stack of books tucked between his arm and his hip, he walked out the front door and jogged through the rain to his car. Inside, he wiped the accumulated drops off the spines, then, under the dim illumination of the dome light, carefully read the back cover copy for each of the six books. When the dome light dimmed he tossed the books into the backseat, then drove through town to County Highway 12, headed for Brookhaven.

Approaching the house from the southeast with storm clouds massed behind it, her house looked like a fanciful ship, the sharp corner of the wraparound front porch poised at the peak of the hill. Rain sheeted from the figurehead's streaming hair and white Grecian gown, her arm outstretched, pointing west, tilting at an odd angle. The windows at floor level were clear glass, and the inset windows above were all made of stained glass, but not in the typical geometric forms. Rather, waves of blue and gray gave way to the warm colors of the sunset.

On a windy fall day, the prairie unbroken to the horizon, the house looked like it was about to launch off into the swells of windblown green grass. He looked at it, blinked. Barked out a laugh. That wasn't the Brookhaven he remembered, with peeling white paint and a vaguely abandoned, ramshackle air about it. No, the house was now utterly unconventional, passionate, unique.

He blinked again, and it was just an odd old house, cobbled together from bits and pieces of architectural styles and auction junk. Where the hell had she gotten a sailing ship's figurehead in South Dakota?

He parked in the circle drive, followed the paving stones around to the servants' entrance, knocked on the door, and found himself braced like he was outside officers' quarters. When she opened the door he was grateful for the stance, because his heart stopped for a split second, then took off in triple time.

She'd always been a tomboy, the kind of girl you'd see in a Michael Bay film, sexy as a centerfold while she kicked alien ass. He hadn't given any thought at all to what she'd wear for a day of apartment hunting. She stood in the doorway in a pair of slim-fitting dark jeans and a forest green turtle-neck sweater that clung to her lean body. Her dark hair spilled around her face and shoulders in tousled waves. A light coat of gloss gleamed on her full mouth, and she'd put on just enough eye makeup to make her brown irises dark and mysterious.

Silence held, then she ducked her head and tucked her hair behind her ear. "What?" she said.

"You look amazing."

That got him a smile. "Thanks. Better than carpenter jeans and work boots, right?"

"Just different," he said. "Jeans and boots work for me."

"You have a thing for construction apparel?"

"Apparently I have a thing for tough girls," he said. His heart thudded against his breastbone, doing an awesome job of sending blood south to his cock. *She said she wasn't sleeping with you again. Take her at her word.* "Grab your coat. The first appointment is at one."

She buttoned herself into a navy peacoat and riffled through her shoulder bag before she stepped out onto the landing to lock the door behind her. He stepped back and gestured for her to lead the way.

"That's a real Navy peacoat," he said as he followed her around the house, to the car.

"It belonged to an old boyfriend," she said as she slid into the car.

Inside the car he could see it was a little big on her through the shoulders, but the right length at hip and sleeve. It would fit perfectly over layers of sweatshirt, turtleneck, and long underwear, though. He started the car and drove back down the driveway, trying to think of something to say. "And you kept it when you broke up with him?" he said, trying to inject a little humor into the situation. The mood in the car vibrated with tension: sexual, emotional, everything. Or maybe that was just him.

"Actually, he left it behind when he went back east," she said lightly. "He was a stained-glass artist doing a residency at SDSU. Showed up in town in June, stayed until December, then went home. We bartered for windows in the great room. I paid for the materials and let him use the barn as a workshop while he was here. In return he did the design and installation. When he wasn't working he would drive all over the countryside, taking pictures, sketching. I went with him. I've lived here my whole life and after a summer with him I saw eastern South Dakota in a whole new way."

He didn't have anything to say to that, because irrational jealousy fisted around his throat, making it hard to swallow and impossible to form words. He reached into the console for a folder containing the pages he'd printed from the computer workstation he'd set up for his mother years ago so they could Skype during his deployments. "These are the apartments I'm looking at today," he said. "First place is on top."

She paged through the stapled sheets, pausing at addresses. "Okay, I know where we're going."

They came to the four-way stop sign at the county highway south of Brookhaven. Left took them east, into Walkers Ford. Right went west, into the next town over. He went south through the intersection and forty minutes of silence later, they were on the outskirts of Brookings. Lost in thought about the books in his backseat, he missed the exit for the university. "Don't worry about it," Marissa said. "You can backtrack up 22nd Avenue. Pull in here," she said as they neared a grocery store.

"You need to stop?"

"A cup of coffee sounds good."

The store had a Starbucks inside, near the customer service area. He pulled into the parking lot and they trotted through the rain to the automatic doors. Inside she inhaled deeply and smiled, then got in line.

"A Venti bold," she said when they got to the counter, then turned to Adam. "What do you want? My treat."

"I've got it," he said and reached for his wallet. "Grande Americano," he said.

She claimed her large cup while he paid, and went to the stand to add cream and sugar. "You like Starbucks coffee?" he asked when he joined her.

"It doesn't taste all that different from Gina's," she said. He gave a little huff of laughter, but she continued. "I just like . . . I don't know. It's a treat. It's something I see on TV when I zone out, people with their cups of coffee in New York City or Las Vegas or Miami. When I have to come to Brookings I treat myself."

This little insight into Marissa's mind amused him. "So you like holding the cup?"

"I like holding the cup," she said. "Why? You don't like it?"

"It's fine if you need a kick, but it tastes bitter and burned. Most people put cream and sugar in the coffee, so they don't notice the taste."

Amused, she said, "So Gina's coffee tastes bitter and burned?"

"Gina's coffee tastes like it was brewed with stagnant swamp water then left on the burner for a week."

She eyed his cup. "What did you get?"

"An Americano. It's a shot of espresso with water."

He offered her the cup. Keeping one eye on the road, she took it and sipped, considering the flavor. "Smoother."

"Let's go hold Starbucks cups while we look at apartments."

The first appointment on his list was at a complex near McCrory Gardens. They parked in the visitor spots and found the management office on the first floor of one of the buildings. A woman in her twenties dressed in tight black slacks and a low-cut shimmery blouse led them down the hall to an empty unit.

"Usually our leases run through the school year," she said as she unlocked the door, "but the tenant dropped out and the unit's available. When do you need occupancy?"

"Now," Adam said as he looked around. The door opened into the kitchen/eating area that faced the living room, carpeted in a cream color that had seen better days, even with the smell of a recent cleaning hanging in the air. Two small bedrooms were at the back of the unit, with bathroom, walk-in closet, and washer/dryer hookups opposite. It was more space than he'd ever lived in.

Marissa peered into closets and ran her free hand over the countertops. The leasing manager eyed her, then asked, "What do you think?"

"It's his apartment," she said. "I'm just here for moral support."

The tour took less than five minutes. "Do you want to fill out an application today? I'll need paycheck stubs and tax returns, plus a credit report, or proof of student loan disbursement if you're at SDSU."

"I'm looking at a couple of other places," Adam said. "I'll take the paperwork, and if I decide to take it, I'll bring it by later today."

"That's fine," she said, and stepped back to let them out.

"So, what do you really think?" Adam said as they hurried back to the Charger.

"I think that's the ugliest shade of green I've ever seen in my life," Marissa said, casting a disparaging glance at the exterior of the buildings. "They redid the kitchen recently but with the cheapest commercial-grade fixtures you can buy."

"You think it's ugly."

She sipped her burned coffee. "I think *ugly* is generous. It's worse than ugly. It's . . . cheap. Soulless."

He nodded. "On the other hand, I've lived in barracks for the last twelve years. It's a big step up from the barracks. Lots of closet space."

"That sounds like something Delaney would say," she said lightly.

"It was something Delaney said. Frequently."

"You can do better," she said dismissively. "Let's look at something else. Anything not in dragon-scale green."

They saw townhouses on the other side of McCrory Gardens, closer to campus, with a reasonably attractive exterior, but a raucous party was going on in the unit next to the available one. Music thumped through the walls, and empty beer cans collected in recycling containers outside the door. The complex manager smiled, excused himself, and knocked on the next door. The music dialed down in seconds, but Adam refused the offer of paperwork.

"Not in the mood for a built-in party?" Marissa asked when she got into the car.

"I don't have the patience to live next to that."

Still holding the cup in one hand, she paged through the printouts in the folder on her lap. "Last one," she said.

The final option for the day was on the opposite side of campus, in a historic building renovated into apartments. The building's exterior was red brick, with a recessed entryway accessed through three large arches. "Looks like it used to be a school," Adam said as he parked on the street at the end of the block. "Look at those windows."

"That," Marissa said, "is not soulless." The coffee had to be cold and coagulated by now, but she still carried it out of the car and paused under a bare oak tree. Rain dotted her hair as she absently tucked it behind her ear. "That is a building worth living in. No air conditioners jutting out of the siding. Whoever redid the brick knew his craft, too."

"Nice location," Adam added. "Walking distance to campus."

"It's a mile," Marissa pointed out, "maybe more. Or is that walking distance for someone who's used to foot patrols with a hundred-pound pack?"

He shrugged. The complex manager waited for them just inside the portico and shook hands with them both. "I have one apartment to show you," she said as she led them down the wide, wood-floored hall. "It's our smallest, unfortunately, but it's available immediately."

"Oh," Marissa husked when she stepped through the door.

The slight noise registered in the back of Adam's brain while the apartment's details occupied his thoughts. Loft ceilings. Hardwood floors, darkened with age but gleaming with a pale patina. Windows that started at mid-thigh and stretched overhead, past the reach of his outstretched fingertips. Rain coursed down the panes, but in sunlight the whole apartment would glow like the interior of a fine sailboat. The same windows illuminated the bedroom, the shadow of the oak tree outside dappling the space where a bed would go. Marissa stepped into the room, and he had a sudden flash of making love to her in all the different lights that would stream through those windows: sunshine, gloomy rainy days, spitting snow. The rooms were small, the kitchen and eating area not much bigger than Marissa's galley kitchen, but beautiful, content as a cat in their role as a welcoming space.

"You have to provide your own washer and dryer," the property manager said apologetically, "and parking is an extra monthly fee."

Coffee cup still in hand, Marissa shot him a look that said *as if that matters.*

"It's smaller than the other places we looked at," he said to no one in particular. By half. He might actually be able to fill this space with all his worldly possessions.

"Size doesn't matter," Marissa replied as she ran her hand along marble windowsills aging more gracefully than the steps to the Walkers Ford library. "Harmonious proportions, the relationship between form and function, how it's used all matter more than size."

She'd not meant the words provocatively. He knew that by the way her cheeks flushed, and the way she suddenly refused to look at him. He let the words hang in the suddenly warm air for a few moments, then turned to the manager, who gave him a bland smile.

"Paperwork?" he said.

She handed him a folder. "Get it back to me as soon as possible," she said. "We've already had several interested parties tour the apartment."

"Couple of hours, max," he said.

They left the building and stood blinking on the sidewalk. Marissa walked to the end of the street and chucked the now-empty cup in the trash can on the corner.

"You sucked every last bit of coffee out of that cup," he said.

"It's a treat. That's what I do with treats," she replied, glancing up and down the street. "It's close to the Children's Museum."

"And the county courthouse," Adam said. "I don't plan to spend much time in either."

She snickered, and looked at him like she used to look at him, eyes gleaming, lips curved in a smile that made him feel like he might be okay, all because he'd made her laugh. It was no easy task making Marissa laugh. Even as a teenager she'd been solemn, serious, weighted down.

"Size doesn't matter?" he said, hoping for another laugh.

"Oh, please. Thanks for leaving me hanging there, by the way. I'm sure she thought we were together."

"We were together."

The laughing light in her eyes flickered off. "Not that way."

So much for connections. "How about another coffee while I fill out this paperwork?"

They drove back to the Starbucks. This time she got an Americano and watched him rip through the paperwork. He was paging back through, double-checking signatures, when she spoke.

"You don't have anything to worry about as a lover."

"I was teasing you," he said without looking up. "You laugh less than you used to, and I didn't think that was possible."

"Why aren't you defensive about this? Most guys would be."

He capped the pen he'd borrowed from the barista, then tossed it on top of the paperwork and sat forward, elbows on knees. "About having reached the advanced age of thirty and slept with two women, instead of two dozen, or two hundred?" When she nodded, he added, " 'Quantity equals quality' is just another way of saying size matters, and I'm not most men." He pulled his cell phone from his cargo pants pocket and called the property manager. "Linda, it's Adam Collins," he started, but she cut him off.

"Adam, I'm sorry," she said. "Another person brought the completed paperwork to the office right after I showed you the apartment. I'm running the credit check right now, but I doubt they'll have any problems."

Marissa was watching him, legs crossed, hair spilling loose along her cheekbones, both hands wrapped around the coffee cup so her fingers met at the mermaid. He felt his face go blank, even as he spoke. "Of course. I understand. Are there any other vacancies coming up?"

"None until May, when classes end," Linda said regretfully.

Fuck. *Fuck!* He should have stayed with her, filled out the paperwork in her office, but he'd wanted to get Marissa another coffee. He blew out his breath. "Okay. Would you keep my name and number, in case a vacancy comes up unexpectedly?"

"I certainly will," Linda said. "Good luck with your search."

He tapped the screen to disconnect. "Someone else is renting it right now," he said without looking at her.

"You shouldn't have brought me," Marissa said, then set her coffee cup on the table and folded her hands in her lap. "My timing's always been crap."

"Hey," he said. He leaned across the table and nudged the cup toward her. "It's fine."

"Should we go back to one of the other complexes?"

He shook his head. Now that he'd seen that building, living somewhere else felt like settling, and he was done settling. Frustration seethed inside him before he locked it down, then considered the equally quiet woman sitting across from him. "We should get some supper and go home. Both of those places are last resorts."

"Supper?"

"Yeah. I dragged you down here and made you look at shitty architecture in the rain. The least I can do is buy you supper." Which would give him a great opportunity to ask her about the books in the back of his car, and try to figure out what was going on with her and Brookhaven.

"You didn't drag me down here," she said. The words were

soft, mild, as she ran her middle finger along the underside of the cup's lid. "I could have said no. I didn't."

The implication being she might say yes to something else, something far more pleasurable than looking at apartments in the rain. "Why did you say yes?"

"Because I didn't believe you when you said you were here to stay."

7

ADAM SAT BACK in the blond wood chair, laced his fingers together behind his head, and glanced at the paperwork, then at her. "Do you believe me now?"

Marissa shrugged more nonchalantly than she felt. Something odd, something strange was happening, something that started in the bedroom of that gorgeous apartment when she stepped into the tracing of bare branches in the square of light on the floor. She felt it, saw it in Adam's darkening eyes, almost could have believed it; but like everything else, the timing was off. Someone else rented the apartment, and the thought of his staying, even in Brookings, was laughable. "Not really," she said.

"Why would I go through all this if I wasn't staying?"

Again, she shrugged. "Something to do?" That wasn't right, either. It was like he had something to finish, and this odd excursion was part of it. Whatever it was, her involvement was a huge risk.

"Why wouldn't I stay?"

"Why would you?"

"I'm from here. I'm enrolled in a graduate program at SDSU." He said the words without inflection, and she wondered if he knew how much space he took up beyond his sheer size. His biceps and triceps bulged under the soft cotton of his shirt. He'd always been tall. Now he was both tall and bulky. He had the untouchable, locked-down appeal of a monk, or a happily married man. Except he was neither. A little thrill zinged through her at the thought of unlocking him.

"You've been gone for twelve years," she pointed out.

"This is home." His gaze sharpened. "Why are you still here?"

"I never left."

"You could leave. People do it."

She laughed. "Do you have any idea how much money I have tied up in Brookhaven? I'm not going anywhere."

"Have you tried to sell it?"

"No," she said, more sharply than she intended. "Restoring Brookhaven is the only dream I've ever had. I'm two weeks away from living that dream." Two weeks away from showing everyone in town, from longtime families like the Walkers to newcomers like Alana, that being a Brooks meant more than dreaming big. It meant making a dream a reality, restoring the Brooks name to its original status. To get so close to that goal only to have it slip through her fingers, and at Delaney's wedding reception, no less, wasn't an option.

Then why are you sitting in Starbucks rather than getting the mantel you need? Are you familiar with the concept of self-sabotage?

"Five generations of Brookses are buried in the cemetery, including my husband. I'm not leaving. And you're not staying."

"Maybe we're both wrong," he said. "Supper?"

A faint alarm went off in her head as she stared at him, but she shook it off. He had to be here for a reason, going through the motions of squeezing those broad shoulders into a life that was two sizes too small. Whatever motivated him didn't have anything to do with her, but she'd bet money she didn't have that it had something to do with Delaney. A meaningless bet. She didn't have any money. A man with Adam's control would do nothing randomly. He never had. Recklessly, yes. Randomly, never.

She might as well have supper. "Okay. Where?"

"How adventurous do you feel?"

"What do you have in mind?"

"A new Thai restaurant opened a couple of months ago."

She considered this. "I've never had Thai food before. Have you?"

"Sure," he said. "It's intense. Really spicy, but they can tone it down if you ask."

She shouldn't. She should go home, heat up soup, take a bath, and go to bed. Alone. She needed to focus for the next two weeks, and Adam was a very potent distraction. But he was leaving. She felt the separation coming, even if it was weeks down the road. When he'd done whatever he was in Walkers Ford to do, he'd leave. Again. The smart thing to do was say no.

"Sounds good," she said.

This time when they trotted through the rain to the car, Adam opened her door for her. She smoothed down her damp hair, then twisted it into a coil at her nape. "Sorry about your hair," he said when he got in. "I never think to carry an umbrella."

She glanced at his squared-off buzz cut. "I suppose you don't," she said as he started the car. "It doesn't matter. I work outside in all kinds of weather. Usually it's in braids."

"You curled it, though."

Her cheeks heated, and not just from the hot air blasting from the vents in the dash. She rarely cared if she looked pretty, but today she'd wanted to fit into whatever metropolitan aura Brookings possessed.

And look nice for Adam. Which he noticed.

You're not in high school anymore, Ris.

"I knew it wouldn't last," she said, wedging her chilled fingers between her thighs to warm them. "It's rained for two weeks straight, and from the looks of the forecast it's going to rain for the next ten days, at least. How's your mom?"

He smiled. "I shocked the hell out of her when I showed up on her doorstep."

"Why didn't you tell your mother you were coming home?"

"I wanted it to be a surprise."

"Last I saw her was August. I renovated her bathroom and she gave me some green beans and tomatoes from her garden."

"Marble countertops, a custom tile design in the shower stall, wainscoting," he mused, then cut her a quick glance. "What did you charge her for?"

"I found most of the pieces in remainder bins. We bartered for the labor," she said.

"Must have been one hell of a sewing project. She does curtains, cushions, slipcovers, but I didn't see a sofa in your apartment."

"I haven't asked her to make me anything yet," she hedged, and she really didn't want to talk about this.

A muscle jumped in his jaw. They found parking across the street and two doors down from Khao San Road, the red letters visible in neon above a steel-gray sign. Despite the now-sheeting rain, he parallel parked the Charger with swift turns of the wheel, then cut the engine. "Mom doesn't need anyone's charity, and you deserve to be paid for your work," he said. "How much?"

"That is between me and your mother," she said stiffly. "It's none of your business, and it wasn't *charity*."

The muscle jumped again. "Stay there," he said, reached into the backseat for a lightweight jacket, then got out of the car.

The driver's door slammed, and behind her something slid to the floor. She peeked over her shoulder to make sure it wasn't anything fragile or important and saw her stack of books slipping forward in an elegant domino sprawl. *The Essentials of Living Aboard a Boat* edged toward the floorboard, then thudded on top of *How to Sail Around the World*.

Her interlibrary loan books, the ones she'd told Alana to ship back to their home libraries, were in Adam's backseat.

The passenger door jerked open. Adam stood in the opening, the jacket held above his head.

"What are you doing with my books?"

His gaze flicked to the backseat, then met hers without a hint of apology. "Can we discuss this after we get out of this monsoon?"

Now he minds the weather? She met his gaze for a moment longer, then stepped out of the car. He held the jacket over their heads as they dashed across the street, into the restaurant. He shook the jacket outside the door, then hung it up on a coatrack next to the cash register. A cheerful hostess in a black skirt and a white shirt said, "Two? This way, please."

They were seated at the back of the restaurant, in a dark corner lit mostly by candlelight. Adam held her chair for her, then slid into the booth seat opposite. The hostess handed them each a menu. Marissa set hers down, flattening the napkin perched on the appetizer plate.

"Why do you have my books?" she said, fighting to keep her voice low.

"Before I picked you up I ran into the library to pick up a couple of books on public speaking. Alana asked me if I was going to see you soon. When I said yes she gave me your books to bring to you. Is that a problem?"

"Just . . . don't say anything to anyone about it."

"Why not? Is it a secret?"

"No," she said, then added rather nonsensically, "I just don't want anyone else to know what I'm reading."

"Sure," he said easily. Too easily. His knee bumped hers under the small table as she met his gaze, like getting shocked in two places at once. Tension thickened the air, but it wasn't all from the intimacy of sitting in a dark restaurant, talking about secrets. Desire eddied around their ankles like a rising tide. The dim light picked out the planes of his cheekbones and forehead but threw the rest of his face into shadow. When he didn't say anything else, she picked up the menu again.

"You got books on public speaking? Pretty serious stuff for a best man's speech," she said as she looked at the menu.

"Delaney's marrying my best friend. It's a big deal. I'm not going to do it half-assed," he said.

And there was Delaney again. Keith, too, but this wasn't about Keith. It could be a good diversion to get his mind off the books. She didn't need him curious. "Why did you break up with Delaney anyway?" she asked as she began to scan the menu options.

Silence. She lowered the menu to see him looking at her with a completely unreadable, nearly cold expression on his face. Big, big mistake, but not because he was angry. He was . . . nothing, absolutely nothing. Shut down in every possible way, a pulse, a breath, nothing more. While her goal had been to shift attention from her to him, she'd meant to stay superficial, not go deeper. His reasons for ending his engagement to Walkers Ford's good girl clearly went straight to the heart.

"It's none of my business," she backtracked.

"I'll tell you, if you really want to know."

"I don't," she said, then looked around the restaurant. Anything to not see the emptiness in his eyes. Buildings. They could talk about buildings. They had that, at least. "Bamboo flooring," she noted. "A contractor I know down here put it into a yoga studio when they couldn't find enough reclaimed oak or maple." He'd said the studio owner would have killed for Brookhaven's floors, but Adam didn't need to know that.

"It's getting popular as a renewable hardwood resource," Adam replied. He flicked Marissa a glance over the top of the menu. "Want some help?"

"Desperately," she said. "I don't recognize half the ingredients, let alone the names."

"We'll get a few things so you can try them all," he said. She sat back into the utterly unexpected pleasure of watching a man order for her. He chose a range of appetizers and main courses in varying heat levels, then added what their waitress said was the house specialty. He ordered a beer, while Marissa stuck with a diet soda.

"Why this restaurant?" she asked after the waitress brought their drinks.

"I like Thai food," he said. "During one WESTPAC cruise we had a few days' R and R in Sukhothai, and another time our LT arranged a sailing trip in Phuket."

He put it out there casually, leaving it up to her to acknowledge that yes, she knew that Phuket was a prime sailing location in the Indian Ocean, had seen pictures of greenery-draped limestone cliffs rising over white sand beaches. "You went sailing in Phuket?" she asked, mimicking his pronunciation.

He nodded, his stance lazily casual, his eyes anything but. The appetizers arrived. The waitress set the tom kha gai in front of Marissa, the spring rolls in front of Adam, and the lettuce wraps on the table between them. Marissa dipped her soup spoon into the broth and lifted it to her mouth. He watched, a half smile on his face, as she hesitantly sampled the soup. Surprise and delight widened her eyes. "It's good," she said, and tried a more satisfying mouthful. "Really good. What's in it?"

"You got me," he said. "I like Thai food but I've never tried to make it. Be careful, though. Takes a while for the burn to build."

She nodded in agreement and swapped him the bowl of soup for the spring rolls. "They're like little egg rolls," she noted, and examined the contents after she bit into one. After tipping the sauces onto her plate she tried each one. "Too hot," she said as her eyes began to tear up. She drank most of her water trying to kill the burn, then a couple of swallows of Adam's beer.

He dipped the tip of his finger in the sauce and sampled it. "You might want to skip the kaeng phet. So far so good?"

A smile and a nod, then, "Tell me about Thailand."

"The first time I was there I went to Sukhothai, which was the country's first capital. Great ruins, great backpacking along the river."

"Who did you travel with? Other Marines?"

"Yeah," he said. "There were always a couple of guys who wanted to see something other than the tourist district and the inside of bars and whorehouses."

Her eyebrows lifted, but he paused while the waitress arranged dishes on the table. She scooped a generous helping of rice and a little of each dish onto her plate, and asked for a soda and some more water.

"Whorehouses?"

He shrugged. "Sorry about the language," he said.

"I've heard worse," she said with a smile. "You're not the only ex-Marine in the area—

"Former Marine."

"What?"

"You're never an ex-Marine. You're a former Marine, because you're always a Marine, just not on active duty."

"Does that explain your bumper sticker?" She'd seen the yellow sticker with red lettering one of the times she rounded the back end of the car to hop into the passenger seat. "To err is human. To forgive is divine. Neither is Marine Corps policy," she quoted.

He shrugged, and added more rice to his plate.

"So if you're not human, and you're not divine . . . you're a Marine?"

"Something like that."

No mistakes, a policy she could understand with lives at risk in a war zone, but how did a man avoid making mistakes? What transpired inside when the inevitable happened?

"I'll remember that," she said. "Anyway, some of the former Marines end up at the lumberyard, waiting to get a truck loaded. After a while they forget I'm there." They talked over, around, and past her, striving to outdo each other with stories.

"No, they don't," he said. "Maybe other women get forgotten. Not you."

His eyes were heavy lidded, and the flush sitting high on his cheekbones wasn't just alcohol and spicy food. The air between them popped and crackled, lifting the hair at the nape of her neck.

She smiled, then tucked her hair behind her ear and sampled another dish. Working her way counterclockwise around her plate she sampled everything he'd ordered. He ate most of the kaeng phet while she made a dent in the pad thai.

"So you traveled to avoid temptation," she said.

"Among other things. Ship duty is one thing, but it's hard when you're deployed to come down from the adrenaline rush of combat. Sitting on a beach sipping drinks with fruit on little umbrellas didn't appeal. I figured I'd marry Delaney and settle down in Chatham County, so I got everything I could out of it. The LT had two speeds—*off* and *balls to the wall*—so he didn't want to sit around on beaches, either. One day we're sitting in the mess and he drops a map of Thailand on the table with a mountain circled and says 'Next shore leave I'm climbing that. Who's in?' But his first love was sailing, so we started planning sailing excursions. He's been sailing all his life and didn't see being deployed as a reason to stop."

She watched him come alive in front of her eyes, glowing from the inside out as he talked. "So that's how you did it. Stayed faithful to one woman for twelve years."

He pushed what was left of his rice around on his plate. "It was part of it, yeah."

"What was the rest of it?"

"Tell me about the books."

She'd tweaked him over Delaney to change the subject; now he'd tweaked her right back. "It's no big deal," she said.

"Whenever someone says that, they usually mean it's a very big deal."

"I've got a lot of free time on my hands," she said, striving for casual. "When I've got a job, I work, sleep, and eat, but when there's no work, I've got hours of free time. I read. I read lots of different things. This is just what I'm reading now."

"What else have you read?"

"Construction books to work on Brookhaven—wiring, plumbing, framing—tons of stuff on architecture," she said promptly. "I've also read everything in the library's Classics section—although I can't get into the Russians—most of the

Poetry section, and a good chunk of Biography. My interests vary, and I go off on tangents. That's all this is. A tangent."

"Alana called it 'your average, run-of-the-mill obsession.'"

She and Alana were going to have words when she got back to Walkers Ford. "It's not."

He sat back and studied her, the focused gaze threatening on so many levels. "You've never been sailing."

She laughed. "I'm fifteen hundred miles from the nearest ocean, so only in my dreams, as they say," she said lightly.

"Speaking of dreams," he said. An odd sensation expanded in her chest. "I want to help with the paneling."

It took her a moment to recognize disappointment, the emotion unfamiliar because she'd tamped down what caused it—unfulfilled anticipation. She'd anticipated that Adam would say something else, like, *Let's go sailing,* a laughable statement when South Dakota was last covered with ocean during the late Cretaceous period; or even, *Let's go to bed.* Instead he brought up Brookhaven. Her real dream. Her obtainable dream. Because she wasn't going sailing, and he was leaving.

She shouldn't do this. One day with him and they were already right back where they left off. *Not quite where you left off* . . . Maybe getting Adam involved would make her take the step she couldn't seem to take. "You've got other things to do," she said.

He held up one long finger. "Prepare a best man's speech." A second finger went up. "Find an apartment so my mom gets her garage back. That's it."

"Somehow I don't think that's the whole truth," she said, and was rewarded with a slight widening of his eyes. But the last thing she wanted was Adam Collins rising to the challenge. "We can talk about it on the way home."

8

THEY RODE IN silence back to Walkers Ford. Marissa had spent plenty of time riding shotgun with Adam, both in the passenger seat of whatever car he was fixing up and driving, and on the back of that dangerous motorcycle. Sometimes they talked. More often than not they just drove around until they found their way back to Brookhaven's barn. She knew his silences as well as most people knew their lovers' words, so she sat in the stillness heating between them as the car prowled the county highways, toward Brookhaven. In the cocoon created by the car's solid feel, the rhythm of the windshield wipers, and soft rock playing on the radio, the mood in the car shifted. He didn't touch her, didn't look at her, but she didn't need a hand on her knee or a quick glance to know what he was thinking. What he finally, finally would do.

What she'd always wanted.

He parked at the apex of the semicircular drive, and when he got out of the car to open her door, the gesture no longer felt gentlemanly. He stayed close, letting her bump into him, feel the heat and strength of his body as they walked around to the servants' quarters entrance. While she unlocked the door he ran his palm over his buzzed hair and flung the col-

lected water to the side, and something in that automatic gesture stripped away her resolve.

"I told you about the books," she said. "Tell me how you
stayed faithful, seeing Delaney once or twice a year."

"It loses something in the telling," he said. "I could dem-
onstrate, though."

Her pulse stuttered, then shot into high gear. She liked
men, loved sex, wasn't afraid to own her sexuality. Given
explosive chemistry with a man disciplined enough to remain
utterly faithful to one woman for twelve years, the possibilities
for sexual exploration were endless, intriguing. Silently she
pushed the door open in invitation. He tilted his head. *Ladies
first.* She walked into her tiny kitchen and flicked on the wall
sconce over her little kitchen table. Dim light pushed at the
shadows in the room.

"Would you normally do this after a first date?" he asked,
his head bent as if he was studying the floor.

"That was hardly our first date," she said lightly. When he
lifted an eyebrow, she relented. "Depends," she said.

"On what?"

That was harder to answer. "On lots of things. The guy.
The date. How long it's been."

"How long has it been?" he asked, still not looking at her.

"Three days," she said. "You were there. Shots of whiskey,
pantry. Remember?"

Then he lifted his head and nailed her to the wall with his
heated hazel gaze. "Before that."

Months. Months and months and months alone, because
she was busy in the summer, and worn down, and in the
winter the weather kept her off the roads. The longing for
touch, for a man's hands on her body, against her body, swept
through her. Maybe it was a betrayal of honor and self-respect.
The night in the pantry probably was. But she'd long since
given up denying what her soft, animal body wanted. Needed.
"A while," she said.

"I know how that feels," he said.

"I expect you do," she said. Longing surged in the room like a rising tide, engulfing them by degrees, rhythmic, predictable.

"It's an ache," he went on. "Low and tight. Heavy."

Her mouth went dry. "Yes," she said.

He crossed the tiny kitchen in a single step, backing her against the wall by the door to her bedroom. One elbow braced by her head, he laid his big palm flat against her lower belly, not quite cupping her sex. "Here. It's steady. Relentless. After a while it doesn't matter if you get yourself off or not. It never goes away."

Air slowly left her lungs, drawn to the heat simmering between them. She inhaled shakily and looked up at him, then cupped the thickening bulge in his jeans. "Is it the same for you?"

He shifted, rubbing against the heel of her hand, while his fingers gathered the loose fall of her hair. "Lower," he said. "Right at the base, and in my balls." When she turned her wrist and applied a little more pressure, he groaned and ground against her. "It's a need," he said, low and rough. The hand slowly twining in her hair tightened for a split second, then released. "But the Marine Corps taught me how to deal with needs."

Two steps, her retreating, him advancing into the dark, warm air of her bedroom, and they were up against her double bed. She stopped but Adam didn't. He slipped an arm around her waist and lifted her, bearing her back onto the unmade bed, breaking their descent with his other hand. He was braced on one arm, stretched out beside her, his hazel eyes dark with restrained desire. Her heart thudded hard against her breastbone. This was a moment she loved, when the promise of sex began to permeate the air. But they were both fully dressed, and something unknown glimmered under the building heat.

His long fingers curled under the hem of her sweater, caught under its bottom, and began to tug it up. Adam, a bed, darkness, and privacy—her teenage dream. Cold air kissed her belly, then her ribs, puckering her nipples inside her lace bra. A little shifting and he tugged her top over her head and dropped it on the floor.

"In boot camp you never refer to yourself in the first person. No 'I' or 'me.' It's 'this recruit,' with the objective being to graduate from recruit to Marine. Before Receiving, I had needs," he said, then bent to the exposed skin. She expected a kiss and got the scrape of his teeth over her collarbone, then the kiss, a softer touch that zinged straight to her nipples, then to her clit. The shudder that ran through her had nothing to do with air temperature. "'This Marine' closed his mind to everything that might cause him to fail. This included all images and thoughts of sex." His tongue slid into the valley between her breasts, then gently under the scalloped edge of black lace. "For example, 'this Marine' didn't look at porn."

The distancing effect heightened the sense of untouchability she found so desperately desirable. "No porn?" she said.

"We're not supposed to have it in Muslim countries, but we did," he said, dark amusement in his voice as he shifted over her. "'This Marine' didn't think about breasts or nipples, either," he said as he released the front catch, then brushed the fabric off to the sides. He gently squeezed the firm flesh, pursed his lips and blew a soft stream of air over her nipple. Her sex clenched as sensation wicked through her body. "Or about the way your nipples darken as you get aroused."

"You didn't," she said unsteadily.

"No. Stay in the moment. Cleaning my rifle, packing for a mission, listening to a briefing, standing watch, running, lifting weights. Never let your mind drift."

"You're very disciplined." It would have been easy to mistake his fidelity for a lack of sex drive. In fact, it was the opposite. Adam was an intensely sexual man, and just as intensely disciplined.

A smile she felt as much as saw, then he caught one nipple between his teeth, laved it with his tongue, then pressed it gently between his fingers while he turned his attention to the other nipple. She slid her hand into his hair, her attention divided between the way the lengthening buzz cut flattened under her palm and the hard biceps flexing under her other hand. A particularly firm pinch sent heat streaking along her nerves, and she arched and whimpered.

" 'This Marine' didn't think about sounds. Breathing."

One warm hand skated down her breastbone to her abdomen, and indeed, anticipating the move lower made her breath catch. Everything he didn't think about became the object of her attention, her taut nipples, her shallowing breath, and his responses. The heat and strength of his body, pressed against hers. The way his voice deepened, the words running together as his erection pulsed against her thigh. He gently stroked her flat abdomen with his fingertips, leaving her sensitized nipples to throb in the dark, warm air.

"Or buttons, or zippers," he continued as he unfastened her jeans, stroked the swell of her hip above the waistband, then slid his hand inside to work them partway down. "No thinking about curves, either." He paused, his gaze roaming her disheveled state, then traced a fingertip from her lowest rib along the flare of her hip, to the point where her jeans were stuck, along with the elastic of her panties. He tugged her jeans down her legs and off, leaving her bare to his gaze.

"I didn't think about having you naked and spread for me," he said.

He was looking in her eyes as he spread her legs, and for a moment Marissa's heart stopped. Something dangerous and edgy flashed there, and the half smile that quirked the corner of his mouth shaved only the thinnest layer off the palpable tension.

He'd thought about it. About her. And whoever *this Marine* was, the only man in the room was Adam.

Still positioned between her legs, he sat back on his heels and pulled his shirt over his head. She sat up, drawn to the finely honed muscles of his shoulders and chest, but he pushed her back to the bed. "I definitely didn't think about touch," he said.

He eased down, the breadth of his shoulders widening her thighs. One hand curved under her leg and over her hip to stroke the soft curls at the top of her mound. With the other he urged her legs to open more. "This was off-limits," he said. He stroked her folds with his index finger, opened them, but avoided her clit. "The soft, delicate skin, the scent. How vulnerable you are right now."

He'd thought about that, too, about how each step in the dance heightened a woman's surrender. When he bent and blew gently on the exposed nub, she made another soft noise.

"So slick," he murmured, but she didn't know whether that was an observation, or something else he wouldn't allow himself to remember. His finger traced her inner folds, then slid inside. "So hot, and very, very tight."

At the words, she spasmed around his finger. He bent his head and put his tongue to her clit. Her eyes dropped closed as all her attention focused on his tongue and what it was doing. A slow circle, another, then he stopped when she shivered and laved several deft strokes on the more sensitive side. "There?"

"There," she said.

"Hmmmm." A satisfied purr from the broad male chest.

The hand resting on top of her mound didn't move, so she brought her hand along his arm and linked her fingers with his as he did it again, and again, the touch of his tongue light, almost teasing, enough to strike sparks under the swelling skin but not enough to satisfy. He dipped lower, circled her soft opening, then slid back up, developing a slow, steady rhythm.

Their fingers still linked, she reached down and spread her folds for him. This time when his tongue stroked along her clit, she bucked toward his mouth. The hand under hers flattened on her mound, holding her down, and then it was game on. He went down on her like he had all the time in the world and no end in mind other than her complete and total devastation. He worked two fingers inside her, stroking in a lazy, gentle reminder of what it would feel like when he fucked

her, and drew tight, desperate gasps from her as molten pleasure built and built. When he turned his fingers and stroked
the bundle of nerves in the swollen inner wall, ecstasy went
supernova. She lifted into his mouth and sobbed out her pleasure as she came.

He backed off a little when she subsided, kissing her trembling inner thighs, the hand still clutching his at her mound, a
veneer of lazy amusement over the intensity in his eyes. He
straightened, looming over her as he shoved off pants, socks,
and boots. Then she got her first good look at the body of a
fighting-strength United States Marine.

Amazing. Hard, not an ounce of fat with the muscles so
sharply delineated. Darker brown hair dusted his pecs and
tapered to a line down his abdomen before thickening around
his erect shaft. Completely unselfconscious, he removed a
condom from his wallet and smoothed it on. The dim light
from the kitchen starkly illuminated his broad shoulders as
he knelt between her legs. He planted one hand beside either
shoulder. She let out a moan when the broad head of his shaft
stretched skin made vibrantly sensitive by foreplay and an
orgasm.

He slid inside, slow and relentless, stretching her unbear-
ably. She drew tight around him, the movement as involuntary
as the helpless little gasp she made. He lowered his body
to hers, taking some of his weight on his elbows, but she
felt the strength and power of his torso covering her, the
clench of his abdominal muscles as he withdrew and pushed
back in.

"That's my secret, Ris. I focus on whatever I'm doing. I
block out everything else. Now I'm focused on how tight you
are, how you're slick and hot, and I'm paying attention." He
stroked in once, twice, and pleasure began to simmer. "That's
good," he said. Then he adjusted the cant of his hips and his
next stroke glided over the sensitive bundle of nerves inside
her.

The contrast was electrifying, the difference between trun-
dling along in her truck and screaming down dirt roads on

the back of Adam's Hayabusa at a hundred and thirty miles an hour. Her toes curled, her fingernails dug into his biceps and nape, and a new, higher-pitched, demanding noise clawed its way from her throat.

"That's better," he said, and did it again.

"God, yes," she said.

The only facets of her world were his voice, low, rough, utterly self-assured, utterly masculine, and the slow, slick glide of his cock into her sensitized channel. She was beyond thinking, adrift in a sea of hot, dark pleasure. His heart pounded against his sternum, the pulse reverberating into her body. Without knowing why, she cupped the back of his head and turned his mouth to hers. The taste of her juices lingered on his mouth, but then the kisses were deep and hard, as much an exchange of gasps and huffs of air as a battle of tongues and teeth. He fisted his hand in her hair and turned her head so his mouth brushed her ear. "I won't forget, Ris. Next time I'll remember this, and I'll use it against you."

She came, and this time her orgasm made her vision close to a pinprick. He thrust through the contractions, holding his breath, then let it out with a stuttering groan as he ground against her and came.

He lifted some of his weight onto his elbows, and the shift only heightened the sensations where they were connected. His hair-roughened legs against her inner thighs, the super-sensitive flesh where they were joined. The muscular strength of his biceps alongside her upper arms. His fingers, entwining with hers as the tension ebbed from their bodies, but she was glad he couldn't see her face.

"Very interesting demonstration," she said. "How long did it take most people to go from 'me' or 'I' to 'this recruit'?"

He nuzzled into her hair, then stretched out on his side, his head braced on his palm. "A few weeks."

She turned toward him. "And you?"

He tucked her hair behind her ear and looked at her with those unreadable hazel eyes while his hand cupped the back of her skull. "Two days."

For a long moment they lay together, then he shifted down to the end of the bed, and off. Cold without his body generating heat next to her, Marissa pulled the layers of bedclothes over her body. The scent of him, skin, sweat, and sex, remained in the sheets. She was trying to decide if she should ask him to stay, when he came out of the bathroom and tugged on his khakis and buttoned up his shirt. Decision made, she snuggled into the bed and watched as solid muscle and bone disappeared behind twill and cotton and his leather belt.

"What time are we leaving to get the paneling?" he asked as he sat down at the end of the bed to put on socks and boots. She peered at him, but his face, cast in shadows by the light from the kitchen, was difficult to read. "I owe you, Ris," he said. "I'm the one who destroyed it."

Clarity sometimes came in darkness. Adam defined himself by control, not by notches on his bedpost, and *this Marine* was having a hard time adapting to civilian life. "I've got a siding job coming up," she said evasively. "I was going to wait for a clear stretch, but this late in the season I'll settle for a relatively dry stretch. I could use the help."

"Great. Just let me know when." He stood at the foot of her bed, then reached behind him for the light switch that controlled the lamp on her nightstand. "Wait!" she exclaimed, and sat up, but she ended up covering her eyes against the light. In her mind's eye she could see Adam standing at the foot of her bed, hands on his hips. When she lowered her hand, he rapped a knuckle on the wall running the length of her bed.

Five pictures hung there, neatly spaced. Each black frame held a yellowing photograph of Josiah Brooks's yacht *Dreaming Seas*, the boat he'd left behind in Rhode Island when he went west, to the High Plains. In two shots the sixty-foot yacht was moored along a dock, in three others moored off an island. The rocky beach and pine trees curved away in the distance; the camera must have been set up on the beach. The photographs were in the trunks her father left her when she died, yellowing, fading, the cardboard frames stained from both handling and neglect. Her heart had skipped several beats when she'd found them. She'd studied them until the cardboard fell apart, then spent money she didn't have to get them archivally framed.

"I have excellent night vision," Adam said with a glance at the wall. "What's this all about?"

How could she describe this? A hobby? She lived in South Dakota, smack in the middle of the North American continent, a region of the country that hadn't seen salt water for several geologic eras. All she knew was that the oldest photographs of Josiah Brooks at the bottom of the trunk were taken on sailboats. Big ones, with sleek lines and teak decking, canvas sails furled or unfurled. He stood among men in white suits with vests, and women in white dresses with sashes and parasols, and he looked young and happy. When she saw the boats, something inside her vibrated slow and deep and long, like she was standing inside a giant bass speaker at a concert, but the music playing was the distant, primal rush and pull of the tides.

"Josiah Brooks owned a sailboat in Connecticut," she said. "A yacht, really. I saw pictures in the trunk in the attic. I was curious about sailing."

"And you call it a tangent." He picked up the sextant, propped on a shelf above one of the pictures, then carefully examined the chronometer resting next to it. "Nice instruments," he said.

Should she mention the boxes of composition notebooks, full of notes she'd taken to familiarize herself with lines and rigging and sails? Should she mention the lists of things she would need for an around-the-world voyage, or the much-revised itinerary?

The first item on the list was *Buy a boat*, something that wouldn't happen as long as she owed the lumberyard six years of her average annual income.

She gave a dismissive little laugh. "I said TV was boring."

"Most people read novels," he said.

"Why would I read about made-up people when I could

read about things real people have done?" Laughter huffed in his chest, and the corners of his mouth quirked up just a little. "They're part of the Brooks family history," she said stiffly, clutching the sheet and blankets under her chin. "The prelude to Brookhaven. I've framed other pictures and hung them in my apartment."

"Not over your bed. Not where you read," he said with a nod at the books stacked by her nightstand. "Not where you dream."

"It's nothing," she said because that was all it could be. "Don't make something out of nothing."

"Making something out of nothing is a Marine's specialty," he said. "It's what you're doing with Brookhaven. You could make it a habit."

She reached for the lamp on her nightstand and turned it off manually, plunging the room back into darkness. Adam's broad shoulders remained backlit in the doorway. A long moment passed before he spoke. "I've been sailing. It's amazing. A purer rush than the bike."

Her breath caught, because she knew how much the bike meant to him, but she couldn't get words through the thickness in her throat. Eventually, he turned and let himself out.

9

ADAM PARKED THE Charger in front of the Walkers' house, situated on the fourteenth green of the Chatham County golf course. From the front the house didn't look like much, a single story with a brick entryway, brightly lit windows in the dining room to the right of the front door and in Mr. Walker's home office to the left. The ground sloped away from the garage on the left. A bottle of wine in hand, he jogged up the driveway and rang the doorbell.

Delaney answered. "You don't have to ring the doorbell," she chided. "You're practically family."

Practically family wasn't a son-in-law, and he knew it. He just nodded and stepped into the foyer. Inside, the house's size and luxury became more evident. A fire popped and cracked in the fireplace in the living room, and the dining room opened into a large, eat-in kitchen with stainless steel appliances and a large island with wrought-iron stools tucked underneath. Big windows looked out over the deck that ran the back of the house, and the golf course, still lushly green and empty thanks to the rain. The furniture was upholstered in heavy, dark greens and blues, with maroon accents, as were the curtains.

"Your mother made the curtains," Delaney reminded him, the bottle of wine tucked in her crossed arms.

"They look good," he said shortly.

"Come in," she said, and set off for the kitchen. She wore her work clothes, a simple pair of black slacks, a blue blouse with a ruffle along the neck, and a darker blue cardigan. "Dad's still helping Mom get dressed, but let's go ahead and open this."

Yeah, they were all going to need alcohol to get through this. Delaney handed him the corkscrew and the bottle. He had the cork out in the time it took her to pull a tray of sliced vegetables from the fridge and set it on the island's raised counter, next to the cheese ball and crackers.

He watched her, the woman he'd planned to marry. Once loved. Her hands were smooth, pale, the same words he'd use to describe her lipstick. Marissa was the bottom of the ocean—deep, fathomless, seemingly endless—Delaney was like a meadow in spring sunshine. People settled down around her, relaxed. He had.

He poured for them both. Delaney lifted her glass and sipped. "That's good," she said. "How are you, Adam?"

She meant it, those words spoken in clear bell tones. She always meant it when she asked, had from the night she sat down next to him at a party hosted by Keith at his parents' lake house. They'd been twenty. She was home from college, he was home on leave, and she asked him how he was. He didn't tell her the truth, but she'd meant it, and that was enough. He'd awkwardly offered to pick her up for the movies the next afternoon, then spent the rest of his leave with her and her friends. When she'd asked him to e-mail her at college, he had, and snail-mailed postcards, then letters, then packages filled with candy, books, mix CDs, the perfume she wore. At the time he'd had only the vaguest clue why he went after her so relentlessly. In hindsight, with her he felt everything he didn't feel with Marissa. He felt nothing at all, and that felt safe.

"I'm fine," he said. "Glad to be home."

She picked up a baby carrot, dipped it in ranch dressing, then asked, "How's your mom?"

"Good. Keeping busy. Lots of orders." She'd laughingly

refused to tell him what Marissa asked for in exchange for renovating the bathroom. He'd come at it from another angle, another time. "How's your mom?"

"The drug regimen seems to be working," she said. "The progression of her symptoms has slowed again." Delaney's parents appeared from the master bedroom, off the sunken living room. "It takes her a while to button her blouse, and she can't get her earrings in on her own," Delaney confided in a low voice.

His gaze sharpened. "That's recent." The last time he'd seen Mrs. Walker, before his last deployment, she'd had tremors in her left hand and a slight balance problem.

"It got worse shortly after this last deployment," Delaney agreed. They both watched Mr. Walker escort his wife across the slick floor. Delaney's room was on the lower level, next to the family room with sliding doors that led to the pool, and the guest room that was ostensibly his when he was home on leave. It made for an idyllic lovers retreat, one her parents turned a blind eye to when he produced a ring box.

"How does the roast look, Delaney-dear?" The endearment was automatic; Delaney once told him she thought her name was Delaneydeer until she started kindergarten and realized they were two separate words and her middle name was Marie.

"I'll just check it, Mom. You catch up with Adam."

She did just that, taking his arm with a surprisingly firm grip and giving him a sound kiss on the cheek. "We're so glad you're home," she said. "Safe and sound and for good. When do you start school?"

They discussed the architecture program while Delaney and her father set the dining room table with four places. "Delaney seems okay," he said.

"Oh, yes," she said, watching her only child fondly. "She wasn't, for a while, you know. You took us all by surprise. Some folks think you repaid a decade of loyalty pretty poorly."

He could always count on Walkers Ford to rush to judgment. "I wasn't the right man for Delaney," he said.

She looked at him, her head wobbling but her pale blue eyes sharp. "Don't you think that was for her to decide?"

"Yes, ma'am," he said noncommittally, watching Delaney precisely align knife and spoon at each place. Her blond hair slid forward against her cheek. She tucked it back, revealing skin the color of cream. Even here Delaney absorbed whatever animosity her parents felt toward him. The engine of the Walker house hummed smoothly. Even before he produced the ring box, *this Marine* fit in here, knew who he was, who he would be. Delaney's husband, the father of her children, a much-needed professional in the larger community.

And now? Where does *this Marine* belong now?

"She had her friends," Delaney's mother said, ending his train of thought. "And Keith. You've all been friends for so long. I hope this won't affect that. In the end, relationships are what matters in life. Family, friends, people you love and who love you."

Spoken like someone facing a slow decline and an early death. "Yes, ma'am," he said again.

"Stop that, Adam," she said, but fondness eased the exasperation.

Delaney appeared in front of them, holding the roast on her mother's wedding china platter. "Adam, would you escort Mom to the table?"

He locked his elbow and offered it to her. Delaney and Mr. Walker followed with the potatoes, squash, peas, and rolls. Adam took his seat next to Mrs. Walker with Delaney opposite her mother, at her father's left hand. They were in the process of passing food when the front door blew open. Rain and wind pushed Keith into the foyer, where he stood dripping on the welcome mat.

"I thought you couldn't get away in time!" Delaney exclaimed. She pushed back her chair and hurried to Keith's side, giving him a quick kiss after he took off his coat.

"Opposing counsel called at the last possible moment," he said. "The hearing's off, at least for now." He crossed the tile, his hand held out. "Don," he said to Mr. Walker, then bent to give Mrs. Walker a kiss on the cheek. "Marie," he said. "How are you feeling? I hope you don't mind if I join you."

Delaney was already returning with the bottle of wine and a plate and silverware for him. There was no mistaking the pleasure in her eyes. He shook Adam's hand across the table then took his seat next to Delaney.

"What've you been up to?" he asked as he helped himself to roast beef.

"Getting settled," Adam said just as genially. "I looked at some apartments in Brookings a couple of days ago. Sorting boxes in my mother's garage."

Delaney exchanged a quick glance with Keith, who managed to look both sheepish and overworked at the same time. "Did you . . . ?" Delaney asked.

"We need to talk about tux fittings," Keith said easily. "Meet me for breakfast tomorrow?"

Adam kept his expression utterly even. "Sure. Heirloom at eight?"

"Perfect. What did you think of Brookhaven?" Keith asked.

An interesting choice of conversation topics. "She's done an incredible job," Adam said.

"I thought the same thing," Delaney said. "She's certainly poured her heart and soul into the renovation. My goodness, the sheer size of that house. It's at least the size of the clubhouse. So much work."

"I never thought she'd pull it off," Keith said. "She made any progress on that paneled wall?"

Adam wondered if God would strike them all down if they used her name. "Marissa said she's got it under control," he said mildly.

"It is a pretty amazing turnaround," Keith said. "The house was trashed for years, then the next thing you know it's like a movie set for one of those PBS Masterpiece shows. Except for the missing wall."

The next thing you know was more like hours and hours and hours of equity sweated into the house by a five-foot-eight-inch, hundred-and-twenty-pound woman who'd taught herself everything she needed to know. She'd rebuilt that house on the strength in her back and arms.

"How did you find out about Brookhaven?" Adam asked Delaney.

"Dad mentioned how far along the renovations were," Delaney said. "He'd been out to the house on business."

Delaney's father was the latest member of the Walker family to serve as president and chairman of the board of Chatham County Bank and Trust. Most everyone in town banked there, although the national banks were making inroads into rural communities. Adam had an account with one such national bank in Brookings, and transferred money into his mother's account at the CCB&T. If Mr. Walker went in person to Brookhaven, it was to verify the property was worth enough to secure a loan. The fact that Marissa had a home equity line of credit for the renovation wasn't surprising. Mr. Walker's recent visit to the property was.

Her father, normally silent in the presence of his wife and daughter, spoke. "Delaney and Keith wanted to get married as quickly as possible," he said in measured tones. "The club wasn't available until February. I thought perhaps we could make a deal with Miss Brooks."

"It's perfect," Mrs. Walker said. "The room, so romantic in candlelight, and such a unique venue. The whole county will be talking about it."

"As long as she gets that wall repaired. She's been working on the house for forever, and it's still not done. I'm glad you let me add the partial repayment clause to the contract, Don."

"It was the prudent thing to do," Mr. Walker said. "She's made great strides on Brookhaven. Whether she can follow through to the finish, or meet a payment schedule, remains to be seen."

Everyone in Walkers Ford would see Keith's care for the wedding, his attentiveness to Delaney. Adam saw the son of the town's lawyer and the daughter of the town's banker up against the daughter of the man who lost the last remaining symbol of a fantastic East Coast inheritance. Adam's jaw set.

"Does she miss deadlines on paid projects?" he asked, striving for a mildly concerned tone.

A quick glance between Delaney and her mother. "Not that I've heard," Delaney said. Her mother nodded. "Everyone who's hired her has been pleased with the results."

"Good thing Brookhaven just jumped to a paid project," Adam said.

The clink of silverware against china reigned for a few moments, then Delaney spoke. "What's she going to do out there in that big house?" she mused. "It's so isolated."

"Maybe she'll give the country club a run for its money," Keith said carelessly. He'd finished his wine and poured what remained of the bottle into his glass as he slumped back in his chair.

"Maybe she'll get married again," Mrs. Walker said. "Her husband might love Brookhaven as much as she does."

"She's a Brooks," Mr. Walker said with the unerring confidence of a big fish in a small pond. "Their hearts belong to that piece of land, to that house, even when they can't muster the financial wherewithal to take care of what they own. Maybe she's the Brooks who can hold on to the house. They've lost that property in stages since Josiah Brooks died."

"If she can't . . ." Keith rubbed Delaney's thigh under the table. "You want to raise kids in the country, sweetheart?"

"We just put the down payment . . . oh," she said, then glanced at Adam. "You're teasing me."

Mrs. Walker explained. "They've bought the house just around the corner."

"We're getting some painting done, new carpets laid, while we're on our honeymoon," Keith said.

"The backyards are practically touching," Delaney said.

Adam could fill in the rest. Adjoining backyards would come in handy when Delaney wanted to send the kids to see her parents. She could watch from the deck as they ran through the grass to Grandma and Grandpa Walker. She'd moved out of their house, to an apartment more centrally located for her school psychologist's duties, but moved back in after her mother's Parkinson's diagnosis.

"The wine's good," Keith noted in the silence, then picked up the bottle and looked at the label. "Where did you get it?" he asked Mr. Walker.

"Adam brought it," Delaney said.

Keith looked at Adam. "A grocery store in Brookings," he said.

"Oh," he replied casually. "Find an apartment?"

"Not yet." He laid his napkin on the table, and Delaney rose to collect plates. He bent low to Mrs. Walker, struggling to get to her feet, and said, "I've got it, ma'am."

He stacked the vegetable dishes on top of the roast platter, and followed Delaney into the kitchen. When he went back for the rest of the plates, Keith and Mr. Walker were in a low-voiced conversation about a land deal. Back in the kitchen, Delaney was rinsing plates into one sink while running hot, soapy water into the other side. Mrs. Walker's wedding china couldn't go in the dishwasher.

"Thanks," she said. "No, don't help me wash. I've got a system."

He leaned against the counter, keeping one eye on the conversation taking place in the dining room, and watched her for a minute. "Are you happy, Delaney?"

She swirled the sponge around a plate, then rinsed it before she answered. "Yes," she said.

"Your mom said you had a hard time of it for a while."

"I did," she said simply. "I wasn't ready for what happened."

"I suppose not," he said. He watched Keith for a moment, bent forward in his suit coat, his elbows on his knees, making points in a low-voiced, emphatic manner to his soon-to-be father-in-law. It didn't escape Adam's notice that Mr. Walker hadn't spoken to him all evening, or, for that matter, at Brookhaven the night he got home.

"Good thing Keith was there for you."

She ducked a plate under the running water, and her

diamond winked as soapy bubbles dripped off her hand. "I don't regret being engaged to you. I'm sorry it wasn't right for you."

She'd never been one for regrets, for second-guessing, perhaps because she'd never done anything regrettable in her life, or because she'd always followed her heart. "Good," he said. "That's all I wanted to know."

He strode back to the dining room. "Thanks for supper," he said with a nod for Delaney's father. "It was good to see you all again. Good night."

"Wait," Mrs. Walker called. "Where's your jacket?"

"Don't need one, ma'am," he said with a grin, just for her. Then he headed into the rain-swept night, thinking about one woman's heart and where she belonged.

10

MARISSA HAULED OPEN the library's front door just as Alana came around from behind her desk, dressed for the weather in an ankle-length raincoat, a laptop bag slung over her shoulder and another tote dangling from her elbow. "I had a feeling I'd see you today," Alana said, one eyebrow lifted.

She was too tired to maintain any emotion above resignation about Alana's giving her books to Adam. She was trying to be helpful, but she didn't know the whole story, and getting angry at her wouldn't change anything. "I would have been here earlier but I had to load siding. It took longer than I thought."

Alana crossed the library's flooring, her boot heels clicking in the silence. "Adam gave you the books, right? He said he'd see you."

He saw her, all right. It was like old times, driving around with him, and new experiences. Grownup experiences. Apartment shopping, having supper at a new restaurant. Having sex. It was everything they'd done and everything they hadn't done, rolled into one night. The memories alternated between making her smile and gripping her heart in a tight fist. "I told you to send them back."

"I thought you should take a look at them," Alana said. She crossed the floor and tapped down the light switches, leaving only a single light burning behind the circulation desk to ward off the fall gloom. "You didn't bring them back already. Tell me you looked at them."

"No," Marissa admitted. She couldn't bring herself to return them. Not yet.

Alana's gaze softened, then she opened the front door. "Have you eaten?"

"Not since breakfast. It was a very long day." Loading the siding, piece by piece, into her truck, then unloading it onto pallets in Mrs. Carson's side yard, was all her in a race against daylight. Dull, hot pain stretched from her shoulders to her lower back.

"Come on. I'll cook," Alana said, and locked the library.

She followed Alana three blocks into town and parked on the street in front of the small house Alana rented from Chief Ridgeway. In the kitchen Alana shed her coat, then turned up the heat and put a kettle on to boil water before ducking into the bedroom. Marissa shed her flannel-lined Carhartt coveralls, leaving her in jeans and a sweatshirt, then eased into a chair at the kitchen table, and rested her head on her folded arms.

"Feel good to sit down?" Alana asked, now wearing a pair of fleece pants and a belted wool cardigan. She turned off the flame under the kettle and opened a cabinet for tea bags and mugs.

"You have no idea," Marissa said without lifting her head. Water from the tips of her wet braids beaded on her red fleece. She'd get up and help with supper in a minute.

A moment later Alana set a cup of tea in front of her, then turned on the local NPR station for background noise while she poked around in the fridge. "Stir-fry okay?" she asked.

"Sounds great." The announcer moved to a story about four dead Marines in Helmand Province, and she cocked her head slightly to catch all the details until she remembered Adam was home, whole and sound.

When she refocused on the kitchen around her, Alana was watching her, a knife in her hand and a head of broccoli on the cutting board. "I get the feeling I shouldn't have given him the books. I asked him how well he knew you and he said he'd known you all his life. I thought he knew."

"He would have, if I'd been interested in sailing before he left. All I talked about then was Brookhaven. I guess it doesn't matter, because he's not staying. He says he is, but he isn't. Can you see him living here? He's totally out of place now."

Alana looked at her, then added oil to a nonstick pan and turned on the heat under it. "Because it's so strange that someone would want to live here, in the flyover states?"

"No. This is my home. Five generations of my family have lived here. But . . . what's here for him?"

"His mother and a graduate degree?" Alana swept the broccoli into a bowl and went to work on a red pepper. "I seem to be missing a key point. Maybe you better start at the beginning."

A spicy-sweet aroma drifted up from the tea. Marissa inhaled, then sipped. Warmth spread down her throat and into her stomach. "Now that he's home, I'm sure someone with *good intentions* filled you in on the history."

"Several someones," Alana said. She scraped pepper innards into the trash, then dumped mushrooms onto the cutting board. "I prefer to hear it from you. Is this a Hatfields-versus-McCoys thing?"

Marissa laughed. "It's more of a grasshoppers-and-ants thing. The Walkers are ants, through and through. They work hard, save what they make, marry prudently, live quietly. The Brookses, on the other hand, are grasshoppers. We sing all summer, and we throw the best parties," she said, looking over at Alana. The other woman smiled at her. "Always have. I have pictures from Brookhaven in the twenties when there must have been a hundred people staying at that house. They pitched tents in the backyard, bathed in the creek. Some of the old-timers around here remember those parties, or remember their parents talking about them. The way Brookhaven used to be." The way the Brookses used to be. Flying high, and taking everyone else along for the ride.

Mushroom caps fell to slices under Alana's deft hands. "What happened?"

"The stock market crash, for one. We never really recovered from that. Droughts. A series of investments that went bad. Like grasshoppers, we made big leaps, usually in response to the last crisis, always in the opposite yet somehow wrong direction. Whatever scheme failed, we came up with a bigger, better dream. That's why my mom left. She was from Rapid City, and married Dad on nothing more than promises and dreams. She left when she figured out she couldn't count on him for anything more. She married a rancher in Wyoming. Dad finally couldn't even pay the taxes and we lost the house when I was fifteen."

"But you bought it back."

She watched Alana add sliced beef to the hot oil. The meat sizzled for a few moments, then Alana tipped the bowl of vegetables into the pan as well. "Because my husband, Chris, got an inheritance. He wasn't much better than I am when it came to practicalities. He was in construction. Buying it back so we could renovate it and use it as a showpiece was my idea. He could teach me what I needed to know." She stopped for a second. "He died five months after we got the deed."

And I lied to him. I never, ever would have sold Brookhaven.

"Why even bother to renovate it after he died?"

"I was tired of everyone in this town looking at me like I was just another big-dreaming Brooks. Living that way for another sixty years didn't appeal to me. Plates or bowls?"

"Plates. I'll have a glass of wine, too. So, if the Brookses are grasshoppers and the Walkers are ants, what are the Collinses? I don't know Adam's mother. She doesn't come into the library."

Marissa got up and pulled two purple stoneware plates from the cabinet, then added two wine glasses from the rack under the cabinets. "Darla Collins is a grasshopper trapped in an ant's world," she said as she set the table. "She was a single mother back before getting knocked up by a stock car driver was no big deal. She had big dreams of going to New

York and making it in the fashion world. The driver made big promises, all of which included getting her out of Walkers Ford, but skipped town alone when she got pregnant."

"What about Adam?"

"Adam then, or Adam now?" she asked as she got forks from the silverware drawer. Her stomach grumbled as Alana tipped steaming, seared vegetables and meat onto the plates, then carried them to the table.

"Adam then. Let's start there."

She speared a piece of broccoli, chewed and swallowed while she considered this. He'd had a dream then, of going on the motorcycle racing circuit, but time and the Corps replaced dreams with a plan, and completely eradicated his emotions, too. "Then was one running battle between testosterone and willpower. He was the life of the party, the strategist behind every prank, skating through school on charm and just enough to get by."

"Girls?" Alana asked, her eyes bright.

"What's the old Marine Corps slogan? Many were called. Few were chosen."

"So he and Delaney weren't high school sweethearts."

"No."

"Were you?"

There are no words for what we were. Love isn't big enough. Lust isn't deep enough. Lost covers it. We were lost in each other. "No."

"That's why he looks at you like you're the one who got away."

I didn't get away. He left. "He doesn't look at me like that," she said firmly.

"Oh, but he does. And now? Who is Adam now?"

"I don't know. He's doing all the right things, saying all the right things, but it's like he's not actually in his body. He says he's here because he's home, and maybe that's true, but it's not the whole truth. Yesterday we went apartment hunting in Brookings. Then we had supper." She finished off the last of her wine. "Then we had sex."

Alana lifted her glass in a toast. "Sounds like a date."

"It wasn't a date. He's here for the wedding, and being home early has something to do with Delaney, too. I just can't figure out what."

"Tell me why he's best man in that wedding?"

It always surprised her that there were people in the world who didn't know every intimate detail of the Walker/Brooks/Herndon history. "He and Keith were best friends. The Herndons have been here for fifteen years, which is a drop in the bucket compared to us Walkers and Brookses, but Keith's dad is the only lawyer in fifty miles. When he retires, Keith will be the only lawyer in fifty miles."

"I can't see Adam Collins and Keith Herndon as best friends."

"They were. Keith liked Adam for the same reason the rest of us did. Things happen when he's around. They always did. For better or for worse, things happen when Adam Collins is around. Keith . . . encouraged those things. None of us thought about it then, but Keith had a safety net Adam didn't have."

"People keep mentioning an accident," Alana said quietly.

"We'd lost Brookhaven by then. The house was abandoned, but it was easy to get inside, and somewhere along the line it became the party house. As long as we weren't too out of control, the sheriff turned a blind eye to the drinking. One night, things got out of control. Adam and I had put two hundred miles on his motorcycle that afternoon and watched the fireworks from Brookhaven's roof. Then kids started to show up. There was a lot of alcohol. Someone decided to build a bonfire—"

"Using the wood paneling in the great room," Alana finished.

That's when she knew Brookhaven, and by association, herself, mattered to no one but her. She'd tried to stop them, but once Adam got in on the act, hauling a long, rickety wooden ladder out of the barn, she'd failed. When Adam was around, things happened. "After that, it was really out of hand. Adam's motorcycle was there, and this other kid, Josh

Wilmont, got one as a graduation present. Adam challenged him to a race, Josh accepted. It had rained the day before and the dirt roads were still a little slick. Josh lost control taking a corner, and died."

She'd never forget that moment when she heard Adam's screams over the drunken shouting. Never. Within seconds kids were piling into cars and running down the road, headlights picking out wheat in the fields, the dust plume from the bikes, homing in on Adam, on his knees in the stagnant water in a ditch, next to a crumpled, twisted scarecrow wearing Josh's faded jeans and flannel shirt.

Adam's hoarse, unearthly screams.

"Neither of them were wearing helmets, although at their speeds, I'm not sure it would have mattered. Josh died. He'd planned to join the Marines at the end of the summer. Adam joined in his place. Keith and Delaney went to college. I got married, and bought back Brookhaven. The end."

"Maybe that's why he's back," Alana said eventually. "Maybe he's got something to prove."

Marissa bristled. "It was a mistake. A stupid, horrible mistake. He was seventeen. No one here expects him to pay for that for the rest of his life." She collected the dishes and took them to the sink.

"We all have something to prove," Alana said with a small smile.

The sound of a car door slamming cut off Marissa's response, and the moment was gone. "Thanks for supper. I should get going," she said. "I've got a date with a hot bath."

"I've got a date with a book," Alana said, and opened the kitchen door to the driveway to let Marissa out. Chief Ridgeway looked up from greeting his dog, Duke, to give Marissa a nod of greeting before transferring his level gaze to Alana. Marissa climbed into her truck and turned the engine over. When she paused in the street to shift from reverse to drive, Alana and the Chief were still looking at each other. The only change was the pink flush high on Alana's cheekbones.

A steady drizzle persisted the whole way to the house, and

when she got home, Adam's Charger lounged at the top of the driveway. She pulled in under the oak tree, shifted into park, and got out of the cab. Adam stood under the sheltering porch, one shoulder braced against the post, watching her.

"Hey," she said. "Everything okay?"

"Define 'okay.' "

A little laugh huffed from her nose as she came to stand in front of him. He'd stood there, still and waiting, long enough for the drifting mist to seep into his button-down shirt and cargo pants. She lifted her hand to his cheek. A tremor ran through his big body, but he didn't move.

"You're cold," she exclaimed, then brushed her thumb over his lips. Even those were cool to the touch.

"I don't feel cold." His voice was distant, remote, as if the forty-degree temps and fog had chilled his voice, too.

She let her hand slip down his jaw to rest on his chest. He looked down at her, physically present, emotionally in the cold emptiness of space. "Says the Marine. I know cold. You're cold."

He reached up to pluck her hand from his chest and bring her hand to his lips. Warm breath gusted over her chilled fingers, then his tongue touched her knuckles. "So are you."

Heat zipped sharp and electric deep in her belly. "I'm always cold." The porch light behind him turned the drops on his hair into scattered diamonds set in the thick, lengthening bristle cut, and cast his face in shadows. "Are you coming in?"

He followed her into the tiny kitchen, and stood on the welcome mat while she hung up her coveralls and sat down to unlace her boots. "I'm going to take a bath," she said.

His gaze focused ever so slightly. "Hard day."

"Average," she said. She went into the bathroom and turned on the hot water tap, sending water gushing into the deep claw-foot tub. When steam rose into the cooler air, she plugged the drain so the tub would fill. Adam still stood in the kitchen.

"In or out," she said. "I close the bathroom door to trap all the heat."

He followed her into the small room, closed the door, and stood, arms folded across his chest, with his back to it. She started shedding layers, starting with the red fleece and her fleece-lined jeans, then stopped to test the water temperature. Plenty hot. She added some cold to the mix, dumped in two cups of Epsom salts for the aches and pains, and resumed undressing under Adam's increasingly interested eye.

"Where were you?"

The tone was too remote to be accusatory. "I had supper with Alana," she said. "How long have you been here?"

He lifted one shoulder, an eloquent dismissal of the passage of time. He wouldn't sit around home in a button-down and khakis, so he'd been somewhere, but wherever it was, he didn't want to talk about it. Next came her turtleneck, and a waffle-weave long-underwear shirt and matching pants, leaving her standing in front of him in her bra and panties. He sank down, butt to floor, back to door, and braced his forearms on his knees. Well aware of what she was doing, less sure of why, she faced him while she unhooked her bra and let it fall, then pushed down her panties to stand in front of him, naked.

His pulse throbbed at the base of his throat as his gaze traveled from the top of her head to the tips of her toes, lingering in places that picked up the beat of his heart. For a moment water lapped at her senses, gushing into the tub, pattering at the roof over her head, streaming in rivulets down the porthole window overlooking the back meadow, turned to liquid heat in the crux of her thighs. Even Adam, solid and strong, blurred at the edges like a watercolor painting.

She could slip under so easily. Instead, she turned off the water, then lit candles on the shelves under the window and behind the tub. Adam reached one long arm up over his head to flick off the light, sheltering the room in flickering candlelight and the steady rain. Water lapped at the tub's curved rim as she climbed in, then sank down with a low moan.

"Oh, that's good," she said. Cradled in blessed heat to her hairline, her muscles eased enough for her to relax. With her eyes closed she pinned her braids to the top of her head.

"How was Alana?"

"Fine," Marissa said, eyes still closed.

"Don't blame her for giving me the books. She asked if I'd known you a long time. I said yes."

"It's fine."

"I thought I knew you."

She turned her head to look at him, and realized the blurry edges to Adam's face and neck were from a sheen of sweat. "You do know me."

"Not like I used to."

She smiled. "According to some standards you know me better than you did twelve years ago."

"Sleeping with a woman only makes her more complex, not less."

Shadows darkened his hazel eyes. "I'm the same person I was then, Adam. Aren't you?"

"No." The word was emphatic, required no explanation. "I'd better not be. You aren't, either."

The wine and heat combined to ease the pain in her back, and loosen her tongue as she looked at the tin-paneled ceiling again. "Alana didn't know anything about what happened," she said. "I forget that most people don't know. She's been in town for just a few weeks, so she didn't even know the history between the Walkers and the Brookses."

"Did you fill her in?"

"I gave her the short version."

A little huff of laughter, which was, aside from the sweat now beaded on his temple, the first sign of a thaw. "What did she say?"

"Not much. She's a good listener. Doesn't judge. Maybe she's not invested in the community enough to judge us." Curiosity got the better of her. "Where were you tonight?"

"I had supper with the Walkers."

That got her attention. "Why?"

"They invited me." He nodded at the tub. "Long day?"

"I picked up the siding for Mrs. Carson's house and took it over there. It's stacked in her side yard, protected by tarps. This rain better let up, and soon, or I'm going to be working on that house when it's ten degrees out."

He stood up, unbuttoned the top two buttons on his shirt, and pulled it over his head. "How big is it?"

"About the same size as your mom's house. A small rectangle. The only difficult parts are the windows, and the cuts around the utility meters."

"So if you had help, you could be done in a couple of days." He set his hands to his buckle, and she tried not to stare.

"Uh, yeah."

"We'll start tomorrow," he said, and shoved his shorts and pants off, then stepped out of them. His erection jutted away from his abdomen.

"You're taking a lot for granted," she said. "I thought I had to ask."

He looked down at his shaft, then back at her. "I'm not taking anything for granted. It's got to be ninety degrees in here," he said. "When a gorgeous woman strips to her skin in front of me, I'm going to get hard. It doesn't mean tab A will be inserted into slot B."

That was it, the problem, the crux of the matter, the issue, the elephant in the room. All that was wild and reckless now subdued under an iron will that locked down everything unpredictable. Like emotions, and not all of them were happy, sunshine feelings. He was strung tight, and the urge to comfort him rose with the steam from the tub.

He stood there, hands on hips, while she looked him over. The hot water melted her muscles, and her resistance. "Are you getting in this tub or not?"

"Ask me to," he said without moving.

Her pulse throbbed in her throat, her temples. "Adam, please get in the tub with me."

The tub held two quite nicely. With his added mass, water lapped dangerously close to the rim, and she sat forward to drain enough to keep the floor somewhat dry, then leaned back against him. His body cradled hers, his erection pressed hard and hot against her lower back, his legs stretched alongside hers. He lifted his hands to one braid and loosened the elastic, then the hair. He repeated the process with her other braid, until her hair hung around her face. He swept it back, then his big palm cupped her forehead and tucked her head into his shoulder.

Her eyelids drooped. Immersed in water that sloshed against the sides of the tub, with only the candlelight for illumination, she could pretend she lay on a bunk in a sailboat in the Caribbean, warm inside and out. With Adam.

"That's nice," she murmured.

"What is?" His voice rumbled low and rough in her ear as his hands skimmed her thighs, hips, up to her breasts. Maybe she wouldn't have to ask for anything else tonight.

"Nothing," she said. "Just dreaming."

11

ADAM WOKE UP curled into the fetal position he'd adopted as protection against the futon's frame. The direction of daylight, at his back rather than over his head, was his first clue he wasn't in his mother's house. The dead giveaway was the warm, naked female body tucked into the curve of his, hair spilling across the pillow wedged between his arm and her head.

Marissa.

She stirred, stretching her legs out and rolling partly onto her stomach. A pretty average morning wood hardened to desperate need in the space of two breaths; he tightened his grip and pulled her close, barely resisting the urge to growl possessively into her hair.

"Are you making up for lost time?" she asked, her voice sleep-rough, amused. By the time he'd lifted her from the tub and dropped her on the bed, he barely remembered to put on a condom before he sank into her. The hot, wet temptation of rubbing against her naked flesh as they lay in the tub together stripped away what passed for control around Marissa. He'd come home with no intention of making up for everything he didn't do that summer, but if she asked, he was there.

Last night she'd begged. He'd spread her legs, braced a

hand on either side of her head, nestled the tip of his cock just inside her, and kissed her through her pleading little gasps, all the while pretending he'd gone stone deaf. He'd sunk into her when she dug her fingers into his ass and shimmied her way onto his cock, an undulating, writhing movement that nearly blew the top of his head off. His tough girl was stronger than she looked.

He swept her hair back from her face, and out of his mouth. She turned enough to look up at him sleepily, her dark eyes soft, her mouth red and swollen. "I have no idea what you're taking about," he said.

A little swivel of her hips. "I'm talking about *that*."

"You have to ask me for *that*, Ris."

"I asked quite nicely, and very frequently, last night," she said, and rolled onto her back. "Can we agree that you've cured my initial resistance to sleeping with you?"

"We can agree to that," he said very seriously, "except for one thing."

On forearms and knees he straddled her, bent to her jaw, kissed the soft, hot spot under her ear, then licked his way down her neck to her collarbone.

"What's that?" she asked, her voice still soft and rough. Her hands slid along his upper arms to his shoulders, where her fingernails left several somewhat tender dents.

He kissed each pebbled nipple, then blew on one. They had to be sensitive. He'd been far less tender last night. "It makes me very, very hot when you ask, tough girl."

"I don't ask," she said, then whimpered and tried to spread her legs when he lapped at the flushed tip. "I beg."

"I'm trying to be politically correct."

"Politically correct is for the rest of my life, not bed, and if it makes you hot, it's probably not politically correct anyway."

"I could pretend," he said, then kissed his way down her belly to the trimmed dark curls. "I could be very formal. *Yes, ma'am*," he said, and spread her legs with his palms. "*No, ma'am*."

Her hands slid from his shoulder to the back of his head as he peered up to meet her gaze. "Save that for when I'm making you beg," she said.

Heat cracked through him. He curved one arm under her ass and around her hip to part the tender folds of her sex. Maintaining eye contact, he dipped his head and circled her clit with the tip of his tongue. On the second pass her eyelids fluttered, then closed. Her fingers slid into his hair, tightening on his skull when she couldn't get a grip in the short strands.

"Please," she husked, then, "*Adam.*"

His name, softly whispered, tightened like a fist around his heart, squeezing emotion into his throat and gut. He inhaled her girl scent and focused on the moment. Nothing more. She was so easy, holding nothing back as he layered pleasure with his tongue until she shuddered and cried out. When she subsided, he found his wallet on the floor, and opened it.

No condoms. He'd used both of them up last night.

Mother*fucker.*

A stifled laugh from the woman splayed underneath him. "You should see the look on your face," Marissa said, then reached for her nightstand and opened the top drawer. He reached inside, grabbed a strip of condoms and tore one off. He took a deep breath and reminded himself to go slowly. She winced once, but when he stopped to let her adjust, she flattened her palms at the small of his back and urged him on.

Who knew lazy could be so intense? His strokes were thorough but gentle, no athletics, not a hint of frenzy. Just him and Marissa, in the dove gray daylight that made her pale skin glow. He watched her watch him, her lower lip caught between her teeth as the pressure climbed his shaft and spine at the same time. His heart pounded crazy-fast, wildly out of proportion to the physical effort involved, but he didn't close his eyes, not until release pulsed at the tip of his cock. Two more slick strokes and he was the one shuddering helplessly in her arms.

She stroked his shoulder blades, then traced her fingers up

and down his spine, not seeming to mind his weight, or realize he'd shattered into little pieces in her bed. Desperately racking his brains for something casual to say, he took a deep breath and pulled out of her body to sit back on his heels, then got a good look at the clock.

"Oh, fuck me," he groaned.

"What?" She struggled up on her elbows and watched him duck into the bathroom. He ditched the condom, then bent over the pedestal sink to splash water on his face. "Do you have an extra toothbrush?"

"Medicine cabinet," came through the six-paneled door. "What's the matter?"

He tore open the packaging like he'd once torn open an MRE after a long, brutal march, and used the thirty seconds he spent brushing his teeth to strive for calm. He dropped the green toothbrush into one of the three empty slots in the silver holder, dried his face, squared his shoulders, then opened the door.

"I'm meeting Keith at the Heirloom at eight."

She quirked an eyebrow at him, then looked at the clock. "You're going to be late."

"Yeah." He grabbed his clothes from the bathroom floor and dressed. "This won't take long. I'll head home for work clothes, then meet you at Mrs. Carson's in an hour, maybe less."

When his head emerged from the open collar of his half-buttoned shirt, she was looking at the rain coursing down the windows. "We're not siding today," she said.

He couldn't take another day in his mom's house with nothing to do. "What are you doing today?"

"Nothing I need help with," she said as he yanked up his pants.

"The paneling?"

She pushed herself to a sitting position and pulled the covers over her bent knees to her chin, a move he knew had nothing to do with the cold. Her gaze drifted from the rain-streaked windows to the five framed pictures of her great-great-grandfather's yacht. Picture, picture, window, picture, window, picture, picture. The photos' frames were roughly the same size as the windows. When she lay in bed, she'd see sky and boats above the pale blue wainscoting.

Daylight gave him a new perspective on the room. The wainscoting was painted in shifting shades of blues he recognized from hours and hours on, in, and near the ocean. The hues lightened to grays at the top of the wainscoting, then returned to blues, this time the paler colors of the sky that deepened to midnight blue near the ceiling. The room's furniture consisted of her double bed, which really wasn't big enough for the both of them, but he wasn't complaining; the nightstand; a single lamp; and a bookshelf. Even from his position at the foot of the bed he could read the spines. Sailing books. Novels. Lots of nonfiction. Biographies, but not about famous politicians or celebrities. *My Old Man and the Sea. Adrift: Seventy-Six Days Lost at Sea.*

Run-of-the-mill obsession all right. At least she was reading about the worst that could happen.

"And now you're going to be really late," she said.

He snagged his wallet from the floor and slid it into his cargo pants pocket. "He can wait."

"That's not how things work around here," she said. "You don't keep Mr. Billable Hours waiting."

Ignoring the little dig at Keith's occupation, he folded his arms across his chest and said, "I'm going with you."

"Maybe I'm not going anywhere."

Sure she wasn't. The wedding was days away, and based on that conversation last night, he knew the bank president wouldn't hesitate to add interest to her loan if she didn't make his daughter's wedding perfect. "Great. I can't think of a better way to spend a rainy day than in bed with you."

Her eyes narrowed. "It's eight o'clock and it's twelve minutes into town."

"Marissa," he said quietly. "Please. Let me help you with the mantel."

Making her ask for sex was a joke, bedroom games, but

he was dead serious about this. Maybe she was accustomed to doing things on her own so she didn't have to pay a second set of hands. He'd do this for free, if she'd let him.

Whether she was worried about Keith getting pissed off at him, or just wanted to get him out of her apartment, she nodded. "Meet me back here when you're done in town."

Breath eased from him like snow falling on a still prairie. "Okay. Thanks. What's your cell number? I can call you when I'm on my way."

"Don't have one," she said with a shrug. "Everyone I know lives in Chatham County. They know where I live, and usually where I'm working. I'm not hard to find."

"Okay. I'll call here when I'm on my way." She rattled off the phone number, the same one her father had when she was a teenager, he noticed, and he keyed it into his phone. Then he strode to the bed, dropped a kiss on her mouth, and jogged to his car through a steady downpour. He pulled into the parking lot of the Heirloom Cafe, a mere twenty minutes late, lucked into a parking spot by the door, but sat in the car for a moment. Through the big front window he could see Keith and Delaney sitting together. Their hands rested on the table between them, their fingers linked, as Delaney spoke in her measured way and Keith leaned forward to listen.

When Delaney rose, Keith helped her with her coat, then gave her a kiss good-bye. For a split second Adam wondered how much of a relationship depended on that simple thing, a kiss good-bye in the morning, another when returning home. The daily routine he'd never forged with Delaney.

He waited until Delaney was in her Camry before heading into the restaurant. The bell over the door tinkled prettily, and customers—including Lucas Ridgeway, sitting alone in a booth in the corner—automatically swiveled their heads to see who the newcomer was. The room quieted considerably for a few seconds, then talk resumed when Keith, dressed for his workday in a suit and tie, raised his hand in greeting.

"Hey," he said as Adam pulled back a chair. Two menus sat on the green checked tablecloths, Keith's open to the skillet section. He looked Adam over quickly, then sat back and grinned. "Last night's clothes? Nice. Anyone I know?"

Adam pushed the menu toward the waitress who materialized at the side of the table, a pot of coffee in one hand, her order pad tucked in her white apron. "Just coffee," he said.

"I'll take the garden skillet, no onions, and coffee," Keith said.

The waitress returned with coffee and a smile for him. Keith watched her, waiting until she left before he leaned across the table. "Come on, man," he said conspiratorially. "Who was it?"

"Why? You're not in the market anymore."

"Living vicariously, my friend. My player days are over. The ring's basically on."

"This was on the floor when I got up," Adam said. It wasn't a lie. His clothes were on Marissa's bathroom floor when he got up. "What's up?"

"You need to get fitted for your tux," Keith said. He pulled his wallet from his suit jacket pocket and removed a card. "Here's the address. The store is in Brookings. Go in for your fitting and make arrangements to bring them back to Walkers Ford the day before the wedding."

"Who else is standing up with you?"

Keith shrugged. "A couple of guys from college, another couple from law school. It's no big deal. You need to go to the university before classes start? Kill two birds with one stone?"

Adam glanced at the card and recognized the store's name embossed in black on the white business card. It was the same place Delaney wanted to use for tuxes when it was his wedding. "It's no trouble," he said with a shrug. "Anything else I need to handle? You want a bachelor party?"

Keith's gaze remained steady on his. "I wasn't going to ask you to do anything else."

"You'd have done the same for me, if things had worked out."

"I'm sorry they didn't," Keith said. "Are you sure you're okay with this?"

Chatter ebbed and flowed around them as Adam met Keith's guileless blue gaze. Adam remembered when Keith's family moved into Chatham County. It was sophomore year of high school, and Keith, with his easy manner, quickly made friends in all the high school cliques. Jocks liked him, brains liked him, dopers liked him. Even the hard-core rebels he ran with were drawn to Keith because he seemed so far above high school. He'd graduate, go to college, go to law school, and join his father's small-town practice. Keith took it for granted, didn't seem to care if it happened or not. He'd sought Adam out early on, rode along on some of the craziest rides, just as easily had Adam over to play video games or to watch movies. He'd been a good friend, a solid friend, and he hadn't been there that night. Neither had Delaney.

One hand on the green-rimmed coffee mug, he slouched back in his chair. "Why wouldn't I be okay with it?"

"Come on," Keith said. "Your best friend. Your ex-fiancée. It's awkward."

"Multiple deployments are hard on a relationship. Lucky for Delaney she had good people around to help her pick up the pieces. Yes or no on the bachelor party?"

Keith shook his head. "Delaney's had weekly meetings with her bridesmaids and her mother for the last three months. They've all got color-coded binders. I'm keeping things low-key. Delaney doesn't need the extra stress. Just get the tux and be at the church. It's no big deal."

"In front of God and Walkers Ford, I'm standing up for your marriage. It's a big deal to me."

The waitress slid a steaming platter of fried potatoes, vegetables, and shredded cheese in front of Keith. "Sure I can't get you anything, hon?"

"I'll take a couple of the caramel buns to go, and two cups of coffee," Adam said.

"For sure," she said and hurried behind the counter.

"Bringing treats to your lady friend?"

"If by 'lady friend' you mean my mother, then yes," Adam said. "She loves them."

"Oh," Keith said. "Hey, I know she's made some wedding dresses, but Delaney wanted to get hers from this boutique in Minneapolis. I hope her feelings weren't hurt."

His mother would have loved the opportunity to work on the couture-style wedding gown Delaney could afford, but that wasn't an option, even when she was marrying him, not Keith. "I know," he said. After a pause, Keith tucked into his breakfast. "I'm working on the speech."

"For the reception?"

Adam nodded.

Keith sat back. "Look, man, nobody expects you to get up in front of all of Walkers Ford and wish us a long and happy future. It's enough that you're there."

"It's part of the best man's job. Unless there's some reason you don't want me to do it."

The waitress arrived with a white paper lunch sack and a to-go cup of coffee that looked a little like the Starbucks cup Marissa secretly and hilariously coveted. "It's on me," she said as she set the bag and cup in front of Adam. "Welcome home."

"Ma'am, I can't let you do that," he started.

"Can't stop me, either," she said with a smile, and hurried away.

"Must be nice," Keith said.

"Yeah," Adam said. "The perks are unbelievable."

Keith's fork halted halfway to his mouth. "Hey, I didn't mean it that way."

"I know," Adam said. He pulled a twenty from his wallet and tucked it under his coffee cup. "Email me the schedule for the rehearsal and wedding day. I'll get fitted in the next couple of days." He pushed back his chair and reached for the to-go coffee and caramel buns.

"So was it Marissa?"

The question was too casual to be casual. "What makes you think that?"

"My amazing powers of deduction. The two of you disappeared that night at Brookhaven."

"That's your evidence," he said.

A masculine grin flashed in Keith's tanned face. "Why the hell not? She's hot enough. Hotter than in high school. Got a look in her eye that tells you she's an emotional freak show but the ride will be hot as hell. Shit taste in men."

"She turn you down?"

"Twice," Keith said without blinking an eye. "Told me to go fuck myself the second time. Girl never did like me. She liked you, though."

Adam looked around the restaurant. No one paid the slightest attention to their conversation. "What do you mean, 'shit taste in men'?"

"Her reputation's worse than in high school," he said. "First Chris, just like you but with an '85 Mustang instead of the motorcycle, and just like her, all talk, no action. Then there was the stained-glass artist who did the windows in Brookhaven, then a guy from Mitchell who specialized in plaster restoration we all thought was gay, but apparently wasn't because he was around for a while. Those were just the guys who lasted more than a night or two." He laughed, the tone of the chuckle knowingly regretful, the way people did when they were about to say something cruel disguised as advice. "Marissa will make your bathroom or your kitchen or your sun porch look like something out of *Architectural Digest*, but she had a string of men teaching her what she needed to know, and she paid them the old-fashioned way."

A fire-breathing dragon of rage swooped up in Adam's torso, beat leather wings at his temples, clawed under the skin of his hands and forearms. He wanted to roar, rattle the Heirloom's windows, scorch Keith to ashes with flames and fury, but clamped down on the beast clawing and snorting fire in his chest.

But you, old pal, didn't have anything she thought was worth learning, did you?

He swallowed hard because he was sitting in the Heirloom Cafe with his best friend. His *best* friend. Swallowed again, but the dragon stuck in his throat, sharp, bitter edges of wings and claws burning and scratching on the way down. "I'll get the fitting done ASAP."

A beat passed, then Keith shrugged and said, "Thanks, man. Hey, stop by the house some night. Mom and Dad want to see you."

"I'll try," he said. "Later." He collected the paper bag and coffee cup in his left hand and pulled his keys from his pocket as he walked away.

Lucas stood just outside the Heirloom's door, a cup of coffee in one hand, his phone in the other. Adam didn't fool himself into thinking Lucas's seemingly relaxed attitude meant he'd missed the nuances of his conversation with Keith. "We really should get that beer sometime soon," Lucas said, then looked up, a hint of humor in his eyes.

Adam gave a short laugh. "Yeah. I'll call you."

Back in the Charger, he stared bemusedly at his white-knuckled grip on the steering wheel. He shook out his hands, felt the muscles and tendons ease slightly. When the acid crawling up his esophagus receded, he started the car and turned into Main Street traffic, heading for home.

His mother was dressed for work in slacks and a blouse in a shade between green and blue. She didn't say anything when he walked into the kitchen, but the relief was clear on her face. "Hi, Mom," he said, then held out the white bag.

She took the bag and gave him a wry smile. "Time was, you'd sneak out, come through that door, hungover and reeking of cigarette smoke after I'd been to church without you, and ask me what was for supper."

He'd been hell on his mother from the time he could walk until his induction into the Marine Corps, maybe the only institution short of prison that could have disciplined the wild streak out of him. "That's breakfast," he said.

"One for you and one for me," she said as she peeked in the bag.

He'd intended them both for her, one for now and one for later, but thought better of it. "Let me get a shower first," he said and headed into her sewing room to grab cammies, boots, and a thick USMC sweatshirt from his duffle. The light was on over the sewing machine, and fabric spread out on the cutting table with a dress pattern half-pinned to it. "I'm heading out again in a few minutes," he said as he emerged from the bedroom.

"Where are you going?"

Her tone was curious, not judgmental. "I'm going to help Marissa get the pieces she needs to repair the mantel at Brookhaven," he said.

She smiled. "That's nice of you, sweetie."

"That's where I was," he said. "Last night, after supper with the Walkers. I was with Ris."

His mother opened a cupboard and took down two plates, then reached in the silverware drawer for two forks. "I thought that might be the case. She could use a friend."

We're more than friends, Mom. We always were.

He gave her a short nod, then ducked into the Marissa-made bathroom for a fast shower. Dressed and sitting at the kitchen table, he dug into the caramel bun and asked his mother the question he'd mulled over on the way into town. "Did Ris ever say anything to you about the ocean?"

"No," she said promptly.

And that was that. He finished off the bun, scraped the caramel off the plate, then kissed his mother on the cheek. "Don't wait up," he said.

He was halfway out the door, work gloves in hand, when she spoke. "Adam."

One eyebrow lifted in inquiry, he turned and looked back in at his mother.

"She never said anything with words."

He stepped back inside the kitchen. "What do you mean?"

"That's all I can say about it, sweetie."

Back in the Charger, he lifted the coffee cups to gauge the remaining heat, then reversed out of the driveway and headed for Brookhaven. The point of coming back early was to clear up loose ends of one sort or another. Clean out the garage. Spend some time with his mother. Sell the bike he wouldn't look at and probably couldn't get a hundred bucks for. Fulfill his duty to Keith and Delaney. Hooking up with Marissa Brooks wasn't on the list, or had he purposefully excluded it? But he was here, sleeping with her, getting caught up in the woman who held all of the girl's vibrant sensuality and a woman's mysterious depths. He'd improvise. Adapt. God knew he owed her.

And if you think you're doing this because you owe her, you're as dumb as dirt.

That less-than-comforting thought and the memory of Keith's acid-sharp assessment of Marissa warred in his mind. He was almost to the turnoff on County Road 12 when a flash of red caught his eye.

12

THE ROAD WINDING through the Walkers Ford cemetery was a dirt track with what remained of the green summer grass clinging to the high ground between the ruts. Marissa coaxed her truck over the peak of the hill where five generations of her family were laid to rest, parked, and turned off the truck. Without the growl of the diesel engine, the rain hit the truck's roof like pebbles and sheeted down the windshield. She reached for the flowers and the umbrella on the passenger's seat; outside the cab the rain nearly drowned out the thump of her pulse in her ears. Cold seeped through the twin layers of flannel and khaki work pants, numbed her fingers through her gloves. The high today might reach forty-five. If the cloud cover didn't break soon, South Dakota would be underwater for the first time in seventy million years or so, or suffering the highest snowfall since the long winter.

Just off the dirt track lay the Brooks family plot, at the peak of the hill, giving her dead ancestors a fine view of Brookhaven to the north and Walkers Ford to the south. Had her father seen what she'd accomplished? If he had, he'd see her failures as well.

She cleared her throat, looked to the north, at Brookhaven.

Undaunted by the water and wind, the figurehead pointed west, her red hair a smudge against the house's white clapboard siding. From up here the house that loomed so large in her mental landscape was uncharacteristically small on the rolling prairie, nearly insignificant. She looked down at her father's grave, then laid the bouquet of prairie crocuses on the headstone carved from the same Black Hills granite as the earlier generations'.

Remember who you are. You're a Brooks. You belong to the house as the house belongs to you.

"I know, Dad. I could use some help today. I've got to do this," she murmured. The rain seemed to drown the words before they left her throat, but then she realized the sound was the low, prowling engine of a muscle car. It shut off, then a moment later a car door slammed. A shiver skittered across the nape of her neck, but not from the chilled breeze. She turned to find Adam behind her, bareheaded, no umbrella, holding two cups of coffee from the Heirloom.

"What the hell are you doing out here in a pounding rainstorm?"

"Talking to the dead," she said promptly. "What the hell are you doing out here with two cups of coffee and no umbrella?"

Water streamed off his nose and chin. "Is it raining?"

"You're crazy," she said.

"If you don't mind, it doesn't matter."

Not crazy. Stoic. The shoulders of his sweatshirt were soaked through, and he'd been out of his car for less than thirty seconds. "I'll trade you one half of my umbrella for that coffee," she said.

He ended up holding the handle and one cup while she had the other. To stay dry and absorb some of the heat he radiated she leaned against his arm. They stood in a cylinder of dry air while the water streamed off the umbrella's edge.

"How did you know I was here?"

"Saw red when I turned onto the road to Brookhaven." He nodded at the bouquet, pounded limp by the rain but still vibrant pinks and purples against the gray granite. "Nice flowers."

"Prairie crocuses. They carpet the meadow at Brookhaven when spring's here to stay. I grow some in pots because Dad loved them."

"I remember," he said, then lifted his coffee cup to his mouth. "Do you talk to the dead a lot?"

She shrugged. When her dad first died, she came alone every day, then once a week, then every couple of weeks, just to talk. Then, when she and Chris bought Brookhaven, daily again, eager to tell him all about her plans and progress, until the work overwhelmed her. "Brookhaven was so important to Dad. He'd want to know what's going on."

"I remember," he said again.

Memory flashed bright in her mind, the living room in the house her father rented after he lost Brookhaven, sunlight filtering through dusty sheer curtains onto Adam, uncharacteristically still as he sat with her father and paged through the family albums, a fresh set of ears for the tales Marissa heard as bedtime stories as a little girl.

Tell me the one about supper for the Governor, Daddy. Tell me about the plates, and the cakes, and the pretty dresses.

Her dolls' tea parties took place in Brookhaven's great room. In the stories she wrote for school, princes rescued maidens from the veranda off the master suite. "It's strange, but sometimes Dad's stories about Brookhaven are more vivid in my mind than he is. That's my inheritance. Dad's dreams."

Adam didn't say anything, just stood beside her and sipped coffee in silence. "Dreams aren't a bad inheritance," he said finally.

Said the man who grew up without a father. "Do you think about your dad?"

For a few moments, the rain was her only answer, then he said, "I used to. Somewhere in the middle of my second tour, I stopped."

Your father could skip town before you were little more

than an embryo and still impact every decision you made, every thought you had. "Do you have any dreams?"

"Yeah," he said. "Bad ones."

Uncertain, she glanced up over her shoulder at him, but his face was totally expressionless. The Marine Corps probably didn't allow dreams of any kind. "That's not the kind of dream I meant," she said.

"Your dad dreamed enough for the three of us," he said. "Where's Chris?"

She tipped her head. "Over the hill with the rest of the Larsons," she said.

"Drunk driving accident, right?"

"He blew the stop sign at 16 and 140 and a tractor-trailer T-boned him," she said. "He never was much for doing anything half-assed. Raising hell, driving, chasing girls, whatever. When he worked, he worked all out, did a beautiful job. When he went on a bender, he did that full tilt, too."

Adam's big, warm body never moved against hers. She had a type, all right. The type was moving at a high rate of speed. Purpose and direction mattered less, at least back then.

"I'm sorry," he said. "When did he die?"

"A couple of years after Dad did."

"That's a lot of grief."

She lifted a shoulder. She went on. There wasn't another option, when there were bills to pay, and no one else providing a roof or food. But he had grief enough of his own, and she'd long since come to terms with hers. "Life's like that," she said. "Are you ready to go?"

"Depends on whether you're okay with making a detour to Brookings first," he said. "I need to get this tux fitting out of the way. The rental place is in Brookings. I can go, then come back and pick you up."

"No problem. That's fine," she said, trying not to sound relieved. "The house is near Colton, between Brookings and Sioux Falls. I'll drive. You can leave your car in the barn."

He walked back through the rain to the Charger. Before she left, Marissa crouched down by her father's headstone and straightened the flattened bunch of prairie crocuses. "Bye, Dad," she said quietly.

The rain washed away the words. Inside her truck, the drops hit metal like nails pinging onto tin, a high-pitched sound that set her nerves jangling. Hopefully Adam's presence would settle her down. The alternative, shaming herself in front of him, was too horrifying to contemplate.

Adam followed her along the curving dirt track back to the iron scroll arch over the cemetery's entrance, then back to Brookhaven. The barn sat at the bottom of the hill, nestled back in the trees that lined the property's creek. She parked off to the side and got out to unlock the barn, then swung the doors wide and guided his car into the open space in the center of the main floor. He cut the engine and got out, absently running his palm over his hair, then flicking the rainwater to the side as he surveyed the dim interior. "Where did everything go?" he asked, his voice echoing in the empty space.

When the county took the property for taxes, they'd had an auction to clear out over a hundred years of Brooks family discards. Her father saved only what they could store in their small house in town. Everything else went under the auctioneer's gavel, boxes and trunks, faded and broken furniture, tools, a tractor from the 1940s, harness and wagon parts from even earlier. "Sold when the county took the house," she said. "We kept pictures, a few trunks and other personal items, mostly what Dad remembered from his childhood. That's when I found the chronometer and the sextant. Josiah Brooks brought them with him when he came west."

The roof was solid, rain cascading down past the open barn doors, but inside was dry, if not warm. Hands on his hips, he looked at the ladder that ran up to the loft. They'd made a cozy little nest up there, stowing blankets, a battery-operated lantern, and a radio. From the look on his face, he remembered, too.

"It's all gone," she said. "Just bare plank floors up there now."

He transferred his gaze from the loft to her face. A small, secret shudder rippled through her, hardening her nipples and halting her breath in her throat. "Would you do it again, Ris?"

He meant that spring, that intense, wild spring, desolation all around. She didn't know how to untangle the threads of a life. If she said no, maybe Josh would still be alive. Maybe Adam would have gone to SDSU, met someone there, moved away. She wouldn't know this dull emptiness all the time, this sense of loss and longing. She wouldn't have the memory of hot, brilliant days with Adam, on the back of his bike, under him in the loft.

She wouldn't have Brookhaven. Her dad would have lost the house, but would she have met Chris, loved him, planned a future with him, only to see it broken and bleeding on a table in the county morgue? Love and loss. Dreams and hopes smashed by unexpected death, but she couldn't change the past. All she could do was keep moving.

"Would you?"

He looked at her. Some trick of light revealed regret and remorse and awareness flashing under the surface of those impenetrable hazel eyes. She waited, then he turned away to snag a backpack from the Charger's trunk. "We should get going."

They climbed into her truck. Without thinking about it, she braced her arm behind the passenger seat and twisted to look over her shoulder as she reversed up the track to the barn, onto Brookhaven's circular drive. When she faced forward Adam was smiling, just a quirk of his lips, but the smile sat like an amused cat in his eyes.

"What?"

"You drive like a man," he said.

She'd heard that before, about more than her driving. It wasn't usually a compliment. "So?"

"It's pretty hot, tough girl."

"Really," she said.

"Strong is hot."

Brookhaven sat at the top of the largest swell of land in the county, the barn down in the hollow, near the flat land that was once cropland but was now thirty years back into prairie. Even the stone circle that held the bonfires was nearly invisible, overgrown as it was by tall, pale grasses. "I don't feel strong," she said finally. "I feel like I'm hanging on by my fingernails."

"What happens if you let go?"

"I don't want to find out," she said, and shifted the truck into drive. Adam opened the backpack and drew out a book. "What are you reading?" she asked, wondering if his choice of reading material would given her a peek into his inner world.

"I've never given a speech before," he continued. "I want to do a little research before I start writing. It may only be sixty seconds, but it's a big deal for Delaney. I'm not going with some formula of a joke plus a story plus a toast."

Jealousy flared, hot, green, bitter acid searing from her gut up her throat to her mouth. She swallowed hard and fixed her gaze on the road without seeing anything more than the broken yellow line separating the lanes. It always came back to Delaney. Always.

"Why did you want to come back?" she asked. "What are you really doing here?"

A moment passed before he answered. "I came home, Ris. That's all."

On the surface it made sense: after a decade away and five tours, he truly wanted the quiet, uneventful world of eastern South Dakota. After Adam broke up with Delaney, the town delightedly rehashed their entire history, down to multiple reenlistments. Delaney seemed genuinely bewildered and hurt, but held her head high and refused to comment. The general consensus was that Adam had done something unforgivable, but covered it up by ending their relationship before Delaney found out.

"Go ahead and ask me," he said.

Startled out of her reverie, she shot a quick glance at him, but he was still looking at the open book on his lap. "Ask you what?"

"Why I broke up with Delaney. What happened."

The statement was a challenge, not an invitation. "Rumor was that you changed your mind and were going to make the Marine Corps your career—"

"That was never the plan."

"But it's none of my business," she finished.

"Then you're the only person in Walkers Ford who thinks so," he said, head still bent.

She shrugged and slowed as they entered the Brookings city limits. "If you want to tell me, you'll tell me."

"Do you want to know?" he asked as he turned that mocking, cynical gaze on her. "It's really good gossip. Juicy. Dirty. You'd be the first to know the whole truth."

She almost said yes. She was human, curious, and none too proud of the shiver of delight that followed on the heels of shock when she heard the news, but the tight line of his mouth promised the pain under the dirt.

"I don't gossip," she said bluntly. "I've been the talk of the town too often to do that to someone else, especially you. You can tell me if you want to, but whatever you say stays with me."

She parked on the street in front of Gentleman's Formal-wear and cut the engine. Adam gripped her arm when she put her hand on the door handle, keeping her in the truck.

"Keith had something to say about you being the talk of the town," he said.

Heat climbed into her cheeks, but she didn't look away. "You told him you were with me?"

"No. He guessed. I didn't confirm, or deny. Then he offered some free advice."

"Keith's advice is never free," she said, then tugged her arm loose from his grip. "Someone pays for it."

He let her go, and met her at the door. While he conferred with the sales clerk, Marissa wandered through the aisles, brushing her fingers lightly over the shoulders of suit jackets hanging in a row in size order, and two tables of silk ties. The clerk reappeared with a tuxedo under plastic and handed it over to the tailor. Adam ducked into a changing room and came out a minute later wearing the pants and jacket over his button-down shirt. Expressionless, he stood in front of the three-way mirror, adjusting his sleeves while the tailor hovered. She drifted over to the fitting area.

His gaze caught hers in the mirror. "What do you think?"

"It looks loose, but you've got more experience with formalwear than I do," she said, thinking of the Marines' distinctive, form-fitting dress uniform.

The tailor smiled at her. "Broad shoulders and a narrow waist. Difficult fit. I'll take it in," he said, and pinched and marked the back of the jacket with a flourish.

Adam ducked back into the changing room and dressed in his cargo pants and boots again. At the front counter he arranged to pick up the tuxes and bring them to Walkers Ford the day before the wedding.

"That didn't take long," she commented when they were back in the truck.

"You mind if I work on this while you drive?"

"No," she said.

He opened one of the books and got out his legal pad and a pen, then settled in to read. It was like someone drew a curtain over a window; the frame and glass were still there, but the interior view of the house disappeared. Adam's face was a study in concentration as he pored over the book, making notes on his legal pad. He braced himself against the jolts and shifts as the truck hurtled along, seemingly unaffected by its aging struts. His unflappable demeanor and flat-rolled shirtsleeves reminded her that he'd spent a fair amount of time working in a moving vehicle, and on subjects more important than a speech at his ex-fiancée's wedding.

His world was so large, but she didn't believe that size mattered any more to a meaningful life than it did to a well-crafted apartment. Her world would stay small, centered on family and history, roots that ran deep into Walkers Ford. She would finish Brookhaven, restore the house to its original grandeur, make right what had gone so very, very wrong.

Then what?

The little voice she'd thought was strangled inside her spoke up. Clear and faint as a bell in the distance.

Then I live my dream.

It's not your dream.

It's enough, she thought back. *Dreams fulfilled are for TV shows and stories in movies. We make do.*

She navigated them westward out of town and twenty minutes later turned onto a county highway. They bumped along the sloppy road; each jolt sent acid sloshing in her stomach, and the nauseated feeling made her heart beat faster. Adam gave up on the speech and stuffed books and notepad on the dash. A dingy white mailbox that tilted into the ditch at the end of a long driveway marked the end of the road. A brass plaque on the side read The Meadows, the words readable only because the black tarnish that gathered in the deep grooves stood out against the weathered metal. She parked and cut the engine.

Adam looked around the empty prairie. "Where are we?"

"Near Colton," she said. She nodded out the windshield at a large, forlorn house, set a quarter mile back from the road. Distance couldn't mask the paint peeled in long strips from the exterior, like bark from a birch tree, exposing black and rotting wood underneath. One side of the long front porch listed, empty gaps in the spandrels and railing giving the impression of a bar code. The glass in the windows was dirty but unbroken, curtains drawn in all the rooms downstairs and missing from the second floor. Automatically she began to assess needed repairs. New plumbing and wiring, new siding, shutters, and paint, new windows upstairs and down, new furnace. All of that assumed the foundation wasn't cracked and the hundred-year-old framing had held up.

It's easy. Start the truck. Drive up the driveway. Park the truck. Open your door. Get your tools. Knock on the door.

Start with turning the key in the ignition.

She reached for her keys and felt her stomach slide hot and thick up her neck to settle at the back of her throat. Moving slowly and carefully, she rested her hand on her thigh. Her stomach retreated, reluctantly.

His elbow braced on the door, his hand on his thigh, Adam studied the house. "Looks abandoned."

"It's not," Marissa said. "Mrs. Edmunds still owns it. She's ninety-four. Henry Dalton Mead was also an East Coast transplant, and he went on to build houses in the Dakotas, Colorado, and Nevada. The trend back in the day was toward heavy, bric-a-brac, Victorian style, so Brookhaven's open floor plan and simple design were the anomaly, not the norm; but he kept a few features, like floor-to-ceiling wood paneling in a large main room for the family."

"How do you know he repeated the details?" he asked, his attention still focused out the window.

"I went to the architecture school's archives and did some research on Mead," she said, then swallowed hard. Her voice sounded odd in her ears, tinny and distant. "Did some more research on the Internet. There's a wealth of photographs online."

"What's your arrangement with Mrs. Edmunds?"

Explaining the details was beyond her ability at the moment. "It's mine," she said. "All I have to do is go get it." She shook her head, and immediately regretted it because her stomach took a roller-coaster ride from her throat against her rib cage to deep in her belly.

"Then we'd better get started."

"No," she said, and closed her eyes. Sweat broke out along her hairline, prickled on her nape. She felt hot, frantically hot. She was *never* hot.

He paused in the act of reaching for the door handle, and looked at her for the first time since Brookings. Her face made him let go of the handle and sit back. His eyebrows drew down ever so slightly. "Okay," he said. Very, very calmly. "We won't get started."

"That's . . . I'm fine . . ." She took a deep, shuddering

breath, exhaled hard. The rain sounded like an entire baseball team was beating on the truck with bats. "Just give me a minute."

"Ris," he said. The word slipped into her brain under the thunder of the bats. "Marissa," he said more loudly.

She opened her eyes. "There's no need to bark at me."

"You're having a panic attack," he said.

"I am not." As long as she didn't reach for the keys with the intention of driving up to the house, she was fine. Or open her eyes. She flattened her palms on her jeans, smoothed them back and forth. "I don't do this anywhere else."

His hand landed on her knee, the heat and strength anchoring her, dialing down the bats' volume. "Talk to me, Ris."

"I know why you came back to Walkers Ford," she said without opening her eyes, but she didn't need to see him to sense his muscles tensing. "You have to know what comes next. You need a direction, and grad school gives you that. I get that. But I don't know what comes next. What happens next? I've never done anything else. I don't know how to do anything else. I'm thirty years old, and all I know how to do is dream of Brookhaven, reborn."

He relaxed subtly, his pants shifting against the fabric seats, his breath exhaling. "You taught yourself to remodel, build, design," he started.

"Oh, I do believe Keith told you I had some help there," she said.

They were so connected she felt him stop breathing, but he continued. "And you'll teach yourself to do something else. Find another dream, Ris."

"I'm a Brooks," she said. "There is no other dream."

"What about sailing?"

"That will never happen," she said. "It's a rich man's pastime, not for women living in the middle of the continent with a sizable home equity loan to pay off."

"Ris. Open your eyes." She did, found that with his hand on her leg she could focus on his face, his tanned, gorgeous face. Just like that, longing grabbed her by the throat. God, she missed him. He jabbed out the window with his free index finger. "Remember when Brookhaven looked like that? If you can take Brookhaven from *that* to what it is now, you can do any damn thing."

Her stomach did a lazy flip-flop, so she closed them again. "I can't see it, Adam," she said. "I just can't see it. I could see Brookhaven, but not beyond, and I certainly can't see sailboats and oceans and cruising. I just need a couple of minutes."

They sat there together, the noise of the rain alternating between bats and drumsticks. Eventually he said, "Do you want me to go in and get the panels for you?"

"No," she said. "I can do this. I have to do this."

More time passed before she heard him open his door. Cold air gusted into the cab, bringing with it the damp, earthy smell of failure. "Slide over," he said, then slammed the door and walked through the downpour to the driver's side of the truck. Without opening her eyes, she crawled across the bench seat and curled up in the warmth left by his body. Silently, he adjusted the seat for his longer legs, then the mirrors, then he cranked the engine over and executed a neat three-point turn in the muddy road. Humming with shame and something worse, Marissa closed her eyes again and let him drive her back to Brookhaven, empty-handed.

THE WOMAN LEANING against the passenger door with her eyes closed and her arms folded across her chest wasn't in any condition to talk on the way back to Brookhaven, so Adam drove in silence and reflected on the epic, slow-motion meltdown he'd just witnessed. The *thwap-thwap* of the windshield wipers set the rhythm of his thoughts. Twelve years ago he knew, as much as any eighteen-year-old boy could, that Brookhaven mattered to Marissa, and he'd gotten wasted and pulled down hundred-year-old paneling with a crowbar, then set it on fire.

Psychologically, what he'd done must have felt like an

assault. No wonder she'd put off replacing the woodwork until the last minute. No wonder she balked at the driveway.

Everyone had a breaking point. Everyone had an edge hidden behind their everyday armor, something they protected or avoided or ignored, but it was there. Drill instructors had an uncanny knack of finding those weaknesses and exploiting them. You faced what you feared because if you couldn't handle fear in boot camp, they wouldn't send you into combat with other Marines depending on you for their survival.

He was a veteran of five tours in war zones, so he knew all about breaking points. He'd never hit his, because his fear wasn't dying in combat. But he'd watched other guys hit their breaking points, and shatter. In combat, breaking points came after particularly vicious, prolonged skirmishes; IEDs; losing a fellow Marine to a bomb or a bullet; or the overlap with the civilian world. Dear John letters. News of a spouse or girlfriend's infidelity. Missing birthdays, funerals, weddings. Money woes.

Delaney's wedding was pushing Marissa right up to her edge. In an ideal world she would have finished the house on her schedule, not Delaney's. Maybe she never would have finished it at all. He shot her a quick glance, but her eyes were closed. She'd regained color in her face, though. For a few minutes she'd been the color of kindergarten paste, gray and waxy, her eyebrows and eyelashes the only color in her face. The thought of finishing Brookhaven clearly scared Marissa, but the other option made his gut clench. If she didn't finish Brookhaven, it was entirely possible she'd live the rest of her life like her father did, suffocating under the weight of a dream she couldn't achieve.

She needed vision. God knew she could work toward the goal, lay down her life in service to the vision. She wasn't lazy, or weak, or fragile, and she sure as shit wasn't a victim. But inside she was falling apart. He'd come back to Walkers Ford with a single purpose in mind, but Marissa needed direction, a purpose, a dream. Some people were afraid to risk themselves in pursuit of a goal, afraid that failure would destroy them, but the truly strong knew that the real risk for someone like that was no goal at all. Take away the anticipation and some people got disappointed, then moved on. A ravenous soul would turn inward and consume itself.

She needed a new dream.

The rain went on, steady and relentless as machine-gun fire. Adam turned onto the county road leading to Brookhaven. Marissa, who probably had distances in eastern South Dakota carved into her bones, opened her eyes and pushed herself upright.

"You working on Mrs. Carson's house tomorrow?"

She leaned forward and peered out the windshield at the low, leaden sky, probably calling to mind the forecast for more rain. "Probably not," she said. "Look, it must have been something I ate. Next time I'll be fine."

The wedding was a week and a half away. "When's next time?" he asked as he floored the engine to get the truck up the hill to Brookhaven.

"Adam, it's better if I—"

"Don't," he said, and braked to a halt under the tree by the servants' entrance. "Just . . . don't."

She looked at him. "I don't need an enforcer to get this done."

"No, you don't," he agreed. She needed the exact opposite of an enforcer. "But you don't have to do it alone, either."

"It won't be tomorrow," she said.

"That's fine." That was perfect, in fact. They got out of the truck into the steady rain, and he tossed her the keys. "I'll see you later."

He waited until she was inside. The house swallowed her up, he thought. Except for the faint light coming through the porthole window in the bathroom, the house swallowed her like the whale that got Jonah. She was falling apart, and no one noticed. Well, not no one. Keith called her an emotional freak show, but Keith had never loved Marissa, only wanted her.

He jogged through the rain to the barn, opened the doors and backed the Charger out, then closed the doors and pointed the car toward Walkers Ford. He made a quick stop at Mrs. Carson's house to double-check the tarp covering the siding stacked in the side yard, anchoring the one loose end with a brick before heading home. His mother was delivering reupholstered sofa cushions to a customer. Adam went for a run, and this time he didn't detour around Oak Street. He was back, facing everything he'd left behind. He could run past 84 Oak Street. He kept his gaze on the cracked cement, his focus unwavering as he navigated the cracks and potholes, but as he drew even with the front door, he stumbled.

Mother. Fucker. His heart leaped as fear of falling washed along his nerves. He'd tracked the conditions of both pavement and weather, and his stride, input pouring into his brain as he ran. It wasn't the road. It wasn't a joint. His knee didn't buckle, and the hip flexor he pulled just before leaving San Diego didn't give way. He just stumbled and nearly went down, in front of Josh Wilmont's house.

Speaking of panic attacks . . .

His mother still wasn't home when he blew into the kitchen, soaked to the skin. He toed off his running shoes, showered and dressed, then mopped up the rain and got water boiling for spaghetti and meatballs. Then he pulled back a dinette chair and sat down to scroll through his contacts to make a call.

Marissa wasn't the kind of person who put a quaint little picture/suncatcher on her fridge to remind her of her dream. She turned a five-thousand-square-foot house on the prairie into a sailing ship, and no one saw it for what it was, a primal scream of not belonging.

Time to show her some options.

13

THE PERSISTENT, EVEN rapping at her door woke her from a sound sleep into predawn blackness. Marissa stumbled from bed and padded through the kitchen, her sock-clad feet curling away from the cold stone floor. She'd fallen asleep immediately after Adam dropped her off. The not-quite-panic attacks left her as limp as the prairie crocuses on her father's grave. Hunger woke her around eight. She'd made a simple salad for supper, then taken a hot bath and given in to the urge to skim the books Alana refused to take back.

The advice on cruising in a sailboat of her own was simple, straightforward, and pragmatic, but with the weight of Brookhaven on her back, not achievable. However, if she spent the next ten years paying off the home equity loan, and the next ten saving, she could do it, if she could come to terms with selling the house.

On that cheery thought she'd fallen asleep again somewhere after 2:00 a.m. Pushing her hair back from her face, she blinked blearily at the clock on the microwave. Six a.m. On the dot. As if there were any question as to who stood under the tiny overhang protecting her door, she peeked through the curtains covering the window. Adam stood on the tiny porch, dressed in cargo pants, a button-down shirt, and running shoes, looking like he'd never needed sleep in his life. Steam rose into the cold air from the Heirloom to-go cups in either hand.

She opened the door and reached for the coffee. He pulled the cup away from her grasping hand. "It is the crack of dawn," she said, then cleared her rusty throat and added, "One of those better be for me."

"We're leaving in thirty minutes. Get dressed and pack an overnight bag."

"Are you insane? I'm not going anywhere today."

"Yesterday you said you weren't working on Mrs. Carson's house or getting the woodwork from The Meadows. Twenty-nine minutes and counting, or I drink both of these myself."

"You're serious."

"Completely."

Cold air eddied into the kitchen. She stepped back and let him in. "Where are we going?"

"What you wore when we looked at apartments is fine," he said as he sat down at the tiny kitchen table and flipped the lid off the coffee cup.

"That's not an answer," she said.

"It's all the answer you're getting."

She stared longingly at the second cup. "Can I have that?"

"Once you're dressed, packed, and in the car, yes."

He had a completely different sense of purpose in the way he held himself. She stared at him, trying to figure out what was going on.

"Twenty-eight minutes and counting," he said, then flashed her a grin so full of then-Adam her heart flipped over in her chest. "If we're not on the road in twenty-eight minutes you don't get the coffee."

She splashed cold water on her face to wake up, brushed her teeth, then pulled together a pair of dark jeans, a silk long-underwear shirt for warmth, a soft violet turtleneck sweater that clung to her curves from shoulder to mid-thigh, and put on black ballet flats. She pulled her hair back from her crown in a silver barrette at the base of her skull, leaving the lower layers to spill loose over her shoulders and down her back.

"One night away?" she asked as she found a simple tote with a zipper.

"Affirmative."

"This is insane," she repeated.

"Twenty minutes and counting."

She threw clean underwear, a nightie, and a change of clothes into the tote, then went into the bathroom and swept her cleanser, moisturizer, lotion, lip balm, toothbrush, toothpaste, and hairbrush on top of the clothes. When she walked back into the kitchen, Adam looked up from his phone, did a very gratifying double take, then got to his feet. "Wow."

The old-fashioned, respectful, chivalrous response made her blush and tuck her hair behind her ear. "I'm ready."

He held her old peacoat for her, then carried her tote to the Charger and held the door for her, which seemed ridiculously formal for 6:22 in the morning, but she let him do it. Once out of her driveway he headed toward the highway. "Do you want breakfast? We'll be on the road awhile."

"Where are we going?"

"That's the surprise."

The way energy hummed around him intrigued her. "It's too early to eat," she said. Wherever they were going would have more interesting breakfast options anyway. "I think I've earned my coffee," she said.

He handed her the cup, her reward for following orders, then navigated onto the highway leading to I-29. Once on the nearly empty interstate he kept their speed steady at eighty miles an hour, zipping right through Brookings with only a glance at the clock on the dashboard.

"We're not going to Brookings?"

"Nope," he said, a pleased smile on his face.

In a little over an hour they arrived on the outskirts of Sioux Falls. He took the West 60th Street exit, toward the airport, then turned down a road before reaching the main parking area and terminal. A sign at the corner pointed to charter flights. Adam parked in the lot and opened his door.

"Wait here, tough girl."

"Okay," she said, feeling more like bewildered girl than tough girl, but he was out of the car, striding through the rain to a man in a blue suit with gold braid at the cuffs and a pilot's hat on his head. Behind him sat a small jet, with five windows down the side and a short stairway built into the open door. Adam shook the man's hand. There was a short conversation, then the man looked at his watch and said something. He turned back to the plane and Adam jogged back to the car. He opened her door and hunkered down beside her.

"You coming?"

"On *that*?" she asked, pointing out the Charger's front window at the airplane.

"On that," he confirmed.

"What is *that*?"

"*That* is a Gulfstream G150 jet."

The words meant nothing to her. "Is it *yours*?"

"No," he said with a smile.

She waited, but he kept smiling that pleased, cocky smile. "That's all I'm getting? Who does it belong to and why are we flying on it? For that matter, *where* are we flying on it?"

"I'll answer all those questions when we get where we're going," he said. "Unless you won't get on the plane without knowing. Then I'll answer them now. But . . . wait. It'll be worth it."

She looked at him, anxiety and excitement warring in her stomach, not sure what to think, let alone say, wanting to know, not wanting to spoil whatever surprise he'd planned that lit him up inside. He was as alive as she'd ever seen him, as alive as he'd been at seventeen, his hazel eyes glowing nearly green, his high cheekbones stained with red from the cold, damp air.

"Trust me, Ris," he said quietly. "Let's do this."

"It's really small," she said thinly.

His hand dropped to her knee, squeezed gently. "The pilot

is former Air Force. He has thirty years of experience flying everything from F-16s to Boeing 777s to gliders."

"I've never been on a plane before," she admitted.

He blinked. "You've never flown anywhere."

"Adam," she said in a whisper, "the farthest away from home I've been is the Black Hills."

"How about you take your first plane ride today?"

She nodded wordlessly and got out of the car. Adam grabbed their bags from the backseat and escorted her toward the plane. The pilot appeared in the doorway, reaching down for her hand to help her up the stairs. "Watch your head, ma'am," he said.

She was so busy watching her head she tripped over the plush carpet. The cabin's interior made her eyes widen. A row of single caramel leather seats lined the aisle, with polished wood accents on the folding tables and cup holders. Televisions folded flat against the interior walls. The interior smelled like leather cream and new car.

"Any seat's fine, ma'am," the pilot said. Marissa sank into the one opposite the door. Adam set their bags in a closet at the front of the plane and sat down next to her while the pilot closed the cabin door and shut himself in the cockpit. The seat belts fastened over her shoulder like they would in a car. The engines revved and the plane turned toward the runway.

"How does he know where to go?" she asked.

"That's what we were talking about while you were in the car," Adam said, studying her. "You know what you need?"

She shook her head mutely.

"You need a Starbucks cup to hold," he said, his eyes twinkling.

The gentle teasing startled a laugh from her. "I'll try to enjoy myself without it," she said.

Rain lashed at the little window while the jet taxied to the end of the runway. The pilot's voice came over the intercom. "The flight's about an hour, folks. Ride up's gonna be a little choppy, so buckle up tight. Once we're airborne I'll let you know when you can help yourself to the pantry. Sit back, relax, and enjoy the flight."

Marissa turned her attention to the tiny window beside her, watching the runway move past, listening to the engines ramp up as the plane taxied to the end of the runway and took off. Her heart clawed its way into her throat as the plane bounced and struggled to clear the ominous clouds. At the second jolt she gripped the armrests. Adam reached across the aisle and offered his hand. She took it, weaving her fingers through his, and squeezing hard. The warm, solid strength of his hand seeped into her cold fingers, and her heart rate slowed a little.

Without warning they broke free of the clouds. Sunlight streamed through the small window, blinding her. She closed her eyes against the sudden, shocking light, but even with her eyes shut the light seared into her brain. Adam's fingers tightened on hers, and she turned to face him. Sunshine gilded his face, dusted his eyelashes and eyebrows with gold, brought out the gold flecks in his eyes.

"It's the sun," she said through the lump in her throat.

"It's always there, Ris," he said gently. "Sometimes you just have to go searching for it."

The ride smoothed out as if by magic. After a few minutes the plane leveled out, the engines barely audible in the plush interior, and the pilot's voice came over the speakers.

"We're at cruising altitude, folks, so the pantry's now open. Help yourselves to whatever you like."

At ease in the small plane, Adam unclipped his seat belt and got to his feet. Marissa reached for her own belt, and together they stepped to the small closet. Adam made a pot of coffee while she poked through the selection of muffins and fresh fruit, assorted teas, juices, and cold cereals. She chose a muffin, still warm in the linen-lined basket, added an apple, and a second cup of coffee, then returned to her seat. Adam handed the pilot a cup of coffee and closed the door between the cockpit and the cabin, then extracted the folding wood table from its slot along the body of the plane and sat down with his own breakfast.

While she ate Marissa peered out the window. The clouds below them gave way to a rolling countryside, the orderly progression of farm fields in square miles except where roads curved along river- or creekbeds. Towns clustered around highway intersections.

"We're flying east, right?"

He nodded while pushing the last piece of banana-nut bread into his mouth, but said nothing more. She thought about what lay east of Walkers Ford. Minneapolis-St. Paul came to mind, a destination definitely reachable in less than an hour. But the flight stretched over thirty minutes and suddenly the patchwork quilt of brown fields gave way to a large body of water. The plane gradually descended as it banked, and the water turned to urban skyline. She peered out the window, and a montage from a television show meshed with what she saw.

"That's the Sears Tower," she said, pointing.

"It is," Adam agreed.

"You're taking me to Chicago?"

He nodded, his hazel eyes dancing with delight.

"I'm speechless," she said.

"There's more," he replied.

The jet landed with an almost imperceptible jolt and braked hard down the runway before coming to a halt at the edge of a cluster of similar jets. Marissa stowed their plates and glasses in the pantry while Adam gathered their bags and the pilot opened the door.

"That was my first flight," she said, pausing in the door way. "It was wonderful."

His smile widened from polite to genuine. "My pleasure, ma'am. Enjoy your stay in Chicago."

Adam guided her to a black Lincoln Continental parked near the hangar. A man in a suit leaned against it, and as they approached he straightened. "Mr. Collins? Ms. Brooks?"

"That's us," Adam said. The driver reached for the bags

and put them in the trunk while Adam helped Marissa into the backseat. A few quiet words with the driver, and then they pulled into traffic.

"How did you do all of this?"

"I made a call," he said.

Things sure did happen when Adam Collins was around. The trip took them along city streets and through more traffic than she'd ever seen in her life. She gave up any appearance of sophistication and pressed her cheek to the glass to look at the buildings, the people, the cars, everything she could see. Sunlight poured over the cityscape, glinted off reflective glass in skyscrapers, making her blink.

"Look at the sun," she said, mostly to herself.

Beside her, Adam pulled out his cell phone and made a quick call. "We're here," he said, then leaned through the partition again. "How long?"

"Five minutes," the driver said.

Adam repeated the information into the phone and hung up. The driver turned off the main road and parked next to a sign that read Chicago Yacht Club. Her heart pumped in solid, hard thunks that made her dizzy, and her stomach began to flip-flop around the blueberry muffin and apple.

She looked at Adam, knew her eyes must be as wide as saucers. He just smiled. "Out you go, tough girl."

A tall man wearing shorts, deck shoes, and a windbreaker with the Chicago Yacht Club logo on the chest was waiting by the sign. His closely cropped blond hair glinted in the sunlight as he reached into the trunk and set their bags on the sidewalk. "That's all of it," he said to the driver, who nodded, got back in the car, and left.

Adam and the blond man gave each other a back-slapping, bear hug of an embrace. "Good to see you, man," Adam said, and put his hand at the small of Marissa's back to guide her forward. "This is Nate Martin. We served together."

The man held out his hand, his aged-whiskey eyes seeming to see straight into her soul. "Welcome to Chicago, Marissa."

"Thank you," she said, but it was all she could do not to

stare past him at the water stretching to the horizon. A forest of white masts swayed at their moorings. Did Nate work there? Could he show them around? She looked up at Adam, not sure what to say, much less what was going on.

"Nate owns a boat," he said gently. "He's going to take us out on the lake for the day."

Earth dropped out from underneath her. She looked at the boats, then at Adam, because in all that was completely unfamiliar, he was the only thing she knew and trusted. "We're going sailing? Right now?"

"As soon as we can cast off," Nate said with a smile. "Ready to work?"

According to the large clock set into the side of the yacht club, it was ten minutes until ten. Four hours earlier she'd been asleep in her bed in Walkers Ford. This was no time for terror. "Yes, of course," she stammered.

They followed Nate down a series of platforms to the docks, then along one to a sailboat Marissa estimated to be around forty-five feet long. The oak deck gleamed, the white lines and sails neatly stowed. Nate climbed aboard first, then held out his hand for Marissa to help her traverse the gap between the pier and the cockpit. Adam dropped their bags on a blue-padded bench near the wheel, deftly unwound the lines from the cleat on the pier, grabbed the ladder, and climbed on board.

"Your stuff's downstairs," Nate said as he started the engine. A gold band glinted on his left ring finger.

"Thanks," Adam said, then looked around. "Where's Julia?"

"Good question," Nate said, his face expressionless.

Adam gave a short nod and disappeared into the small opening as they idled away out toward open water.

"First time on a sailboat?" Nate asked as he handled the large round wheel.

"First time on any boat," Marissa admitted from her seat next to Nate. "I'm from South Dakota."

He cut her a worried glance. "You can swim, right?"

"Yes," she said. "I swim for exercise in the winter, usually for an hour five or six days a week. It's low impact."

She stopped herself. She was babbling like a fool while her body registered every dip and sway, the sense of motion as the boat gathered momentum and pushed into open water. Nate didn't seem to notice either the way her fingers gripped the bench cushion or her rambling. "You don't have to wear a life jacket, but don't fall overboard."

"Okay," she said.

Adam reappeared in shorts, deck shoes, and a windbreaker, and started digging in a bag he'd brought from below deck. He pulled out a brand-new pair of shoes exactly like Nate's brown, battered ones and handed them to her. "Those shoes won't get much of a grip on the deck once it gets wet," he explained, "and he wasn't kidding about work."

She exchanged her ballet flats for the deck shoes and wiggled her toes experimentally. "They fit." Of course they did. He'd conjured a private jet and a sailboat out of thin air. Learning her shoe size was child's play.

"I looked inside your work boots before I left last night. Nate picked them up this morning."

They'd cleared the marina and were in open water now, the sun warm on her face, the wind equally cold. Adam pulled a bright red jacket from the bag and handed it to her. The coat had a liner and a hood, and a drawstring at the waist to keep the drafts out. "Take out the liner if you get too warm," he said.

"Thanks," she said, and shucked her peacoat for the warmer, lightweight, waterproof jacket. It cut the wind, and in moments she began to warm up. Adam handed her a hat, again a newer version of Nate's battered, stained wide-brimmed hat, and showed her how the cords kept it secured to her head no matter which direction the wind blew from. She'd left Walkers Ford without her sunglasses, and while she soaked up the sunlight glittering off the water, a little shade was a good thing.

Nate wore a similar hat much the worse for wear, and

Adam clapped one on his own head after she'd gotten hers adjusted. The gear was all brand new, and clearly expensive if he'd bought her the women's version of everything Nate wore. She looked around, reconciling things she'd seen only in books or videos to the reality of a big, luxurious yacht.

"Don't worry," Nate said as he cut the engine. "I'm not going to give you a pop quiz."

Adam hauled on the lines with practiced motions. The sails rose into the air, and just like that, the boat skimmed across the surface of the lake. She tilted her head back. Breezes and sunshine spilled down her face and neck.

"Want to take the wheel?" Nate asked from the captain's chair.

"I couldn't," Marissa started.

"We're in the middle of Lake Michigan. You can't hit anything and you can't tip us over," he said. "She won't bite."

She stood beside Nate, then slipped into the seat he'd just left and put her hands on the wheel where his had been. Immediately she felt the tug of the keel in the water as the wind caught the sail, as if the boat were a living thing connected to the lake beneath her and the wind around her. Energy flowed through her, the wind filling the sails, the boat following, and she braced her feet, let out her breath.

"She's all yours," Nate said.

In her dreams. Adam was stretched out on a bench, knees bent, face tipped to the sun. "I missed this," he said without opening his eyes. "You get out here often?"

"More than usual, lately," Nate replied.

The handset squawked. "*Resolute, Resolute, Resolute*, this is *Big Deal, Big Deal, Big Deal* on one six. Do you copy? Over."

"*Big Deal*?" Adam asked dryly.

"He's compensating." Nate picked up the handset. "*Big Deal*, this is *Resolute*, over."

They switched to another channel, and Nate directed her attention to a boat off in the distance. "It's Jack McCallister. He's got a new boat, and wants a race," Nate said. He pressed the button on the handset. "Sorry, Jack. I've got a first-time sailor on board. We're just pleasure cruising this afternoon. Over."

Marissa heard regret in his voice. "Don't hold back on my account," she said.

Nate's grin didn't get anywhere close to his eyes. He looked into the binoculars at the other sailboat. "He's an egregious asshole. Bought the boat, then furloughed two hundred people to keep his stock price high. Want to help me kick his ass?" At her eager nod he lifted the handset to his mouth and said, "The lady wants a race, so you're on, Jack." He pointed at Marissa. "Stay there and do what I tell you to do."

"What?" she yelped.

Adam rolled from catlike lounging to forward movement in the time it took Nate to hang up the handset. Both men hurried along opposite gunwales, toward the lines.

At first they stalled in the water, the mainsail flapping limply as the breezes seemed to come from every direction. Nate checked the rigging and the bearing, then glanced off into the distance, his gaze intent. Then, as if he'd known all along where the wind would come from, a giant, invisible fist swooped up and slammed into the *Resolute*'s slack mainsail. The boat leaped ahead like a shark smelling blood in the water. Adrenaline spiked high, blasting away any shred of nerves as she struggled to keep the wheel aligned according to Nate's shouted commands, using every muscle in her body.

Nate called back to her and she adjusted the wheel, watching Adam drop to his belly to escape being flattened by the boom swinging across the deck. He was back up in an instant, adjusting the tension in a line, then securing it.

"How are we looking?" Nate yelled at her.

"We're gaining on them," she called back, trying to sound blasé about the whole thing, and failing spectacularly. Another strong wind filled the sail, lifting Marissa's hair in a wild tangle, and in that instant the edges of her body blurred into water, wind, and sky. The keel sliced through the water beneath her feet, the wind filled the sail and her chest, her consciousness disappeared into the expansive blue sky arching overhead. She flowed into boat and wind and water, the sensation of movement transcendent and obliterating, and for a few moments, nothing else existed, not even herself.

The sails trimmed to his satisfaction, Nate clambered back down into the cockpit, jolting Marissa back into the now. She kept both hands on the wheel but stepped aside, intending to transfer the wheel to Nate's more experienced hands.

"No, you've got her," he said, his voice calm and steady. He looked at the sails, the compass, the boat off their port side. "He's got too much sail out," he said. "See how the edges are flapping? You think more is better, but it's not. It's about trimming the right sails to the wind. Jack never did figure that out." He grinned at her. "You like?"

The smile transformed a thin-lipped, uncompromising face into something transfixing, leaving her with the sense that she'd joined a secret society. "I love," she said.

"We're going to win," he said confidently. "Smile nice and big, okay?"

They did exactly that, the *Resolute* gliding past *Big Deal* to the buoy with a couple of lengths to spare. The handset chirped again, and Nate picked it up.

"Nice race, Jack. Enjoy the rest of the day," he said casually and hung up on a pissed-off response. "Want a tour belowdecks?"

14

ADAM TOOK THE wheel and rigged the sails to take them farther out onto the lake. They had hours before sundown, and he wanted to give Marissa as much sun and wind as she could absorb today. Watching her transition from mildly peeved when he showed up at her door to bewildered when they arrived at the airport to utterly astonished when he said they were going sailing combined to lift a weight from his heart. This was a thirty-six-hour reprieve for both of them, a sliver of dream sliced from day-to-day reality. When he'd returned to Walkers Ford he'd had nothing more on his mind than tying up loose ends.

This was more than a loose end.

Marissa followed Nate down the narrow stairwell, into the boat's oak-appointed interior. Everything was neatly stowed, as befitting a disciplined former Marine, but while Adam was unpacking the bags Nate picked up for Marissa, he'd seen the razor in the head, the fresh supplies in the tiny kitchen, and the books organized in the inset shelf in the larger berth. Unless he missed the mark, his former LT was living on the boat, not with his wife.

Nate's low voice rumbled, describing the boat's features much as he'd run patrol briefings: crisp, clear, concise. They examined everything from the engine room to the head together for several minutes, then came back upstairs to pick their way through the neatly organized lines leading to the sails, where Nate gave a quick, basic lesson in sailing. As Adam watched, Marissa gathered her wind-tossed hair at her nape and focused intently on Nate.

When they finished, Nate helped her back into the cockpit. "I've got to make a couple of calls," he said. "Got her?"

Adam nodded. Nate went below and Marissa said, "He said he'd brought a light lunch. Adam, there's enough food down there to feed us for a week! Three kinds of salads, cold chicken, fresh fruit, French bread, and a chocolate cake."

"That's Nate for you," Adam said. "C'mere." He stepped to the side, keeping one hand on the wheel until Marissa reclaimed it. Then he settled onto the bench seat, stretched his arms along the back, and studied her. "It suits you," he said.

The hat's brim didn't quite hide her eyes. Something wild and vibrant glowed there, as hot and steady as a welding flame, and when she turned to look at him, the connection was like gripping a live wire in his bare hand. "Thank you," she said.

He held the connection as long as he could stand it, then looked away, because seeing her so alive reminded him of more than he could bear. He shrugged, and pretended to check the tension on the lines. "I just made a call. Nate did the rest."

"That was his jet?" she asked.

He nodded. "His personal jet. His company owns several for business trips, but Nate's scrupulous about keeping personal and work trips separate."

Nate reappeared with bottles gripped in his fist. "I've got white wine, beer, and a variety of nonalcoholic beverages," he said. Marissa accepted a glass of white wine and studied Nate as he popped the tops off two bottles of beer and handed one to Adam, then sat down across from him.

"Wondering what a guy who owns a private jet and a yacht was doing in the Marine Corps?" Nate asked with a mild smile.

"We all wondered, once we found out," Adam said. Officers all had college degrees, but not many came with Nate's pedigree.

"I wanted to do my life instead of thinking about it," Nate said. "I was two years into college at Penn when I decided not to spend the summer interning on Wall Street but at Officer Candidates School instead. I was commissioned a second lieutenant when I graduated, and stationed in San Diego."

"What did your parents think of that?" Marissa asked.

Nate laughed, short and hard. "Military service is an admirable, honorable profession if you don't have options. They hadn't spent nearly three-quarters of a million dollars on twelve years of prep school, a gap year in France and Italy, and an Ivy League education to ship me to Afghanistan to fight in the dirt with some Hispanic kid from the South Side." He looked at her. "That's not what they said, but it's what they meant. I felt differently."

"Lucky for us," Adam said, staring off toward the setting sun. He couldn't captain a race like Nate, but he'd spent enough time on boats to feel comfortable at the wheel. "Your intuition got us out of some tight spots."

Nate settled onto the bench and tipped back his beer bottle. "What got you interested in sailing, Marissa?"

Adam feigned indifference even as he tuned out everything else, the thud of the rigging as the wind caught the sail, the waves lapping at the hull.

"My great-great-grandfather came to South Dakota from Connecticut," she said cautiously. "The family owned mills and kept a yacht in Newport."

"So that would have been, what, the eighteen-seventies? Newport was the yachting center of the US back then. It still is. We members of the Chicago Yacht Club are bumpkin upstarts," Nate said.

Adam stifled a smile at Marissa's slightly surprised expression. No way would Nate judge her crazy or even impractical for a passion that had no logical roots. No way would Nate judge her at all. When she continued, her voice was a little less hesitant. "My dad and I were cleaning out some old trunks and found pictures of his grandfather on the family's yacht, logs from his trips, and his navigation equipment."

Nate's gaze sharpened. "What did you find?"

"A sextant, a chronometer, a brass torpedo log with a piece of line attached, old almanacs and tables, a double slate in an oak case with a hinge, a box compass, ebony parallel rules, and brass dividers."

"That's quite a collection," Nate said. "The sextant and the chronometer might be worth a fair amount, especially with your family provenance behind it," he said.

"Oh, I'd never sell," she said. "I couldn't. It's part of the Brooks family history."

You could accuse Marissa of many things, Adam thought, but not disloyalty. When times got tough, when the chips were down, she stuck. Past the point of logic and reason, sure, but she stuck. He understood that quality. Respected it.

"Why did he leave everything he knew and go west?"

"In his journals he wrote about feeling called to leave for new country, for a fresh beginning in an untouched place. He had a dream, I guess."

Nate nodded as if that made perfect sense, then stretched out on the bench seat. "Do you want to take over?" Marissa asked.

"Nope," he said and closed his eyes. "I sail her by myself all the time. Relaxing while someone else does the work sounds just fine right now."

They made the return trip with the sun setting at their backs, burnishing the city's skyline in an opaque reddish orange layer of light. He and Nate lowered and stowed the sails. Marissa relinquished the wheel to Nate when traffic heading back to shore grew heavy. Adam sat on one of the cushioned benches, his arms stretched out along the back as he gazed into the distance. To his surprise, Marissa snuggled in beside him. The chilly air must have been cold on her bare feet because she tucked them beside her and pulled a blanket over them.

He could get used to this.

"Have a good time?" he murmured in her ear.

"This is the best day of my life," she said, her eyes closed. Even he could see the lights flickering across her eyelids as she replayed the day. Sunshine, glittering waves, wind, the creak of the boat, the sensation of movement at its purest.

"I'm glad," he replied, and pulled her in close.

The engine rumbled as Nate guided them into the yacht club's docks. Adam leaped over the side of the boat and secured the lines. While Nate powered down, Marissa helped Adam gather their belongings from above and belowdecks. He steadied her while she stepped onto the dock, then joined her. She swayed a little, unsteady on her land legs after only a few hours on a boat.

Nate made no move to leave the boat. "You want a recommendation for dinner?"

"Somewhere local," he said. "A neighborhood place, not a tourist trap."

Nate squinted up at him, a grin creasing his face. "I remember you eating at local places all over the world and getting sick as a dog from them."

"So somewhere local that won't make me puke my guts out on the sidewalk," Adam said.

"Lou Malnati's has the best Chicago-style pizza, and good pasta if you don't want pizza," Nate said. "The State Street location is fairly close to your hotel."

"Want to join us, or are you headed home?"

The smile disappeared, and he looked at the ring on his finger, twisting it with his thumb. "Spending a few nights on the boat," he said.

"You can still join us."

"Thanks, but no. You two have a good time."

"Nate, thank you so much." She looked out at the lake, where a gleaming silver path reflected the light of the moon. "I can't describe what today meant to me. Thank you."

He cocked his head and gave her that rare wide smile. "Adam told me you had the bug," he said. "I love sailing, and

I love introducing people to the sport. Come back anytime and we'll go again. Just call the pilot a couple of hours before you're ready to leave, and he'll get you home."

Adam exchanged one last handshake with Nate, then hoisted the bags in one hand and took Marissa's chilled fingers in the other to walk along the pier. Several boats were lit, and a party was going on both above and belowdecks on one big yacht. They climbed the stairs to the club and walked out to the street, where a cab was waiting for them. The bags went back in the trunk, and he followed Marissa into the backseat, then gave the driver the restaurant's cross streets.

Marissa was slumped in the seat, her eyes closed. "Did you feel the way the boat handled in the wind? I didn't want to ask, but I think that was one of the original Herreshoff S-class yachts. They built America's Cup winners in the late eighteen-hundreds on into the twenties. People like the Vanderbilts bought yachts from Nathanael Herreshoff." She opened her eyes and looked at him. The connection was still like handling a live wire. "And I sailed one today. I sailed one of the finest boats ever built." She laughed, a mixture of astonishment and delight in the sound. "I can't believe it."

The cab pulled up in front of the restaurant, but when Adam handed money through the window the cab driver said, "It's been paid for, sir."

"Dammit, Nate," Adam muttered. Despite the driver's protestations that the tip was included, Adam handed a ten through the window. They retrieved the bags once again.

There was a short wait for a table, so they found a seat at the bar. Marissa glanced around as if a casual Italian restaurant in Chicago was as foreign as Mumbai or Thailand. She looked completely different, her eyes alight, inquisitive, shining. "Tell me more about Nate."

Adam tipped back his beer and swallowed. "We used to call him ESP rather than LT, because he was fucking spooky, like he was with the wind today. He knew where things we couldn't see—enemy fighters—were going to be before they got there. He probably knew before *they* got there. He says he's good with angles and probability. All I know is he took twenty-two men to Afghanistan twice and brought all of them home twice. He owns that boat and half of Chicago, and when I called him last night to see if he could recommend a company to take us out, I thought I'd get voicemail and a call back when he left work at ten. Instead he answered the phone and said he'd send his jet for us."

She tilted her head quizzically. "Half of Chicago?"

He gave a short bark of laughter. "Okay, maybe a quarter of Chicago. He never talks about it. I'd served under him for over a year before I had any idea what kind of money he had."

"Things don't sound ideal with his wife," she said.

"I'm not sure what's going on there," Adam said quietly. "Deployments are hard on a marriage. He did two in four years, and I don't think his wife was any happier about his decision than his parents were." The offhand comment hit too close to home, so he changed the subject in a hurry. "Tell me what you thought about today. Start when I showed up at your door."

Marissa laughed and the mood shifted again, flashing quicksilver, as unpredictable and vivid as her eyes. Every guy at the bar turned to look when she hitched herself up on a stool, her hair tousled and tangled down her back, her face pink from the sun and wind, her dark eyes glinting in the light. She looked alive, like she could look. Like she should look.

His heart skidded in his chest, tumbling and skittering like rocks presaging an avalanche, and for one brief moment he let all kinds of things he'd locked away flare in his brain. What he felt for Marissa. What he'd done for her, and maybe to her by making one phone call. Because this would change her. She might not know it, but it would. Experiences did that to a person with a soul like Marissa's. Deep and shadowed. On the surface it was as simple as making a call to a friend. Underneath, to a soul starved for water and wind and sun, it was the kind of experience that changed a life.

She might not believe she could be different, but after

today she was, and the fact that he'd done that for her locked them together. He'd shown her she could be the woman she'd only imagined, and that connected them more intimately than sex. He could get deep inside her body, but to open a window in her mind, let in water and sun and wind, that . . . that was connection. That was experience. He'd stood with her while she looked at the swaying forest of masts and the endless expanse of Lake Michigan, and realized that even landlocked, root-bound Marissa Brooks could go sailing.

He wanted to do it again.

He wanted to be the only man who ever did that for her, and he'd been a fool to think he'd be able to resist her. Something inside her called to him, brought him alive. Against his will, against all common sense and the consequences of his past experiences, he'd fallen for Marissa Brooks, for her tough-girl attitude and her vulnerable, dreamer heart.

That wasn't part of the plan.

HER SEEMINGLY ENDLESS stream of words dried up during dessert. The change was as subtle as Brookhaven's creek succumbing to a summer drought, a babble becoming a murmur, then a trickle, then nothing. Marissa lifted the last bite of profiterole to her lips, and when the powdered sugar dissolved in her mouth, the words, like water on the prairie, were gone. The city wasn't so much dark as missing light, and the day already seemed like a dream.

They'd shared the ice-cream-filled pastry, and Adam let her have the last bite. He'd watched her all day, from the moment she opened her door to him until now. The light from the single candle brought out the gold flecks in his eyes. He leaned back in his chair, an odd half smile on his mouth.

"You're sunburned," she pointed out, then touched her own nose to show him where.

"So are you," he said. "Not bad. The hat helped."

"How am I going to explain a sunburn to Walkers Ford?" she asked.

His gaze sharpened. "You don't have to explain anything to anyone, ever," he said.

The waitress arrived with their check, then waited as Adam slid a credit card into the plastic slot without even looking at the total. "I thought we'd walk, unless you're cold."

"I'm not cold," she said. She'd never felt more alive, like her skin held the day's sunlight and wind inside her.

He scrawled his signature on the receipt. Outside the restaurant she zipped her new coat to her chin and pulled up the hood. Adam stuffed her peacoat in his half-full duffle, slung the bags over his left shoulder, looked around as if getting his bearings, then held out his free hand. She slid her hand into his, and set off down the sidewalk.

The night was crystal clear, the fall air sharp but without the breeze she expected from the Windy City. A few stars glittered overhead, barely a fifth of what she usually saw at home, but she wasn't here to stargaze. Instead she focused on the architecture along Michigan Avenue, and Grant Park until they turned left at the marble steps and arches of the Art Institute. A couple of blocks later Adam led her into the lobby of the Palmer House Hilton.

"Wow," she whispered as they walked through the lobby to the front desk. Ornately decorated ceilings soared overhead. Oriental carpets lay under chairs clustered in groups, and tall vases held floral arrangements larger than the fireplaces dominating Brookhaven's great room. She gripped his hand more firmly and tried not to gawk.

"Just one night?" the clerk asked with a smile.

Adam confirmed, and the smiling desk clerk gave them two plastic key cards and pointed the way to the elevator. They had the dark-paneled rectangle all to themselves. Adam led her down a quiet hallway, then inserted the key card into the door, and the light switched from red to green as the lock clicked open. He held the door open for Marissa and let her walk through, into luxury like she'd never seen. A king-sized bed draped with a cranberry-red spread and apple-green cushions took up most of the space along one wall. Across from it was a flat-screen television hung over a dark wood dresser. A little table with two chairs sat in one corner, but it was the view that drew Marissa. The curtains were open to the city's skyline, with the dark expanse of Lake Michigan and the sky in the distance. It called to her, the darkness, the unknown, the depths.

Adam came up behind her, swept her hair away from her nape, and kissed her ear. "You got cold on the walk back," he said.

"It was worth it," she replied. "I feel like I've been here, not just flown over it."

"We'll see more tomorrow," he said as his hands slid down to hers. Warmth seeped into her chilled fingers. "The room doesn't have a tub, but it's got one hell of a shower," he said. "Go get warmed up."

Distance widened between them. She didn't look at the bed as she walked past it to the bathroom. They'd fooled around in the backseat of a car, on the back of a motorcycle, on a blanket by the creek, in a cozy nest in the loft, in her pantry, but only twice had they had sex in a bed, an experience that nearly annihilated her. Comparatively speaking, the king-sized bed in this silent, elegant room looked like a hedonistic playground.

Would she have to ask?

The thought sent heat shimmering through her, hot longing swirling through her cold body like cream in coffee. She peeked over her shoulder, saw him watching her, knew he was thinking the same thing.

Maybe she wouldn't have to ask. Maybe she already had.

The bathroom was a work of art, tiled in marble in subtle, dusky shades of brown. It boasted a shower almost the size of her bathroom back home, tiled on two walls, the other walls glass. Marissa ran the water hot enough to steam up the glass, stripped and left her clothes on the counter, and stepped into the glass cocoon.

She closed her eyes and let the day play across the movie screen of her mind. Adam at her door. The jet. Breaking through the clouds. The yacht club, boats jostling against the docks. That heart-stopping moment when she realized she, Marissa Brooks, fifth-generation South Dakotan, was going sailing.

The moment when her body disappeared into limitless water and sky.

Holding hands with Adam as they strolled through Chicago. The feel of his palm against hers, his lips brushing her ear.

A gentle tap on the glass startled her. Adam stood just outside the door. Water pounded around her, but the look on his face, the intensity in his eyes, was unmistakable, and drew an answering nod from her, even though he said nothing. When he'd undressed, she opened the door to let him in. He stepped into the enclosure, set a condom packet in the soap dish, then closed the door on the cool air in the bathroom. The water pelted them both, stinging hot and loud, but he didn't say a word. He just stepped into her and held her, and she buried her face in his chest.

The silence between them rang with things said and things better left unsaid. The water trickling down his defined pectorals caught her attention; without thinking, she bent her head and lapped at one rivulet, tracing it back up his chest, over his nipple to his collarbone. She did it again, felt his cock thicken and nudge at her thigh. Again, and again, each time following the water flowing over his shoulders and chest. A nip to his collarbone, then with the next trail of water she went on tiptoes to lick his chin and flick her tongue against his lower lip. The second time she did it his hand cupped the back of her head and held her mouth to his.

Again, that shocking moment of dissolving, but while the *Resolute*'s keel anchored her on the lake, Adam's mouth and hands kept her from soaring into the void. Then he turned his back to the tiled wall and sank to the floor, taking her with him.

She straddled his lap. His cock notched against her sex as he cupped her head and held her mouth still for his. The ocean rhythm of her breathing rushed and ebbed in her ears when he covered them with his hands; or maybe it was the water, all around them, pouring over their heads, down her back and his chest, heated to steam in the air they were breathing. She was drowning in water and Adam and life, no longer safe on solid ground. Laying her hands flat on either side of his jaw, she took kiss after kiss after kiss from him, her nipples rubbing against his slick chest. When he pulled her away to stare into her eyes, his hair was plastered to his forehead, his eyes dark.

The thumb and fingers of one hand held her mouth for his as they traded kisses; the other roamed from her hip to her breast and back, the pace leisurely, the sensations anything but. When his fingers found her nipple and pinched, she gasped and arched into his palm. She slid against him, her body's slick fluids and the water easing her movements. When the shock of sexual electricity subsided, she eased back down and felt his cock stretch her swollen, sensitive opening. Her body took over, working him inside while the water beat at the tiles and steam swirled around them. Her heart pounded against her rib cage, making her lightheaded, or maybe that was the intense energy surging under her skin.

Then his eyes widened. He gripped her hip hard enough to stop her. Hard enough to hurt. "Condom," he said.

She froze. That's why it felt so good. Skin to skin, nothing separating his erect shaft from her yielding flesh. The water droplets transformed his muscular body into a stone-cold, oiled-up warrior. Her inner muscles spasmed in response to the image, the words, his hands on her naked, vulnerable body. This was Adam, pure control over himself, over her, the boy she'd loved in a man's body.

"You don't have to," she said. She was on the Pill. She always insisted on condoms, and she wanted him to let go, to give her his trust, his vulnerability so she wasn't alone in this. She wanted more than *this Marine*. She wanted Adam.

His eyes closed briefly, and she felt more than heard a low rumble in his chest, but after a short, hot expanse of time, the hand on her hip tightened and lifted. He reached overhead and found the condom in the soap dish.

Mildly disappointed, she plucked it from his hand and tore open the wrapper, then pulled his erection away from his ridged abdomen. She locked her gaze with his, then placed the condom on the tip of his shaft and rolled the thin latex down, covering him in tiny increments. When his eyelids drooped, she stopped. His hands tightened on her hips and his breath eased from his broad chest in one long, hissing groan. When he opened his eyes, she resumed, stroking each inch before sheathing it, stopping to caress his balls before seating the condom at the base of his shaft.

His dark gaze bored into hers. Her head was empty of everything except the water pounding all around them and the heat in his eyes. "Jesus, Ris," he said.

His hand covered hers at the base of his shaft, pulling it away from his belly. The hand on her hip tightened, urging her down. Looking deep into his eyes, she took every hard, hot inch in a slow, slick glide that had her trembling against him when he was seated to the hilt inside her.

She'd never felt closer to anyone in her life.

His eyes dropped closed. "Fuck," he whispered.

She bent and kissed him, wet and passionate, her tongue rubbing the roof of his mouth, flicking against his while she kept her lower body completely still.

"That's not helping, Ris," he said.

"You feel so good inside me," she whispered.

"It feels so good to be inside you," he groaned. "I can't . . . fuck. I can't." He wrapped his arms around her and pulled her against his chest, one hand urging her face into the curve of his neck. "Just sit still for a minute, okay? While I—"

"Recite the Pledge of Allegiance?"

His mouth smiled against her temple. "Something like that," he said.

Naked and slick and hot, they sat on the tiled floor of the shower, water splattering around them, while time stood still, the tension hovering at a plateau. After a few moments—or perhaps an eternity—passed, he fisted his hand in her wet hair and gently tugged her face away from his neck.

"Slow," he said. "Really slow. Like it has to last forever."

She looked deep into his eyes and lifted herself, the granite-hard shaft caressing her swollen pussy lips until the head of his cock was barely nestled in her folds. Then she sank down again, watched the banked fire in his eyes flare infinitesimally hotter. Her knees skidded on the wet tile, so he braced his hands on either side of them to hold her in place.

"Touch yourself," he murmured, and the command, low and rough, flicked through her. She lifted her hands to her breasts and pinched the nipples as she picked up the pace. One hand slipped down her belly to circle her clit, but she didn't need it, wanted the build without the nitro burn. She lifted her fingers to his mouth, let him lick water and her juices off the tips of her fingers before returning the hand to her nipples. Her hair hung in wet strands against her forehead and cheeks, partially obscuring her vision, but she saw enough, saw the sexual heat climb up his throat and merge with the hot flush on his cheeks, saw the muscles tighten in his chest and arms as he held her in place on the wet tile.

"So hot," he said, and the words disappeared with a hiss into the steam.

A rope of desire tangled deep from her sex all the way to her throat, and each clinging surge of her hips tightened the knots. She didn't want it to end, but longing drove her on until she tipped over the edge. Each hard pulse unraveled a tangle of nerves and emotions inside her, until her bones and muscles gave way, leaving her limp against him.

Unlike her, he was rigid with tension, tremors running through his muscles, on the ragged edge of control. She lifted her head and looked at him, trying to discern what was going on inside him. His gaze was as steadfast, but behind those glittering hazel eyes simmered vulnerability, maybe even fear. Not *this Marine*. Not Adam, either.

She lifted her hands to his jaw and kissed him, soft, delicate, precise impacts on his lower lip, the corner of his mouth, then full-on, openmouthed and wet and hot as she rose and fell, enveloping his cock in her body. Each measured stroke brought a soft sob up from her lungs. She couldn't hear them over the water and the electric noise in her head, but she could feel them much the way she felt his shaft thicken inside her. He reached out, gripped her hip and her hair, pulled her down so her mouth rested on his, breaths gusting together. His muscles contracted and his eyes dropped closed as he jetted into her, warm, liquid pulses deep inside her.

He came, but she was the one who came apart.

Her vision contracted sharply and her head throbbed. "I've got to get out of here," she said. "I'm too hot."

A huff of laughter from that broad chest, then he gently shifted her to the side and stood. She reached for his extended hand to get to her feet, then gripped it tightly when her vision faded to black. Adam turned the water to a cooler temp and stood her under it. Air drifted into the shower stall when he stepped out, and returned several moments later. He handed her a tiny bottle of shampoo. She began to work lather into her hair while he unwrapped the bar of hotel soap and unself-consciously soaped up. It was an intimate little dance, him rinsing off while she worked shampoo through her hair, then used the conditioner as well.

"I'll be outside," he said, and stepped out of the shower. Unaccountably shy, she took her time getting the conditioner out of her hair, then turned off the water. The towels, thick and plush and warming on a towel rack, were luxury in themselves. She found a mini-bottle of lotion in the basket by the sink, and used it on her face.

In the room, Adam was stretched out on the bed, wearing his shorts, one hand behind his head, the remote in his hand as he surfed through the channels. He looked so handsome, dark stubble shadowing his lean jaw, his body muscular and relaxed on the bed. He gave her an appraising glance, a quick smile, then turned back to the basketball game.

It hurt, that he'd give her such a beautiful gift as the day of sun and water and wind, but not himself.

Do you want him to give himself, then leave? Because he will. Live in this moment. It's enough.

She pulled on her nightgown and went to sit by the window, using the towel to dry her hair, then her brush to finish the job, pulling the bristles through the strands in stroke after stroke as she looked out over the skyline and the enigmatic darkness of the lake beyond.

15

SHE AWOKE THE next morning in a burrow of down comforter, sheets, pillows, not completely sure where she was. A rough fingertip stroked the sensitive skin and delicate hairs at her nape, raising a shiver completely unrelated to the air temperature and calling her from the sleep of the dead. She rolled toward daylight and tugged the sheet down to peer out. The cream paint and apple green valance oriented her. A hotel room. Chicago. Sailing.

Adam.

He lay beside her, head braced on his hand, the sheet at his waist, his dark hair, tanned skin, and hazel eyes vivid against the sea of white around them. Under the sheet he traced a line from her nape to her tailbone and back. "Sore?" he asked.

Shifting her weight fired her muscles, reminding her that a day of sailing used different muscles than a day of construction work. She was indeed sore but she wouldn't admit to it in the cold light of day.

"Nothing I can't handle," she said as she lifted herself on her elbows to look over his shoulder at the clock. "It's eight o'clock!" she yelped.

A firm hand between her shoulder blades pushed her back to the mattress. "Do you have to be somewhere?"

"I don't know. Do I?"

His hand left her back to tuck her tumbled, sleep-warmed hair behind her ear, but his face didn't change. "Whatever you want, Ris," he said softly. "We can play it by ear. I just need to give the pilot a couple of hours' notice before we leave so he can file a flight plan."

She reached for something casual, informal, something that wouldn't feel like too much. "Let's start with something simple. Breakfast. Maybe just coffee." She pushed back the covers and got to her feet but ruined her easygoing approach by wincing when her muscles protested. Limping only slightly, she made it to the coffee pot sitting on a tray on top of the mini-fridge and grabbed the small glass pot.

"Halt."

She halted and looked at him.

"We're in a city, Marissa, a real city with real coffee shops. We're not drinking watery instant swill from a packet on the minibar. Go take another hot shower. We'll get coffee while we're sightseeing."

"I don't need another shower," she protested.

"Fine, tough girl. Stand up straight."

She tried, and winced as things cracked.

He lifted one eyebrow. "The heat will loosen your muscles."

"You're bossy when you're right."

Humor flickered across his face. "It's called 'command presence,' and I've got it when I'm wrong, too," he said. "Go on."

She secured her hair in a topknot so she wouldn't waste time drying it again, and stretched under the warm spray, felt her muscles loosen and ease. Fifteen minutes later she was dry, her teeth brushed, and dressed in her jeans, sweater, and the deck shoes. She brushed her hair into loose waves, then secured it low on her nape with her barrette. Back in his cargo pants and windbreaker, Adam brushed his teeth while she packed. After a quick conference with the concierge to pick up a Chicago tourism booklet and identify an acceptable coffee shop for her coffee snob, they strolled through the sumptuous lobby, down Adams Street to Michigan Avenue, then along Millennium Park to a sleek coffee shop called Intelligentsia, where Adam snagged the last copy of the *Chicago Sun-Times* and they waited in line.

"What on earth are all these choices?" Marissa said under her breath.

"Coffee," he said, the word vibrating with satisfaction and anticipation as he folded the laminated street map and tucked it in his back pocket. "Unburnt coffee. Different roasts, different beans from different parts of the world."

She chose a large dark roast, with room, and a cranberry muffin from the case. Adam got an enormous blueberry muffin and his own cup of coffee, no room. They settled into a table by the windows. Adam pulled the Auto section from the paper and pushed the rest of it across the table to Marissa.

She sipped the coffee, then blinked. "Oh my God," she said.

Humor glimmered in his eyes. "I know. You can get a bag to go so you can treat yourself at home. Just ask them to grind it for you."

She did exactly that, looking around as she waited, automatically comparing her jacket, jeans, and deck shoes to what the other women in the shop wore. The tourists were easily identified by their Chicago sweatshirts or windbreakers, while the women she guessed were residents carried brown bags with gold letters in the leather and wore scarves draped in a variety of ways. In her sailing jacket and shoes she didn't look out of place. Like no one knew that twenty-four hours earlier she'd woken up in South Dakota.

Engrossed in the paper, elbows braced on his knees, Adam sat by the window, completely at home.

"Have you been here before?" she asked while she tucked the coffee into her tote bag.

"No," he said.

"How do you know where to go?"

"The Marine Corps taught me how to find things," he said casually. "If I can find my way through gullies in Helmand Province at night, I can find a coffee shop on clearly marked streets in broad damn daylight."

"I can't believe I'm here," she said. "I'm sitting in a coffee shop in Chicago, drinking the best coffee I've ever had, and deciding what to do with my day. Is this real?"

"I'm doing the same thing," Adam said, his gaze back on the newspaper, "so we're either hallucinating together or it's real."

"Can I try your muffin?"

Still focused on all things automotive, he pushed the plate across the table to her. She broke off a piece and popped it in her mouth, then flipped through the sections of the newspaper. Arts and Leisure caught her eye, so she pulled it out of the stack and opened it. Articles about the ballet; two concerts, one pop, one classical; a traveling dance troupe; and a new exhibit at the Art Institute. The tourism booklet boasted some of the world's best shopping along the Magnificent Mile. She flipped to the map, found their location, and smiled.

"We can do whatever I want?"

He nodded.

"Here's the plan. I want to go to the Art Institute, but it doesn't open for a couple of hours, so until then I want to walk along Michigan Avenue. We can window-shop and look at the architecture."

She wasn't sure how a US Marine would feel about shopping, followed by a museum to see Impressionist art, but the odd light in his eyes matched the half smile on his face when he nodded again, then pulled the map from his back pocket and slid it across the table to her. "Want a coffee to go?"

"Better make it decaf," she said and stepped outside to orient herself.

He stuffed her tote bag in his larger backpack, then shouldered it. They opted for the sunny side of the street for the stroll up Michigan Avenue. They crossed the river, stopping on the span to study the Wrigley Building and Tribune Tower.

"They don't make buildings like that anymore," Marissa said. "Ornate, elaborate, meant to represent a company or a place's history and give it a sense of permanence."

Adam leaned his elbows on the bridge railing, his sharp eyes taking in the buildings lining the river as he spoke. "Maybe that's what's different between now and then. We know nothing lasts forever."

"That doesn't mean it's not worth trying." She sipped her coffee, then pointed at the bas-relief sculptures on the granite pillars supporting either end of the bridge. "That effort is worth honoring."

His gaze turned to hers, the sharpness tempered with understanding. "There's a difference between honoring something and sacrificing yourself for it."

She just lifted her eyebrows at him. The sun streamed along the river, a winding path of water and light through the towers of stone and glass nearly surrounding them.

He straightened and reached for her hand. "Come on. We don't have much time."

She let him lead her off the bridge and into the thick of the Magnificent Mile's upscale shopping. The windows fascinated her, works of art in fabric and color, impossibly thin mannequins dressed in impractical clothes. "Your mother would love this," she said absently, because the Banana Republic window caught her eye. Adam said nothing when she pushed through the doors, just followed her inside to a long wood table covered with a dusky fabric.

What appeared on the model to be a thin scarf was actually a large wrap, approximately six feet long by three feet wide, saved from bulkiness by the thin silk fabric. One side started a dark, midnight blue, the color paling through twilight and periwinkle to summer sky blue. The other side was a single shade of grayish blue, or bluish gray. The colors were an exact match for the range of sky she saw on Lake Michigan the day before. Embroidered triangular shapes resembling sailboats quilted the two pieces of fabric together.

Her heart hiccupped as she looked at it.

"Pretty," Adam said beside her.

It was the most beautiful item of clothing she'd ever seen, meant to be worn over a sleeveless dress to a fancy party, and therefore completely impractical for a construction worker in Walkers Ford, South Dakota. She stroked it with her index finger anyway. The fabric was so fine she registered the sensation of coolness before she felt silk. The price tags were all carefully turned over so only the Banana Republic logo showed, not the actual cost, and when she turned one over she knew why. Three hundred dollars. She turned the tag back over so it matched all the others at the edge of the mahogany table and stepped back.

"Try it on," Adam said.

"There's nothing to try on," she replied lightly and took another step back, right into Adam, warm, solid, and unmoving. "One size fits all."

He reached around her and unzipped her jacket. "Humor me."

He draped her jacket over a chair next to a long, single mirror, then picked up the nearest scarf. For something so large it weighed almost nothing, like the wind. He gathered the fabric and draped it behind her neck, then caught the trailing end and pulled it around and behind. The graduated colors shifted like waves, and the pewter backing was the exact color of a stormy sky. Her hair was caught under the wrap, and as she looked at her reflection in the mirror, she didn't recognize herself.

"Beautiful," he said.

"It's not for me," she replied and unwound it from around her neck. It was for all the sophisticated women living in Chicago, getting their coffee at Intelligentsia and going to the Art Institute every weekend.

"Why not?"

"Where would I wear that?"

"You're always cold," he reasoned. "Wear it to weddings and funerals and everything between. Hell, wear it to watch TV. Sleep with it."

The thought of her wearing Polartec pajamas, fleece-lined

slippers, and a silk wrap in all the shades of Chicago to watch reruns of *Ice Road Truckers* made her laugh. "I'm too old for security blankets, and I don't need it," she said and flipped it back onto the table like she'd flip a top sheet onto the bed. Silk fluttered through the air toward the table. "That's good because I can't afford it, either."

He watched the fabric settle into stillness, then looked at her, an indecipherable look in his eyes. She broke the stare and picked up her empty coffee cup from the floor. "Did you see a trash can anywhere?"

"By the door. I'm going to find a bathroom. I'll meet you down there. The museum's open."

She threw the cup away, then watched people walk across the street, merging and separating on their separate ways. It was about timing, she decided as she waited for Adam. When they stepped off the curb, their speed and direction. Sometimes they made it to the sidewalk without dodging someone. Sometimes they didn't.

Timing was everything.

Adam came up behind her, the backpack over his shoulder. "Ready?"

They didn't linger on the trip back to the Art Institute. As they waited in line for tickets, Marissa got her wallet from her purse.

"Put that away," Adam said.

She turned and looked up into his face. In close quarters and flat shoes she realized how much shorter she was. "Please," she said quietly. "Let this be my treat."

His gaze searched hers for a second, then, to her surprise, he put his wallet away and kissed her. "Thank you," he said.

She smiled, ridiculously pleased. "My pleasure."

They stored their bags and jackets in the coat check. The galleries were an education in themselves. She lingered in the Impressionist rooms, then found Adam in the Architecture and Design galleries. They had lunch in the small cafeteria. She chose food she'd never had before, asparagus quiche and a rich chocolate torte for dessert. The gift shop took another hour as they browsed through books before she chose a magnet, bookmarks, and splurged on a couple of books. Sunshine lifted the temperatures above normal, so they spent the afternoon wandering through Millennium Park until Adam called the pilot and set a departure time.

"We have to leave," she said.

He nodded, and stepped to the curb to hail a cab. This time she knew what to expect and got back in the plane a seasoned traveler. Takeoff was smooth as silk, but the descent through the thick clouds into Sioux Falls left her gripping Adam's hand hard enough to leave dents in his skin. The ride back to Walkers Ford was quiet, Marissa sorting through her memories, slowly but surely returning to reality, because the wedding was now less than a week away. They turned down the road that led to Walkers Ford, the lights of the town visible to the south, and Brookhaven's silhouette barely visible a mile down the road.

The weekend away, as short as it was, only convinced her of two truths. She was home, and he would leave.

"Why do that for me?" she asked.

The only sound in the car was the thwack of the windshield wipers and the modern rock station, on low since they left Sioux Falls. Then he said, "Because you're drowning, Ris. I'm just trying to throw you a life preserver."

"I'm not drowning. I'm rooted," she said, but even as the words left her mouth, she knew she was lying. Lying to him. Lying to herself. "Do you think I'll somehow figure out a way to cancel all my debts and pull up over a hundred years of roots and leave South Dakota forever? One day on a boat doesn't make me a sailor any more than reading every book ever written about sailing does."

"Only because you don't think you can do it," he said. His voice was even, but his grip tightened on the steering wheel. "You can move mountains, Ris. You've done it before. All you have to do is commit."

She pursed her lips, but didn't respond.

"Fine. Forget I said that. I did it because I thought you

would like it, because it was a gift within my reach to give you." He paused, then said, "I did it for me, too. I'm coming down off an adrenaline high, trying to avoid the crash."

That was the most truthful thing she'd heard him say since he walked through Brookhaven's front door. "So why are you going to school to be an architect?"

Now he blinked. "What?"

"If you want the rush, why stick yourself in an office, drawing elevations and blueprints?"

"I like to build things."

She stared at him, disbelief in her open mouth and wide eyes, but he braked to a halt at the top of Brookhaven's circular drive. "And when did you figure this out?"

"I have to do something. The SDSU program focuses on sustainable design, and the state needs more architects. It's as good a job as any."

"So how come you get away with 'as good a job as any' but I have to see new possibilities? How come I get to go sailing in what will probably be the best day of my life, ever, and you get to join the Marine Corps, then live in a cube farm? Let's talk about your dreams," she said, warming up. "Let's go there."

"I don't get a dream, Marissa."

Using her full name meant he was pissed. So was she. "Because of what happened to Josh? I was there, too, Adam. That night I was right there with you. My house, my land, my mantel on the bonfire."

A muscle jumped in his jaw. "That's another reason why I don't get a dream. You weren't on the bike," he bit off. "You didn't say what I said, you didn't take the turn too fast on roads as slick as snot, knowing you could barely handle it and Josh couldn't."

"So you pay forever?"

His profile was carved from stone, eyes bleak. "Why not? Josh did."

"Josh *died*. You didn't. I know you, Adam. You like speed, movement, people. You like hard things, testing the limits.

You're smart as hell, but you're not going to be happy at a desk job. You make things happen. You make other people believe things can happen. That's why everyone wanted to be where you were in high school, that's why Keith befriended you when he couldn't take you down. Architecture sounds like Delaney's idea of a perfect white-collar, double-income life, maybe enough to let her stay home with the kids. Was it your idea, or hers?"

She was shouting now, gesturing wildly enough to smack her hand against the Charger's dash. The pain flashed her back twelve years to arguments in the front seat of his old Challenger, fights that led to make-out sessions that went nowhere. They'd been like caged animals then, trapped behind bars they couldn't see, only feel.

"It doesn't matter whose idea it was," he ground out. "I'm in the program, and I'm going through with it."

Taking Josh's place in the Marine Corps and serving five tours was payment enough for the mistake he'd made. She scrambled for options, anything to make him reconsider. "Can you defer a year? At least take some time and think about it."

"No. No more time. All this time with nothing to do is making me crazy. I'm in. I'm going to lease one of those apartments. I'm going to grad school. That's final."

She unfastened her seatbelt. "Exactly," she said softly. "I'm going to finish Brookhaven. I'm going to pay off the home equity loan. And *that's* final."

"Fine," he said. "There's no reason for us not to pick up where we left off twelve years ago." He'd conducted the conversation while staring fixedly out the front windshield, but now his gaze flicked to hers. Anger and a very familiar sexual arousal mixed with something deeper, something anguished glimmered in the hazel depths.

Longing, hot and sharp, speared through her. "Oh, no," she said. "One of us is delusional about our futures, and it's not me. I can't afford to fall for you. You being here makes no sense. You don't belong here, and you won't stay. But I will, and I can't go to pieces like I did the last time you left."

She hefted her tote from the floorboard and opened the door. He gripped her forearm and prevented her from getting out of the car. His gaze was hot, enticing, everything he'd been twelve years ago, everything he was now. "Fall for me, Ris. I'm staying."

How could he give her the space to be someone else, if only for a weekend, yet box himself off so rigidly? She tugged gently. His grip tightened, then relaxed enough for her to pull free. "Thank you for a lovely weekend, Adam. I'll remember it forever."

She'd left the porch light off when she took off thirty-six hours earlier, so she fumbled in the gravelike darkness until she got the key in the lock. Once inside she flicked on the kitchen light. Her tiny apartment remained exactly as she'd left it. She hung her jacket on the row of hooks by the door, got herself a glass of water, checked the weather for the next couple of days, then set about the business of fitting her new self into her old world.

A bath would help. Hot and liquid and engulfing. While the water ran into the claw-foot tub, she put away her few toiletries. Next she found her new hat. Her underwear, night-shirt, and sweater went into the laundry basket. She pulled out Ben's peacoat and hung it next to Adam's gift, her brand-new, bright red jacket, then went back into her bedroom.

The plastic bag at the bottom of her black tote was dark blue, so only the white *ana pub* lettering caught the light from the lamp on her nightstand. Slowly she reached in and pulled it out. It didn't weigh much, only as much as a weekend shaped out of wind and dreams. The drawstring was pulled tight. She opened it, drew out neatly folded tissue paper, and upended it.

Three hundred dollars of beautiful, useless silk slid into her lap. "Adam," she said quietly. "Oh, Adam."

She snipped the tag off, stood in front of her full-length mirror and wrapped the scarf around her neck, then pulled it off and draped it over her shoulders. As the fabric shifted and slid in the dim light, the colors blended, water and sky and rain around her shoulders. Still wearing the wrap, she went to the kitchen and picked up her old rotary phone and dialed his cell number.

"Hey," he said gruffly.

She rubbed her forehead with her palm. Where to start? "Thank you."

A pause. "You're welcome."

"You shouldn't have," she said. It was so much, the plane ride and the hotel, the day of sailing, the Art Institute, the wrap. The start of something she thought was doomed and he thought was a new beginning.

"I wanted to," he said, still gruff, even a little defensive. "I wanted you to have it. I wanted you to have everything you can dream, everything it's in my power to give you."

She swallowed hard. "I'm sorry I said . . . everything I said in the car."

"No, you're not, tough girl," he replied, amusement clear in his rough voice.

She laughed. "Okay, that's true. But I feel the same way about you. I want you to dream, too." In the silence that followed she heard the Charger's engine shift into idle. "You're home."

"Yeah. I have to see what Mom's been up to. Tomorrow I'm going to Brookings to get an apartment. Want to ride along?"

"I can't."

"You're going to get the mantel."

Her heart clawed its way into her throat, and birds' wings fluttered at her temples. "No," she said quickly. "The weather's just cloudy with a chance of showers for the next couple of days. I need to re-side Mrs. Carson's house."

"Ris," he said quietly.

She cut him off. "Then . . . then I'll get the mantel."

"I'll put off the apartment," he said. "What time are you starting at Mrs. Carson's?"

"I don't need help with either project."

"But I need something to do, so you're doing me a favor. What comes after that?"

She rubbed her forehead and walked into the bathroom to turn off the water running into the tub. "I have to clean the great hall. The event planners arrive on Friday to start decorating, and the caterer needs to get into the kitchen no later than noon."

"You know, I need a date for this wedding," he said offhandedly.

"Let's not do that," she said.

"Why not?"

"Because if you show up with me, it'll be scandal and gossip and I'm tired of people talking about you and me."

"You weren't invited to the wedding, were you?" His flat, hard voice made the question a statement.

"I'm not friends with Delaney, and I think Keith's one life-form removed from pond scum. Why would I be invited?"

"Your house is the reception location."

"Oh, I'll be there," she said lightly. "Working. In the background, making sure the event planners and caterer have everything they need."

She didn't catch all the words that tumbled out of his mouth, but *motherfucker* featured prominently in the low growl.

"Better clean up that potty mouth," she said. "Welcome back to Walkers Ford."

16

MARISSA NEGLECTED TO give him a starting time for Mrs. Carson's re-siding project, but Adam figured sunrise, or seven thirty, was a good bet. On his way to the job site he swung through the Heirloom Cafe. He waved off the hostess and leaned against the counter to order two large cups of coffee to go. The waitress working the counter went off to pour them. Coffee at the Heirloom wouldn't win any international awards, but it also wouldn't taste like week-old battery acid. Their little inside joke, bringing her a cup she could hold. He tried to remember if he'd had anything like that with Delaney. In the beginning she'd been a textbook military girlfriend. Regardless of whether he was stateside, on a WESTPAC cruise, or deployed, packages arrived every week or so, filled with magazines, supplies, and homemade treats his fellow Marines fell on like wolves. He'd matched her efforts with cards and e-mails, flowers, gifts ordered online and shipped to her door in his absence. It was all very Delaney, the right thing to do. But what were their inside jokes, the things that bonded a couple on more than one level?

"Are the books you checked out proving adequate?"

The town's contract librarian, her brown wool coat buttoned to her chin, a summer sky-blue scarf trapping her loose hair, leaned against the next stool over. "Yes, ma'am," he said. "Thanks for your help."

"It's my pleas—"

Marissa's name and a low laugh drowned out the rest of Alana's sentence. Her gaze sharpened. "Yesterday I taught a class on computer research at the high school," she said, her voice just a little louder than before. "While I was there I picked up several of their better books on public speaking and rhetoric. Unfortunately I don't have them with me, but please stop by the library later today, if you're interested."

Whether he needed the books or not, he'd get them and at least skim them. "I appreciate that, ma'am. Thank you," he said.

"—good at finding a man to teach her what she needs to know."

The words, spoken by an older man at a table behind Adam and to his left, dropped into that sudden hush that falls over crowded spaces at odd intervals. They so closely mirrored what Keith said to him a few days ago that Adam knew Keith was the one to frame Marissa in that particularly unflattering light. The characterization stank of his particular wit, stinging and smarmy and accurate all at once.

Adam exhaled sulfur, long and slow, as he lifted the lid off one of the to-go cups and stirred cream into Marissa's coffee. Something hot, leathery, and dangerous shifted inside him, testing the chains holding it inside. He looked at Alana, twin red flags staining her pale cheeks as she fit the lid on her oatmeal with brown sugar and raisins. Her precise movements and high color told him he couldn't have asked for a better straight man. "You know what we're taught in the Marines?" he asked.

"I know very little about military service," she admitted.

The conversations at the periphery of the dropped stone of gossip now halted as most of the heads in the restaurant turned to stare unabashedly at Adam and Alana. He ignored them all, just stood ramrod straight, arms folded across his chest. Projecting command presence into the space around him. "We're trained to fight in pairs. A Marine alone is hard to kill. Two Marines together are nearly impossible to kill. Three or more, with thirty seconds to plan and weapons made from things you can find on this counter and we will wreak havoc."

Fuck you up is what he meant. *Wreak havoc* came out at the last minute as he remembered where he was. "A Marine who learns everything he can from someone who knows more about a weapon or a terrain or a situation is a smart Marine. Resourceful. Adaptable. Someone you want in your platoon." He swallowed a mouthful of his own coffee, noted with intense satisfaction the absolute silence in the restaurant. Still moving with a precision totally at odds with the fierce creature seething inside him, he snapped the lid back on Marissa's coffee.

"How interesting," Alana said. She extracted her wallet from her leather bag and withdrew a bill, then tucked it under her oatmeal. "Allow me to buy your coffees this morning, Adam."

"That's not necessary, ma'am," he said. Something about her formal cadence had him braced like he would for a conversation with a visiting general or dignitary.

"It would be my honor," she said.

"Thank you." He balanced both cups in his palm and followed her through the still-silent dining room. She pulled on gloves and gathered her breakfast, then he opened the door for her.

"And say hello to Marissa for me," she said as she swept through.

Despite the fury boiling inside him, he had to smile. "I will, ma'am."

Outside she ducked her chin into her scarf and gave him a mischievous grin. "That was fun."

"Yes, ma'am." Damn this place. *Damn* it for labeling Marissa, defining who she was, how her life should look when she wanted so much more. Could be so free. Thoughts were flying thick and fast now, with emotion hard on their heels.

"Stop calling me 'ma'am.'"

"Sorry," he said, barely cutting off the automatic *ma'am* her imperious tone inspired. "Old habits die hard."

"I understand," she said. "Do you want to stop by the library now? I was heading home, but I can open the building for you."

"Maybe later this afternoon," he said, remembering the library's official afternoon hours. "I don't want this coffee to get cold."

He put the coffees in the Charger's cupholders and drove across Main Street to the older part of town. The wide streets were lined with small houses on good-sized lots. Marissa's red diesel dualie made it easy to identify Mrs. Carson's house.

For a moment he watched her unload siding board by board from the truck bed to a location alongside the garage. She wore paint- and caulk-stained overalls, and her red fleece zipped to her chin underneath. Her hair lay in brown braids over her shoulders, topped with a red fleece watch cap. Her cheeks were pink either from the cool air or the exertion.

Nothing about what she did, the way she moved, was calculating. She was just being Marissa, but she had to know what people thought of her and she wasn't even trying to deflect attention.

He got out, reached back in for the coffees, closed the door, and joined her by the tailgate. He handed her the fuller cup then hefted a piece of siding, a movement that exerted more effort than he'd expected. "What is this stuff?"

She looked at it. "Fiber cement. Best siding on the market. When I'm at the auctions I look for construction overbuys and leftovers and pick them up. I found it at an auction when Mrs. Carson said she wanted to re-side her house. The color's neutral. I'll put it on now and if she doesn't like it, I'll paint it in the spring. It's heavy, though."

"Who helped you load it?"

"At the auction or today?" she asked over the rim of the coffee cup.

"Either."

"The guy running the auction had a forklift, so he put both pallets in the back of the truck for me. I unloaded it into the barn piece by piece back in July, then reloaded it to bring it over."

The single piece of siding still straining his biceps, he looked at her, long and hard enough to get her attention. "I can barely afford to pay myself, Adam. I don't have the money to hire a second set of hands, and there's a limit to what I can trade."

The concept of bartering brought back the way Walkers Ford's citizens cut her down to their size at the Heirloom. He looked at the house. The old, vertical siding was still on it. The house wasn't big, maybe a thousand-square-foot ranch style with a single-car attached garage, but there'd be ladder work. Remove the old siding and heft it into the back of her truck to take to the dump. Unload it. At least she could just back up and shove it off. Tack on the new weather guard/rain barrier. Measure, cut, hang, and nail on the new siding, piece by piece, in the damp fall rain.

"Why are you working in construction?"

"That's what Chris did, remember?"

He did. Vaguely. Chris's father was a handyman/jack-of-all-trades, doing whatever didn't require a building permit from the county. No electrical work, but a little plumbing. His father hurt his back young and Chris picked up his tools, and his drinking habit.

She held the cup in both hands, inhaling the coffee-scented steam. "I had a couple other jobs after high school. I waitressed at Saddles and Spurs, worked as a checkout clerk at the convenience store, but I didn't like being inside all day, or standing in one place all the time. I just started going to work with him. I figured if I could help, he'd get through a job faster and could take more work. When the opportunity to buy Brookhaven came up, we thought we'd renovate it, get experience, then sell it."

He lifted an eyebrow. "And he bought that?"

Her gaze flicked to his face, then off into the distance. "Yes," she admitted. "I sold it pretty convincingly."

He wasn't ready to go there yet. "Did you get the panic attacks when you worked on the house with him?"

"They're not panic attacks," she protested. "It was different work. Before he died we rewired the house with the help of an electrician friend of his, and were most of the way through the plumbing. That next fall, when the paying work slowed down, I started on the ceilings and walls. Come summer, Brian helped me with the windows. Then I tackled the floors."

From a construction-plan standpoint, her strategy made perfectly logical sense. There was no point in replacing the mantel and woodwork only to have to remove it or cover it while she was rewiring, plastering, painting. But that wasn't why she couldn't drive up Mrs. Edmunds's driveway. "So the panic attacks are about the mantel."

"They're not your fault," she said.

"Sure they're not," he scoffed, then pinned her with his gaze. "I destroyed it. You'd be done by now. That's on me."

"The physical damage is your fault," she said quietly, "but you're not responsible for me."

Because you left. The words vibrated in the air as surely as if she'd spoken them, and therein lay the rub, as they said. He'd left, forfeited any right or claim to Marissa Brooks, and no matter who did the asking, she wasn't ready to give him a second chance.

He couldn't blame her, but that didn't make hearing the gossip any easier. She didn't need a knight in dress A's to sweep her off her feet. She needed a second set of hands to finish this siding job, and a friend at her back when she went to do what she had to do.

She set her coffee cup beside the wheel well and pulled on her work gloves. "Let's get the siding off the side of the garage."

He'd brought some tools from his mother's garage. She wedged the split end of her pry bar under the nail head and tapped on the opposite end to pop the nail out, then lifted her eyebrow at him to check his understanding. When he nodded, she asked, "Low or high? Low's hard on your knees. High's hard on your shoulders because you've got your arms over your head."

"High," he said. He had more upper-body strength than she did.

She went to her knees in the grass and efficiently popped the nails. He watched her technique for a second to get his bearings, then went to work where the siding met the soffit under the gutter. For a few minutes the only sound was the screech and jerk of nails tearing free from wood and the thud of the hammer against the pry bar. When the sheet of siding sagged away from the framing, Marissa stood up. He popped the last nails loose, then they took down the sheet of siding, rotted and crumbling at the bottom, and carried it to Marissa's truck and slid it into the bed.

"I've been to the Architecture school at SDSU," she said as they walked back to the house.

He hefted his pry bar and hammer. "Yeah?"

"They have a collection of photos and newspaper articles about old houses in the upper Midwest. Original plans and elevations. That kind of thing. It's kind of interesting."

"If you could do anything for work," he said, putting his full weight into a stubborn nail, "what would you do?"

Screech. Pop. "Truth?"

"Always."

"This," she said.

He looked down at her. "Really?"

Her blue eyes were wide, challenging. "Why is that so surprising? I couldn't handle a desk job. I like the challenge of redesigning a space, making it reflect a person's character or personality. Your mom and I had a blast working out her bathroom reno. It's not buildings, but it's satisfying, and I'm good at it."

"Even after going out on the *Resolute*?"

"That's not reality, Adam. It's a dream. That's all."

"I thought it was a tangent."

Screech. Pop. Then she cut him a glance. They worked in silence for the next few minutes. "What had you so pissed off when you drove up?"

"Nothing," he said.

"Give me three guesses," she said but continued before he could agree. "You heard some gossip about you and me down at the Heirloom."

He put a little extra force behind the hammer swing. "Close enough. It was just about you."

Bitterly amused laughter huffed from her as she gripped the bottom edge of the siding in her work gloves. "They're just too intimidated to talk about you so openly," she said.

"They should be," he said with a grunt. He hoisted the rotting sheet of siding himself and dropped it into the truck bed.

She finished the rest of the coffee. Her breath condensed in the cool air. "The merry widow of Chatham County. That's what Keith used to call me when I did start going to Saddles and Spurs after Chris died. He was home from law school by then."

"Because you were so fucking merry?"

"I was the life of the party," she said, so blandly he couldn't tell whether she meant she'd gotten drunk and danced topless on the tables, or she was as reserved and remote as she was now.

Did it matter?

"Why did you do it?" he asked. "You know how this town talks. Why carry on like you did?"

"Like I do," she interrupted, lifting her cup.

A hot flush of anger replaced the cold-air flush on his cheekbones at the thought of being the latest in a long string of men teaching Marissa something she wanted to know.

What exactly are you teaching her anyway?

"When you know what they'll say," he finished. "What they'll think."

She shrugged. "I've liked every man I've had sex with. He's liked me. I have a hard time getting worked up about that."

After what I've been through was the unspoken end to that

sentence. It sounded very friends-with-benefits, except she still used that casual, half-mocking tone that removed all emotion from the argument. He waited a minute. He was a slow learner when it came to Marissa Brooks, but he *was* learning. If he gave her time and space, she'd talk.

"It's hard to be alone," she said finally. "I got lonely. I wanted someone to touch me but I didn't want to have to promise undying love or link the rest of my life to his just to be touched."

She'd lived up to everyone's expectations of the wild, vibrant girl who'd go anywhere, do anything with anyone because she'd been going everywhere and doing everything with him.

Almost everything. Not sex. She'd been more than willing. As desperately as he'd wanted to have her in every way he could, he'd refused, settled for the motorcycle, drinking, partying. He'd lived for those nights at Brookhaven.

It never occurred to him that she'd lived for them, too.

"You taught me that," she added. "You taught me how much touch can mean, even without sex. I kept looking after you left."

A steel spike, thin, flexible, razor sharp, slid between his ribs, into his chest cavity. Cutting off his air, his ability to speak. Because he was still silent, she went on. "Good girls make the trade or keep their legs closed. I didn't do either. That makes me a slut."

Physical intimacy was impossible to avoid in the Corps. He'd spent the night in foxholes with three other guys, sharing body heat to stay warm, lived in tents with other members of his platoon where his personal space was his cot and his footlocker. He'd held guys when they cried, carried wounded men down trails and up ravines.

He'd been in fistfights that were as intimate as any sex he'd ever had. Until Marissa.

"Needing touch makes you human," he said before she could say anything else. "That's all."

They worked the rest of the day in a silence broken only

by brief discussions about measurements, techniques, and a good stopping point. He sent Marissa to get lunch, and while she was gone removed the rest of the rotting siding. They had the sides wrapped when twilight fell. He packed his meager tools back in his truck. Marissa hoisted her tools into her truck bed, then stood by her door for a moment.

"Coming back for more tomorrow?" she asked.

Her eyes were bottomless dark pools in her face. "Yes," he said. "What are you doing tonight?"

"Get some food in my stomach, take a hot bath, go to bed. It's a work night," she said.

"Got it," he said, still studying her.

She got in her truck and turned the engine over. "See you tomorrow," she said over the diesel's rumble.

A train of thought chugged through his mind as he drove back into town. Her father taught her to dream. He taught her to need, then left. Consequently, he'd taught her to endure. Neither one of them taught her anything about fulfillment, or dependability. If she knew anything about that, it was thanks to Chris. Now Adam was back, and according to Keith, taking his place at the end of a line of men teaching Marissa something she needed to know.

He didn't want to teach her anything. He wanted to give her everything.

None of this was supposed to happen. None of it was part of the plan. But sometimes a mission objective shifted, encompassed more than was originally thought possible. In that case, actions spoke louder than words.

She needed touch. He could give her touch.

17

MARISSA KICKED THE door closed behind her and slumped into one of the two chairs at her narrow kitchen table. She sat there for a few moments, eyes closed, hands loose on her lap, and catalogued her aches. Hands, shoulders, back, thighs were all beacons of pain, flashing intermittently every few seconds, never at the same time. Adam had been a huge help, a capable assistant who didn't feel the need to tell her how to do something correctly, but his help meant they did more work in eight hours than she usually did in sixteen, so she was just as tired. Sitting for too long wouldn't help the situation, and the only way to stave off muscle tears was heat. She needed to eat enough that she didn't get lightheaded in the bathtub, then have a long soak. But first she had to take off her boots.

The tiny living space held all the warmth she pumped into it, so she pushed her watch cap off and hung it by feel on a lower hook in the double row by the door. Then she bent to her boots, unlacing one, then the other before toeing them off. They also went by the door. She sat for another minute while her brain worried over the mantel situation, then pushed the play button on the answering machine.

Alana's cultured, warm voice bounced around the tiny

space, reminding her that the books she'd ordered through interlibrary loan were due back in a week. Marissa deleted the message, then opened the cupboard in search of a can of Chunky soup she could reheat in the microwave and scarf down while the water ran into the tub. The books dealt with the practicalities around cruising in a sailboat; she'd keep the books up to the last minute, rereading them in light of her single experience with sailing.

Going back to work after thirty-six hours had been much harder than she'd let on. Before her afternoon on the *Resolute*, she'd harbored an obsession about sailing, but had no real experience to back it up. Now . . . now she knew exactly what she dreamed of, and didn't have. She left the unopened can of soup on the counter and walked into the bedroom and picked up the box compass in its lovely wood case. The needle swayed with the movement, but remained oriented north. She knew which direction she would go. West, to San Diego, home of three hundred sunny, breezy days a year.

Knuckles rapped smartly at the door. She set the box compass down and returned to the kitchen. The dark shape cast on the braided mat in front of the door told her who her unexpected visitor was before she put her hand to the knob. She opened the door to Adam, holding a cardboard-topped foil pan of what smelled like hot lasagna. More foil enclosed a loaf-shaped object on top of the pan, which she judged to be garlic bread. Green beans lay in a jumble in steam-condensed sides of a plastic container.

He didn't speak, just gave her a small, wry smile. The delicious scents drifted into her nostrils on a wave of genuinely cold air, and her stomach rumbled like rocks in a tumbler.

"Is that from Gina's Diner?" she asked, like it made a difference.

"Of course," he said.

"Thank you," she said, and stepped back and admitted him into the kitchen, where his wide shoulders and heavily muscled chest promptly took up most of the remaining space and all of the oxygen. He shrugged out of a backpack she hadn't noticed because the straps were the same color as his black long-sleeved T-shirt. The bag hit the floor with a solid thump, then he uncrimped the edges of the metal pan holding the cardboard lid, and steam rose into the air.

"Still hot," he said with satisfaction.

"Did you order that ahead?" she asked. The half-empty pan was the kind of takeout container Gina used when she cooked for a church gathering or the Rotary Club.

"I bought the pan and she took it off the specials menu," he said. "I left some for Mom. She's delivering curtains to a customer in Brookings. Plates?"

Her mouth watered as she gathered plates, forks, knives, and napkins. "Do you want a beer?" she asked.

"Yes," he said as he slid two huge slabs of lasagna onto the plates.

He dished up green beans, then took the plates to the table. She followed with a beer for him, a glass of ice water for herself, the loaf of bread balanced on top of her glass.

"Looks good," she said.

They dug into the food, and once she had a few bites in her stomach she was able to eat more slowly. Gina specialized in comfort food—burgers, macaroni and cheese, steak, lasagna. It was a good, hearty meat-based red sauce, and lots of cheese melted on top. She watched him polish off his helping while she finished a piece of garlic bread.

"Want more?" he asked.

"This is plenty," she said. "Thank you."

The helping of seconds he brought back to the table was as large as the first. She watched him methodically decimate the lasagna, and felt a smile tugging at the corners of her mouth, as if the exhaustion undercut her determination to keep him at arm's length. He finished the bottle of beer, then tilted his head and looked at her, his gaze assessing her. "What?" he asked.

"Nothing. Just watching you." He fit here, with her, at this tiny table. Too bad they couldn't live out their lives in Brookhaven's servants' quarters. "What's with the bag?"

"That's my gear for tomorrow." When she lifted an eyebrow, he added, "I'm throwing myself on your mercy, Ris. The futon's killing me."

She could do this. She could let him into the house but keep him out of her heart. "What will people say?" she asked lightly.

"I don't give a damn," he said. The silence stretched between them, then he said, "I'll earn my keep."

"What do you have to offer?"

His gaze went lazy, heated. "Massage."

Her flirtatious mood disappeared. She sipped her water. "And this has nothing to do with what I said this afternoon about needing to be touched."

"No, it's got everything to do with that."

At least he was honest with her. "It's really not necessary," she said.

"Think of it as an experiment," he said angelically. The tone of his voice made her smile, but the heat in his eyes made her belly drop six inches in a hot rush. "It's just a massage, Ris. You still have to ask me for sex. You have any massage oil?"

As a matter of fact, she did. She nodded, then stood to clear the plates, but he stopped her. "I'll do that. Go get ready."

In the bedroom she turned on the bathroom light and closed the door partway, leaving a narrow swath of light across her unmade bed. She got a bottle of massage oil from her nightstand, stripped, then crawled between the flannel sheets and pulled the covers to her chin to stay warm while she waited.

Adam closed the bedroom door, turned the baseboard heat to high, and stripped down to his boxer briefs. He climbed into the bed but to her surprise he arranged them so he leaned against the headboard, with her back to his bare chest, the covers pulled up to her neck. His heart beat solidly against her spine while he pulled the elastic from the bottom of her left braid and began to loosen the plait.

"What are we doing?" she asked.

"Just relax," he murmured. "I've got you."

He had her, all right, tucked into his body, his erection thickening in pulses against her bottom. But she could handle the inevitable conclusion to this massage—taking him inside her body. It was the possession he took when he learned her secrets that scared her.

He unraveled her right braid, then slid both hands into her hair and massaged her skull with strong fingers. A wave of relaxation so strong she shuddered under its force coursed down her nape and into her shoulders, where it lapped and eddied against her tight muscles. He kept that up for a few moments, fingertips urging the muscles under her scalp to soften, surrender. She let her head tip forward, felt the tight resistance in her nape. Her hair slid forward around her face, darkening her vision while his hands move to either ear. He massaged her earlobes between thumb and forefinger, then moved up the outer curve of her ear and back down again. Her head drooped on her neck.

"Where did you learn to do that?" She'd had massages before, from other guys, usually halfheartedly as a warm-up to sex. They lasted five minutes before the hands on her back shifted to her breasts or her ass. Adam would get there eventually, but he was making an effort. A real effort.

"The base had all kinds of amenities, including therapeutic massages. At twenty bucks for an hour it was a smoking deal. After a week on patrol, humping over a hundred pounds of gear up trails and down ravines, it was worth every penny. Apparently massage heals sore muscles better than anti-inflammatories." Using both hands, he swept her hair over one shoulder, baring her nape. His thumbs stroked either side of her neck before he grunted disapprovingly. "Lie down on your front."

She shifted, automatically placing her hands under her forehead until he guided them down to her sides. He gently tucked the flannel sheet around her hips, leaving her back bare from nape to the top of her ass. With her eyes closed, each sound registered distinctly in the dim, quiet air. The click as he flipped open the massage oil bottle top, followed by a little gurgle as liquid trickled out. The slick sound of the oil between his palms. Then his big hands spanned her back, his thumbs slipping along the groove on either side of her spine, the tips of his fingers trailing over the outer edge of her ribs, curving down to her breasts and abdomen. With a firm, slow touch, he squeezed her shoulders and upper arms, then stroked down again.

"You're tight," he said. "Knotted up." On the next sweeping pass over her back, his thumbs probed at various spots on her back, one just above her left shoulder blade, another at the small of her back, a third just below her ribs.

She stiffened when he pressed a little harder. "You know what you're doing?" she mumbled.

"I can't name the muscles and I don't have a fancy technique, but I won't hurt you."

She felt like she should say something, carry on a conversation while he worked on her back, but the honest truth was that his hands on her skin created a distance between her mind and her mouth. The words would come from very far away, deep inside her soul, seep from her slack mouth and into the cocoon of her bedroom. She'd already said too much, but Adam made it so easy to talk. He'd hurt and been hurt. He'd seen horror and suffering. He was unflappable, and he didn't judge. At the end of the telling, he'd open another door for you. Offer absolution, and a future. Stand with you as you walked through the door.

But she had to take the first step.

A sigh shuddered from her at the thought. To counter it she focused on his hands. The oil coating his palms softened the scrape of his callouses against her skin, but the lingering slight roughness somehow kept the contact from being purely therapeutic.

"Do you have blisters?" she asked, the words sluggish and muffled by the flannel pressing into her face.

"Stop thinking, Ris," he said, his voice low, calm. The repetitive glide of his palms against her back lulled her into that drifting black space, until his thumbs returned to the knotted muscle above her left shoulder blade. He focused on that knot, rhythmically swiping one thumb, then the other, over the tight muscle, deepening the pressure until she felt more than heard a pop and the knot released.

"Better," he said with satisfaction as he continued to knead the spot.

"Much," she said. "You have strong hands."

That was the appeal, having all that strength devoted to giving her pleasure in every sense of the word. Holding the hammer and pry bar, lifting siding, offering lasagna and garlic bread, massaging knots from her muscles, caressing her breasts, holding her hips as he pounded into her from behind . . . all for her. Licking flame flickered along nerve endings he wasn't touching. She shifted restlessly under him.

"Too hard?"

"It's fine," she said. Her erogenous zones were pressed to the flannel sheet, yet heat continued to pool deep in her belly.

"Turn your head to the other side."

She did, and he went to work on the knot beside that shoulder. This one proved more stubborn, and he left it for a minute to knead the slackening muscles along her spine and in her lower back before he returned to the stubborn knot. Unexpectedly, his hand slid up to grasp her nape, massaging her neck with a firm grip that made her all but purr. When he applied both thumbs to the knot again, it dissolved.

With it went the last of her restraint. She'd never known touch like this. Touch meant sex. It meant rough fingers on her nipples, a belly against hers, hair-roughened legs shifting over her inner thighs as a man's shaft stroked into her. It meant a fist in her hair when she wanted it, the sensitive, thin skin of a hard cock stretching her lips, pressing against her tongue. She gave nothing real to the man in her bed, nothing truly herself because he asked for nothing real, nothing truly herself.

For Adam she would give everything. He coaxed longing to life like flame in a campfire, kept it simmering until the edges of her skin dissolved into the space around her. She writhed again, the soft texture of the flannel sheets stimulating her nipples from awareness to need. Trapped and desperate, she braced her forearms against the mattress and pushed, lifting her upper torso off the bed.

"What's wrong?" he asked.

She peered over her shoulder at him. "Lift up," she said.

When he did, she rolled once again to her back and stretched her arms over her head. Sweat gleamed on his face and heavy shoulders, and his cock strained at the elastic of his boxer briefs as he stared down at her exposed torso.

"Please," she said.

"Always," he said, then bent forward, using his body weight to apply pressure to her shoulders, collarbone, and upper arms. The muscles stretched and loosened even as the need tightened deep in her belly. She arched a little, trembling as his hands swept down her ribs to her hip bones, fingers still massaging her back while his thumbs swept over her abdomen. He repeated the movements, with each stroke caressing more of her breasts but never quite touching her nipples.

She held her breath in anticipation, released it on what was rapidly becoming a pleading sigh. When he finally did close his thumbs and forefingers around her nipples, pleasure cracked through her body and into her pussy. She undulated but his hands moved, stroking down along the indentation of her waist until only his thumbs met just above her mound, still barely covered by the flannel sheet. Her gasp wasn't just in anticipation of those thumbs spreading her sex for his tongue; his fingers dug deep into her buttocks, finding muscles tight and sore from kneeling or crouching all day.

A chuckle rumbled from deep in his chest. He did it again, pressure slipping from her collarbone to her shoulders, releasing tension she hadn't known she was holding in. From there his hands curved down to cup her breasts, squeezing and massaging without mercy before drifting down. Ribs, waist, hips, ass, again and again and again until she was somehow both limp with pleasure while need fisted deep in her sex.

This time when she pushed against his inner thighs with

her legs, he shifted and let her spread for him, tugging the sheet and blankets to the foot of her bed as he did. Without his touch to anchor her to the bed, she felt like she was floating as she watched him shove his shorts down and off, smooth on a condom, then kneel between her legs.

His face was oddly intent as he planted his palms beside her shoulders. Braced over her, he held eye contact as the broad head of his cock nudged into the swollen folds. Sweat trickled down the side of his face, trembled on the edge of his jaw, then plunked to her collarbone.

Touch. Oh God, touch. Even with the thin barrier of latex separating his skin from hers, when he tilted forward and slid into her body, inch by slow, excruciating inch, there was no denying the raw, immediate message shooting from her nerves into her brain. This was what she'd been missing all those years. Adam's touch. Inside and out, slow and gentle or rough and careless, it didn't matter. She'd needed Adam's touch.

He withdrew and pushed back inside again, his thick cock surging over sensitive, swollen flesh. Her eyes dropped closed even as her hands found his arms. She wrapped her fingers around his wrists, then slid her palms along taut muscles and hard bone to his shoulders. Without thinking about it she curved her arms over his shoulder blades and pulled.

He settled over her, his cheek to hers, and she reflected on a new facet of touch. Rough-stubbled jaw against soft skin. Breath huffing against her ear as he maintained his pace. The heavy weight of his body pressing her into the mattress. She dug her fingers into his shoulders and clung to him as he moved, pulses of sensation washing from deep inside her out to the edges of her skin. The normally solid boundary between her and the world that disappeared when she took the wheel of the *Resolute* wavered again, then vanished as release flung her into blackness. She was only vaguely aware of Adam's hard shudders as his cock pulsed inside her. Slowly her body knit itself back together, ribs joining to spine, hips and legs, elbows and shoulders and wrists and fingers weaving into the fabric of her body. His belly pressed against hers with each rapid, shallow breath, slowing as the seconds stretched into a minute. He kissed her, soft and sweet, then pushed back and withdrew from her. The sudden sense of being solitary where she'd been united, the flesh of two joined into one a mere moment before, swamped her. Her hands trembled as she reached for the layers of covers that anchored her in her sleep.

Adam appeared in the bathroom door. "Still want that bath?"

"No," she said.

The bed shifted, the displacement telling her he'd sat down beside her. Gentle fingers loosened hair clinging to her sweat-dampened face, then tucked it behind her ear before cupping the back of her skull. "You okay?"

The answer to his question was *Maybe*, because he was in, under her defenses, behind the barbed wire separating her from the rest of the world. "No one's ever touched me like that before," she said, purposefully evading his question.

"What do you mean?" he asked cautiously.

Languidly. Leisurely. As if the touch itself was the point, not sex. "Without it leading somewhere."

His hand shifted to her shoulder. "That went somewhere," he pointed out.

She lifted the shoulder under his palm, not denying the truth. "Only after I asked."

A long silence followed, and she wondered if he was putting together pieces in the silent stretches, or if he just regretted coming over to say hello that first night. Had the dangerous separation of Adam and *this Marine* ruined any chance of him being able to love? Whatever he thought, he moved over her and stretched out between her and the wall, grunting with satisfaction as he stretched out to his full length. A smile curved her lips as she drifted between postcoital haze and sleep.

"Ris."

"Hmmm?"

"We need to get the mantel."

The wedding was just days away, pushing her back to the wall. "I know."

"Tomorrow. After we finish Mrs. Carson's house." He paused, but she didn't say anything. "It'll make for a long day but we don't have much time left."

"I know."

"You won't be alone. We'll do it together."

He needed this as badly as she did, she realized. He needed to repair what he'd destroyed. One way or another, they both needed Brookhaven restored. But then what?

18

THEY WORKED THE next day in near silence. She'd expected a steady stream of chatter intended to bolster her resolve, pointing out what she could do with a finished house. Turn it into a bed and breakfast. Sell it. Offer tours to summer visitors headed for the nearby towns of De Smet or up the interstate to North Dakota. But once again she'd underestimated Adam. From the moment her alarm went off, he limited his comments to questions about the job, double-checking measurements, clarifying next steps, getting her lunch order. Just like yesterday, she completed more than twice the work in half the time.

"That's it," she said after she shot the last nail into the new siding. She looked around the messy side yard. "Let's get this cleaned up and under a tarp again. I'll pick up the leftover siding next week."

He stacked the few remaining lengths of siding on the pallets while she walked around to the front door and knocked. Mrs. Carson opened the door, dressed in polyester slacks and a navy sweatshirt decorated with appliquéd pumpkin vines. "I'm all finished," Marissa said. "If it's all right with you, I'll come back next week to get the unused siding and the pallets. I've got another job to get to."

"That's fine," Mrs. Carson said. She held out a check carefully written in old-fashioned penmanship. "I'll get you the rest next month."

"Sure," Marissa said. She folded the check and put it in her pocket, then trotted down the cement steps to the sidewalk. Adam stood by the driver's door. "What was that about getting you the rest next month?"

"She's on a fixed income," she said. "I let her pay me in installments."

"You're a pussycat, Brooks."

"For good people, you're right," she said.

"I can drive if you're tired," he said.

She walked right up to him, then tipped her head back and looked up at him. He stood there, arms folded, feet braced, shoulders as wide as the window, trying to make this as easy as possible for her. But she had to do this herself. "I'll drive," she said.

This time she took the county roads, avoiding the interstate and a procrastinating coffee run. When she turned onto the road leading to The Meadows, the familiar fear crawled up her chest cavity, sharp-spiked tail swishing in her belly, claws hooking in her ribs, breathing cold ice on her heart and lungs even as her pulse skyrocketed out of the red zone. When the sagging white mailbox appeared in the distance, she focused on the silk-gray horizon, called up the memory of the *Resolute* slicing through the water, and gunned the engine as she jerked the wheel to the right and steered her truck into the two parallel ruts that served as The Meadows' driveway. Overgrown weeds brushed the undercarriage as they bounced toward the house. Adam white-knuckled the door handle, but she braked to a halt just before she hit the rotting steps.

"Jesus *Christ*," he said when his seatbelt locked, then exhaled and looked over at her. "You okay?"

Her blunt-cut nails dug into her palms as she took stock. The fear, the paralyzing fear sat frozen between her diaphragm and her throat, as if shocked into immobility. "I feel like I kicked what I thought was a solid wall and found it was rotted through."

He considered her, his hazel eyes alight. "So you've got one foot in the wall."

"So to speak."

"Let's kick that motherfucker all the way to the ground."

She gave a sharp laugh. The demon-fear inside snarled, but curled its claws more tightly around her ribs. She let go of the steering wheel and shoved her door open, stepping into an ice-tinged wind out of the north. Winter was coming. Come the weekend, Brookhaven would be complete and Delaney and Keith would marry.

Searching the wood for the least rotted path, she climbed the front steps, Adam hard on her heels. "Does it look like Brookhaven inside?"

"The footprint and structure are similar," Marissa said absently. "The difference is in the interior layout. Imagine if Brookhaven's movable walls were permanent, making little rooms. Then imagine those rooms ornately decorated to within an inch of their lives."

"A typical Victorian."

"Exactly."

She rapped at the front door, waited, then rapped again. Eventually she heard the shuffle of slippered feet against wood. The door opened, and in the doorway stood a tiny, slender woman with a puff of white hair and clear blue eyes. She wore faded blue slacks, slippers, and a thick yellow cardigan buttoned over a turtleneck.

"Hello, Mrs. Edmunds," she said.

"Hello, Marissa," she said, her gaze unclouded and unblinking. "Come in, please."

They stepped into a house so cold she could see her breath. Whatever heat remained from summer had dissipated into fall's coldest air, swirling like water around the wood floors. Without a word, Mrs. Edmunds led them through a music room and a library to the family parlor at back of the house. Dominating one wall was a mantel nearly identical to the missing one at Brookhaven, but without the vast space of Brookhaven's great room, the massive piece hulked over the room like Devils Tower over the surrounding plains.

"We've had no wood rot," Mrs. Edmunds said clearly. "No termites. It's sound."

"May I?" Marissa asked.

At the tiny woman's nod, she walked to the windows and drew the curtains. Gray light seeped into the room, dulled by both the thick layer of clouds that threatened more rain and the caked South Dakota dirt partially obscuring the view of the land around the house.

Adam stepped up beside her and ran a palm over the wood. "Good color," he said as he transferred years of dust and dirt to his cargo pants. "Dimensions match?"

"Not exactly. Design elements from Brookhaven showed up in all of Henry Dalton Mead's later houses. He varied size and shape, played with details, but in The Meadows he replicated Brookhaven's mantel almost exactly. He wrote in his journals that the mantel symbolized the family, hearth and home," Marissa said. "I think he was as obsessed with Brookhaven as I am. If I take it all, I hope I can fit the pieces into what's left of Brookhaven's mantel."

"I'm glad you came to take it," Mrs. Edmunds said, her gaze moving fondly over the woodwork. "My son and his wife insist I move into an assisted living facility."

"They don't want The Meadows?" Adam asked.

"They want the money the land will bring," she said. "Every few months a lawyer shows up and makes me an offer. I always refuse. I don't care about money. I care about The Meadows. But I can't take care of the house anymore."

For the first time her voice shook, just a little, before she cleared her throat.

"I'm so sorry," Marissa said. They waited while she pulled a crumpled tissue from her sweater pocket with trembling fingers and dabbed her eyes. Adam stood quietly by the fireplace, not flinching or shifting, his rock-solid presence holding the fear at bay. "We never discussed a price," she began.

"It's yours, my dear," said Mrs. Edmunds.

"Mrs. Edmunds," she said carefully, "a mantel like that would bring thousands of dollars at auction. It's a piece of South Dakota history, and an example of Art Deco interior design. I can't take it for nothing."

"The mantel goes with you as my gift, or it gets bulldozed with the rest of the house. My children don't want their heritage. I'll give it to someone who appreciates it."

In the clear, crisp words Marissa heard the backbone of settlers, a woman who'd buried her husband and two of her children, a proud woman who had nothing left but a house her family didn't want.

She swallowed hard, first her pride, then the lump in her throat. "Thank you."

"You're welcome."

"I'll take good care of it. I promise."

"I know you will," she said.

"I'll get the tools," Adam said.

"I'll get them," she said. The fear was shifting inside, swinging its barbed tail like a cat on the hunt, preparing to pounce on her throat.

Adam reached for her hand and gave it a squeeze. "Stay inside," he said.

"Your husband?" Mrs. Edmunds asked.

"No," she said.

Mrs. Edmunds gazed at the woodwork, a heartbreaking failure creasing her soft face. "I'll be in the kitchen if you need me," she said, and shuffled off.

Adam returned with her tools bundled into the sheets and tarps she'd brought to protect the wood from scratches and the rain, and laid them out on the floor. Marissa picked up a pry bar and went to the far end of the wall. He stood opposite her, each probing for a chink in the finely joined woodwork to jimmy the first piece of wood from the wall.

"I've got one," Adam said, his long fingers wedged in a panel at shoulder height.

She joined him at the other end, and lifted her hand to his. "Feel that?"

She felt both the gap between the wood and the plaster, and his hand, warm and rough and strong over hers. "Yes," she said, and cleared her throat. "I feel it. Good find."

He stepped back to give her room. She closed her eyes and called up the sensation of rocking waves and sunshine, then wedged the end of the pry bar behind the flat walnut stile. It gave easily when she put her weight behind it. Adam caught the stile before it hit the floor.

Their eyes met, hers wide, his calm and assessing. "Doing okay?" he asked.

She could only nod. Each breath shrank the demon-fear, and each beat of her heart thawed a little more of the fear's ice. Then she traded him the pry bar for the stile. "Your turn."

He hefted the thin metal tool, then stepped up to the wall. One smooth motion and the panel dropped free, into his hand. He considered it for a moment, then turned and handed it to her.

Based on the look in his eyes, she wasn't the only one facing down a fear. "Doing okay?"

"Yeah," he said. "I am. Let's finish this."

Once they had the start, removing the rest of the rails, stiles, caps, and shoes went easily. Adam used his greater height and arm strength to pluck the pieces from the wall, while Marissa numbered and wrapped the segments carefully and carried them to the truck. By the time they'd detached the mantel, laid it in the bed of the truck, and secured the tarps, it was nearly nine o'clock. She looked in on Mrs. Edmunds, sitting on a kitchen chair with a cup of tea in her lap, watching television.

"We're leaving, Mrs. Edmunds," she said. "Thank you again."

"A house like this needs people in it," she said, apropos of nothing. "Family, friends staying for long visits, servants. Fill that house with people, dear. Marry that nice young man and fill the house with a family. One person isn't enough."

Heat rushed into her cheeks. "He's not here forever, Mrs. Edmunds."

"Oh," the elderly lady said. "What a shame. Good night." She stared at Marissa for a long moment, then turned back to the television.

Adam waited on the porch, feet spread, arms crossed over his chest as he stared into the night. "I'm starving. Kicking through walls is hungry work."

She joined him on the porch. The endless blackness rolling away from the single pool of light mirrored the feeling inside her. Emptiness. She'd lived with the anxiety and fear for so long its absence didn't bring relief, but rather a vast void.

What next? What do you do next, without this obstacle in your path?

One step at a time. Next step: hang all this woodwork.

"We can drive through somewhere on the way home," she said.

He held out his palm for the keys. She dropped them in his hand, and kept one hand on the truck as she checked the tarp before climbing into the passenger seat. Without an anchor, the slightest breeze might send her drifting into the blackness.

The next thirty-six hours were a blur. They arrived at Brookhaven at ten with the paneling and half-full cups of coffee from the drive-thru run, and unloaded everything to get it out of the rain. Marissa ducked into her apartment and returned with sheets to use as drop cloths and her photo album. Laying out the pieces on the floor sapped what was left of her caffeinated energy.

"Here's a picture of the original woodwork," she said, flipping through the pages until she found the right one.

Hands on his hips, Adam glanced from the picture to the pieces on the floor, and from there to what was left on the south wall. The right-hand side took the brunt of his destructive energy. Panels were missing from the floor, up along the fireplace and over the mantel, and up a good portion of the chimney. The left-hand side was intact, although several larger panels splintered under attack by out-of-control teens wielding a pry bar and hammer.

"So we've got to make this," he said, pointing at the sprawling pieces from The Meadows, "fit onto that," he pointed at the south wall, "by Saturday."

"I've been up for twenty hours. Let's catch a couple of hours of sleep," she said through a yawn.

"You go ahead," Adam said. "I'll sleep later."

His tone reminded her of how he sounded when he was thinking through an engine teardown and repair, the absent look on his face indicating he'd pulled up a mental schematic of the engine and was thinking through possible problems. He stood by the fireplace, hands on his hips as he considered the wall. When she hesitated, he turned to look at her. "Unless you don't trust me to do this."

To fix what he'd wrecked. To repair what he'd destroyed. Defensiveness lay under the even tone, and she walked up to him and gave him a gentle kiss. "I trust you. I just want you to sleep, too. Your weekend's busier than mine."

"I'll be fine," he said. His hand rose under her braids to massage her neck. "You got the panels here, Ris. Let me work at this for a while. Get some sleep."

She did, falling into bed fully clothed after she set her alarm for seven. She woke up alone, and made a pot of the Intelligentsia coffee before padding into the great room in her wool socks. Adam lay on his stomach, his cheek pressed to the hardwood, breathing deep and easy.

In front of him on the floor lay a new version of Brookhaven's gorgeous, fine-grained wall. He'd pried the rest of the woodwork off the south wall and interspersed it with the paneling from The Meadows, rearranging some pieces so the larger panels flanked the fireplace and the smaller ones, interspersed with medallions, rose above the mantel and drew the eye up, emphasizing how lofty the ceilings were, how expansive the room really was.

He'd somehow been able to see what she couldn't, that in order to make the pieces fit, she had to take down the rest of the wall and envision something entirely new, yet true to the house.

Moving as quietly as she could, she set the cups of coffee down next to Adam, then sat down cross-legged beside him and sipped her coffee. Day spread through the room, the dull streaky light less illuminating the wood and the room than grudgingly sharing space with it.

Either her presence or the aroma of coffee penetrated Adam's brain, because his breathing shallowed, and he lifted his head.

"You could have come to bed," she said.

With a grunt, he rolled over and bent his legs at the knees. "Easier to just lie down."

In other words, he'd worked until he dropped. "How long have you been asleep?"

He glanced at his watch, rubbed his eyes, looked again, then said, "Twenty minutes. Plenty of sleep. Sleep's for pussies." He looked at the now-blank wall, then at her. "I had to take the rest of the paneling off to make it work in my head. I'm sorry."

"Don't be," she said softly. He'd needed this, perhaps as badly as she'd feared it. Like her standing at the entrance to the yacht club, he stood just hours away from making right what he'd torn apart so long ago. The dove gray light lay on them as they finished the coffee, sitting in a companionable silence.

His eyes were bloodshot but calm as his gaze skimmed her face. "Got your nail gun?" he asked.

"Ready when you are."

He'd left the shoe pieces on. Marissa picked up the first rail and walked over to the wall. Adam hunkered down beside her and held the flat piece flush and steady. *Thunk, thunk, thunk.* Broad panels interspersed with stiles made for quick work, and before long, they were on their feet, working with small, detailed pieces. They stopped for a quick lunch of soup and sandwiches, then Adam hauled her ladders up from the barn.

"I'm almost done with my to do list for *the wedding*," she said, poised above him as she sent nails into the wood. "What about you?"

"What about me?" He eyeballed the top of the mantel and reached for the level.

She gave him a lifted brow. "How's the speech coming?"

"Fine," he said shortly.

"Want to run it by me?"

It was his turn to raise eyebrows. "You want to hear what I have to say about the sacrament of marriage and lifelong fidelity?"

"Sure," she said.

He tapped the paneling, indicating she should do her part with the nail gun. "You can wait until the reception, like everyone else," he said. "Unless you won't be around at all."

"I need to be available for the wedding planner, in case anything goes wrong."

"What is it with you and Keith?"

"He said something he shouldn't have . . ." She paused, then went on. "I lost my temper and took a swing at him."

He nodded at her shoulders and upper arms, flexed with the effort of holding a piece of paneling over her head. "He's lucky you missed."

She cut him a glance. "I didn't miss. Asshole had a nice shiner for a week."

"What did he say?"

"I ignored most of it. He always was good with words, just funny enough that you didn't notice the sting until afterwards, but when he got drunk he got really nasty. I hit him when he asked what he could trade for a fuck, or even a blow job."

A muscle flexed in his jaw, but his hands held the bottom of a mid-sized panel while she held the level to the top. "Why didn't you tell me?"

"Because this was six years ago, and we hadn't talked for six years. Because it happened just after you got engaged to

Delaney. Because you're his best man." A muscle flexed in his jaw at this list of reasons why she hadn't turned to him. "What do you see in him?"

"Back then I thought he was funny. Up for anything. He was one of the few people who stuck around after what happened."

"You weren't a threat anymore. Of course he hung around. You had something he'll never have. You had . . ." She searched for the right word. "Presence. Even coming from nothing and going nowhere, you were the guy everyone wanted to be with. Including Keith. You were lit up inside in a way he wasn't, and he was jealous, but too smart to let on. He's a master manipulator."

"He didn't manipulate you. Not then. Not now."

"He scares me. Still does. I avoid him."

"Why don't I scare you?"

"You're not that scary, Collins."

"Back then at any given point in time I was ten seconds away from a total flameout. As I proved that night. But you wanted to be with me."

Rivulets of rain coursed down curves of red and yellow glass in the floor-to-ceiling windows stretching from corner to corner of the house's west wall, reminding her of the people crossing Michigan Avenue in Chicago. Timing was everything. "I loved that about you," she said quietly. "You were going nowhere at a hundred miles an hour, but I loved you."

He went still, then looked up at her. "I didn't know how to love anyone then."

Not even himself, she'd bet. "You learn by doing."

The last panel and stile went on in silence, snugging between the next panel, cap, and wall like it was all made to fit the house. Marissa climbed down off the ladder and joined Adam in the middle of the room. He cleared his throat and put his hands on his hips to look at the wall. The walnut wood gleaming around the fireplace, setting off the painted white tiles that had somehow survived decades of use and neglect. "Done," he said with the air of a man who'd tied off a loose end.

"And done well," she replied. "Look." She picked up the photo album and stood beside him. The page she'd chosen held photos of house parties from the twenties, women in white simple dresses sitting on furniture clustered around the fireplace. A man in white trousers and jacket leaned against the mantel, a cigarette clasped loosely between two fingers. "That's my great-grandfather, Reginald Brooks. I'm not sure who the ladies are."

He studied the picture, comparing the image to the wall in front of him, then tapped the picture. "Look at the tables," he said.

"What?" Then she peered more closely at the other details in the picture and saw what he meant. Reginald Brooks held his father's box compass, and the other instruments lay on the tops of the tables on either side of the fire. She'd been too focused on the wall to notice that detail. "Oh."

"Someone packed them away in the trunk in the barn," he said, "but it wasn't Josiah, or even Reginald. I'd say your dream's not as far-fetched as you think."

"I'll dream another dream if you let yourself off the hook for what happened twelve years ago."

He shot her a look, thick lashes narrowing around those changeable hazel eyes. "I don't get to let myself off the hook, Ris. That's not for me to do." He made a big show of looking around. "So, what's next?"

"The wedding's next."

"After that."

She shrugged, then began collecting movers' blankets and tarps and sheets from the floor. "Clean the first floor from top to bottom."

"That's a task, not a plan."

She just looked at him. "My only goal now is to get through today. I'll deal with the rest of my life Sunday morning."

"Fine. Let's go down to the barn and finish what we started twelve years ago."

"It's forty-two degrees out. The barn's not heated."

He stepped close and slid his hand under her hair to cup

her nape. For a moment she thought they'd end up right where it all began, on the loft floor, but this time with nothing stopping them. His hand flexed at her nape as his lips brushed hers, both touches hot and possessive. Lightning cracked deep in her belly, and in her heart. Her hands curled into his sweatshirt even as she gave him a little push.

"I can't. I've got things to do."

Another devastating kiss, then his hand dropped and he stepped back. "Me, too. I've got to run to Brookings to get the tuxes. Rain check?"

She glanced over his shoulder and smiled with lips still tingling from his touch. He followed her gaze, and gave a little huff of a laugh. "It's going to rain on Delaney's wedding day."

"As long as she's marrying the man she loves, then the weather doesn't matter."

Adam's face closed off. "Do you think she is?"

"I'm the wrong person to ask," Marissa said wryly. "I wouldn't marry Keith if he was the last man standing."

"Seriously, Ris. Do you think he's the right man for her?"

Something she didn't recognize lay behind the question. "Even with his many faults, I actually do think he'll make her happy, because he wants to give her what she wants. Sometimes that's enough."

"Is that enough for you? Someone who can give you what you want?"

It took her a long time to find the right words. "It's more complicated than that," she said.

She wanted him, the boy she'd known and the man he'd become, for better or worse; not the defenses he wore like armor, protecting him from feeling anything at all. But while the words trembled on the tip of her tongue, she knew better than to speak from exhaustion, or from the high emotions Delaney's wedding seemed to inspire in everyone it touched.

"See you after the wedding," he said, then bent and kissed her.

19

NOTHING CHANGED HIS morning run routine, not even a wedding. Adam sprinted down Main Street, past the Heirloom; past Herndon and Son, Attorneys at Law; past the library and the gas station and the mini-mart; breathing in desperate, hard huffs, pushing his endurance to the limit. Getting four hours of sleep in the last forty-eight was no reason to slack up on physical conditioning, so he avoided Oak Street entirely. No tripping today. No falling. Today something ended, some element of his past gone terribly wrong, and he wasn't taking any chances that he'd miss it.

Brookhaven was done. Finished. Restored to as good as new, if not better. He'd left Marissa sitting on the floor in the great room, her arms wrapped around her knees, studying the gleaming wall of walnut. Every seam was perfect, every line true. In the peculiar light of a cloudy day, the color in the room glowed as if lit from within. The stained glass. Marissa's red jacket. Her eyes, the dark chocolate pools at once bitter and sweet with the weight of over a hundred years of history and reputation.

As good as new. If not better. So why did she look like she was arming for battle? Why did he feel so old and used up, like all he'd done was put a bandage on a gaping wound?

When he came through the kitchen door his mother was finishing her coffee and watching the morning news. "Morning, sweetie," she said.

"How'd it go yesterday?" he asked.

"Good. She loved the curtains, and asked for cards to give her friends. We'll see. What about you?"

"Brookhaven's done." He bent to unlace his running shoes. "We finished polishing the mantel and wall at four this morning. Marissa's cleaning the main floor before the wedding planner and her team arrive at nine."

"That girl knows how to work," his mother said when he straightened. She switched off the TV. "I'm glad. It's time to close that book, and move on."

He stared at his mother, sitting so calmly in the tiny kitchen. "I've been telling her that," Adam said. "She doesn't seem to think there's anywhere to go."

"Give it time," his mother said. "Some people need more time to let go of what was, and see what could be."

An uncomfortable feeling settled in the pit of his stomach. He got to his feet. "Pictures start at ten," he said. "I'm going to be late."

She just smiled at him with those sad, sad eyes. "Sure, sweetie."

He shaved and showered, then dressed in jeans and a shirt. According to the timeline Keith emailed him, everyone would dress at the church. The photographer would take pictures of the individual groupings prior to the wedding, with the bride and groom carefully segregated to preserve the appearance of Keith not seeing Delaney before she walked down the aisle. He was due at the church at nine with the tuxedoes still hanging from the hooks in the backseat of his Charger, but what occupied his thoughts when he walked into the kitchen was Marissa.

"You said you were bartering sewing for the bathroom with Marissa, right?"

"That's right."

"Did she give you an invoice? I'll pay her. She needs cash if she's going to pay back the bank."

"She didn't give me a bill," his mother said.

"What about an estimate? You paid for the materials, but—"

"Adam, this is none of your business."

He looked at her. "It is my business, Mom. She's dying here. Dying inside. She's got a dream, and she needs money to make it come true. Curtains and throw pillows won't get her there."

His mother returned his look for a long moment, then set her coffee on the table and went into her sewing room. She returned with a picture and handed it to Adam. He looked at it and his heart stopped.

Caribbean ocean and white sand. The background was a white cotton canopy bedecked with flowers, fluttering in the breeze. The blond model wore a wedding dress, or maybe a slip. The relatively demure neckline was supported by two thin shoulder straps. The lines were deceptively simple, perfectly cut to the model's slim curves. The hem ended at her ankles, just the right height to keep the dress pristine as she walked the beach, bouquet of white roses in hand, and smiled up at her new groom.

"It looks simple, but it's not," his mother said. "That kind of tailoring, fitting her body and her body only. It's a fair trade for her work. We both know that."

That was Marissa. So simple on the surface, working construction, fixing up her house, sleeping with men she liked, and all the while as complex as the ocean's depths. "I know," he said. You didn't grow up with a seamstress without gaining some understanding of sewing basics. "When does she want you to make this?"

"She said she'd let me know."

So she had plans and dreams she'd kept hidden from him, even now. Dreams of a beach wedding. A wedding, period.

"She married Chris at the courthouse in her high school

graduation dress," his mother said. "When she brought me
that picture, she said the next time she did it, she'd have a
destination wedding on the beach and she wanted to wear that
dress. It costs nearly three thousand dollars in a boutique. I
can make it for the cost of my renovated bathroom."

Ris would carry red roses, not white. Red for passion. Red
for love. Red for life. With her dark hair and vibrant eyes,
she'd make the model look like a pale shadow. "Does she have
anyone in mind?" he said through his tight throat.

His mother just smiled at him, soft and sad. "Maybe you
should ask her."

Tomorrow. He'd ask her tomorrow, after he got through
this hellish day. He kissed the top of his mother's head and
headed out.

Everything ran on schedule: pictures, the lunch Delaney's
parents hosted, more pictures, signing the wedding license
with the pastor prior to the service. But at ten minutes past
two the string quartet was still playing prelude music, muted
but audible in the vestry. Keith's groomsmen were still half-
tanked and had chosen to sit down in the first pew and breathe
very carefully. Adam stood, feet braced apart, back to the
wall beside the door to the sanctuary with the minister, who
adjusted his clerical collar for the sixth time while Keith
looked at his watch.

"Weddings always begin late," the minister offered Keith.
"Perhaps the rain is causing a delay. The dresses have to be
arranged just so."

The wedding was scheduled down to the minute according
to the timeline Delaney put together, but it wasn't the late
start that had sweat breaking out at Keith's hairline. It was
the close quarters. Ever since Adam got home, Keith had been
careful not to get caught alone with his best man. "Why don't
you go check and see what's holding things up?" Adam
suggested.

"Of course," the minister said. "I'll do that." He opened
the door and slipped out.

Position was everything. The only way out of the room

was through the door Adam stood beside, into a sanctuary full of their friends, neighbors, and colleagues forming the network of relationships that stretched across eastern South Dakota. Nowhere to run, nowhere to hide, and they were having this conversation now.

Adam folded his arms across his chest, and met Keith's gaze.

"You look like shit," Keith said. "Rough night?"

"I spent the last four days with Ris, installing the paneling and the mantel."

"She finished it? Good for her." Keith shoved his hands into his pants pockets and rocked onto the balls of his feet, then back down. He seemed to look everywhere except Adam's face. "Look, man, I know you're not happy about what I've been saying about her, but you haven't been here the last twelve years. You don't know what she's really like."

The sharp cessation of sound that signaled a combination of adrenaline and single-minded focus necessary to stay alive in combat shut out everything except his breathing, and Keith's. *This ends, now. Right now.*

"You're right. I haven't been around for the last twelve years. I may not know what a lot of people are really like. Let's see how I do," he said casually. "So Marissa's an opportunistic whore, trading sex for training."

"I wouldn't go that—"

"Anyone else you want to bring me up to speed on? Like, for example, you? Or Delaney?"

Keith had a good courtroom face. He didn't even blink. "What are you insinuating?"

"You guys were always friends. High school first, then you went to SDSU together, and you were in grad school down there at the same time," Adam said. "It would make sense that she turned to you after I broke up with her."

"Yeah," Keith said casually. "She was pretty upset when you . . . ended it with her. I didn't mean for it to happen, man."

"That's what happened?"

"That's what happened," Keith repeated. "Why bring it up now? I thought we were cool."

"I'd be cool with friends turned to lovers. That's romantic."
A shift in the music pinged in his awareness and he paused,
but it wasn't *Canon in D*, Delaney's wedding march. "What
I wouldn't be okay with is you fucking her behind my back
while I was deployed. That would not be *cool*."

Keith still wasn't blinking, but he stared at Adam like a
mouse stared at a snake.

"I could live with the two of you falling in love while I
was gone," Adam continued. "It happens. I wasn't here. But
sending me a picture of her in a hotel room, naked and freshly
fucked, that is not cool at all. Not for me. Not for her."

"What the fuck are you talking about?"

He was talking about deception, cheating, a backstabbing
betrayal he'd never, ever anticipated, covered up by a bold-as-
brass-balls whirlwind romance. "Keep your voice down,
man," he said easily. "The quartet's not loud enough to cover
you lying at the top of your lungs. You know exactly what I'm
talking about. Ten months ago you took a picture of Delaney
after you had sex with her. Maybe more than one, but you
only sent me one. Based on her expression in the photo, she
knew you were taking it, which is really bold for her. Then
you downloaded it to your computer and sent it to me. You
used an anonymous e-mail address, but they're still linked to
IP addresses. My buddies in intelligence had the location in
ten minutes."

At that, all color drained from Keith's tanned skin. "You
sent that picture to your Marine friends?" he hissed. "Jesus
fucking Christ!"

"No," Adam said precisely. "What Marines do with pictures of cheating girlfriends is print them out nice and big
and post them on a wall of shame. Every time a new picture
goes up guys gather around and trash the latest addition. The
conversation gets sexual and explicit faster than you went
down when Marissa hit you."

Keith's eyes were enormous, his shoulders tensed under
the gray tuxedo jacket.

"I didn't do that, either. I did forward the e-mail without the attachment. Had a response back in twenty minutes. There's no privacy anymore, *man*." He'd never forget opening the e-mail and seeing a screen-filling image of Delaney, her hair tumbled around her face, on her belly on the bed, her ankles crossed behind her. She was smiling at the camera, gaze soft and languid and utterly at peace. Happy. Not a hint of regret at the cheating.

That's what destroyed him. Not the evidence, not the tawdry picture. She had no regrets. He breathed them, swam in them, ate them for breakfast, and she'd just walked away from them.

"It wasn't enough that you stole her, or that you fucked her while I was deployed. You had to make sure I knew. Does she know you sent it?" When Keith didn't reply, Adam said, "Answer me, motherfucker."

The words, spoken in a tone as thin and soft as a coiled whip, cracked into the air, and Keith startled. "I didn't send you any fucking picture," he bluffed.

"They traced the e-mail to your office IP address." Adam rattled it off, then widened his eyes mockingly. "So your dad sent it? Wow. Awkward. Sorry, man. I'll ask him at the reception."

Keith didn't look pale, or red anymore. He wore a greenish tinge that signaled near vomiting. "You wouldn't fucking dare."

He didn't even have to think about it, just let twelve years in the Corps, five deployments, let the dragon inside push against his skin. "And then you asked me to be your best man."

It was the perfect cover. No one would ever consider the possibility of Delaney and Keith cheating behind Adam's back if Keith asked him to be his best man. They'd fucked around on him, and then used him to cover up the infidelity.

"You fucking said yes! I thought you never got it!"

Laughter barked from Adam's chest. "You knew I got it."

"It took you a month to break up with her."

"I was trying to figure out if I could forgive her. When I decided I couldn't, I broke it off."

"She was planning your wedding!"

"And fucking you at the same time."

Keith colored. "Stop saying that."

"Were you *making love with her* in that hotel room? Is that what you whispered when you took off her clothes and spread her legs, that it wasn't screwing around, but *making love*?"

The mockingly snarled words put Keith on the offensive. "You weren't right for her. You were never right for her, not before you joined the Corps, not even after you came home wearing glory and honor like a suit of armor. You never knew what she wanted, what she dreamed about. All she wanted was to have a family. A quiet life. You promised for years and years that you'd come home, marry her, settle down. You broke your promise again and again."

"I was serving my country," Adam bit off.

"That's an excuse. Delaney was one, too, and eventually she figured that out. You didn't love her. You needed her and you used her, but you didn't love her."

"Don't you fucking tell me how I felt about Delaney."

They spat words at each other like bullets, Keith carefully staying out of arm's reach but using his best weapon, twisting words and arguments to his advantage. "If you loved her you would have given her what she wanted. Fought for her. That's what I did. I fought for her," he snarled, color high on his cheekbones. "I've loved her since high school. When she looked unhappy, I went after her."

"Why didn't you fight for her when I was sending packages and calling and writing her in college?"

Keith broke eye contact at that. "Like I could compete with the uniform," he said.

"If she loves you, the uniform's no competition. If she doesn't, then the uniform doesn't matter." This seemed patently obvious to Adam, but Keith just glared at him. "You waited until she was weak, alone. You waited until I was six months into what I'd promised would be my last deployment before I started grad school."

"I waited until the second time you promised that, asshole. I put her first. You made her wait and wait, while all her other friends got married, had babies, grew the fuck up! Playing soldier at eighteen's one thing. Who makes a fucking career of that?"

Adam would not hit him. He would not pound this pussy motherfucker's perfect teeth down his throat and ruin Delaney's wedding. Because while Keith's tactics were street-fight dirty, his analysis was dead-on. He'd promised he'd be out two years ago. Instead he'd volunteered to take another Marine's place in a rifle platoon destined for Afghanistan.

Because, like Marissa and Brookhaven, he had no idea who he was without the Corps.

"You e-mailed a picture of her, naked and unfaithful, to her fiancé. How is that putting her first?"

"Do you love her?" Keith challenged.

Training compelled him to meet Keith's gaze while oxygen evaporated from his lungs like in a vacuum. "Until I saw that picture, I did."

"I *do*. I've loved her since I was fifteen years old. I'm going to give her the only life she's ever wanted. Starting today."

"Why did you ask me to be your best man?"

The mask finally broke, a high-pitched victory on Keith's face. "So you'd know I won. You'd have to watch me marry her and know I'd beaten you."

Adam held his gaze for a beat, then another while some vitally important truth struggled up from the depths of his subconsciousness, not quite pushing to the surface. What did bubble up, however, was that Keith's idea of victory was the saddest thing he'd ever seen. "Delaney was never about winning or losing," he said quietly.

"It's always about winning and losing."

The silence stretched taut, then the string quartet went silent. The minister opened the door and peered into the small room. "The maid of honor ripped the hem out of her dress getting out of the car, but they're finally ready," he said, then looked from Adam to Keith. "Is everything okay?"

"Fine," Adam said. "We'll be out in a minute." The minister prudently withdrew and closed the door.

Keith looked at him, defiance and shame staining his high cheekbones. "Are you going to tell her?"

The air in the vestry was hot and close, tinged with flop sweat and anger, and the smell coupled with the emotions made him slightly sick to his stomach. The whole situation was so fucked up he couldn't tell right from wrong anymore. Tell Delaney, ruin her wedding day, and taint the rest of her life? Tell her and take the chance she already knew? She'd made her choice, made it badly, but she'd made it. Betrayal, anger, revenge, seduction, cheating, deception, malicious intent . . . it was the complete opposite of the life he'd intended to create for himself, and the man he'd wanted to be.

He looked at Keith, and shook his head. "No. She knows what she's done, and she wants this anyway. It's one fucked-up, sorry way to begin a marriage, but this is her dream day. I'm going to give her what she wants."

Keith said nothing. As the muted, gentle prelude to *Canon in D* finally began, their cue to emerge from the vestry and take up position on the chancel steps, Adam opened the door for Keith. When his former best friend reached the door frame, Adam blocked the door with his outstretched arm. Keith flinched.

"It's Marine, motherfucker. Not soldier. *Marine*. Get it really fucking straight in your head, because if I hear one more bullshit rumor circulating about Ris, I'll drive the forty minutes from Brookings and use your face to teach you the difference." Adam let his arm drop. "Move."

The rustling and shifting of bodies cued him to look up from his position behind and one step down from Keith. Delaney appeared in the open double doors leading into the sanctuary, her arm resting gently on her father's, her bouquet of white roses clasped in her left hand. Her hair was smoothed back from her face, and she radiated joy, simple, sheer joy, as if it made no difference that her marriage began in infidelity.

Delaney and Mr. Walker stopped at the steps leading to the altar. Her father lifted her veil and kissed her cheek, then she stepped up beside Keith and smiled up at him. The minister cleared his throat and began the service with an earnest prayer for the families and with that, Adam stood and watched his former best friend and his ex-fiancée marry.

He'd thought about this moment, imagined it in order to determine if he could follow through with Keith's outrageous request. It was supposed to be simple, returning home to clear out boxes and stand up for Keith and Delaney, knowing who and what they were as he did it. Instead of emptiness or righteous anger, all he could think about was Marissa. The dress she wanted for her next wedding, the finished wall at Brookhaven, what the wedding ended and the completed house began. The light in her eyes when she took the wheel from Nate, the completely different yet equally intense glow emanating from her skin when she took Adam inside her.

He'd come home to slam the door on his past, and walk away. Instead his past held hopes for his future, hopes he intended to share with Marissa tonight.

20

SHE FELT LIKE a virgin on her wedding night, all a-tremble with nerves and excitement.

Marissa stood by the flung-wide double doors, ready to welcome the cream of eastern South Dakota's high society: doctors, lawyers, bankers, real estate agents, teachers, guidance counselors from the surrounding counties. The bride and groom greeted the wedding guests by releasing them from the pews, eliminating the traditional receiving line so the guests arrived at Brookhaven before the newly married couple. Car after car pulled under the awning the wedding planner's staff hastily erected at noon to protect guests from the relentless rain. Stacey waved her magic wand and produced rugs to minimize the dirt tracked onto Marissa's shining hardwood floors.

A Cadillac pulled under the awning. Clarence Emmitt, the driver, stooped and balding, emerged from the car as one of the valet-parking staff helped his wife from the passenger seat. Lucille was ninety-five if she was a day, and despite the line of cars extending down the drive and onto the road, she hurried for no one. "My goodness gracious, Marissa," she said as a smiling cloakroom attendant helped her shed her sapphire blue coat. "Brookhaven looks just like it did when your grandfather was alive. I remember dancing in this room when I was a girl. Your grandfather used to have the most wonderful parties here."

She was so astonished it took a moment for the words to register. "Thank you," she said.

"Helen," Lucille said, turning to the next guest arriving. Helen Lamont's husband, sons, and grandsons farmed fourteen-hundred acres just west of Walkers Ford. "Do you remember the parties when we were girls? Helen met her husband here at Brookhaven," she confided to Marissa.

"Oh, yes," Helen said, staring wide-eyed at the tin ceiling and wall sconces. Fires sparked and popped in the great room's two fireplaces, casting flickering shadows into the rapidly darkening room. "I met a few young men here before him, too. The parties lasted for days."

The house filled gradually, the laughter and chatter brightening the great room as much as the light from the candles on the tables. Wait staff circulated with appetizers and drinks as guests headed not for tables draped in linen table cloths and decorated with white roses, but instead admired the gleaming paneling, the smooth plaster, the windows casting muted sunset colors over the great room.

"Good thing we blocked off the staircase," Stacey said. The wedding planner adjusted the discreet earpiece tucked under her carefully styled hair, then nodded at the velvet rope strung between the oak newel posts. A brass sign clipped to the rope read *Private*. "You'd be rousting guests from the bedrooms all night."

She'd done that before, when high school parties got out of hand. Marissa just smiled and basked in the delight infusing the great room.

Brookhaven, newly restored and polished to gleaming, had stolen the show from Delaney Walker-Herndon's wedding.

"I did it, Dad," she whispered. "I did it." Savor the atmosphere, the mood, the sheer happiness suffusing the room. She'd done it. She'd taken the broken-down, hopeless ruin of a house and restored it to glory.

Tucking her silk wrap more securely in her elbows, she moved through the great room as it filled, listening as older folks reminisced, explaining the house's history to people too young to remember anything but a tumble-down shell. She listened to the rain pelt the windows, sputtering and gurgling onto the terrace, and tried to remember Chicago. Sunshine. Wind. Michigan Avenue. The Art Institute. Coffee and scones and a down-filled comforter. A shower built like a seraglio.

"That's a beautiful wrap," Stacey offered.

"Thank you," Marissa said. She wore it with the gray side in, the shadings from light gray to dark blue facing out. For something so thin and insubstantial, it warded off the damp, chilly air quite effectively.

Stacey eyed it covetously. "Where did you get it?"

"Banana Republic in Chicago," Marissa said. With Adam, because he cared enough to give her silk and dreams.

Adam. Somehow, despite her best efforts, Adam was entangled in her life, her dreams. She closed her eyes. Bright sunshine danced behind her lids. The wedding was nearly over. The rain would end. Winter would come, and Adam Collins would move on.

As if thinking of him conjured him out of the rain, he appeared on the terrace. Raindrops dotted the broad shoulders and arms of his tuxedo jacket, clung to his close-cropped hair and the line of his jaw. Moving easily and without self-consciousness, he skimmed his hand over his hair and jaw, then flung the collected water to the side as he crossed the stone terrace. Lightning cracked through her, and her heart stopped.

"He's the best man, right?" Stacey asked absently.

"He is," Marissa agreed.

They watched Adam walk three more strides, then Stacey started. "That means Mrs. Herndon's here!" Barking orders into the headset she wore, she hustled off to the front door, where Keith's Jeep Cherokee was scheduled to drop off the newly married couple, leaving Marissa to open the French doors to the terrace and let Adam in.

"Where did you come from?" she asked.

"I parked in the barn," he said. His gaze skimmed her body like a physical touch, but lingered on her face. He slipped two fingers between her arm and the wrap, and tugged the silk across her shoulders, leaving her in the same outfit she'd worn the day he came home: a black knee-length skirt and the gray satin halter. Her hair tumbled down her back in loose, shining waves. She wore mascara and lip gloss, and Adam's gift.

Based on the heat in his eyes, she might as well have been naked.

"You look amazing," he said, then bent to kiss her.

"Thank you," she said. The chaste brush of his warm lips left her mouth tingling.

"Better than amazing," he whispered, then kissed her again. His tongue gently touched hers, and she shivered. He stepped back and carefully arranged the wrap around her shoulders, then pulled her hair free. "Can't have you getting cold," he said.

Stacey reappeared carrying a battery pack and a lapel microphone. "Here's your microphone," she said, and held it out.

Adam just stared at it. "What's that for?"

"Your speech."

That explained the speakers in the corners opposite the heaters. Marissa shook her head.

"You're serious," Adam said.

At Stacey's nod, Adam took the battery pack and ear piece from her. Stacey faded into the crowd. He handed them to Marissa, then opened the two buttons on his jacket and held the fabric away from his side while she clipped the battery pack to his waistband, the heat of his body radiating against her fingers, then attached the small microphone to his lapel. "The word *circus* comes to mind."

Marissa shrugged and left her hand on his chest. Adam turned on the battery pack. She patted the microphone and the muffled reverberations echoed through the room. He switched it off again.

"Dreams come in all shapes and sizes. Some women dream their whole lives of their wedding day," she said.

"Did you?" he asked.

"No, but . . . if I could do it again, I'd choose a ceremony on the beach at sunset. Something simple," she said. A round of applause signaled the bride and groom's arrival, but Adam's gaze never left hers. "A day of sailing was enough. You don't have to marry me in the Caribbean to make that dream come true."

She'd been teasing him, but he went still, his gaze searching hers. "I take marriage too seriously to make it simple wish-fulfillment," he said.

She blinked. "Where did that come from?"

He looked over her shoulder to where Delaney stood in the center of the room, surrounded by friends and family, glowing with happiness. Her pavé-diamond wedding band caught the weak light pushing through the rain, tinging her wedding dress and the white linens with gray, as if they were washed at the Laundromat with cheap soap in a load of dirty socks.

Stacey wove through the crowded room. "We're ready to begin serving supper," she said.

"I'll find you later," Adam murmured to her.

"I'll make it easy on you. I'll be in the kitchen," she replied.

More compliments slowed her progress to the kitchen. Everyone in the room either remembered Brookhaven at its height or had heard stories from family members. Don Lemmox was engrossed in taking pictures of the paneling, and had to be shooed from his position near the newly paneled wall. Marissa remembered his daughter was recently engaged, which explained the interest in the house and Stacey's careful arrangements. She wasn't sure how she felt about that. The point of hosting Delaney's wedding was to show off the house, not to start a second business.

In the kitchen she settled onto a stool and watched the caterer somehow manage to be in four places at once, overseeing the wine and champagne and trays of delicacies on their way out the door while checking on the prime rib and potatoes keeping warm in the ovens. Food flowed out to the tables, and Marissa did her job of staying out of the way. After the meal Stacey's efficient servers cleared the tables, then circulated with glasses of champagne, the cue for Adam to give his speech. Marissa moved to the door between the kitchen and the great room. At a nod from Stacey, Adam got to his feet, and even at this distance his straight back and squared shoulders marked him as different from the rest of the guests. Men slumped or slouched or pulled at their collars and cummerbunds. He reached into his jacket and turned on the microphone clipped to his lapel.

Marissa could have heard a pin drop in the enormous room. Without preamble or clearing his throat, hands loose and relaxed at his sides, he began.

"The Roman statesman Marcus Tullius Cicero said 'Nothing is more noble, nothing more venerable than fidelity. Faithfulness and truth are the most sacred excellences and endowments of the human mind.' Everyone in this room has known Keith since the Herndons moved to Walkers Ford nearly twenty years ago, and Delaney since she the day she was born. One quality characterizes this newly wedded couple; it's their fidelity to each other, to their families, and to the community.

"The Marine Corps motto is *Semper Fidelis*. Always faithful. It's the core of what it means to be a Marine, underscores everything you do, every action you take. Fidelity to your brother and sister Marines binds you more strongly than friendship to your oath of service, to God and country, but fidelity isn't the sole province of the military. Fidelity is the bond that keeps marriages and families together. It strengthens communities, makes love true, keeps honor untarnished, and it is at the core of the love and commitments Keith and Delaney share with each other, a gift that will flow from them to all of you. They've taken Proverbs chapter three, verse three to heart: 'Let love and faithfulness never leave you; bind them around your neck, write them on the tablet of your heart.'"

From her position at the back of the room Marissa could see many of the older women's mouths move, reciting the verse as Adam spoke, his voice ringing clear and strong. "As you give, so shall you receive. May your marriage be blessed with love, and may we all return to you the love and fidelity you've shown us." He lifted his glass and turned to the newly wedded couple. "To Keith and Delaney."

Keith and Delaney echoed in the room and up from the tent in the meadow below, the call and response as automatic and heartfelt as the most passionate churchgoer's. Marissa wondered if she was the only person to see Keith's jaw clench as he returned Adam's salute, or see Delaney's gaze focus intently on the gathered guests rather than look at Adam.

The tableau broke when Delaney's maid of honor rose to give her own speech, followed by both fathers, before Stacey cued the waitstaff to break down the head table to open the dance floor. Keith and Delaney shared their first dance. Delaney danced with her father, then with her father-in-law. Finally the wedding party retook the floor and the deejay urged everyone to join them.

She was sitting on a stool, out of the chef's way as they packed up the remaining food for transport to the shelter in Brookings, when Adam walked into the room as if he had every right to be backstage at the wedding. Without a word, he crossed to the back door that led out to the kitchen garden, then to the meadow. One hand in his pocket, with the other he held the door opened and tilted his head in a *let's go* gesture.

Marissa looked out the open kitchen door into the rain-pelted night. "Really?" she asked in disbelief.

His edgy smile, a mere flash of white teeth in his tanned face, didn't make it to his eyes. She slid off her seat, folded the silk wrap and left it on the stool, then kicked her heels under it. The ground was too wet for anything less than flat feet.

"Where are we going?"

"The barn. Ready?"

At her nod Adam shucked his tuxedo jacket and held it over their heads as they dashed through the rain, skirting the

enormous white tent before crossing the gravel spread in front
of the big double doors. She held his coat over her head while
he put his shoulder to the door and opened it enough to let
her slip inside. Rain pelted the shingled roof high overhead,
and the interior was dark as night.

Beside her Adam flicked on a flashlight. His white shirt
clung to his heavy shoulders and upper arms, and she didn't
look much better. She was soaked to her waist, and her hair
hung in damp tendrils around her face.

"I must look like a drowned rabbit," she said as she coiled
the heavy mass to wring it out.

"I like the look on you," he said. "Remember?"

Water trickled from her hair to the floor as she looked at
him. She did remember. The water fight, the thrill of the
chase, the heat of the summer sun on her face and back as
they made out in the loft. The feel of him, hard and slick with
sweat against her, the soft, helpless sounds she made and he
made as they pushed the limits further and further. Him saying no, again.

*You can do whatever you want. I want you to do whatever
you want. Please, Adam. Please.*

But he didn't, wouldn't. He'd held back, locked it all away
until, half-crazed with longing, he'd gotten drunk, gotten on
his bike after a vicious summer thunderstorm, and raced Josh
to his death.

"I remember," she said quietly.

The flashlight beam flicked away from her face to the ladder leading up to the loft. "Let's go," he said.

She went up first while he held the beam steady on the
rungs, then he followed her. The light swept over first a heater,
then a battery-powered camping light Adam turned on. The
weak light brightened the space enough to reveal a bed made
of an opened sleeping bag and several blankets in the middle
of the loft.

Memory and longing, that most potent mix of emotion and
desire, shivered through her as she stood by the ladder. Seeing
this, Adam turned on the space heater. "Sorry it's so cold,"

he said. "I didn't want to turn it on earlier and burn down your barn."

"I'm not cold," she said quietly. Uncertain. Touched. Aroused. Very aroused, as the state of her nipples had nothing to do with the temperature. "When did you do this?"

"Between the ceremony and the reception. It didn't take long. It's not exactly the Palmer House," he said, looking around at the makeshift bed, the dark, silent space. She heard only the rain on the roof. In here there was no trace of the wedding, no lights or laughter or music. Just her and Adam, wet and torn by desire, back where it all began.

"Is this some kind of revenge thing, to get back at Delaney?" she asked.

Hands deep in his pockets, rain clinging to his hair and face, he looked at her, unsmiling. "This is about you and me, Ris," he said. "It's always been about you and me."

Intrigued by the purpose in his voice, she lifted her chin and met his gaze, but despite the longing cracking in the air like static electricity, she made no move toward him. Twelve years ago she'd drawn him up the stairs and down on the floor. She'd stripped off his shirt, and hers. Unzipped his jeans, and hers. This time, in this place, with the reality that was oh-so-real outside the door, he would have to come to her. Waiting for him made her heart slam into her breastbone and her breathing go shallow.

He crossed the slight distance between them and turned her so she faced the dim light emitting from the camping lantern, then stood behind her. Another shiver coursed down her spine when his warm fingers gathered her hair and sent it tumbling over her shoulder, then found the ties holding up her drenched halter. Two tugs and the fabric dropped forward. Adam unzipped her skirt, then pushed both skirt and halter to the floor. Light illuminated her bared torso while his body heat radiated against her back.

She wore nothing but black lace panties, her hair, and the shadows hovering all around them. His breath huffed warm and soft against her collarbone as he looked down at her body.

His breathing deepened, rough and slightly unsteady as he looked at her. Her nipples hardened and he cupped her breasts, rolling the hardened tips between his thumbs and forefingers before sliding one hand up her throat to turn her mouth to his.

One hard, demanding kiss and she opened to him. A little whimper escaped her before she lifted one hand to his nape and the other to his ruthlessly shaved jaw. A deep kiss, another slick and hot and teeth-clicking and wet, then he turned her so she faced him. She went up on tiptoes to press the length of her nearly naked body to his and kiss him like she'd kissed him when they were young, without hesitation, without reservation. Holding nothing back.

His hands skimmed down her back and slid into the black lace boy shorts she wore. He cupped her ass, pulling her tight against him, and for a moment she thought they might set the barn on fire with their peculiar, potent chemistry. But he lifted his head to break the kiss, then shrugged out of his tuxedo jacket and draped it around her shoulders. She smiled and slipped her arms into the sleeves. The rain hadn't penetrated the lining, so the jacket was warm and heavy around her nearly naked body. While he unfastened his cummerbund and dropped it on the floor, she examined the black tuxedo studs fastening his shirt, figured out how they worked with the buttons, and began to undo them, dropping the released studs into his jacket pocket.

"Ris," he said.

She flicked a glance at his face to see him focused on her. The open jacket revealed more than it hid as it brushed against the curves of her breasts and her hip bones. She got the front of the shirt open, fumbled with his cufflinks until they came free in her hands, and got the shirt and white T-shirt underneath off as well.

He went to his knees on the sleeping bag and pulled her down with him until he was flat on his back. She straddled his hips, shook back her hair, and kissed him. His hands roamed through her hair, fisted, tugged, then swept down her back to her ass, again and again, until she was undulating against his erection. It was like no time had passed at all. Different season, different decade, two seemingly different people, but it was the same. The heat, the passion, the need, the sense of total rightness; and this time he held nothing back. He rolled her, pushed the jacket to the side, baring her body to his gaze, his hands. His competent, strong fingers trembled when he hooked in the waistband of her lacy boy shorts and tugged them off.

On his knees between her legs, he planted his palm beside her shoulder and moved his finger in slow, tight circles around her clit. Heat blasted at her, from the space heaters, from his body. Open to him, utterly helpless, she stared up into his eyes as the heat built, tightening muscles and setting fire to expectant, desperate nerves. She could feel pleasure washing up her body in ever-growing waves, felt her own gaze grow desperate and demanding and molten all at once. And still she looked at him, fighting the urge to close her eyes and go deep inside her body, wanting, needed to see what was happening in his own eyes.

He didn't look away, either. He didn't look down at his hand, working so intimately between her thighs, or at her pink nipples, or at the way her abdomen tightened and flexed as the pleasure built. He looked at her, no longer avoiding what they felt for each other or how it came out, right there with her in the storm. Rain slapped at the roof in wind-tossed sheets. She arched and gasped under his hand, the noise high-pitched, needy, and almost inaudible over the downpour.

"Go under, Marissa," he commanded.

She did. At the next slow stroke of his finger she let the waves and the rain take her. When she subsided into the padded sleeping bag his hands went to his waistband and unfastened his pants. His erection sprang free as he shoved the black wool down to the tops of his thighs, then dug in the jacket pocket by her hip. When he pulled out a condom, she gripped his wrist.

"Adam," she said. "It's okay. Go under with me."

He went still above her, and for a moment the only sound

in the loft was the steady patter of rain on the roof as she looked at him and he looked at her.

His eyes were dark, mossy green from heat and lust. She could drown in his intense hazel eyes, clear and unguarded in the lantern's steady light. "No unplanned pregnancies," he said. "No mistakes."

No lives ruined.

Her throat tightened. Tears stung her eyes. "Adam," she whispered. She cupped his stubbled jaw and stroked her thumbs over his mouth. "This isn't a mistake. We were never a mistake."

Long moments passed as he remained poised above her, emotions scudding under the blank surface he wore like armor. Her thighs glowed in the light, his hair-roughened legs between hers, his erection above her dark curls. She slid her hands down his ribs to his hips, stroked the soft skin there with her thumbs. "I'm asking. Please. Give me something more than a facade, more than a dream. Give me something real. Give me you."

His gaze searched hers as he lowered his chest to hers. They pressed together, breath to breath, sex to sex, thighs to hips. "Adam, I love you. It's all right. We're all right."

He froze, and long moments passed while his gaze searched hers. She'd never said the words to him before, never told him that truth. But she could, now. Finishing the house made her strong. He made her strong. She could wait for him to finish whatever he'd come home to do.

Time held its heated breath. His response was to align himself with her entrance and push inside. The slick, gliding pressure against sensitive inner walls made her gasp and coil around him. Her heels dug into the backs of his thighs, her arms slid under his to grip his shoulders. "God," she whispered as her eyes dropped shut. "Adam. Oh, Adam."

Still watching her, he withdrew, then did it again. He reached down and adjusted the cant of her hips. Again. Again. Lightning streaked through her, and she tightened around him even more, calling a harsh gasp from his throat.

"Ris. It's too much."

"It's never too much," she whispered with what little air remained in her lungs.

Perfect synchronicity, skin to skin in every way possible, every cell in their bodies working together . . . she buried her face in his neck to stifle her noises, and his hand cupped the back of her head to hold her safe as she cried out and came. Utterly helpless under him, the pleasure wracked her in sharp pulses, sensation heightened with his relentless thrusts until he went rigid above her, and his release joined her own.

He eased down on top of her, taking enough of his weight on his elbows to avoid crushing her, but the heft of his body against hers eased her shudders into trembling, as if trapping the waves and sending them back in on themselves in a physical and emotional feedback loop. *So that's what it could be like*, she thought. *When you get everything aligned, when love welcomes the longing, accepts it, learns to live with it, you make love.*

She swallowed hard against the lump in her throat, inhaled shakily.

"You okay?" he murmured against her hair.

She nodded, unable to do anything more complicated, like talk. Her fingers loosened their death grip on his shoulders, scudded down the damp length of his back, and patted his ass tentatively, prompting a chuckle. He pulled out and reached for a travel pack of wet wipes in a plastic bag by the camping lantern, prompting a chuckle from her as she sat up.

"What's the Marine Corps saying?"

"*Semper Fi*," he said with a grin, then hunkered down beside her.

She plucked wipes from the packet and cleaned up as best she could while he did the same. He found her panties in the darkness and handed them to her, then fastened his pants.

"I'm going into Brookings early next week to look at apartments again," he said as he pulled on his slightly wrinkled shirt. "Want to come along?"

She looked up from stepping into her skirt. "You know, I'm starting to believe you're really staying."

"I'm staying, Ris. I'll graduate, join a firm in Brookings or Sioux Falls, but I want to open an office here in Chatham County and focus on rural sustainable design projects." He gave her a crooked smile. "Brookhaven would make a great space for a home office, and it's always good to have a reputable contractor to recommend to clients."

She felt her heart stop dead in her chest. "You want us to be business partners?"

"I want you to be aware I've thought about it."

She pulled the halter top over her head, then presented her back to Adam. "You don't have to say that because I said I love you," she said, proud of her even tone.

He tied the tapes, then wrapped his arms around her, engulfing her in his warm, solid embrace. "I'm not saying it for that reason. It's always been about you and me, Ris," he said into her hair.

The edge was gone, whatever had simmered under his skin when he arrived from the church, and maybe for the first time their being together made things better for him, not worse. "I know," she said quietly. Always. It had always been Adam, would always be Adam. Forever. And it would be a good life. A very good life. People made very good lives out of far less than the love of a lifetime and honest, important work in the community where her roots ran deep and wide.

Isn't this what you wanted?

Yes, when I didn't dare want anything else!

As if he could hear her thinking, he said, "We'll travel. Not as much as I'd like while I'm in school, but after that, we'll make the time and find the money."

"I know," she said again. It was a storybook ending, the fairy tale she'd never dreamed she could have. Twelve years ago all she'd wanted was Adam, a life with him, whatever life they could scratch together from Dakota dirt and dreams, from sweat equity and passion. But then he'd left, and in the cool, gritty darkness his absence created, different dreams took root and flourished.

She could go back to the old dreams. For Adam she could, and she would. She took a shuddering breath and relaxed back into his heavily muscled body. They stayed like that for a long moment, breathing together. Eventually he kissed the top of her head.

"I should get back," she said. "God only knows what crisis Stacey's handling without me around."

"Stacey could take over supply logistics for an entire battalion and not lose a beat," Adam said, but he let her go.

"Are you staying tonight?" He nodded. "The door to my apartment's unlocked," she said. "Wait for me?"

"Sure," he said, then gave her a crooked grin. "It's my turn to wait."

21

T HE SUNDAY AFTER the wedding was like every other Sunday in Walkers Ford, slow, quiet, traffic on Main Street picking up in time for church, but not before. Adam went home to dig through the last of the boxes; Marissa joined him and his mother at the Heirloom for brunch. The mood in the restaurant was subdued, as if the whole town was suffering from a wedding hangover. Marissa certainly was. They let Adam's mother do most of the talking, a steady stream of chatter about customers and orders, the kind of seemingly trivial background noise that cemented people together. After he took his mother home they went back to Brookhaven and slept for six hours, waking up only for supper and a hot bath that turned into a leisurely, sweet evening in bed.

On Monday, Adam drove his mother to Sioux Falls to pick up a fabric order, and set up appointments with apartment managers in Brookings while Marissa caught up on her books. It was one of the rare fall days when the sun played hide-and-seek with the low gray and white clouds, gilding the very air. Delaney and Keith were off on their honeymoon in Fiji, and Adam was due in a few minutes to pick up Marissa for another apartment-hunting trip to Brookings.

Up to her ears in invoices and billing, the knock on her

apartment door surprised her. Even more surprising was the shape in the window, backlit by the first sun in weeks, too short to be Adam, the shoulders too broad to be Alana.

She opened the door to Don Lemmox, the county's most successful real estate agent. His agency brokered many of the larger land deals in the area, and also auctioned estates like Mrs. Edmunds. She could think of no good reason for him to show up at her door.

"Mr. Lemmox," she said, blinking with surprise. "What can I do for you?"

"Miss Brooks," he said formally, his hat in his hand, "Can I have a moment of your time?"

"Of course," she said, and stood back to let him in.

"I'd like to have another look at the house," he said.

She should have felt a pleased surprise. He could only be back to investigate Brookhaven as a possible reception site for his daughter's wedding, and this was a good thing. The income would help pay the house's operating costs, and pay down her home equity loan more quickly.

"Of course," she said, striving for a smile. "I'll meet you at the front door."

He nodded and resettled his hat on his head. She hurried through the door connecting the servants' quarters to the kitchen, through the great room to the front door. The hardwood floors, efficiently mopped by Stacey and her cleanup crew, gleamed in the intermittent sunlight as Lemmox walked around, examining the plaster, the flooring, the mantel as closely as he had the night before.

"Candlelight hides flaws," he mused, peering at the paneling.

"There aren't many to hide," she said.

"You've done quite a bit of work to the house," he said mildly. His gaze went to the stained-glass windows. "Did you do it yourself?"

"Much of it," she said. "The windows were designed by a visiting artist at SDSU, and Billy did the wiring and the

HVAC. Adam Collins helped me with the woodwork. The rest of the interior and exterior work is mine."

"Where did you find the paneling?" he asked, examining the newly restored south wall in his careful way.

"The Meadows, owned by the Edmunds family."

"Same architect as Brookhaven, correct?" he asked, his two-pack-a-day voice echoing in the empty room.

"Yes."

"It's a good match. That property goes up for sale next week," he said. "She had a stroke last Friday."

She froze, mid-breath, because she and Adam had removed the last, best piece of her house just days before. "I didn't know," she murmured. "Was she . . . ?"

"Apparently she'd had a series of ministrokes last year. It was only a matter of time." He stopped in front of the west-facing windows looking over the meadow that led to the creek. "How much land comes with the property?"

"Twenty acres. All that's left," she said before the odd nature of the question registered. "Why?"

"Last year a woman from Connecticut contacted me, asking about properties in the area," he said, still looking out over the meadow. "She had a Wall Street job and got downsized in one of the recent economic downturns. Apparently she's into yoga and Buddhism, and she got it into her head to open a retreat center, but they're thick on the ground on the East Coast, so she decided to look for untapped markets. She had a business plan," he said with a slightly mocking smile. "I figured her for an East-Coast fly-by-night and told her I didn't have anything to sell."

"Okay," she said, not sure what this had to do with her and Brookhaven.

"Last week I got another call from her, asking if anything new had opened up. 'Somewhere with a little space, so we could build rustic cabins for long-term retreatants,' she said. 'Near water,' she said. 'Something with character,' she said." He looked around the great room. "Something like

Brookhaven. I sent her pictures yesterday. She liked it, and authorized me to make you an offer."

He named a sum so astonishing that for a minute all thinking ceased. Lemmox mistook her reaction for disbelief. "I asked around to find out what you'd put into the house, figured I knew what the land was worth in dollars, but not in family value. This was your family's home for nearly a hundred and fifty years. I told the buyer you probably wouldn't want to sell, so she's making an offer based on the house's newly renovated condition, historical value, and character. It's a fair offer."

He had no reason to lowball her. He'd make a percentage on the sale, so the higher the price, the more he made. But swindling the buyers wasn't in his best interests, either. If the business failed, he'd cheat himself out of an opportunity to sell Brookhaven again. The fair offer, the little voice in her brain told her, was enough to pay off the home equity loan, buy a small sailboat, and leave enough left over for a couple of years of supplies, if she were frugal.

Don't be ridiculous. I don't know how to sail. It's a dream. It's not meant to become reality.

"I got them a good loan through Walker's bank. You'd get a cashier's check on signing." He gave a phlegmy cough, then added, "She wants to take possession as soon as possible."

In one stunning moment the *why* became clear, why she'd felt so driven to finish the house. Restoring Brookhaven wasn't intended to tie her to Walkers Ford. It was intended to set her free.

No angels sang a hallelujah chorus; if anything, the house sat unusually silent. She could leave. She could leave Brookhaven, Walkers Ford, South Dakota, and the entire Midwest; and the thoughts, coming hard and fast, sent a cresting wave of joy through her chest. Thanks to Adam, she now knew what it meant to want something, to desire it, long for it out of the depths of her soul, not out of a desperate loyalty, or worse, fear. Restoring Brookhaven was her duty, one she'd fulfilled without complaint.

Sailing was her desire. That's what Adam taught her, the difference between duty and desire.

A car door closed outside the front door, sending another thought eddying through her frozen brain. Adam was staying. Adam was back home, for good, about to start graduate school, planning their future in eastern South Dakota. Planning it. Not dreaming it.

Your timing always was shit said that oh-so-helpful little voice.

He came through the open front door, his face clearing when he saw her and Lemmox standing in front of the mantel. She gestured him in, and he closed the door, then crossed the wide space, his booted feet loud in the vast, echoing space that was the great room, and her mind.

Adam and Mr. Lemmox shook hands, exchanged greetings. Then Adam turned to her, wary curiosity in his hazel eyes.

"Mr. Lemmox has just made me an offer for Brookhaven," she said in a voice that didn't sound like her own.

Lemmox repeated his story about the woman from Connecticut that wanted to open a Great Plains retreat center, get back to the simple life. The concept of life in Walkers Ford as "simple" made her laugh, the sound startling her back into the chilly room, where she found both men looking at her. She blinked, came back to the oddly lit day, sunlight streaming in patches along the creek and meadow, lighting up one or two windows, then disappearing behind the calico clouds. She came back to Adam, backlit in the windows, his face hidden to her.

The straight spine and squared shoulders told her all she needed to know.

"I need to think about this," she said gently to Mr. Lemmox.

"Of course," he said. "I'll call you tomorrow, see what you've decided."

He walked to the front door and let himself out while she and Adam stared at each other. She couldn't see his face, just the nimbus of sunlight around his head, and she couldn't tell what her own expression was.

"Say something," she said.

"I got the apartment. In the 1921 building," he added. "The guy who rented it got into law school at Michigan. The property manager called today."

"Timing," she said. "It's all about timing, and mine's always been shit."

"Wrong. Your timing's perfect. I've seen that look on your face one other time," he replied. "When we were sailing and Nate gave you the wheel. Right now you look exactly like you did then. You look alive."

"I can't do it," she said. "The house holds a hundred and fifty years of Brooks memories. I belong here. My family is here, buried in the cemetery—."

"Exactly, Ris. They're *buried* here. You're alive. Live!"

She shook her head. "It's an incredible offer, but I can't take it."

"Why not?" He folded his arms across his chest. Braced to do battle with *I can'ts*. "Why not take it and get out of here?"

"I don't know how to sail a boat! One afternoon on Lake Michigan, that's all I've got! How am I going to buy a boat and sail it across the ocean?"

He flung his hand toward the stained-glass windows in the great room as he strode toward her. Now she could see his face clearly, and it was alive as well, passionately intent on making her see what he saw. What he believed. "How did you learn to do any of this? Plaster walls? Plumb bathrooms? Craft windows?"

"Someone taught me," she said quietly.

"Wrong," he said again. "You went after it. You did what you had to do to make your dad's dream come true. Now it's time to make your own dream come true."

The complete reversal in their situations would have been

funny, if it wasn't going to destroy them. "You're part of my dream, Adam. I love you. It's always been you. Not you alone, but you're a part of me. Come with me."

"I can't," he said. "But I'll wait for you."

"Wrong," she said slowly, arms folded, spine straight. "That's what *this Marine* would do, because that's the logical thing to do. You don't have to make up for what you've done, not to me, not to Brookhaven. I need you to love me, to let yourself feel what you felt that spring, what you feel now. Defer enrollment for a year and come with me."

"It's not just you." He shoved both palms over his hair, then turned toward the windows framing the town of Walkers Ford. "I've made more mistakes than walking away from you. I can't keep running from this place. You've done what you had to do to get right with this town. I haven't. I have to stay. Leaving again isn't the answer."

He stood solid and unmoving in the great room. Maybe it was the unusual silence, maybe it was the shift in her internal landscape, but something clicked into place inside her. She finally asked the question she'd avoided asking for the last month. "Why did you break up with Delaney? Why did you come back so early for the wedding?"

He answered without hesitation. "Eight months ago I got an anonymous e-mail. Attached was a picture of Delaney, naked in a hotel room I'd never seen. The picture quality was really good. The sex flush on her face and neck was just starting to fade."

She blinked, not quite comprehending what she heard. "Delaney was cheating on you?"

"So it appeared."

"For how long?"

"I'm not sure. In the picture her hair was the length it is now. She cut it shorter a year or so ago, so sometime in the last year. It may have been the first time, but I doubt it. Delaney wouldn't have let someone take her picture that way unless she was totally comfortable with him."

"Who was she with? Who took the picture?" she asked,

her voice rising with disbelief. "Who *sent* you the picture *while you were deployed to Afghanistan*?" Adam didn't say anything, didn't move, and she made the connection. This was the problem with clearing the fog away. Realizations came out of the blue, hard and fast, things she'd known deep down but didn't want to acknowledge. About herself, about Adam, but not about this. "Keith. She cheated on you with Keith, and that son of a bitch sent you the picture."

"The e-mail address was an anonymous Yahoo! account, but a buddy of mine traced it back to the IP address for Keith's office."

"No one here knew," she said, still in disbelief. "I'm sure of it. Gossip like that would have been all over town."

"It didn't have to happen here. They both have plenty of reason to be in Brookings or Sioux Falls at the same time."

"Did you confront him? Her?" she asked, losing her footing in the conversation as easily as she'd found it. "Who asked you to be the best man?"

"He did." Adam was braced now, legs spread, arms folded across his chest, unmovable. "He never came out and asked me what happened. He was careful about that. Just said he was sorry things fell apart. Then he e-mailed and said they'd been spending time together, and he wanted to know how I'd feel if he asked her out. Would I mind. I knew by this time, knew he'd sent it, knew what he was doing. I wanted to see how far he'd take it, and he took it all the way."

"You never confronted him? You just let him think he'd won?"

"I brought it up in the vestry before the wedding started. Asked him why he'd done it."

A short laugh burst from her lungs. "Because he's a manipulative, self-centered, insecure asshole who gets off on bringing other people low."

His smile was utterly without humor. "You called it twelve years ago."

"Being right about this doesn't make me feel any better. Did he say why?"

"He claimed he'd stood by and watched me string her along for a decade while I went to every school the Marine Corps offered and deployed for guys who had families at home. If I'd loved her, I would have come home to her."

"That's bullshit," Marissa scoffed.

"From his perspective, it's dead-on accurate."

"So you're back, fixing what you think you've done wrong. Me. Brookhaven. Delaney."

"You weren't on the list, Ris," he said with a crooked smile. "You were like you always were, unavoidable. Undeniable. The siren call I couldn't resist."

How could he look at her like that? "I'm not sorry for it," she said.

"Neither am I," he replied, then looked out the windows again. "Keith asked me to stand up at his wedding. I take that responsibility seriously, even if they don't. I had to be sure she was getting what she wanted. Because in the end, he was right. I didn't love her like she needed to be loved."

"No wonder she's avoided you the last month. I thought she was being considerate of your feelings. Why didn't you tell people the truth?"

She knew the answer to that question the moment it left her mouth. When you'd survived vicious gossip, had your name, reputation, and future dragged through the mud, you thought twice about inflicting that pain on someone else. When you'd sweated blood to learn honor and discipline, you thought twice about throwing it away on sordid gossip.

"It's over now," he said. "They're in Fiji. Then they'll come home, and life will go on."

"All the more reason for you to leave Walkers Ford," she said.

"I can't, Marissa," he said simply. "You've had a decade to get right with this place. I spent a decade avoiding what I'd done here. Who I was. Who I am. It's time for me to face that."

"I know who I am," she said. "I'm a Brooks. This is my home. When I was with you, I was something more. I was Adam's girl. Then you left, and I was just a Brooks. I never thought I'd be anything more than that again, but you taught me I could be more. You can, too! You can be more than *this Marine*," she said, her sweeping gesture taking in his straight spine, his cropped hair, his tan, the years of blood and sweat and sacrifice somehow worked into his skin.

"That's sacrilege, Brooks," he said, his humor flashing for just a moment, but then the smile faded. "It would just be more running, and without the uniform and the sacrifice to justify it. The Marine Corps gave me a framework when I needed one. You stayed, and you worked through it. You built the possibility of a future. I left and avoided it. I can't keep running."

His voice was implacable, but she shook her head, felt the tears burn behind her eyes. "Getting the sailboat and getting out of here was just a dream, something to keep me sane."

"That's exactly why you have to do it. It's your dream." He looked around. "This was your father's dream. Construction was Chris's life. It's time for you to live yours. Grab it with both hands."

"I don't need to do it. I'll stay. I'll move to Brookings with you, find a job." She huffed out a laugh. "Maybe I'll go to college. I never had the money before. I could, if I sell the house."

"I want that," he said softly, ache vibrating in his voice. "I want that so bad I feel like I'm dying inside. But I won't keep asking people to put their life on hold for me, and that's what you'd be doing. Living my dream, not yours."

"It's not your dream, either!" she burst out.

"Marissa." His voice cracked into the room. "Close your eyes and think about that day on the lake. Do it."

She did, drawing the memories of the sun and wind from the locked chamber in her heart. A smile spread across her face even as she exhaled against the tears and clenched her fists. "No," she said.

He ignored her. "Keep your eyes closed. Now think about getting an apartment with me in Brookings. Think about trying to find a job there, or going to class at the U."

She couldn't do it. The smile melted, and the familiar sense of clouds and rain settled over her. She opened her eyes, shook her head.

"You have to go."

"No," she repeated. "No. I don't."

"Don't ask me to take you knowing what you'd give up to be with me," he said.

"Don't tell me how much I can bear to sacrifice." The words came out more sharply than she intended, and he went still. She glanced around pointedly at the house that nearly consumed her. "I can handle a lot, Adam. Giving up a dream I had no hope of realizing until last week isn't much at all in the big scheme of things."

"Don't you see?" he asked gently. "I don't want you to give up anything for me. I want to give you everything I have, everything I am, everything you've ever wanted."

"What are you going to do if I sell and stay?" she challenged.

"Ris. Don't ask me to bear that. Please."

The remark stopped her cold, cold enough to feel hot tears spill down her cheeks. He relaxed his arms, and she walked into them, felt him pull her close, hard enough to hurt. One hand cupped her hair as he laid his cheek on the top of her head. They'd never lose the demons, the memories, the what-ifs and could-have-beens and regrets. The regrets weighed more than anything else, and timing really was everything. They stood together in Brookhaven's great room and looked out the window at the hide-and-seek sun.

His throat worked, then he spoke. "This time I'm staying," he said.

She drew in a shuddering breath, and finished his sentence. "And I'm leaving."

22

FOR TWELVE YEARS Adam assumed loneliness equaled emptiness. That's how he felt when he left Delaney at the airport: empty. Having kissed Marissa good-bye and watched her truck head west for San Diego, he now knew how loneliness felt. It was an ache, ever present at the base of his throat, sometimes sending twinges into his gut. The dragon inside didn't bother to rumble or huff, a stillness so unusual he wondered if the damn thing needed antidepressants. She was gone. He was here, contemplating a newfound appreciation for those who were left behind when Marines went off to war.

The unexpected knock on his apartment door Sunday afternoon found him in his new apartment, drinking a beer, half watching the football game while he unpacked. When he opened the door a hand reached into his rib cage and fisted around his heart and lungs. Not from joy, but rather from utter shock, because Delaney stood in the hallway. She wore a black jacket over jeans, and her black leather purse hung from the crook of her arm. The vacation tan couldn't hide the twin spots of color high on her cheekbones.

She wasn't supposed to be here. He'd never, ever imagined seeing her alone, on his territory, on a random Sunday afternoon, thumb working at the shiny-bright rings on her left hand.

"May I come in?" she asked quietly.

He stepped to the side to let her in. She looked around, taking in the empty, flattened boxes, the neatly arranged furniture. The television sat on a stand across from a recliner and sofa set delivered the previous day, and his laptop sat open and active on the kitchen counter. He didn't ask her to sit down, but he did pick up the TV remote and mute the sound. The picture flickered behind him, a high-pitched whine signaling when the screen went bright.

"How did you find me?" he asked as he tapped refresh on his e-mail. The only people who knew his new address were his mother, Lucas—who'd stopped by to finally have that beer after police business in Brookings—and a few buddies from the Corps. And Marissa. It took less than a week to finalize the details to sell Brookhaven and pack her few possessions into the bed of her pickup truck. E-mails arrived daily, something he'd expected. The postcards surprised him, postmarked from places like Bozeman and Las Vegas, reducing him to checking the mailbox like it was the twentieth century.

She'd been gone all of a week, taking her time on the way to San Diego. Her absence taught him the meaning of lonely, but slowly, he was learning to stay in the moment with the emotion, let it wash over him, through him, and then recede. He didn't have to react, or deny, or ignore what he felt, just feel. Simply experiencing emotion, observing it, taking its measure, let him gauge strength and meaning, determine impulse from unshakable, and told him that he was right. He had unfinished business, and until he figured it out and dealt with it, he needed to stay.

Delaney watched him close the laptop lid before she answered. "I heard your mother tell Alana you'd moved into this complex. The building's lovely," she said.

"Does Keith know you're here?"

She adjusted her purse on her arm. "I told him I was exchanging wedding gifts," she said, the color spreading on her cheekbones. "And I was. But I had to talk to you."

He'd automatically braced, he realized. Legs spread, weight on the balls of his feet, arms folded. But he didn't say anything.

"I should have told you a long time ago, but I didn't have the courage." She looked around the apartment, as if searching for a distraction, then sighed and met his gaze without flinching. "Keith and I got together before you and I broke up. We started seeing each other about four months into your last deployment."

He said nothing.

"It didn't start out as . . . anything inappropriate, at least not for me. Keith was always around in college and grad school. He'd take me out, and we'd talk about you, about our plans for the future. He listened to me, to my . . . concerns. I'd turned thirty. Mom was getting worse, and I didn't know how much longer . . . I wasn't married yet, wasn't a mother, either. He . . . helped me stay strong, told me you were worth it, that what we had together was worth waiting for. But then you volunteered for another deployment, when you said you wouldn't, and one night . . ." Her voice trailed off, and she shook her head. "But it wasn't just one night."

"I know," he said. He handled other people like they were Marines, pushed too far, asked too much, goaded them into giving more than they could handle. His edge, he was slowly learning, was way beyond the norm. But not Marissa. Marissa's edge snugged up against his just right.

"I thought you might," she said. "You broke it off so suddenly, but then you said yes when Keith asked you to be best man, so I thought you didn't, you'd just decided we weren't right for each other. Then the way you acted when you got back made me wonder. Your speech pretty well confirmed it."

"If you knew I knew, why are you here?"

"To apologize, and ask for your forgiveness."

Incredulous, he stared at her, but the word triggered a slow skittering of pebbles down a rocky slope inside. He'd heard the sound a thousand times on patrol, a crumbling of stone, a shifting of the earth under him set off by his boots, by a fellow Marine's steps. He didn't have the LT's ESP, but he slowly developed a sixth sense for the sound that was new, the tumble of pebbles with more velocity, more speed. The hair on his nape would rise slightly, his attention shifting to a point in the wadi, his body's reaction to something out of the ordinary. *Pay attention. This is important.*

"Why, Delaney?"

"You promised the fourth deployment would be the last. Then it wasn't," she started, then shook her head. "No." She took a deep breath. "I loved you. You have to believe that. I loved you."

He'd heard that a lot lately. Loved. Past tense.

"After a while I began to love what you stood for, what you'd made of yourself. I thought that was you. But it isn't. It wasn't enough, to love the potential and a shiny surface of a man who was two thousand miles away during a good year and showing no interest in coming home. I wanted someone who was here, now, and ready to be a husband and a father."

"And did you figure all of this out before you started sleeping with Keith, or was that the pillow talk afterwards?"

At that she did flinch. "Both. I agonized over this, Adam."

"And never mentioned it to me." Neither did Keith. Not one word in the e-mails about Delaney's concerns. He'd played to win.

At that she opened her palm, pleading for understanding. "You don't know what it's like to be on the other side. Support the troops, stay loyal, stay true. Put on a front until the front is all you have. I watched my girlfriends get married, get pregnant. I'd been a bridesmaid six times, and I'm godmother to four of my friends' daughters. They have homes and families, and I had a ring and a promise that kept getting extended another year, another year. I was *lonely*." The word so sharply echoed Marissa's explanation of why she sought out companionship on her terms that Adam startled, but Delaney went on. "And I was weak."

"And now you expect me to forgive you for cheating on me with our best friend while I was deployed," he said.

"I don't expect anything," she said simply. "All I can do is apologize, and ask."

And if she doesn't apologize, how could he forgive?

More dirt and pebbles twisted and shivered down his spine. He shook it off. "I hope you'll be happy, Delaney."

She twisted her wedding ring again, diamonds disappearing under her hand, then reappearing between her ring and pinkie fingers, only to disappear again in a slow circle. "He wants what I want," she said. "And I think I'll be good for him."

He was trying to figure out what that meant, when her right hand delved inside her purse and pulled out his engagement ring, the smaller round diamond set in yellow gold. Without a word she offered it to him.

Etiquette dictated she keep it when he'd broken up with her. Now that the truth was out in the open, she was right to offer it back, but he didn't want it. "Keep it," he said.

"I can't," she replied.

"Then sell it and buy supplies for the kids at Pine Ridge, because I won't take it back."

"All right," she said, and put it back in an inner pocket of her purse.

He remembered what Keith had said: that Delaney wanted a small life, a home, a job, kids, to spend holidays and vacations with her family. That was all. He'd wanted her to be his defense, his shield, his protection against everything inside him that scared him. But that wasn't who she was, and in the end, it wasn't what he really needed. He needed a partner, a guide, a sounding board. He needed someone who knew and loved the man under the brightly polished uniform and sword and the jarhead haircut.

He needed Marissa.

"I am sorry," Delaney said quietly.

The words registered somewhere in his consciousness, but he was too busy processing awareness, coming bright and sharp and fast as a sword. Forgiveness wasn't a right, something demanded and expected. It was his duty, made more worthwhile when it was freely offered, and the only thing that would make all of this right for him. Keith and Delaney would always live with the knowledge that their love and marriage began in the sordid muck of infidelity, but he could start over, if he forgave them.

To err is human. To forgive is divine. Neither is Marine Corps policy. The bumper sticker on his car said it all. No mistakes. No forgiveness. *It's a Marine thing,* he'd said casually to Marissa. But life didn't reduce to a bumper sticker, and maybe that was the answer to who he was when he wasn't *this Marine.* Not inhumanly perfect, or unable to forgive. Just Adam. Just like everyone else.

She turned to go, her hand on the doorknob, when he spoke. "Delaney. I forgive you."

There. He'd done it. Three simple, short words. *I. Forgive. You.* He didn't feel smaller, or weak, or taken advantage of. He felt . . . light. Strong. Like he could slice through steel. Was this what Marissa knew that he didn't know? How letting go made you strong?

Tears welled up in Delaney's eyes as she looked at him. "Thank you," she said quietly.

He didn't extend his newfound magnanimity to Keith, and she wisely didn't ask. Instead she opened the door, then turned to look back at him. He got the sense whatever she was about to say cost her more than telling him she'd gone to another man's bed. "I thought Marissa would be here. Since Brookhaven's been sold."

Speaking of blades to the heart. There was a lifetime of animosity and jealousies and envy washed around in the currents of Walkers Ford, and perhaps Delaney hadn't been as immune as he'd suspected. "She's gone," he said.

"Where?"

The small-town curiosity never died. His mother and

Alana weren't talking. He wouldn't be the first to reveal Marissa's whereabouts. "I kept your secret, Delaney. I'll keep hers, too."

"I knew you were together when I saw her shoes and that wrap in the kitchen, just like I knew you were together the night you surprised us all." He neither confirmed nor denied, but something about his expression made Delaney look away. "Is she ever coming back?"

"I don't know. She says she will. I doubt it."

Delaney considered him. "You came back."

"I have unfinished business here." He'd keep explaining that to people until they got it.

Her calm blue gaze never faltered. "So finish it," she said simply, and closed the door.

First Marissa. Now Delaney. He didn't know how many more of these punches to the solar plexus he could take. Was it that simple? Screw up his courage like Delaney had, confess, and ask for absolution?

Why not?

Because what he'd done was unforgivable. Cheating and lying were tiny wrongs compared to causing the stupid, unnecessary, irrevocable death of a beloved son.

Unfinished business, oh yeah. He could stay stuck in the past, shoring up the crumbing walls that held in everything he hated about himself, or he could do the right thing. Face who he was. What he'd done. What he'd become. Deep down, hidden inside behind the structure he'd created to keep himself in line, was the fear of who he would be without that structure. But even if he was no longer *this Marine*, he was still a Marine, and Marines faced their fears.

Marissa loved him. If she could rebuild Brookhaven, he could do this. If he loved her, wanted a future with her, he *had* to confront his worst fear. He clicked off the television, shrugged into his jacket, and snagged his keys.

It was time to face the demons that lay behind the white door of 84 Oak Street.

*   *   *

HE PARKED A couple of houses away, shut off the engine, and sat listening to the engine pop and cool. As the seconds passed, his blood thumping in his ears drowned out the irregular ticks under the hood. He'd been in more firefights than he could count, pinned in ravines by snipers, on choppers taking fire from RPGs, held broken and bleeding bodies while Marines died, but apparently he could still feel fear. His heart raced and his stomach shuddered. Was this what Ris fought outside Mrs. Edmunds's house, the desire to curl into a tiny little ball on the floorboards from nothing more threatening than the obstacle to your future?

He'd been there for her, stood by her and made that right. Made it possible for her to fly. He'd come home to tie up loose ends with Keith and Delaney, and like the events of that summer night long ago, set off a chain of events he couldn't control.

Ris was gone, shopping for boats in San Diego. Warm and safe and free. And here he was, in front of 84 Oak Street, back where it all began twelve years ago.

Fall sunshine bathed the quiet street as he strode up the driveway to the front door. A wooden pumpkin hung from a hook that probably held a Christmas wreath, then a snowman, then a Valentine's Day heart, then something whimsical like tulips for spring. The yard was neatly maintained, the flower bed mulched for the winter. From the outside the family's loss wasn't apparent. He rang the doorbell and waited.

When Mrs. Wilmont opened the front door, he thought maybe he should have taken the five minutes to call first, because her blue eyes, just like Josh's, went wide. "Mrs. Wilmont," he began, "I'm Adam Collins."

"I know who you are," she said clearly, slowly wiping flour-dusted hands on her apron. "Come in."

In some ways she'd aged terribly, and in others, not at all. Some remote part of his brain did the math, and calculated

her age at somewhere close to his mother's, just over fifty.
Silver streaked her chin-length brown hair, and her skin was
smooth and pale, but her eyes held infinite pain.

He followed her into the kitchen, where an afternoon talk
show played on a small television set on the counter, providing
background noise while she made a rhubarb pie. Daily life
for a small-town wife. Mr. Wilmont worked at the manufac-
turing plant south of Walkers Ford. She would have grown
the rhubarb in the garden he saw through the family room
windows.

He should have called first. He felt big and awkward in her
small, clean kitchen. Through the doorway into the family
room he could see Josh's senior portrait. The photographer
had airbrushed away Josh's acne, leaving a smooth-faced boy
with blue eyes and black curls, dressed in jeans, a white
T-shirt, and his letter jacket, smiling confidently for the camera. The family pictures around the portrait began with five
people, Mr. and Mrs. Wilmont, Josh, his two younger sisters,
then shrank to four as the girls aged through high school, into
college and beyond.

The absence evident in those pictures clenched hard
around his throat.

"Can I get you something to drink?"

"No, thank you, ma'am," he said hastily.

She poured herself a cup of coffee. "Sit down," she said.

The chair legs scraped across the linoleum, then he eased
into the seat. She looked at him with those clear, expectant
eyes.

"Mrs. Wilmont," he began, then stopped. He cleared his
throat, rubbed his thumbnail against his forehead. Looked at
Josh's photograph. Looked at Josh's mother.

It was as if the last twelve years hadn't happened, as if he'd
never survived boot camp, or five deployments, as if he'd never
worn the uniform and carried the dress sword. Faced with
blue eyes identical to Josh's, twelve years disappeared in the
blink of an eye and he was seventeen again, scared, boulders
of self-loathing grinding against his heart and lungs. Just a

bike and an attitude, the cockiness covering a scared boy convinced he'd never amount to shit.

And he wouldn't, if he didn't do this.

He cleared his throat again, started again. "Mrs. Wilmont, I'm here to apologize. I'm sorry . . ." Tears filled his eyes. He blinked them back, felt his nasal passages sting anyway. "I am so sorry for what I did."

She said nothing, just traced the curve of the coffee cup's handle with her index finger. Pie dough clung to the nail bed.

"I should have come before," he said. "I should have come when I got out of the hospital, or before I left for boot camp, or after. I should have called you. I didn't, and that was wrong. I'm sorry."

They were the most pathetic words imaginable. To err was human. To forgive was divine. Neither is Marine Corps policy. He understood why now. Because fucking up left gaping wounds that scarred over if they healed at all.

He shouldn't have come, but here he was, flashing hot and cold, sick to his stomach. Ashamed. Absolutely riddled with a shame and regret so visceral he could taste the dirt in his mouth, smell the blood.

He had no right to be here. He waited for the vilification he deserved.

"Will you tell me what happened that night?" she asked gently. "The chief gave me the official version, but I'd like to hear it from you."

He cleared his throat. Started at the beginning. "I had a fight with Marissa Brooks over . . . well. Over something. I was angry and cocky and arrogant, a bad combination for a seventeen-year-old boy. I called a couple of friends to come party at Brookhaven. The next thing I knew, 'a couple of friends' turned into fifty or sixty kids and things got out of hand. I got out of hand."

He stopped. Breathed. Swallowed hard as he met her calm, unflinching gaze.

"I was really wrecked. I only remember flashes of it, but somewhere along the line I got the great idea to rip the paneling out of Brookhaven's main room and burn it in the meadow. Marissa begged me to leave the house alone, but I just shook her off. I remember Josh pulling up on his new bike. He was so proud of it."

This was like lancing a pus-filled boil, the stink and rotting matter oozing out, but he couldn't stop now. "I don't remember challenging him to a race, but it must have been my idea. I do remember that Josh didn't want to do it, and I do remember ragging at him, calling him names until he said he'd do it."

How could she stand to look at him? He hadn't been able to look in the mirror for years.

"I was the more experienced rider, and I knew I could beat him, but Josh rode hell-bent for leather from the moment we took off. I was pushing my bike's limits on the dirt roads north of Brookhaven. Josh angled for the inside around the last corner. I wouldn't drop back and let him in. He hit a rut going eighty miles an hour, maybe a little faster. That's how fast I was going. All I know is one second he was beside me and the next his bike was sliding back down the road. I managed to keep control as I braked. I found Josh in the ditch."

No need to tell Josh's mother the details, how his body was twisted unnaturally, his face in the mud and cattails. He must have hit a rock that dented the side of his skull like a divot on a golf course. His thighbone protruded through his jeans, his pelvis was oddly twisted, like his hips had shifted ninety degrees to the right, and blood seeped from his nose and mouth. No need to tell her that the clarity that came when he saw the body was remarkably similar to how he felt now, how the screams in his ears sounded so very far away yet were loud enough to bring fifty kids from Brookhaven, on foot and in cars.

He looked at Josh's senior class picture and prayed to whatever god would listen to him after all he'd done that this image of Josh, alive, smiling, whole, would replace the shattered face in his dreams.

He came back to the kitchen, to Mrs. Wilmont and the aroma of pie dough and sugar. "I'm sorry," he said again.

"There's nothing I can say or do to make up for what I did, or the fact that it took me twelve years to come here, but I'm sorry. I'm sorry, I'm so sorry."

He was crying, he realized. The emotions from that night, driven deep into the depths of his soul, gripped his throat in a tight fist, the wet, hot drops plunking on his hands, limp and helpless in his lap. He was crying silently when he had no business doing any such thing in front of the mother of the boy he killed as surely as if he'd held a gun to his head and pulled the trigger. And he was saying *I'm sorry* like it was a prayer, like the god who filled his dreams with Josh's battered head would grant him absolution.

Then she reached across the table, not for his hand, but for his face. She cupped his jaw, wet with tears, and leaned toward him. "Adam," she said through tears of her own, shining bright but unshed, "Adam. Listen to me. You were just a boy. I forgive you."

The sobs tore from his chest like a giant hand reached in and ripped them out, one by one, through twelve years of armor that turned out to be no more defense than gauze. He doubled over in Mrs. Wilmont's kitchen, rested elbows on knees and linked his hands behind his neck, and cried out a decade's worth of regret and fear and self-hatred. She patted his shoulder until the sobs tapered off, then got up and found a box of tissues. Her face was full of compassion, and sadness. She knew grief. He'd taught her grief, and that thought was more than he could bear.

"You've been carrying this around since Josh died." He just nodded. "I wondered," she said quietly. "You seemed tightly wound when you came home. Rigid. I almost talked to you several times, but I couldn't give you what you didn't know you needed."

He thought about how he would have responded to her approaching him on the street, or at the Heirloom. He would have been stiffly formal, all walls up, barricaded behind his suit-of-armor identity, desperate to look like he had it all together. He thought about how that would have felt to her—like shame heaped upon shame. "You couldn't give me what I wouldn't admit I needed. I'm so sorry," he said again.

She sat back, a small, unreadable smile on her face. "Twelve years later and I still don't know what to say to that. It's not all right. It's not okay. It's not for the best, and I'm sorry to say this if you're a true believer, but I hate a god who wanted my son with him, not here with me."

She could say these things to him because he understood. He lived the flip side of the same coin. No one ever knew what to say to him, either. They said he was young, and he made a mistake, or people avoided it, because it made them uncomfortable. Except Marissa.

"What I do know, Adam, is that you've punished yourself enough. I don't think a career in the Marine Corps was your dream. Maybe you did it for Josh, or because you thought you needed what they'd give you, discipline and honor and purpose. But for you to waste your own life and talents and gifts is to dishonor Josh. Let yourself live, and love. Let yourself be loved. If you think you owe me anything, give me your life lived as fully as you can live it."

He stared at her, his brain trying to work through this new angle on his life. He did owe her something. He owed her whatever she asked of him, but it had never occurred to him that she might ask for something other than rigid discipline and self-inflicted retribution.

"Do you have any idea what that might look like, now that you're out of the service?" she asked.

The desire to give her a firm answer, a confident plan, nearly overwhelmed him, but he told her the truth. "I thought I did. Then I came home. Now I'm not so sure."

She nodded, as if she understood even that, and he finally realized where he'd seen the look in her eyes. It was the same as Marissa's, the weary perceptiveness that came from going through hell and coming out on the other side, burned and bruised but still standing. Still walking.

"You have time to think about it," she said.

He did. He had a little money, and plenty of time, if he

took it. If he didn't launch himself into graduate school. If he went through the hell he'd avoided for over a decade. He could do worse for guides than Marissa and Mrs. Wilmont.

"Yeah," he said. "I do."

"And you'll take it?"

"I will." The words caught in his throat. He cleared it, and looked her right in the eye. "I will."

She gave him another small smile, patted his hand again, and got to her feet. "I need to finish this pie."

He stood, took a deep, shaky breath. He couldn't earn forgiveness. He didn't deserve it when it comes like the breeze that disperses a lingering, acrid, explosion-tinged fog after a firefight, the grass that grows over ground soaked with blood and urine and shit. Time passes; it came, and accepting it was the only way to honor the gift it was. Words were completely inadequate in this situation, but he said the only thing he could say. "Thank you, Mrs. Wilmont."

"You're welcome, Adam. Let me know what you decide. I'd like to hear from you again."

"Yes, ma'am," he said. "I will."

He walked out the front door, down the steps to the sidewalk, and along the street to his car. He was standing by the Charger, keys in hand and the doors unlocked, before he realized he hadn't tripped over that invisible, ever-present spot in the street that sent him stumbling every time he ran past the Wilmont house. 84 Oak Street. Maybe that was because he was lighter. He felt like he did when he got back from patrol, safe inside the barbed-wire fences enclosing the FOB, behind the sandbags, deep in the foxhole. The red stain of shame was gone. The responsibility still clung to him. That would never leave, but he could go on.

HE DROVE HOME on autopilot, unaware of his surroundings, until he pulled into his mother's driveway. A touch of the garage door opener sent the door creaking up to reveal his mother's Buick and the space cleared when he took his boxes to the new apartment. The interior of the garage smelled musty as he walked to the cover-draped object sitting in the dark, the looming thing he'd pushed to the edges of his consciousness ever since he came home. One tug pulled back the protective poly-cotton cloth covering the Hayabusa.

He draped the cover on the Buick's hood. Still curiously empty, he rocked the bike off the center stand and pushed it out of the garage, into the late-fall sunlight, then walked a slow circle around it. The exterior was clean. Oddly clean. After sitting for twelve years there was no way it would start, let alone run all the way to San Diego. He'd have to haul it into Brookings and have one of the bike shops there do a total engine overhaul and put new tires on it.

Except the tires were ninety-five percent treads and plump with air. The gas tank read full. The keys were in the ignition.

Driven by intuition, he straddled the seat and twisted the key.

It started.

The engine ran smoothly, purring with the high-intensity idle that signaled speed. The vibrations rippled through his calves and thighs, up into his chest cavity. He gripped the handlebars and twisted the throttle. The engine revved into the red zone without a hiccup.

No way in hell could a bike sit for a decade and start on the first try. He throttled back, then a flash of green caught his attention. His mother stood in the kitchen doorway, arms folded at her waist, watching him.

He cut the engine when she opened the door and walked down the cement steps. A little smile danced at the corners of her mouth, half-pleased, half-wry.

"It's as good as new," he said in disbelief. "How?"

"That night, Marissa pushed it into her barn. After your induction ceremony she suggested Clem down at the garage ride it here. Some months I didn't need the money you sent," she said. "I used it to pay Clem to maintain it. He rode it when the weather was good, idled it when it wasn't."

He'd left the bike nearly two miles from Brookhaven. The image of seventeen-year-old Marissa pushing the Hayabusa along those dirt roads and down the slope to the barn made his heart crack wide open. "Why?" he said shakily. "Why would you two take care of my bike for me?"

"Marissa said she thought you might want to ride it again someday," she said simply. "And I agreed."

He bent his head, inhaled carefully, at the thought of his mother and Ris taking care of his dream when he couldn't. "I loved this bike. I thought it was my future."

"*You* are your future, honey. The bike's just a way of getting you there."

He looked at her, saw himself in her eyes. "I'm leaving. I'm going back out to San Diego."

"I know," she said again.

"I'll get a storage unit in Brookings," he said.

She smiled, with a hint of sadness, but she knew how to let him go. "Good. Get a helmet."

"Yes, ma'am." He kissed her on the cheek, then ran his hand over the engine housing. The Marine Corps drilled courage into his soul, his bones, but it paled in comparison to a mother's courage necessary to let her children go, just for a couple of hours, for a few months, or forever. "I'm not sure when I'll be back."

"We'll be in touch," she said. She patted his cheek, then stepped back.

He started the engine again, then opened the throttle and the bike surged forward, kicking adrenaline through his veins. The soles of his boots scraped the cement as long-unused skills came back on the fly. He balanced and the bike gained speed, then he rocketed down the street, driving right into the setting sun. He stayed at the speed limit as he rolled through town, taking one last look around. The Heirloom Cafe, nestled in the main shopping district. The library. The gas station, then the long curve to the highway.

A couple of miles outside of town, Brookhaven loomed to the north, rocking on the ocean swell of the hill like a boat, all white and orange and red, the figurehead pointing west. A toy truck of a moving van sat in front of the double doors as the new owner set up her retreat center on the plains. Adam pulled over to the shoulder and stopped the bike, staring at the house. That's where the dragon was born, in the clash between his turbulent feelings for Marissa and his determination to be something more than just a waste of breath and space. As a teen he hadn't known how to channel passionate emotions; as a Marine he'd learned to ignore them. Love. Longing. Desire. But mostly love.

Marissa taught him how to feel. How to love. And the dragon was gone.

The house receded as he headed south and east, to Brookings. As he rode, he compiled a list of things to do in his mind. Buy a helmet. Break his lease. Move his stuff into a storage unit. Pack what he could carry in his duffle and head west.

Where he belonged. With Marissa. It was time to find his dream.

23

MARISSA AWOKE TO a foreign sound, erratic, gentle, with a faint slap to it. She lay with her eyes closed and absorbed stimuli, the rocking motion under her, the unusual triangular shape of the bed tucked into one side of the bow, warm air on the length of her arms and legs, exposed by a thin pair of cotton shorts and a tank top.

She lay in a bunk on a boat, wearing not sweats, a sweatshirt, and socks under three blankets, but shorts and a tank, one cotton sheet, and a lightweight quilt she'd kicked off during the night. She exchanged the sleepwear for the bikini at the end of the thick pad that served as a mattress, and was dressed for the day. A pair of khaki shorts made the bikini modest enough for casual morning wear, and her wind-and-dreams silk wrap warded off the slight chill of morning in San Diego.

The sounds. A soft thump as the boat drifted against the dock, and not quite a sloshing, not quite a patting. Waves. Waves gently rocking the sailboat she now owned. Her dream came true in the form of a Westsail 32 that needed some interior refinishing but was mechanically sound, simple to sail, and comfortable for cruising. Nicknamed the "wet snail," her new home was no classic racing yacht, but she loved it fiercely, dearly, even after just a few days onboard. In tribute to her past, she'd named the boat *Prairie Dream*.

No one she'd met in the marina thought she was crazy for dreaming of wind and waves. The forty-foot boat next to hers held a family of four, parents and two kids who left a home in Indiana to cruise around the world while homeschooling their eight-year-old daughter and ten-year-old son in both the sailing life and traditional coursework. The kids took great pleasure in teaching her all about her new home, how things worked, cooking simple meals, and the parents were no less enthusiastic about sharing their sailing knowledge. Early in the mornings Ashley often hopped over to Marissa's boat with a blueberry muffin or a plate of pancakes to share. Marissa returned the favor by gently guiding Ashley's husband, Tony, through his cabin renovation project. Apparently carpentry skills would come in handy in a marina.

She scooted to the bottom of the bed and stood up, which put her in the kitchen/dining area. Cabinets with clever little fasteners hung above the stove and over the counter space. She boiled water on the stove, then poured it into the French press containing the last of the Intelligentsia coffee from Chicago. While she waited for it to brew, she unlocked the hatch and swung it open. Fresh salt-tinged air flowed down the stairway and into the kitchen area. For a moment she simply stood there, rocking slightly with the boat's motion, face tipped upward as sunlight and happiness patted her with gentle palms.

Right where I belong.

The thought rose to the surface of her mind. She had no schedule beyond the day's sailing lesson, no plan other than *Make a plan*. The Southern California coastline offered dozens of short trips, opportunities to hone her skills within sight of land before she launched out, perhaps to Seattle, perhaps to Hawaii and on to Thailand, perhaps through the Panama Canal into the Caribbean. She had time, and knew how to live frugally. She owned a boat. Sun and wind and water were free.

What she didn't have was Adam.

They e-mailed and Skyped. She'd seen his apartment through the camera on his computer, everything neatly organized and stowed, heard his plans for spring semester courses and internship applications. But three days ago the contact ended abruptly. He wasn't on Skype and hadn't answered a single e-mail. She told herself he was busy getting set up in Brookings, attending orientation meetings for the incoming students, and reminded her aching heart that some things just weren't meant to be.

She missed him so much that she wondered if she liked what she'd started. Saying good-bye to Brookhaven tugged at her heartstrings until she saw the ocean. Saying good-bye to Adam still knotted her throat. She loved him, both the boy he'd been twelve years ago and the man he was now, strong enough to set her free rather than keep her for himself. But only he could decide whether to stay trapped in his past, or build a new future.

She depressed the plunger on the French press to trap the grounds, poured a mug of coffee and climbed the stairs, expecting to see a rumpled Tony sitting in his cockpit, nursing his first cup of coffee while the kids clambered around like monkeys. True to form, Tony sat in the captain's chair, blearily eyeing the dark-haired, hazel-eyed man sitting on the dock by her boat. He wore a USMC T-shirt with jeans, but dangled his bare feet over the edge of the dock, his boots lined up beside him next to a motorcycle helmet and a single duffle bag. In one hand he held a Starbucks cup.

Adam.

She blinked, then surreptitiously patted the wheel for reassurance.

"You're not dreaming," he said.

"I must be," she said, striving for casual. "You're drinking Starbucks."

"I was desperate," he said, giving the cup a disparaging glance. "I rode into town a couple of hours ago and the first coffee place I saw was Starbucks. I've been awake since Utah."

One phrase had her heart doing slow flip-flops in her chest. "You rode into town?"

"On the bike," he said. "Why didn't you tell me you kept it running?"

Tears of sheer joy stung her eyes. She blinked them away, then sipped her coffee. "If you went looking for it, you'd know. If you didn't, then it didn't matter."

He looked ragged, shadows under his red-rimmed eyes, stubble thick on his jaw. "All that time I was on you about daring to dream, and you'd kept mine alive."

"You thought I needed a little shove," she said. "I thought you needed space. Was I wrong?"

"No," he said. A smile broke soft and sweet in the dark scruff obscuring his jaw, but he stayed where he was. "You weren't wrong."

"Why didn't you wake me up?" she said.

"I got here at oh-four-hundred. I didn't want to scare you." He sipped the coffee, and nodded at *Prairie Dream*. "Nice."

"Nate helped me find her," she said. "She's not pretty yet, but she will be when I'm done with her."

"I think she's beautiful, tough girl," he said as he scanned the sails and rigging with a knowledgeable eye. "You going to sail her by yourself?"

"I could rework the rigging so I could sail her single-handed," she said. "It's been done."

He sipped his coffee and made a noncommittal noise completely belied by the *over-my-dead-body* look in his eye. Single-handed sailing was for people with a death wish and no respect for the international conventions requiring a constant watch on the high seas.

"Or I could try to find someone who wanted to sail around the world with me," she said. "It's not easy to do. It would have to be someone I knew well. Someone who wouldn't spook at the first sign of trouble. Someone I'd seen at his worst, and who's seen me at mine."

"Someone capable, but adventurous," he said, summing up her requirements. "Practical, but enough of a romantic to go after the next sunset. Preferably with more sailing experience than you."

"That part's not hard to find," she said, "but for the rest of it . . . yes. Exactly."

"And you're having trouble finding someone who fits that bill?"

"That depends," she said, her heart in her throat. "Why are you here?"

"I'm following my dream," he said.

"What about architecture school?"

"Not yet," he said. "I'm not rushing into any decisions right now. I'm going to take some time, get reacquainted with who I am, and what I want out of life." He looked at her, his clear, bottomless gaze drawing tears to her eyes. "But this I know, Marissa Brooks, this I've always known. Whatever future I make is empty without you."

She gave a hiccuping little laugh and set her coffee on the hatch. "Well, that's lucky," she said. "I happen to need a first mate."

"Permission to come aboard?"

At her nod, he swung his legs over the side of the boat and dropped into the cockpit. The boat rocked gently with his momentum and weight, tipping her forward, right into his arms. Right where she belonged.

It would take more than her weight and a gently rocking boat to knock him off his feet, so she assumed his knees buckled because he wanted her in his lap on the red cushioned bench. She straddled his hips and flattened her palms along his jaw to kiss him, tasting bitter coffee and hot desire. One hand palmed her butt while the other fisted in her hair, for a very long, very tantalizing kiss.

She broke away and looked over her shoulder at Tony, studiously focusing on his open laptop. "We can't do this here," she whispered. "This is a family-friendly pier."

"Guess you'll have to show me my new quarters."

"So you can sleep." She ran her thumbs gently along the dark circles under his eyes. "You look so tired."

"I didn't want to wait one second longer than necessary to see you again."

"I'm so glad you got the bike out again."

"Didn't even get a speeding ticket on the way here. Riding it, knowing you were at the end of the trip was rush enough. I love you, Ris," he said. "Always. Even when I wouldn't feel it, much less admit it, I loved you. I felt so much when I was with you, and not just teenage lust. Love. Fear. Exhilaration. Mostly love, but I was so scared of what I could do to you that I did something worse to Josh and his family. To all of us."

"You've learned. That's all we do. We live, and we learn, and we keep going." She searched his gaze, but the bitter emotions driving him for so long were gone. "I love you, too, Adam."

That earned her another long kiss, but he was good and kept his hands at the middle of her back. When the kiss broke off, he reached over the gunwale and snagged the Starbucks cup sitting on the dock, flipped off the lid with his thumb, then dumped the rest of his coffee into the water. "We haven't discussed pay," he said. "I work for good coffee."

Her cup still sat on the hatch, miraculously upright with all the rocking. She reached for it, took a sip, then handed him the mug. Heat and love danced in his hazel eyes as he turned the rim to drink from the same place she had.

"We'll lay in a good supply before we cast off for Thailand," she said.

His gaze flicked over the cockpit and rigging. "Have you taken her out yet?"

"Not yet," she admitted. "Nate's guy looked her over thoroughly, but I've been waiting."

"For what?" he scoffed. "You've got the boat, sunshine, a good breeze, and temps in the upper sixties. What else could you need to sail?"

"You," she said simply.

His hand came up and tangled in her hair, then he touched his forehead to hers. "I'm here, Ris," he said. "Let's go."

TURN THE PAGE FOR A SNEAK PEEK OF
ANNE CALHOUN'S NEW NOVEL

Jaded

COMING SOON FROM BERKLEY SENSATION!

ALANA WENTWORTH LOCKED the front door to the Walkers Ford Public Library with one thing on her mind: Chief of Police Lucas Ridgeway.

She gave the brass door handle an absentminded tug to make sure it was secured before setting off at a brisk walk down the traditionally named Main Street. Lucas usually got home a few minutes after she did. With any luck, she'd have just enough time to put on the opposite of her librarian clothes, which consisted of a primly buttoned silk blouse and cashmere sweater over a tweed skirt. The blue scoop-neck T-shirt with the rosettes would do, then she'd put a little extra oomph into her makeup. Figure out her strategy before his truck pulled into the driveway next door to hers.

A quick glance at her watch told her she'd left herself just enough time to get ready, but not enough to talk herself out of what she planned to do.

She stepped lightly in the shallow depressions worn into the marble steps by thousands of residents, and turned for home. With the May 1st late frost date two days in the past, spring had taken a firm grip on the region. The Business District's beautification committee had spent the day hanging planters full of impatiens from the green-painted light poles and set out the half barrels spilling over with tulips and crocuses, but Alana only noticed the hardy spring flowers when a sharp knock on the Heirloom Cafe's front window snapped her out of her reverie. Fifteen-year-old Carlene Winters, dressed in her green uniform, waved brightly and hurried to the cafe's front door.

"Hi, Miss Wentworth! I just wanted to say thanks for the recommendation. I started *Pride and Prejudice* last night, and I can't put it down."

"You're welcome," Alana said. "I really have to—"

"The language was a little tough, but I totally got that Mr. Darcy was being mean to Lizzy," the girl continued. "He says there aren't any pretty girls for him to dance with, but she's more than pretty. She's funny, and she laughs at herself. That should count for something."

Normally she'd love to talk to Carlene about all the intricacies of Darcy and Lizzy's courtship, but not tonight, not when she wanted to start a courtship of her own. Or something resembling a courtship, in a way. In a very indirect way. "It should," Alana agreed rather desperately. "I'm sorry, but I have to get home. Come by the library tomorrow and we can talk about it then?"

"Sure! Have a good night."

An image of Lucas from last Sunday flashed into her mind. He'd caught Alana in her thin robe and nightie, scampering barefoot down the driveway to pick up her newspaper for her Sunday morning tradition of reading the *Trib* in bed with a pot of coffee and Nina Simone on in the background. Dressed in jeans, hiking boots, and a hunter-green fleece pullover, he'd loaded his retired service dog, Duke, into his truck for *his* Sunday morning tradition of taking Duke for a long hike. As usual he'd looked unflappable during the embarrassing encounter, but when she reached the safety of the stoop and looked back, he was still watching her.

The look in his dark-chocolate eyes had sent heat flickering through her despite the early-morning chill. Even now, two days later, her nerves still held the charge of that look.

"I hope to," she said to Carlene, then set off again, impatient with the delay, but mostly impatient with herself.

Once again she'd left something important until almost the last minute. Well, this wasn't the last minute. The last minute would be two weeks from today, when her contract with the town of Walkers Ford ended and she left town to drive back to Chicago. But her habitual distraction and procrastination meant yet again she was scrambling to do something she'd always meant to do, then didn't.

Like working in a public library, the goal she'd set when she got her MLS then let slip through her fingers after graduation. The whole point of this diversion was for her to learn to be more proactive in her life, to make things happen rather than let them happen to her. Including Lucas Ridgeway, assuming he had no objections to being one half of the oldest clichés in the book—a whirlwind affair between a repressed librarian and a cop.

She hurried down the street to her rented house as nature put on a show in the expansive sky at the end of the street. There was the Hanford house five doors down, then there was nascent twilight streaked with the sunset's reds, oranges, and pinks. It should have clashed horribly, but the prairie sky wore the colors with a magnificent lack of concern that reminded her of her sister, Freddie. Freddie wore jeans, ballet flats, and a faded blue button-down shirt in front of fifty thousand people and within minutes *#preppiestyle* trended on Twitter all over North America and Europe.

Nothing ever just happened to Freddie. Freddie made things happen. Their mother often complained that one daughter got all the initiative and the other got all the absent-mindedness.

She hurried up the driveway, trying to remember if the shirt she wanted to wear was in her dresser or on the closet shelf, when Lucas's police department Bronco pulled into the driveway next to hers. The transmission ground when he shifted into park and cut the engine.

Too late. The story of her life, but she resisted the urge to

write off the rest of the night. Instead, she climbed the front
step and waited, pretending to thumb through the mail while
she watched him greet Duke. Maybe it was the untempered
affection he had for the dog that tugged at her heart. He hunkered down to scratch the dog's throat and whisper, "*You're
a good boy yes you are*," into his upturned muzzle. Duke spent
his days on the screened-in front porch of his house next door.
Every time Lucas came home, Duke pranced and danced and
rubbed his white-furred snout against Lucas's legs, his fawn-
colored tail wagging frantically. The raw blast of emotion
from the dog and Lucas's gentle scratching tightened Alana's
throat every time she saw it.

Tonight was no exception. When the reunion ended, Lucas
got to his feet, then glanced her way. He wore a navy suit and
a gray tie, with his badge and service weapon clipped to his
belt.

"Evening, Chief," she said.

"Ms. Wentworth," he replied.

The way he said it shouldn't have made her heart beat a
little faster, but her name in his mouth always did. She could
salvage this, still take her few minutes to get ready. "I wonder
if you'd have a moment later tonight," she said. "The bathroom sink isn't draining properly."

"It's not the kitchen sink this time?"

"Sorry, but no," she said.

He looked at his watch, a no-nonsense Timex. "I've got a
couple of minutes now," he said. "I'll get my toolbox."

Damn!

Alana carried her bags inside, turning on lights as she
moved from the kitchen to the dining room and down the short
hall to the bedroom she used as an office, where she dumped
the bags, then continued down to her bedroom. The house
was lovely, with gorgeous hardwood floors, walnut cabinets
built into the corners of the dining room, brick molding, and
charming window seats in the two bedrooms. When she first
looked at the rental property, Lucas had told her his

grandparents lived out a seventy-year marriage in the house. Love seeped from the woodwork and floors to give texture to the light that poured through the picture window overlooking Mrs. Ridgeway's famous rose beds. Chief Ridgeway had scrupulously pointed out the house's defects—leaky windows, ancient plumbing—but to Alana, bundling up during the winter was a small price to pay for the chance to see those roses bloom as spring turned to summer.

She smiled wistfully at her cluelessness. The roses wouldn't bloom until long after she left town, but the possibility had charmed her into ignoring the plumbing problems.

After opening the kitchen door, she poured herself a glass of wine, turned on NPR, and more attentively sorted through her mail. The stack included the usual bills as well as invitations, personal notes, and birth announcements on Crane's finest paper. She slit open the formal announcement of a party in a few weeks' time honoring her stepfather's contribution to efforts to ameliorate global poverty. Her mother had set the date for the celebration months earlier, but receiving the formal invitation made it all real. Alana's time in Walkers Ford was almost over. She should start packing, another task she was putting off, but she'd brought so little with her. A few hours one evening and she'd be ready to leave.

Lucas knocked at the kitchen door with the Maglite she recognized from the sports bag he carried to and from work each day. Glass of wine still in hand, she crossed the kitchen and let him in.

"You're still dressed for work," she said, stating the obvious. He'd left the gun and badge in his house, though.

"Town council meeting tonight," he said as he turned sideways to get past her. He carried an old-fashioned wooden toolbox weathered gray. A hammer and a neatly organized set of wrenches lay on the top shelf, other tools stored in the compartment underneath. His broad shoulder brushed hers as he managed to avoid hitting her knees with the toolbox.

Every cell in her body lit up, and heat bloomed on her

cheekbones. His gaze, normally so controlled, flicked down just enough to let her know he saw the blush. Silence. The air between them heated.

"I'll just . . ." he said with a tilt of his head toward the bathroom.

"Of course," she replied, and stepped to the side to let him down the hall.

Her experience with Marissa Brooks and Adam Collins a few weeks after she arrived had taught her about small-town values, and gossip. She couldn't just start up a torrid affair with the small town's Chief of Police. Yet she wondered how to tell him in no uncertain terms that she wanted to go to bed with him and stay there until she couldn't remember her own name, preferably without sounding like a shameless tart.

A sophisticated woman would know how to go about this. Freddie could probably do it while polishing a paper for an international conference on human trafficking. Alana wasn't Freddie, though, or her mother, or her stepfather, the senator. In a family characterized by brilliance, wit, and a talent for far-reaching policy development, Alana was quiet, observant, content with the background. *Just stand still and smile,* her mother used to say with resignation. *You have such a pretty smile.* So her pretty smile graced the walls and corners first of school dances and mixers, then college parties, then cocktail parties and receptions when she went to work for the Wentworth Foundation.

But not even time spent on the edge of the limelight matched the long, heated moments when Lucas Ridgeway gave her his full attention.

"It's a budget meeting," he said as he set down the toolbox.

"Sorry?"

He shrugged out of his suit jacket and draped it over the linen closet's doorknob. "I'm still dressed for work because there's a town council meeting tonight. Budget meeting."

"Oh. Of course."

The tiny, rose-pink bathroom was barely large enough for Alana to dry off after a shower. Lucas could brace one shoulder against the wall and rest his palm on the mirror opposite, something he'd done the day the pipe draining the shower cracked and leaked peach-scented water into the basement. He'd been cursing steadily and quite prolifically under his breath then, but not tonight.

He yanked the stopper free and peered into the drain. "It's clogged again."

"I could use a drain cleaner."

"It'll eat right through the pipes," he replied. "They're seventy years old. Some weekend soon I'll replace the drain line and the P-trap. Maybe that will help. In the meantime . . ."

He handed her the flashlight, then stretched out on his back and wedged his torso into the cabinet under the sink. One hand fumbled in the toolbox. He lifted his head to see better, banged his forehead on the cabinet, and grunted.

"Sorry," Alana said hastily, and shone the light on the offending pipes.

It took only minutes to clear the pipe, then reattach the stopper to the drain lever, each stage punctuated by curt instructions given by the big male maneuvering in the small room. He twisted, his legs pushing against the opposite wall so his knee pressed into her shoulder.

"Do you wash your hair in the sink?" he asked.

"No," she said, pulling a handful forward to consider it. It was thick and poker-straight, cut in a bob that swung just below her jawline. It's only redeeming characteristic was the natural, pale blond color. Freddie bemoaned her regular appointments at Chicago's best hair salon to maintain the same shade. "There's just a lot of it."

"I can see that," he said to the interior of the cabinet. His dress shirt pulled free from his pants, revealing the waistband of his dark blue boxers. A thin line of hair ran from his navel into the waistband. Muscles flexed as he tightened the joint, and with each moment the scent of male skin and laundry soap permeated the air.

Don't let this chance slip through your fingers.

According to the thriving small-town gossip he wasn't

seeing anyone, which gave her an excellent reason to use what she'd heard described as the oldest technique in the book to get over what happened with David. She was going to get under Lucas Ridgeway. Tonight. A single, uncomplicated interlude without any awkwardness because he'd leave for the town council meeting.

She should probably attend, too. The town was in the process of conducting a search for a permanent librarian, one capable of ushering the library into the digital age. That was her research focus during her master's program, but while she'd given Mayor Mitch Turner a fairly lengthy document outlining a wide variety of possible approaches to upgrading the library, she had no real long-term business in town. It was an interesting challenge. The library, built with money donated by Andrew Carnegie in the early 1900s, was a beautiful old building dangerously near the point of being unrepairable. Something would have to be done, soon, although she assumed the something would be done by whoever they hired full time. . . .

The wrench thudded back into the toolbox.

Stay focused.

"Do you want a beer?" she asked.

"Yeah. Thanks."

In the time it took him to extract himself from his contortionist's position under the cabinet she went into the kitchen and snagged a bottle from the fridge. Back in the tiny bathroom she handed him the bottle. He twisted the cap off and tossed it on the counter, then tipped the bottle back. His throat worked as he swallowed. Her heart skittered in her chest.

Then he turned sideways to step through the door just as Alana made the same move. They ended up chest to chest in the narrow doorway, her breasts brushing that rock-solid chest with each breathy inhale. An electric charge sparked between them, heating the air as she looked up at him. He didn't move closer, or take her mouth. He simply stayed a breath and a heartbeat away, waiting for her to close the distance.

She went on tiptoe and brushed her lips against his, slow

and hot, striking sparks. His arm tightened around her waist, pulling her against his body as he leaned back into the door-frame, adding to her breathlessness. He wasn't like any other man she'd kissed. He let her lead, waited for her tongue to touch his before responding, somehow both completely male and completely available to her all at once. As she grew bolder, drawing back to nibble at the sensitive corner of his mouth, she pressed herself against him, and felt his erection thicken against her lower belly.

With a growl, he backed out of the doorway and down the hall until the backs of his legs hit the boxy arm of her black leather sofa. He tipped backward. She landed on top of him, forcing a grunt that became a groan as they shifted up so that his head lay against a red throw pillow. The vivid color soft-ened his brown eyes, or maybe that was the simmering heat radiating from his big body. She wove their legs together, gripped the armrest over his head, and kissed him through the groan with hot, sexy demand. He looped one leg over hers and rubbed his erect cock against her hip and belly.

Her hands found his lower abdomen, warm skin and ridged muscle that sent a hot zing along her nerves. She looked down. His pants had ridden down again, revealing his erection strain-ing against his boxers waistband. Starting with the lowest button on his dress shirt, she worked her way up to his throat, then spread the fabric wide. He looked at her, his body bared to her, his gaze unapologetically, unashamedly sexual.

And for good reason. He was built, ripped, whatever the current slang was for not an ounce of fat under skin stretched over workout-honed muscles. She looked him over, her fingers winding in that tantalizing line of hair.

"That doesn't tickle?" she asked.

His abs tightened but his smile loosened. "Not enough to distract me from how close your hand is to my cock."

Heat flared in her cheeks. "Very close," she said as she trailed the tip of her middle finger down the chestnut brown hair, then squeezed the hard shaft straining against his zipper. A few moments of one-handed work, all very slow and awkward and yet somehow sexy, and she'd unzipped his pants, then tugged the fabric to the tops of his thighs. He didn't help, just lay there, the fingers of one hand tangled in her hair while the other flexed on her hip, and let her strip him.

The combination of utter availability and remoteness was so hot.

Then hard hands closed on her ass. "Take this off," he growled as he worked the hem of her sweater up over her hips.

"Why?"

He looked at her, the gold flecks in his brown eyes glowing in the lamplight. "Because I like watching you blush."

"That's a relief," she said as he tugged the cashmere sweater over her head. Static electricity lifted her hair in a wild nimbus. He smoothed it down again, hands cupping her ears as his gaze traveled from her eyes to her lips, then to her throat and the tops of her breasts. "I do it all the time," she added breathlessly.

"All the time?" he asked, as if he hadn't noticed.

She nodded.

"Show me."

THE WAY ALANA Wentworth blushed damn near slayed him. Every. Single. Time.

Blushing usually meant innocence, but the combination of soft hands on his body and the heated slide of her tongue banished any illusions he had about sheltered librarians. When she unbuttoned his shirt and spread the fabric to either side of his chest, the color on her cheeks darkened from the pale shade of his grandmother's Pierre de Ronsard roses into Fragrant Cloud, a color he would associate forevermore with arousal.

He waited a long moment, letting the heat coursing down his spine show in his eyes, until she kissed him again, her lace bra chafing his chest. Her nipples pebbled as the kiss extended, her tongue rubbing seductively against his before she nipped at his lower lip. He reached behind her and unfastened her bra. The sweet, hot pressure of her breasts made his heart pound. He shifted and tightened one arm around her waist while cupping her breast in his other hand. Her thigh pressed hard against his erection, and for a few moments he indulged himself in the tantalizing, erotic tease of making out on the couch, lips pressed together, tongues sliding. Her hair tumbled on either side of his face, snagging on his five o'clock shadow.

Duke barked. Hands firmly gripping her seriously luscious ass, Lucas paused to listen.

"What is it?" Alana murmured.

The last time a woman purred into his ear that plaintively he'd been deep inside her, moving slow and hard and steady. Maybe the spring weather revitalized Duke enough to go after a squirrel.

Another bark. Alana lifted her head and peered in the direction of his house. Since they were in her living room all she could see was a wall of bookshelves, but he got the idea. He relaxed his grip and groaned low in his throat. "Someone's at my house."

That got an unexpected reaction. She sat up, snagged her bra and sweater, and all but levitated backward into the bathroom where, based on the sounds of lace and silk against skin, she was dressing like a teenager whose parents came home without warning. For his part, he sat up slowly, rubbed his face with both hands, then stood to button his shirt. Tucking his shirt back into his pants only confirmed how frustrated he was. He took a deep breath, thought about cold nights in cold cars staking out coldhearted criminals.

Not working. Blood thumped slow and hot in his veins.

Alana reappeared beside him, arms tense with the effort of holding the toolbox. "Here. This will . . . I'm sure it won't look like . . ."

He took the box before she dropped it on her bare feet, but didn't move. "Hey. We're two consenting adults."

"I know . . . it's just . . . you have a position to maintain in the community, and I'm not . . ."

Was that some kind of code for *I don't want anyone to know what we were doing*? He lifted the corners of his mouth in what passed for a smile for him these days. "Relax. I'm fine. You're fine. It's all fine."

She breathed in, smiled back at him. "Okay. Good. But—"

Next door his screen door slammed. "Lucas? You around?"

Mayor Mitchell Turner.

"We'll talk," he said, and headed for the kitchen door.

The door closed behind him. Still gripping the toolbox, Lucas rubbed the back of his neck and took a deep breath.

Where in the hell did *that* come from? Alana always seemed too—he hated to say innocent because a decade with the Denver PD and five years on the DEA task force had trampled any notions of the existence of innocence, but that was sure what it seemed like. She blushed, for God's sake, and she did it a lot. She'd blushed as she signed the rental agreement on the house next door to his, and Lucas hadn't been able to get the memory out of his mind. It was so completely small-town librarian, which she wasn't, and so innocently sexy.

He was beginning to suspect she wasn't innocently anything.

He knew she watched him, but the only time she ever said anything was when something broke. Then, after he'd gone over and fixed whatever it was, she'd turn on a throaty jazz singer, hand him a drink, and struggle to make small talk. Which was strange in itself. In his experience, women as polished as Alana knew what they wanted and how to ask for it, but Alana turned the color of his grandmother's roses every time she had to ask him for anything.

And yet she'd come on to him tonight. And he'd let his hard-on dictate his response. She was an enigma he'd have to figure out later—after they finished what they started.

He inhaled deeply, reaching for his composure, trying to reroute blood from his cock to his brain. Then he crossed her driveway to his house. The purple-blue twilight glittered and carried the scent of a greening prairie, the texture of starlight.

Maybe he'd take a couple of days off and go rock-climbing in the Black Hills. It had been years since he'd been cranking, long enough for memories to fade.

He'd go. After Alana left. Just in case she wanted to take what happened tonight to its natural conclusion, then maybe do it again.

That's an excuse, and you know it. You're procrastinating. For a very good reason . . .

"Hi, Mitch," he said to the man standing on his front porch.

"Lucas." Mitch said as Lucas climbed the stairs and opened the porch. "Some guard dog you've got here." Duke leaned against Mitch's leg, eyes closed in satisfaction as Mitch scratched the sweet spot behind his ears.

"What's up?" Lucas asked. He opened the front door and walked inside. Mitch and Duke followed but stayed in the living room as Lucas stowed the toolbox in the kitchen.

"I thought we'd head to the meeting together," Mitch said.

Lucas narrowed his eyes at the mayor, who played the political game with the savvy of a Washington insider. Most of the time he went to council meetings on his own. There'd been a small but noticeable spike in burglaries lately, which meant that the discussion about renovating the library would face opposition from people more concerned with public safety. While Mitch wasn't one to sell his seed corn to pay for the harvest, he'd been pretty tight-lipped about why he'd hired Alana temporarily, or how committed he was to a large-scale library renovation. Tonight he wanted to show up with the chief of police by his side.

"What are you up to, Mitch?"

"Just wanted some company." Mitch unwittingly copied Alana's move and glanced significantly at the living room wall. "Problem next door?"

Lucas kept his face blank. "Just seventy-year-old plumbing," he said noncommittally.

"You should replace it, or just sell the house."

"No time," Lucas said shortly.

"Huh," Mitch said. "Let's go. We can talk on the way."

* * *

ONCE THE MEETING started, Mitch morphed into Mayor Turner in formal business mode and ran efficiently through the budget. A few minutes later, Alana slipped into the back row of the high school auditorium, still dressed in her work clothes. Lucas had his moment in the spotlight addressing the burglaries, reminding people to lock their doors and report anything suspicious. Alana picked up a handout discarded by local rancher Jack Whiting and paged through it, seemingly half listening to the various line items and totals. The general rustling of people slipping into spring jackets and tucking handouts into purses and coat pockets halted when Mitch spoke again.

"Ms. Wentworth, I read through the information you compiled on the options and costs around renovating the library. Would you run through the situation for us?"

Clearly surprised, Alana got to her feet. When she moved, her perfume drifted into Lucas's nose, straight to the back of his brain. Not possible. They were thirty feet apart, maybe more, but there it was. It took a moment, but he realized her perfume was on his skin.

"As you know, the building's in dire need of renovation. The plaster needs repairing and the brickwork and roof are long past their best days. The Carnegie libraries are a national treasure. It would be an absolute shame to lose that building. The budget for books is adequate, but the shift in technology to e-books and e-readers means making a commitment to new technology. The computers are adequate, for now, which means in a year they'll be hopelessly obsolete."

"And what exactly do you recommend?"

Alana blinked. "I didn't . . . that is, all I did was gather information about possible directions you could take the library. But the real question that must be addressed before any renovations or shift in fund allocation occurs is what purpose does the library serve in the community? Without an answer to that question, you can't direct the funds you have to best meet your needs."

Don Walker, the local bank owner and spokesperson for the fiscally conservative segment of the town, spoke. "Miss Wentworth, we're the last town this side of Brookings to keep our library open at all. We barely have the money to do that, let alone upgrade computers or repair a hundred-year-old building."

"There are technology grants available," she started, but Mr. Walker cut her off.

"We're not in the business of supporting national treasures. What percentage of the community uses the library?" he asked. "We've got high-speed internet access now. Based on what I've heard from Chief Ridgeway, we need to upgrade the police department's vehicles and consider making David Wimmer a full-time officer. You're asking us to commit a fairly sizable investment to a resource that, as you said, is well on its way to becoming obsolete."

"That's not what I said at all," Alana replied. "Nearly a quarter of the county's residents live below the poverty line. Those who can afford the service have high-speed internet access. Many in Walkers Ford and the surrounding county cannot. Access to information is one of the greatest divides between rich and poor in this country. I think we'd all agree that poverty fuels crime."

"Let's keep this impartial and balanced, Don," Mitch said. "We've got an expert here, and it doesn't cost us anything to work up a proposal. Ms. Wentworth, why don't you put something together for the renovation project, talk to people, give us something to work with? Present it in a couple of weeks, just before you leave. How does that sound?"

As one, the audience turned to look at Alana. Her mouth opened, then closed, then opened again. "I could do that," she said.

"Good," Mayor Turner said. "I'm calling a special session in two weeks. Ruth, make sure the meeting announcement is posted in all the appropriate places, and book the auditorium. Talk to Ms. Wentworth about the A/V setup she'll need for the presentation. Folks, if you have any questions or ideas, feel free to contact Ms. Wentworth. For any other business, you can contact me, or any of the council members, or Chief Ridgeway."

Lucas recognized the tone in his voice. Mayor Mitch "Sandbagger" Turner strikes again. What the hell was that crafty old bastard up to?

He'd barely had time to formulate the question in his head before he was surrounded by people with questions about the break-ins, information about suspicious activity occurring down every remote dirt road in the county, and a whole slew of other questions. He glanced past Don Walker's shoulder at Alana, who was similarly surrounded. Mrs. Battle, the former English teacher who'd come out of retirement to work part-time at the library, stopped to talk to Alana before leaving.

Alana looked over Mrs. Battle's head, straight at Lucas. Electricity sparked along the invisible connection between them, an involuntary tug of attraction he hadn't felt in a long, long time.

Ever so slightly he lifted one eyebrow at her. *Later?*

She gave him a compact shake of her head, just enough to indicate *Not now,* and loosen her hair from its mooring behind her ear. The shiny blond strands slid forward in slow motion, setting off a sympathetic flex of his hand as the nerves remembered the sleek feel of her hair between his fingers, the curve of her hips in his palms.

If secrecy mattered to her, they could work something out. She'd leave in a couple of weeks, which was plenty of time for him to explore every nuance of her blushes. Hell, thanks to the plumbing, they had a good cover story to explain his being in her house.

Based on their chemistry, he had even better reason to be in her bed.

An imperfect pair . . .
perfectly matched.

FROM THE *USA TODAY* BESTSELLING AUTHOR

JENNIFER ASHLEY

The Duke's Perfect Wife

Lady Eleanor Ramsay is the only one who knows the truth about Hart Mackenzie. Once his fiancée, she is the sole woman to whom he could ever pour out his heart.

Hart has it all—a dukedom, wealth, power, influence, whatever he desires—and every woman wants him. But Hart has sacrificed much to keep his brothers safe, first from their brutal father, and then from the world. He's also suffered loss—his wife, his infant son, and the woman he loved with all his heart though he realized it too late.

Now, Eleanor has reappeared on Hart's doorstep, with scandalous nude photographs of Hart taken long ago. Intrigued by the challenge in her blue eyes—and aroused by her charming, no-nonsense determination—Hart wonders if his young love has come to ruin him . . . or save him.

penguin.com

LOVE
ROMANCE
NOVELS?

For news on all your favorite romance authors, sneak peeks into the newest releases, book giveaways, and much more—

"Like" Love Always on Facebook!

f LoveAlwaysBooks

Discover Romance

berkleyjoveauthors.com

See what's coming up next from your
favorite romance authors and explore all
the latest Berkley, Jove, and Sensation
selections.

See what's new

~

Find author appearances

~

Win fantastic prizes

~

Get reading recommendations

~

Chat with authors and other fans

~

Read interviews with authors you love

berkleyjoveauthors.com

M1G06